I0728055

First Edition.

Ebook ISBN: B09R3HDWZZ

Paperback ISBN: 9781916521124

Publisher: Dirty Talk Publishing

Editing: Mom Loves Books Editing and Proofreading

Cover Design: JMaddison Cole

Formatting: Emma Luna at Moonlight Author Services

CONTENTS

Deprived beings without genetic mutations make the worst saviours.

I was wrong. So very wrong. I used to think love was a weakness, but now I draw on its strength to survive. Too bad I'm more alone than ever. Deemed useless by the deranged owner of Afterlife Asylum, every step I now take in the human world is a struggle. With a bitter chill gnawing at my bones, refusing to let me sleep, I long for the fires of the underworld. Although, I know from the chasm residing in my chest, those are not the fires I'm longing for.

Stuck between two worlds and not a part of either, I keep grappling onward with one goal in mind - save Hoax. Hell is my salvation, but I can't be at peace with my adoptive demon mother until I see this through. Yet with Pyro still trapped and no way to help him, I must turn to the irritating prick who has always hated me and abandoned us in our hour of need. Always ready with a sarcastic answer and condescending smirk, I'll need to work with Ghost to help free his brothers, no matter the cost. I'm on my last life. I have to make this one count.

AUTHOR NOTE

TRIGGER WARNING

This novel is the second book in a dark paranormal RH trilogy, and it does end on a cliffhanger. Certain themes such as sex, self-harm, death and controversial beliefs are featured. However, those who always fall for the twisted, deranged villain and never question their own sanity about it, then come on in. The Afterlife Asylum is the place for you.

If you enjoy the All My Pretty Psychos series, please consider leaving a review on Amazon and Goodreads.

Reviews help authors get more recognition and promotion, and it's also helpful to get your feedback.

If you find any spelling or grammatical issues in this book, please don't report them using Amazon's new feature.

Instead, contact me using the details at the back of this book, and I will ensure they get fixed straight away. Contacting me directly ensures it gets fixed quicker.

Please also remember that despite being a UK based author, this book is based in the US, and uses US English spellings.

Thank you for reading and supporting me!

DEDICATION

I dedicate this
book to
my supportive family
and
my lack of sanity

KINGS OF MADNESS

ALL MY PRETTY PSYCHOS BOOK TWO

MADDISON COLE

PROLOGUE

I manage to stagger into the elevator, keeping most of my composure intact until the doors begin to shut. Enzo's arms close around me just as my legs give out, easing my fall. The wash of guilt expanding through my chest crushes inwards, my heart struggling to beat. I did what I had to do. Hoax is defenseless, but now even his spirit is gone. A rising tide of panic crashes over me that I might have seen him for the last time. Maybe I've seen all three of them for the last time, after Ghost left and Pyro will never have anything to do with me again. But only I know the truth. Only I hold the key knowledge that would bring Hoax back. In an attempt to become his savior, I've possibly doomed us all.

The stress is too much, the wires in my brain are not matching up to what I keep trying to tell myself. This is for the greater good. I did a selfless, noble thing. One that has left me feeling like utter shit. The elevator traveling downwards messes with my head, causing me to sway in Enzo's arms when he tries to pull me to my feet. I cough, spluttering in an effort to inhale fully and then something snaps. Breaks so viscerally, it catapults me backward. Not even Enzo is quick enough this time as I hurtle into the wall and crumple into a heap. Agony writhes in my veins, blinding me with its intensity.

Vaguely, I register the doors pinging open and the sound of a conversation happening over me.

"I think there's something really wrong, Sir. Should I take Mania to the Infirmary?" Enzo frets, brushing my hair out of my face to assess me. The lights glare, slamming a headache through the base of my skull. Rolling myself over to expel the contents of my stomach onto the floor, a shiny dress shoe steps into view. Kicking me onto my back, a pair of icy blue eyes track the length of my body with a scowl engrained between his brows. Christopher's gruff voice leaks through the internal crisis I can't shake, his words filling me with a further reason to vomit.

"Seems she's human now, therefore, no longer any use to me. Get rid of her by any means necessary."

HOAX

I've always preferred my solitude. Even without my memories, I know this. It's carved into every fiber of my transparent being. Yet now I have just that, the solitude I'm trapped in has become my new personal hell.

Mania exits the café over the road, clutching a disposable cup in her gloved hands. Winter hasn't fully set in, yet Mania's skeletal frame is hidden beneath a huge parka jacket and fur snood. Whether to conceal her shivering or her once mutated appearance, I'm not sure. I've tried to stop following her as closely since she was tossed out of the Afterlife Asylum, although this is as far away as I can handle. Every day she suffers a little more as she adjusts to life as a feeble human, after the fracture of Pyro's bond left her completely defenseless. At least from this distance, I can still watch over her like a loyal protector, even if she can no longer see me. No one can.

Crossing the street just before the light turns back to green, Mania flinches at the blaring horn of a red truck as it revs forward at her. Anger rises within me, and I swing my arm out, my fist disappearing into the head of the closest person while they remain none the wiser. Shoving off the building I'm pretending to lean on, I walk through the passing vehicles and follow after her. This town is the fourth Mania has tried, alternating between dilapidated squatter's pads and internet cafes in search of her prey.

This town, however, is the shittiest so far. Every other store is either closing down or looking for new owners. There are healthier stray cats than there are humans; the rat population thriving in the sewers below our feet. I walk through a long line queuing outside the church, hoping for a bowl of soup or a bed for the night. Women and children sob. Men with lifeless eyes stare at the ground and I scowl at them all. If only Mutes had been accepted into society, life could have been better for us all. Sure, there are assholes in every species, but similarly, there are those who'd have helped without needing to be asked. Pyro would have single-handedly warmed the world before his heart was crushed to dust.

Tall, gleaming new builds in the distance belong to a nearby major city, mocking those who scrimp for food in the outskirts. All the while, commuters pass through with their loud exhausts and disapproving glares. If I didn't find humans vile creatures before, I certainly do now.

All except for the one I'm so deeply in love with, gaping holes within are shredding my soul apart, aching to be filled with her. The ashy smell of her hair, the roughness of her cracked lips scraping over my skin, the way she craved me in a way I instinctively know no one ever has before. I had nothing to offer, no memories or experience to rely on, yet she accepted me anyway. That's why I can't leave her completely, regardless that my brothers probably need me more. Not that there's anything I can do for anyone.

I catch up to Mania as she ducks into a back alley, scanning every inch of the brick walls for the bumblebee graffiti marks she's been trailing. Every time a new sighting pops up on the conspiracy webpage she found, she sneaks onto a bus and follows it. Most of the website members believe it's part of some cult to save the planet, but we know the truth. Bee's brothel is where Mania found her answers last time, and although it appears to have vanished from its previous site, she's desperately clutching at the hope of being given a valuable lead once again.

Downing her steaming coffee, she tosses the cup into one of the many dumpsters and pulls the notepad from her gigantic parka pocket. Finding this alley to either be a bust or recently scrubbed clean, she scratches out the street name and moves on to the next one. And the next, and the next until the sun is beginning to settle on another wasted day. Entering the last one on the list until Mania can steal another wallet to afford the internet café again, her options seem to have run out for today. Not to mention the vicious growl her stomach makes at that exact moment.

Throwing her back into a wall, Mania sighs and slumps downwards. The weight of the world is visible in her glazed, red eyes, my heart breaking even further when I thought it couldn't anymore. I kneel in front of her, cupping her cheek in the hopes she might feel my presence. She never does. Her bond to Pyro has been broken, hence so has ours. Yet walking away isn't an option. I remain in front of her as she scans her list of crossed out street names, shrinking further into the fur snood around her neck. Finally tossing the notepad aside, she looks ready to give up and waste away in this alley, alone and forgotten by everyone except me.

Flicking her eyes up, Mania stills and her head tilts to the side. I look over my shoulder to see what her eyes have narrowed on, spotting a bumblebee sticking out from behind an old mattress. Jolting through me to get a closer look, Mania pulls out a piece of cardboard I'd imagine propped in front of a homeless person. There's four bees in total, cornering a message scribbled in marker pen. '436, Morrison Station. 20:30 daily.'

I crawl closer, a surprised grunt leaving me and Mania's head whips to the side. I freeze, my eyes wide as she looks straight at me. Her blood-red eyes shine like the rarest of rubies, her pale skin beckoning my touch. If I were alive, this would be a heart-stopping, breath-held moment, so I pretend both of those things are happening. Maybe with a flare of hope, our connection has been revived enough for Mania to see me again. Long lashes flutter in disbelief, her teeth pulling her bottom lip inside her mouth. This is it. She can finally see me again. A smile grows across my lips, my mouth opening to speak when a drunken man staggers into the alleyway.

"Oi! That's my sign, get your own!" he slurs and Mania slowly stands upright. A glass bottle scrapes against the wall and I realize now she wasn't looking at me but through me. Of course it wouldn't be that easy. This nightmare isn't going to have a quick fix, especially when I haven't bothered to check in on Pyro and if he's started working on reviving my body yet. My eye line falls upon the battered trainers Mania swapped her last food voucher for, her feet rammed inside and ready to break through the cotton.

"S-sorry," she mutters. I stand now, turning to hover over her shoulder in some form of comfort. As the drunk moves forward, she takes a step back into me and I wrap my arms around her. So precious, so fragile now she's lost her ability to come back from hell. Mania is on her last life and she knows it. When the man with aged skin and unfocused eyes doesn't stop coming, Mania jumps to the side and he falls into the old mattress, bouncing onto the ground with a yell. Neither of us wait for him to get back up as Mania is already out of the alley, darting through the crowd waiting by a pizzeria.

Mania doesn't stop running until she reaches Morrison Station all the way across town. It's the same one she arrived at in the cargo hold of a bus last week. Using a lamp post for stability, she shoves down the parka zipper and heaves great gulps of air in, wheezing like a heavy smoker. My eyes drink in her body, encased in stolen clothes from another squatter back at the abandoned hotel. Sweat beads her forehead, but she's shivering again, hastily zipping the coat back up.

Clearly, the eternal flame from Pyro didn't just keep Mania coming back to life but gifted her with the vitality she's grown to depend on. As merely human, I don't know how long her body will hold out. I've considered every way that we could be together again, whether alive or dead, but I can't seem to skip between earth and the underworld while our link is broken. And trust me, I've tried.

Once Mania has regained her composure, she crosses the road and finds a bench. Dropping down heavily, I feel her sigh to the depths of my non-existent soul. For all the good it won't do, I lower myself beside her, wrapping a transparent arm around her shivering body. The station is surprisingly busy this time of night, even more apparent by the lack of buses coming and going. Shadows loiter among the large columns holding up a stone overhang. Wind whips inside, howling through the rows of filled seats in a waiting area. Dragging my attention back from over my shoulder, I curl into the woman at my side, the one I wish I could shroud in my warmth and comfort with my kisses. The one who blew into the underworld like a fallen angel, pulling me back from the fringe of immortality with her love. I wish we'd had a chance. Just a little bit more time, if nothing else.

We remain there until the clock tower opposite slowly turns to half eight. As if conjured by the minute hand nudging into place, a pair of headlights brighten the station and nearly blinds us. We hear the music long before the hot pink coach pulls into the station, slotting between vivid white lines sprayed onto the tarmac. This isn't a usual coach, but more like a kitted-out party vehicle containing the cast of Rocky Horror. Don't ask me how I know that, but instinctively, the thought pops in my head when a six-foot woman with an Adam's apple more defined than mine steps out. Her cinched corset is as black as her mane of curly hair and leather platform boots.

"Tickets, boys," she calls and a rush of businessmen in suits appear out of the waiting area, scrambling towards her. A younger crowd at the back catcall and whistle excitedly, their matching t-shirts claiming them to be 'the Pussy Posse.' Mania also stands, my heart leaping into my throat as she does. She can't go in there, not with a bunch of horny guys looking for a good time, no matter the cost. The drag queen raises an eyebrow at her, seeing the rest of the men in before signaling for Mania to step forward. "Do you have a ticket to ride this bus honey?"

"I'm looking for someone," Mania states, devoid of all emotion. "A Mute I believe to be a regular customer of yours. He has white eyes and hair, can walk through walls. Has a particular taste for human women." By now, I'm over Mania's shoulder and able to see the hint of recognition in the drag queen's eyes.

"Seems like you're asking Mama Kay a favor, and since you don't appear to have a ticket, there happens to be something you can do for me too." I uselessly try to grab for Mania as she tips her head along the length of the bus in thought, trying to pull her back into me. There's no fucking way she'd agree to-

"I'm not having sex with anyone," Mania says coldly. My mouth drops open, my un-beating heart sinking. Mama Kay grins, extending her hand to help Mania up onto the bus and peels her parka off as she passes. The tiny denim skirt and gaping fishnet tights Mania's been hiding become visible, as does the long sleeve top she's tugging down to cover her gloves. A round of cheering sounds from the stag party within, making my fists clench and teeth grit so hard, I almost miss the bus beginning to pull away.

Jumping through the now-closed door, I dive inside, acting like Mania's shadow. Screw keeping my distance, I can't let her go through this alone. At least we're both suffering together, since that seems to be the closest to a relationship we're going to get. As the speed increases, the overhead lights fade out, leaving strips of color-changing LED's to illuminate the converted shell of the bus. Feather boas decorate the window panes and flower petals dust the floor, all the way down to the stripper pole at the other end.

Women showing more skin than dignity use rails to slink along the length of the bus while it's in motion, a silver tray in their hands. The businessmen take their champagne flutes and faked affection, but the stag do's hungry gazes are solely on Mania further down the bench. A growl is drawn from my throat when one whistles and beckons her to him like a dog. My hand uselessly flashes out to grab her thigh in an effort to keep her seated, not that she has any intention of moving anyway. Hanging my head in defeat, it's apparent that I was wrong before. This, right here, is my new personal hell.

I keep my eyes dipped low, my hands clenched between my thighs. Music bleeds from the speakers, the repetitive chorus of 'fuck the pain away' along with flashing LED lights making me wince. Goodbye dignity, hello headache. Inhaling in short pants, as the low hum of body odor and sweat burns my nostrils, I shimmy down the long leather bench to retrieve my coat and pull it over my legs. A few of the men still staring at me grumble, alerting Mama Kay, who immediately whips it away once more.

I imagine she is mistaking my behavior for shyness, but I'm just that fucking cold. Words can't describe how hard it has been to adjust to living as a pathetic human, but it's the loss of Pyro's warmth that hurts the most. Both physically and mentally. I hadn't even realized it was there, dulling my other senses with the ferocity of his love. The love I didn't deserve or cherish until I lost it.

I shove those thoughts aside, focusing on the mission that's the only reason I haven't curled up to die somewhere for the final time. Finding Ghost, he's the only one who will believe what I saw in the Afterlife basement. He can use his ability to go back and get Hoax's body, hopefully convincing Pyro to work his eternal flame to bring their friend back. Then what is anyone's guess, but at this stage, nothing except bringing Hoax back to life matters.

The bus pulls up at yet another location with nothing distinguishable from the darkness outside. Opening the doors, Mama Kay calls for 'couples only' this time and I look up to see a line of humans walking arm in arm. I hadn't even seen most of them get on, preferring to focus on my feet instead. Dread has my stomach in knots while I scratch the back of my neck like I have fleas. My skin has been extra sensitive lately and clothing labels are my new nemesis.

With the return of my senses, including taste buds which can only handle the blandest of foods, came the joys of the delayed puberty I never had. Dying at eight years old and being revived by Pyro's flame meant I missed all of that, but now my body is playing catch up and it fucking sucks. My first period, for example, was horrific. I was so worried about bleeding out, I went to the ER and got laughed out of there. At least some charity worker collecting donations in the reception took pity on me, introduced me to the puppy training pads for my vagina and gave me the parka coat, which has become my lifeline. I smile sadly to myself, recalling the night of 'truth or dare' a bunch of us played at Bellemare once. If it wasn't for a drunken night of truth or dare with a Mute called

Modify, I never would have had a woman's body to work with at all. Wouldn't that have been a shame?

Laughter breaks through my thoughts and I look around to see what has everyone excited. A human female with long hair is upside down on the stripper pole, her legs spread into the splits while men around her see how many items they can balance on her ass. Three whiskey glasses and a random shoe so far. I roll my eyes, hugging my arms tighter around myself. I'm dreading what favor Mama Kay has in store for me. I can barely jog without getting a stitch these days, so hopefully it doesn't involve too much physical activity. The bus jostles to a stop and a pair of black platform boots come into view.

"This is you, Sweetie. Tell Mr. Large you're his cover for tonight and he'll be able to help with your request." Mr. Large? What kind of a name is that? An over-compensated one, I imagine. I stand with a nod, waiting for the Pussy Posse to pass by first. The last one blows me a kiss and tells me to save a blowjob for him. I don't hide my look of disgust and that seems to make him smile wider. Creep.

Mama Kay is standing by the door, whispering and passing my coat to what I presume is a bouncer. He stuffs it under his arm and leads me along by the wrist, ignoring my protests to have my only possession back. Literally, my sole possession since humans aren't allowed into Mute City without some bribery involved and so I was unable to retrieve my stuff, least of all - my money. My teeth chatter and puffs of my own breath cloud my vision as I step off the bus, my toes painfully jammed into these battered Converses.

Struggling to see around the bouncer's large frame, he drags me forward into the night. He's fully dressed in black fatigues, except for a reflective stripe across his front. The darkness concealing his forehead suggests a mop of dark hair that leaks into his eyes. Not the usually clean-cut look I'd expect from a bouncer but maybe I'm too used to the guards from Afterlife. Bald, unathletic, naive.

The bus skids away behind us, taking the only source of noise and light with it. The stag party walk casually at the bouncer's other side, clearly knowing where they are going while I remain clueless. At some point, I become complacent being tugged along, resigned to the fact I can't escape, even if I wanted to. At the very least, I'm not leaving until I have a valuable lead to finding Ghost and hence, a reason to keep existing.

The bouncer abruptly stops, causing me to crash into his back. My bones scream in protest and I groan slightly. I hate feeling so fragile and goddam tired all the time. Peering around his side, I notice he's reaching out to poke his index finger into thin air in some sort of strange pattern. A long beep sounds and in the middle of the desolation with nothing around us, a door opens inwards. Colored lights burst out, as does the heavy bass of loud music, splitting the night in two.

I blink in shock, trying to make sense of what I'm seeing. There's no visible building or structure, just an open doorway in the darkness like a portal. The stag party whoops and run inside, chatting excitedly while apprehension holds me rooted in place.

"What the hell? Where did that doorway come from?"

"Really?" the bouncer comments dryly, using the light from inside to eye me suspiciously for the first time. I tilt my head and cock my eyebrow, silently demanding for more than his sarcasm-laced, rhetorical question. "For someone who looks like one of us, you sure are fooled easily."

"Us?" I query, taking him in properly now. Stark yellow eyes reflect in the lighting and peer out from beneath his hair, his muscles seeming bigger now than when I first stepped off the bus. His hand whips out so fast it makes me flinch and him chuckle.

"Endurance," he states. I smile weakly, slipping my hand into his.

"Mania." Whistling low at my name, Endurance doesn't elaborate on the irony I'm all too familiar with. By nature, my name would imply hysteria or that I'm a crazy, fearless bitch. Yet I flinch at a handshake and see my final death looming around every corner. I'm thankful when he reverts back to my original question instead of probing.

"Bee's brothels are owned by a powerful Mute called Camo. F. Large. Some concealments are better than others," he trails off. Patting a hand beside the door, a wall briefly becomes visible until he removes his palm once more. "This is his best establishment and where he's based, hence the strength of his ability here." I swallow thickly as my fears are confirmed this is a brothel. A major, invisible one at that. Any belief of leaving unscathed suddenly vanishes as images flash in my mind with what I might be asked, or forced, to do here, sending another shiver through me.

"A Mute who owns a chain of brothels and strip clubs under a human alias," I try to focus on anything else. "Why?"

"Can you think of a better way for a Mute to make a fortune in this world?" The bouncer answers easily and I nod in agreement. He's right. Our - I mean, the Mutes only chance of survival outside Bellemare is to remain hidden and lie, cheat or steal in order to survive. In fact, the more I think about it, I'm starting to think this Mr. Large might be onto a gold mine.

Endurance's hand is still encircling my wrist and he uses it to ease me inside. Less forceful this time, he guides me into a long corridor, the door behind us closing of its own accord. Color-changing bulbs lining the ceiling flash from one shade to the next, signaling the way like an airplane strip. A muffled voice makes an announcement inside the next room and a crowd cheers wildly, betraying the sheer amount of people stowed away in this hidden building.

Drawing me closer to the door at the far end, Endurance swiftly diverts into a thinner corridor. Then another, leading down a flight of stairs and beneath the music playing overhead. Depositing me into an empty dressing room, he takes a long look at my face before handing my coat back.

"You've been to hell and back, haven't you little human?" I wrinkle my nose at the name, hating that I can't deny it.

"You have no idea," I sigh. Understatement of the century. His yellow, reflective eyes lower as he sighs, showing the first hint of emotion I've seen from him.

"Mama Kay is good to her word and Mr. Large always honors her deals. I hope you can find the Mute you're looking for, before this place swallows you whole." The last part was said beneath his breath but I heard it, alarm bells blaring in my head to run now. But then what? Accept a life of hiding in an abandoned hotel and stealing each meal. Sounds too much like giving up to me.

The bouncer pulls the door closed between us, leaving me alone and I circle the room, wondering what I'm supposed to do. Each dressing table along the two rows holds an oval mirror, an assortment of aerosol cans and trays upon trays of makeup. Across the far side of the room, multiple rails of skimpy fancy dress costumes draw me closer, I see a cat, lizard and a unicorn. I run my fingers over the sequin-embedded leotards, my frown deepening as the door is slammed open.

"Fridays are the best night of the week!" a female shouts, her bra stuffed with paper notes. I spin and shrink back against a large feather boa, eyeing the flurry of color, glitter and scales that burst into the dressing room. Other than her tiny red bikini, the brunette speaking is wearing a pair of diamanté, black leather boots, a strange fur-lined hat. It's black and rounded high above her head. "Tonight's tips alone will buy me a whole new wardrobe." She shouts yee-haw, spanking a topless male across his chiseled abs with the riding crop she's holding.

"Only because you were requested by the stag do. You haven't even done anything yet," another female rolls her eyes. She's the owner of the scales, shimmering from jade green to purple from the neck down. I catch a glimpse of her eyes, piercing blue like gleaming aquamarine stones which are both starkly beautiful and painfully shrewd.

"It's called a deposit, Siren. I can't help if my tail brings all the boys to the yard while yours is a bigger flop than my right ear!" Siren's lower half is tightly constricted in a mermaid's tail but even I can see the high heels poking out the side, breaking the illusion. The women start to argue and my eyes then become transfixed on the white fluff ball sticking out of the brunette's thong. What the fuck have I stumbled into?

"Now, now girls. We need to change and get back up there before those men start using the dreaded 'R' word," the male wearing only the tightest pair of see-through white pants says, gently pushing his way in between them. He shakes out a mane of glorious blonde hair that even I'm ready to swoon over.

"*Refunds,*" the two females and everyone else piling into the room all shudder together. I huff out a small laugh, gingerly stepping out of the boa. Eyes snap to me at once, a mixture of surprise and suspicion passing through the crowd of faces. It's the bunny/rider who breaks away from the crowd first, looking me over with a growing smile.

"Ooooo," she rubs her hands together like she's trying to start a fire. "I like this whole day-of-the-dead thing you've got going on. So unique, the clients will love it." My eyes widen at her wink and everyone begins to disperse towards their stations, not wasting any more of their precious time gaping at me. I start to shake my head but the female has already moved on, fishing out another slip of a costume from the rail. This one is a sexy fox - an orange faux fur corset with white trim, matching boot covers and gloves. Prying off her bowler hat, the female shakes her head and two lengthy white rabbit ears pop up from her head. The right one then flops back over, just as she described.

"Guys love the whole Fox hunting and the rabbit routine," she winks when she catches me gawking. "I'm Hare-iett." I take her outstretched hand and give it a brief shake.

"Mania," I reply, my voice sounding small. I wish I could find some of the blasé attitude that used to guide me through life before my soul shattered into a million pieces. Before I began mourning the love of the two men I could never really have. Clearing my throat, holding onto the image of Hoax's firm nod in my mind, I lift my chin higher. "I need to find Mr. Large. I'm his cover tonight."

"Camo is fine," a deep voice states and I flinch out of my undead skin. "Mr. Large sounds so pretentious." I spin to see a figure materialize out of a nearby dressing table, his body shimmering slightly as the illusion of the mirror fades from his skin. His fine suit blends from a sandy, wood hue back to its normal colors and he strides over to me with a grin. Was he...watching me the whole time? I immediately dislike him; his creepy, all-knowing smile grinding me in all the wrong ways.

Instead of addressing me again, he walks passed to the rail, shoving a costume in my arms and directs my shoulders towards an empty booth. I wriggle out of his touch, narrowing my eyes on his reflection in the mirror now in front of me. Short, cropped hair hinting at an olive green shade reflects the color of his mischievous eyes.

"Scowl harder," he lowers his head to speak directly in my ear. "The punters upstairs are going to lap up something different from the usual smiles and giggles." He toys with a lock of my hair and I shudder for a whole different reason. "Maybe you'll out-rank Hareiett one day."

"Wait!" I call as he begins to walk away, spinning with panic flooding my system. "I'm just doing this tonight so you'll give me information on a Mute I'm looking for!"

"I overheard your request, but I can't believe Mama Kay implied this favor was just for tonight?" Camo doesn't wait for my answer, heading over to check on his other employees. My heart plummets and my mind racks back through everything Mama Kay said. Shit. She didn't specify the length of the favor, I'd just presumed. My head lowers and I now notice the costume in my hands. Black, stretchy material with a skeleton's ribs and pelvis printed across the front, a spine down the back, no ass cover in sight and matching stockings. How has it all come to this?

I drop into the seat, kissing the rest of my fleeting self-respect goodbye. The topless male from earlier is sitting at the station beside me, now wearing an open plaid shirt and rubbing cream into his face. I open my mouth to ask him something, but the question escapes my mind as a beard begins to sprout along his jawline. It grows longer and fuller beneath a materializing mustache. The Mute runs his hands over the beard that is now down to his chest and then turns his attention to the blonde hair upon his head. The yellow fades into the color of melted chocolate while the hair itself loses its buoyancy. Now straight, he is able to tie it up into a top knot. Catching my eye, he smirks at my stunned expression.

"Follicle," he states his name, explaining it all. I stare until a cackle of laughter draws my attention across the room. A small group of females are peering around a mirror facing the opposite way to get a glimpse of me. I frown slightly, but more at the fact their hair makes up all the colors of the rainbow. It only now clicks that the dressing room is full of Mutes, and only Mutes. I shrink into myself, dipping my head so my hair acts as a curtain and hides me from view. I no longer fit in here. I'm a fraud. I wonder if Camo would throw me out if he knew I was merely a human or if he wouldn't care. I get the impression only appearances seem to concern him.

"Moping isn't going to help," Hareiett states, rounding the front of my chair and dropping to her knees before me. "Look, this is no one's first choice. But we're all here together and getting paid for being ourselves. That's not a common occurrence for people like us," she smiles sadly. I decide then, opening up to anyone about my… predicament won't help. I can't handle being outcast yet again and I need to find Ghost, no matter the cost. "So suck it up and let's get you ready. You'll have fun up there, I promise." I seriously doubt that but I fake a smirk and straighten my back anyway.

Soon enough, I'm being rushed out of the dressing room at the sound of an overhead alarm. There's a layer of white powder on my face to make the dark circles around my eyes more prominent. Curled tendrils of my hair frame my face, the rest of my black and red locks tied back into a slick ponytail. My cracked lips have been left bare, because apparently 'they're perfect for my niche.' I sincerely hope there's not many guys upstairs who dig the deceased appeal so Camo might give me the info I need and send me on my way as soon as possible.

I've also dragged on the offensive piece of clothing, trying to ignore the way my real bones protrude against the stretchy material and how my stomach is aching from hunger, despite the pastries I scoffed down on my way out of the dressing room. Apparently everyone else is watching their weight while I'm fading away over here.

"Just breathe, you'll be fine," Hareiett winks at me as we wait in a line leading up the metal staircase. Above us, an audience roars with each Mute announced onto the stage and I reluctantly take another step closer.

"Without sounding judgmental, how did you end up in a place like this?" I lean closer to ask in a low voice. I mean, Hareiett is model-worthy beautiful. Her rich brown waves are a stark contrast to the pure whiteness of her long bunny ears. Her eyes crinkle in the corner, two orbs of hazel-specked marble watching me closely. And on top of that, she seems to have such a genuine heart. Surely there's somewhere else in the world she could fit in, even if it was simply teaching at the Bellemare Elementary school. I bet the Mute children would love her.

"We're all rejects here," she shrugs as if that's the criteria for strippers. Maybe it is, I wouldn't really know. "It's the Mute matron who has the real power. She busts tables, posing as a waitress but really, she's pouring lust into the clients. Keeps business booming, even on the slow nights." My eyebrows raise and I stash that information away for later.

"Rejects how?" I ask to help distract myself as I have to climb a fateful step towards the stage and the strobe lights up ahead.

"Well, there's Script, who can name any font, and Disappointment, who we keep out back for obvious reasons. Then Siren, who can't hold a tune to save her life," Hareiett snorts and I giggle too. Siren's icy blue eyes suddenly find me from further down the metal staircase and I immediately restrain myself, shuffling aside to disappear from her view. Hareiett doesn't seem to notice as she sighs and continues.

"Then there's me, I suppose. I can take on the characteristics of any animal, but only once. I learned that the hard way when I flew up to the top of a volcano on albatross wings, and later jumped off to find I couldn't summon the bird in me again. Managed to conjure some dragon wings before my face met the ground, but now I've used up my dragon card." She huffs, genuinely annoyed at that. "But doesn't matter now. I'm happy as a hare; it brings in good money and saves me changing my name every time I switch animal."

"Small wins," I half-smile, half-wince. A name is hardly a consolation prize for being stuck a certain way for the rest of your life. Hareiett shrugs one shoulder, pressing on.

"If Camo deems you of use in other ways, he'll soon pull you out. There was a male who came once for the chance to be free like the rest of us. Holy hotness, he was drool-worthy. Stone-cold eyes, tattoos across his scalp and rock-carved abs. Fucking yum. I'd have happily shown him the advantages of my bunny tail," she winks. "Rumor has it he could conjure buildings from the ground with his bare hands, so typically he never even saw the stage." The Mute two ahead of me is announced through the speakers and a lump of bile rises in my throat.

What am I even supposed to do when I get up there? Swan around and attempt to look sexy? My knees knock together, alerting me that my shivering has taken on a whole new level. I need a way out of this and fast.

"Hey, can I ask you a question?" I suddenly blurt to Hareiett, clutching for an out. "I'm looking for a Mute called Ghost. Have you heard of him? I don't know where else-." Her giggle interrupts me and I cock an eyebrow, missing the joke.

"Oh I know Ghost, everyone does." When she doesn't elaborate and I'm ushered onto the top step, I start to grow angsty and crack my fingers against my palms.

"Well, do you know where I can find him? I know he favors human women and they seem to be lacking around here, but can you point me in the right direction?" I leave out the part that means I'd run for it if she does and retain any slither of dignity I have left. Annoyingly, Hareiett mimes zipping her lips and turns me around. The sound of blood rushing in my ears means I missed the last announcement and I'm now facing an open stage. Fuck.

'We have a special treat for you all this evening. Fresh from the grave and looking for someone to warm her zombified carcass. Introducing the undead widow!' I'm sorry, the what?! I don't have time to argue as Hareiett nudges me forward, tears pricking the back of my eyes. Why do I feel like after the next few minutes, my future will be sealed and I'm never going to get out of here? Hoax's secrets will die with me and Pyro will never know why I broke his heart.

With a deep exhale of acceptance, I step out onto the stage as the house lights go up and I'm immediately greeted with a pair of milky white eyes in the front row. Well, that was easier than expected.

GHOST

T he noise in the room falls away as my gaze snags on the one woman I never wanted to see again. My chest halts mid-breath, my lungs constricting with a burning need. The hand stroking my torso also stops, sensing the tension suddenly raking through me. Slowly, I release the breath I was holding and make three quick judgments.

Number one, Mania looks like shit. Number two, she's here. Number three, and this is the one that has me restrained in my chair with dread, she wouldn't be in a Mute strip club and looking like a haunted whore if Pyro was here. No. If Pyro had finally had Mania the way he's been dreaming of all these years, he wouldn't leave her side for a second. So in conclusion, Pyro is either trapped and/or in trouble, and someone is about to die. Right now.

Pushing to my feet, I turn on the heel of my dress shoe and stalk to the back of the room. My name is shouted from behind by Mania and my date, but I ignore them both. Instead, my feet eat up the glittery, lino floor until I reach the bar and I throw my fist straight into the jukebox. Camo bellows, appearing out of the machine and clutching his busted nose. I know him well enough to know his usual resting places, after all I'm his main investor. Grabbing the scruff of his shirt, I walk through the nearest wall and throw him down onto his desk.

"There's no way she's here by coincidence," I grit through my teeth, getting right into his face. I don't need to clarify who I'm talking about, not when I'd confided in him while blind drunk on my first night here. Not when I'm sharing his fucking apartment upstairs. "So why the *fuck* is she up on that stage?"

Camo splutters as he gasps for air, clearly winded but I don't let up. Grabbing his shoulders, I ram them down onto his desk and snarl at him to start talking.

"I-I-" he strains against me. "I thought it'd be poetic," he chuckles and I thump him in the chest. Pacing away, I realize an eerie tune has begun to play in the next room. Oh hell no. Fisting my hands, I storm back through the wall, ready to knock out every man and Mute who's laid eyes on Mania. Luckily for them, it's a rabbit/fox combo spinning around on the pole center stage and my rage lessens a fraction. My eyes search the room frantically, failing to locate the female who's here to ruin everything. Again.

"Ghost," a small voice breathes from behind the bar and I briefly close my eyes to brace myself. Twisting my head to the side, I scowl at her. She's across the counter, but so much closer than before. What happened to her? She's skinnier, if that were even possible. Her face is gaunt, stretched over protruding cheekbones and her bottom black cracked lip is trembling. But it's her blood-red eyes that strike me the most. Glistening with misery, grief and regret. Whatever for, I'm about to find out and make her pay for it for real. None of this 'crying into a pillow' bullshit – proper pain.

Striding through both the bar and Mania, I allow my hand to materialize at the last moment to hook around her slim wrist. She doesn't fight as I'd expected but merely allows me to drag her through the cheering crowd and into the room of my choice.

Spinning the moment we've entered, I slam Mania into the wall and close my hands around her throat. Her eyes bulge and she flails, but it only serves to encourage me. To feel her pulse flutter out beneath my fingers will soothe the ache inside I haven't been able to shake. I broke the moment I left Afterlife, and if it weren't for her, I wouldn't have done so alone. Taking her life will be a balm to my soul, easing me of my guilt. I've been dreaming of a moment like this, and the excuse to execute it. Now she's here, and fuck, how dare she come here. How dare she bring whatever bad news is inevitably following her to me. How dare she not be with Pyro, after I left him so they could be together. Just like he wanted.

"Don't-" Mania rasps, kicking her legs out and digging her nails into my arms. "I'm….human." My whole body freezes, my hands still clasped tight as her words filter into my mind. Then I instantly release her and she crumples to the floor. Killing her has suddenly lost its appeal if she won't come back to haunt me. I don't waste time on that thought, backing away as if she's contagious.

My back bumps into the booth from one of the private rooms. A curved sofa in deep purple is sprawled out at the rear, optional drapes in the same color hanging either side. A lone chair, like one I'd expect to see at a dining table, sits in the middle of the room for those who have only paid to watch, not touch. Fitted with a personal pole and glass-topped sideboard, displaying a range of bondage restraints, this is one of the more expensive suites. No cameras in here, I think to myself while checking the corners of the dim room. Probably for the best, before Camo thinks I've gone soft. All I've spoken about for weeks is wanting the chance to kill the little demon that destroyed my life. Granted, I can't blame her for everything that's gone wrong *ever*, but it sure feels good.

"Tell me everything," I grunt, dropping onto the sofa. I untuck my shirt from my jeans and spread my legs, getting comfortable. Mania strokes her throat, taking much longer than expected to recover and drags herself up onto her knees, where she stays.

"I've been looking for you," she croaks. Folding my arms, I don't respond. Not out of patience but in simmering rage. The silence stretches on until Mania has managed to stand and make her way to the other end of the sofa, lowering herself down so gently, I can't take it anymore.

"Why are you so fucking fragile? What do you mean you're human? Where's Pyro? Why are you here and what do you want from me?!" My voice grows louder as the questions pour out of me. Once I got started, I just couldn't stop until it had all come out. Yet after all of that, Mania can only give me a one word answer.

"Christopher." That name causes acid to claw up the back of my throat and settle in my mouth. I haven't been able to think about anything else since the day I left, fucking left my brother behind, but hearing it out loud draws it back out of my memory. Makes the pain of my betrayal too real. Tension ripples through the veins in my arm as I flex my hand into a fist and back out again, repeatedly. A minuscule thread of my consciousness is begging me to stay calm, to notice that Mania is clearly as broken as I am, but I can't control the underlying threat laced within my voice.

"Tell me Pyro got out," I demand, low and dangerous. Those blood-red eyes slowly flick up to me, the agony in them so clear, I have my answer. "Fuck!" I shoot to my feet, ignoring the way Mania flinches, and kick the offensive chair into the wall behind. It doesn't nearly shatter enough so I continue my attack, bringing my dress shoe down on the wood until it's splintered in every possible way and beyond repair. Still, my blood runs at a scolding level. The foolish hope that Pyro has run into the sunset with his girl and never looked back crashing down on me. I knew it was a lie, a pretty fairy-tale I've been clinging onto, but it dulled my senses enough to keep going.

"You," I turn to glare at Mania. She's pulled her knees up to her chest, leaving her bare ass exposed to me in that ridiculous costume. Heat of a whole different nature courses through me but I shove it down, telling myself I don't just want to see my handprints marring her ass, but the evidence of my anger all over her. She fucking left him. After he went back for her. Knowing she's human now only means I need to squeeze every drop of information from her black lips before sealing the deal. Her death will be on my hands, and I will relish it. "You abandoned him to play stripper at a Mute joint. Whatever he's going through right now is on your head, and I will see that you suffer for it."

"Me?!" Mania's spine suddenly straightens and her legs drop to the floor. Gone is the pathetic act and instead, the defiant female I remember is marching over to me. Jabbing a feeble finger into my chest, she glares daggers right into my face. "You left him first! I watched on the CCTV as you left Pyro long before I did, so you're as much to blame for this situation as I am. At least I had a good reason for betraying Pyro, you were just plain selfish. I should have known I'd find you cozied up in a strip club with some whore all over you."

I'd completely forgotten about my date but the twinge of jealousy in Mania's tone makes this predicament almost laughable. Almost, if I wasn't fucking fuming at everything else she just said. Her finger is still pushing into my chest, although I barely feel it. Still, I grab her wrist and twist her around, pinning her arm behind her back. My other hand snakes up to circle her neck in what I hoped would be a warning, but I instantly realize my mistake. I gingerly move my crotch away from her ass, shaking myself to focus.

"Tell me, Mania," I spit her name like a curse. "What kind of reason could possibly justify leaving your soulmate behind?" I hate calling Pyro her soulmate but I wanted to drive the point home of how much worse her betrayal is than mine. Wrenching her arm up a little further, she yelps in pain but I hold her in place.

"I had to leave Pyro to save Hoax," she cries. My teeth grit harder, that answer sounding too much like a cop-out for my liking. Tightening my fingers around her slender throat, I only need to twitch my thumb to break her damn neck.

"Hoax is already dead," I mutter to myself but she heard me.

"Not completely," Mania breathes and my body stills. What the fuck is that supposed to mean? There's no such thing as partially dead. Releasing and spinning her in one swift move, I walk Mania backward before kicking her legs out from under her. She drops onto the edge of the sofa with a small shriek. I'm over her in a second, bracing my arms on either side of her head, crushing her with the weight of my body. This isn't a sexual moment, I tell myself, but an intimidation tactic she couldn't have seen coming. My eyes are inches from hers, her breath mingling with mine, her body pinned. She has nowhere to hide.

"My patience has run out. Explain yourself or fuck off so I can get back to the club." For a millisecond, her eyes drop to my lips and I increase my death glare.

"Hoax's body is underneath the asylum in a tank and his

consciousness is on a hard drive. I think it's why his spirit came to me, because we were both tethered to Pyro but he's not a complete soul that can enter hell either. Christopher believes Pyro doesn't know the extent of his ability, that he can create eternal flames to keep those he loves from dying, or in my case – from staying dead. He's going to use Pyro to bring back Hoax and then what...Well, I wasn't kept around long enough to find out." Her eyes trail away from mine, misery claiming her features again but I jerk her back to me, imploring her to keep going. Now she's loosened her lips, I want the full truth; no withholding information that will come back to bite me in the ass later.

"Christopher said I had to break Pyro because as long as he loved me, he would never stop fighting to be free. I refused, but then they turned off Hoax's tank and...I saw his body dying before my eyes and I couldn't take it. I broke Pyro's heart and now our bond is shattered. I was thrown out of Afterlife, I'm cold all the fucking time, I've spent weeks looking for you and I'm constantly starving because all that I am now is just...just..."

"A human," I finish for her. A lone tear leaks from Mania's eye and I don't move to wipe it away. Instead, I watch it drip into the shell of her ear while mulling over her words. She betrayed one of my brothers to save the other? What am I supposed to do with that? Where am I supposed to direct my anger now?

"Christopher," Mania repeats his name again with such venom, and I now realize I huffed that last question out loud. The air shifts slightly, a slither of agreement passing between us. The anger hasn't lessened, but it's not fully directed at each other. For that brief moment, then I remember that without her in the equation, Pyro and I would be fully immersed in a video game and elbow deep in pizza right now. He went back for her. He *chose* her over me. I push away, needing to put some distance between us. Clawing a hand through my hair, I open my mouth to speak when a soft knock sounds at the door.

"Ghosty?" my date calls and I freeze. Fuck, I forgot about her – again. Lifting a finger to my lips as a signal for Mania to remain quiet, I straighten my shirt and pass through the door. Isabelle's eyes light up when I appear in front of her, relief washing over her pretty face.

"Oh, there you are. I've been knocking on doors searching for you. I've seen some things," she whispers with a mischievous wink. I reach for her right hand, raising the reddened knuckles to my lips and placing a gentle kiss there.

"Forgive me, I thought I saw someone I knew," I reply with a smile as smooth as butter. Tucking a strand of her black hair behind her ear, I cup her cheek in my head. "I've had a great time tonight but I'm feeling drained," I fake a yawn. "Would you mind if we reconvene tomorrow night?" Disappointment flares in Isabelle's porcelain face but she quickly regains her composure.

"Sure thing. My husband is on a night shift tomorrow so I'll be yours for as long as you want me." I force out a pleasured groan, lowering my head to swerve at the last moment and kiss her cheek. Her chest pushes into mine, her arousal palpable. After a long moment, Isabelle drags herself away and bids me goodbye, swaying her hips exaggeratingly and looking back to check I'm still watching.

Only when she's disappeared from view do I shove my arm through the door, my palm held up in invitation until I feel Mania's smaller one slip inside. The simple contact does more for me than Isabelle's revealing dress and tight curves have all evening but I push that aside and yank her through the door.

"You're such a fucking sleaze," Mania remarks from beside me. I leave her with that impression, not bothering to divulge my intentions to the person who came between my best friend and me. No, my brother and I. It's none of her business that Isabelle's husband happens to be Dwayne, the bald guard at Afterlife, nor that I've been biding my time to build her trust. Turns out, gaining entry back into the asylum after leaving wasn't exactly as easy as I'd hoped. After locating Camo, I'd planned on dragging him straight back while disguising us both, so I could pull Pyro's stupid ass straight out. Alas, I can't fucking find the place.

"Hey, I don't suppose you remember your way back to the site where you were ejected from?" I ask, cocking a brief eyebrow in Mania's direction. She merely shakes her head, seeming confused by my question but there's not enough time to explain it now. Even if there was, I reckon the walls in this place have ears.

"Come on," I grumble. With her hand still in mine for some strange reason, I yank Mania through the network of hallways until we breach the back door, where I promptly chuck her on the back of my motorbike. The MV Agusta was a gift from Isabelle when she found out I didn't have the transport to visit her, not that I've used it for that purpose once. Throwing my leg over the middle, I bark at Mania to hold on as I twist the throttle and speed off, her arms barely closing around my middle and a scream ripping from her throat.

It's not a long journey, but somewhere along the way, Mania's legs snake around mine and I realize she's still practically naked, thoroughly human and on the back of my bike for all to see. No wonder so many trucks have blared their horn in appreciation, although I'd thought it was for the bike. Now the rush of adrenaline pumping through me has quelled some of my anger, I absentmindedly reach down with one hand to touch Mania's thigh. Fuck, she's ice-cold. I pull the accelerator harder and gun it down the freeway, weaving in and out of vehicles until the turnoff comes into view. From there, it's just ten more minutes of speeding before I'm pulling up at our destination. Well, her destination.

"Home sweet home," I state, lifting Mania off the bike and giving her a gentle shove in the direction of the doorway.

"Is this some kind of joke?" she complains, as ungrateful as ever. I look over the old chapel, from the thick cross over the doorway to the cemetery. It's not much, but it's as good a hideout as anywhere. I learned from past mistakes, i.e. the explosion of our bunker that left us with no options and nowhere to go. Now, I have secret lairs all over the place, fully stocked and ready to provide Pyro and I refuge. Once I've rescued him, that is.

"I thought you'd be comfortable here," I smirk. "You'll be snug as a bug in the crypt and there's plenty of candles for some heat." I leave out the stash of supplies I've also compiled down there, not wanting her to be too excited about stealing one of my hideouts. She might never leave otherwise. Hopping back onto the bike, I nudge the kickstand away when Mania's panicked voice calls out to me.

"Wait, you're leaving me here?" The scoff leaving my throat turns to rumbling laughter, but there's no humor in it. Her eyes duck away, embarrassment claiming her cheeks with a pinkish hue against her alabaster skin. I'll never say this out loud, but the pitiful display before me kinda makes me wish for the old Mania back. The one who always had a comeback and challenged as much as she riled me. I suppose losing her bond with Pyro has truly broken something deep within. That's it. Her spark is missing and I can't help but wonder how much of that was thanks to Pyro's flame.

"As if I'd choose to stay here with you," I snarl, my voice dripping with disdain when I finally stop laughing. "I have a plush apartment and a flock of women to warm my bed back at Bee's."

"You know what," Mania huffs, half turning and I think she's going to leave when she twists back and punches me straight in the face. I barely move, the crack of her knuckles on my jaw and the howl escaping her throat like music to my ears. My eyebrow cocks slightly, a glimmer of the restrained respect I used to have for her flickering back to life. Well, that was interesting. Mania hugs her hand into her chest, her eyes blazing with her newfound spunk.

"You can keep up this act all you like, but I know you, *Ghost*," she adds extra emphasis onto my name like a curse. "You push your self-directed anger onto others because you can't face the truth. You don't hate me. You hate that you want me. I know because the feeling's mutual, but at least I'm Mute- I mean, human enough to own it. Not you though. If you hadn't been so petty and jealous, Pyro wouldn't have had to choose between the two of us. He'd have been at that strip club with a girl clinging to his arm to soothe his broken heart. Just. Like. You. It's both our faults he's trapped, so the least we can do is be assholes together and punish each other for the shitshow state we've found ourselves in."

I remain in place after Mania has spun with an impressive hair flick from her high ponytail and marched inside. A frown is etched into my brows, my eyes flicking from side to side as I contemplate Mania's words. It's only when I taste blood in my mouth that I realize her punch actually caught me, my bottom lip split on the left-hand side. It unnerves me how good of a read she got on me when I keep everything bottled up so tightly. Maybe I'm not as closed off as I thought. I may be able to walk through walls, but in no way does that make me transparent.

With that thought in mind, I pull my leg back off the bike and walk it around the side of the church. Securing a sheet of tarp and leaf-covered netting over the MV, I swallow my pride and make my way through the front door. A chill runs through me as I step over the threshold, and now I know a bit more about how Pyro's flames work, I can't help but wonder if this decision means I've just distanced myself from him further.

I hate to admit it, but I am surprisingly at home in the crypt. Around the size of my old shack with higher ceilings, the stone walls are dotted with brass plaques, each one suggesting up to twelve bodies have been thrown into the same tombs and forgotten. Any empty spaces have been crammed with Ghost's supplies, packaged neatly in air-tight bags. On a heightened step against the far wall is a single tomb, surrounded by columns on each corner. Quietly peaceful and neglected. I kinda love it.

Hidden beneath the church in a forgotten pocket of the earth, I snuggle down, finally slightly warmer in an oversized tracksuit with fur lining. All of the stashed emergency clothing was intended for Ghost or a man his size, which means I can use them both as clothes and a wearable blanket, all rolled into one. A cracked hole in the concrete slabs filled with a thick duvet has become my bed for the night and I curl up inside with another cover on top, finally able to stop my teeth from chattering. Shadows dance across the walls from the flickering candles while Ghost sits cross-legged in front of me, trying to convince me to play this dumb game with him.

"Look, it's easy. My two index fingers are the Chopsticks. I nudge your hand to make your one turn into three. You nudge mine to make four, then my nudge makes yours five and you're out. Then we do the other hand and you can go first. Simple."

"Stupid," I correct. "We literally both win a round every time."

"That's the point," he huffs and finally stops pointing his fingers at me. He's changed into a matching pair of tracksuit pants to the ones I'm now wearing, a fitted, charcoal gray t-shirt and the fluffy socks we fought over. I think he secretly wanted me to try to punch him again but when he held the socks high above his head, I knew it was pointless. I'll steal them off him when he's asleep instead.

"Forget it. I suppose now is as good as time as any to clear up a few things." I exhale slowly, dragging myself up into a reclined, sitting position. I knew this conversation was coming but now it's here, I'm unsure where to start.

"I pretty much told you everything I know," I confess. Everything happened so quickly on the day Christopher revealed his hand to me, and I lost so much. My mind struggles to comprehend it all, even now. "I was naive while we were at Afterlife. I don't expect you to understand, but I've been mostly alone my entire life and fending for myself since I can remember. Suddenly, I had Hoax and Pyro, a place to stay, people who seemed to want me around. Maybe if I hadn't become complacent..." My voice trails away and Ghost shrugs since none of that matters now.

"Where is Hoax's body being held? Tell me exactly what Christopher said to you. Don't leave anything out." He shuffles forward slightly, hanging on my next words.

"It was just a room in the basement with huge cylinders and computers everywhere. The scientists believed I was the answer to bringing Hoax back from the dead, which is why they wanted me to join their side. But then Lorraine turned up with some photograph-"

"Wait, Lorraine? As in the woman who raised us at the Hermitage orphanage?"

"And Christopher's daughter." I nod and watch the cogs in Ghost's brain churn behind his flickering eyes. "She's been keeping tabs on you all, said something about experimenting on hundreds of others to make sure they were ready for Pyro. I think trapping and killing Hoax was all part of their plan-"

"Where did she come from?" Ghost cuts me off and I frown at his question, thinking back to the smaller details.

"Erm, the elevator I guess." After grunting, Ghost urges me to continue so I clear my throat. "Anyways, this photograph was aged and from a top window or surveillance camera at Hermitage. It showed the moment Pyro and I first laid eyes on each other, and there was a fiery thread connecting us. They're calling it his 'eternal flame,' meaning he gifted me a portion of his fire so I couldn't stay dead. You and Hoax no doubt have it too." Ghost tries to hide his surprise, briefly looking at his own hand as if it'll suddenly combust. The silence around us thickens as Ghost stews on what I've said, although his expression remains stoic.

"What about Hoax? What's he got to say about all of this?" I look away now, unable to answer that question. It must be obvious because Ghost releases an 'ahh' and my heart begins to sink all over again. I hadn't realized how good it felt to finally share the stress-load I've been carrying alone up to this point. Terrified that if something happened to me, Hoax's secrets would never be heard. It becomes clear now, human or not, I need to see this through. I've come too far and hurt too much to give up now. Mostly, I need to meet Hoax in real life, at least once. My stomach rumbles then, loud enough to be heard through the layers concealing my frail body and Ghost rolls his eyes.

"How are you still hungry? You ate a week's worth of Spam." He gestures to the pile of empty tins by my feet. Snuggling back down into my cubby hole, I wrap my arms around myself in an effort to hide the noise. Despite Ghost's moaning, he stands and walks over to the tomb where he's storing his food supply. He lifts the lid with one arm, his upper body appearing bulkier than I remember in the hindered lighting, and plucks out a packet.

Returning to sit before me, he holds up the cake bar, waiting for me to take it but all I do is wrinkle my nose. I'm not getting out of this cover for anything and, that came out of a tomb. A literal tomb with a skeleton inside. Gross. At least in hell, the souls keep their scorched skin so there's no decomposing bones hanging around. I groan out loud at the thought of missing hell and Ghost mistakes it for my disgust at his offering.

"Oh shut up and eat it," he hisses. Pulling the bar from its packet, he tugs on my jaw with his free hand and stuffs it in my mouth. "I'm not listening to your growling stomach all night. Fucking humans," he mutters the last part. He sits and waits until I've chewed and swallowed, showing him my tongue before scooting over to lean against the wall by my head. I glance up at him and he makes a shooing motion with his hand. "Sleep."

I don't argue, for once. After weeks of fending for myself in the shittiest conditions, I'll revel in the gift Ghost doesn't realize he's giving me. Warmth, a place to stay, food. It was these things that made me so complacent to stay at Afterlife without looking too closely beneath the surface, but at least here I know what I'm getting. An asshole for a roommate and preserved snacks for dinner. Practically paradise at this rate.

I wake to the sounds of grunting, temporarily forgetting where I am. My back instantly screams to be stretched out, the stiffness in my neck making my movements slow. Eventually, I bow out of the hole in the ground and roll onto the concrete like a flattened sausage. Once again, I hear the grunts and huffs and perk up to see Ghost lost to a workout. He's facing away, switching between one-handed push-ups and planks, topless and glistening with sweat in the burning candles. I will myself to sit upright, merely watching for a moment. It's not a trick of the light; he's definitely bulkier than before and now I can see why.

"Breakfast's by your feet," his voice suddenly echoes around the crypt and I jolt. Could he sense me staring? Looking along the ground, I spot a box of granola bars. "Eat up, I've decided you can help me out with some jobs today."

"I should punch you in the face more often," I smirk until I flex my hand and feel the strain on my knuckles. Yeah, maybe not. It was worth it once, but twice would be plain stupid if I feel like using my hand anytime soon. Reaching for the bars, I nibble through each one with my knees drawn up to my chest while continuing to watch Ghost work out. It's not like there's anything else to watch, I tell myself.

The rest of the morning, which I'm guessing it is, Ghost takes his sweet time exercising and using a liter bottle of water to wash with. I force myself to look away, not wanting to give either of us ideas. After passing it my way, I scrub the leftover makeup from my face and pull on a fresh pebble gray tracksuit. The waistband needs to be rolled up until I have a wedgie and I tie a knot in the white tee before slipping the hoodie over.

I find Ghost waiting for me in the doorway, having tidied up the covers, clothes and pile of wrappers I'd accumulated. His gaze lingers on my body, the emotion I can't get a read on disappearing as soon as he catches my eye. On a sharp nod, he leaves and I'm left to follow like some kind of puppy. I bet Ghost would peg me as a yippy chihuahua and usually, I'd have agreed. Currently though, I feel heavy and drowsy like a dopey bulldog.

"You going to tell me where we're going?" I ask when he continues stalking away once outside the church. I don't get an answer. Ghost turns and lifts me too easily, dropping me onto the leather seat of his bike before hopping on, behind this time. I brace myself on the handlebars, ignoring the strong pair of arms that box me in. Firm muscles press against my arms, thick thighs squeezing me snugly. A feeling similar to pins and needles prickles my skin and I swallow thickly. This isn't right. I hate Ghost, and he hates me.

"Okay, why are you being….not a shithead to me?" I peer over my shoulder and instantly regret it as his heated breath washes over me. Too close, way too close. Ghost doesn't look my way, his eyes glued to the road ahead.

"You're the only one who's seen the inside of the lab where Hoax's body is."

"The basement," I correct but Ghost shakes his head.

"I don't believe so." The bike rumbles to life, the vibrations awakening a whole new sensation between my legs. Fuck, it's been way too long for this kind of intensity. Maybe I should have taken one of the stag do guys up on their catcalls, although I instantly know I couldn't have.

"What does that mean?!" I yell, hoping he can hear me as we rev away. "Hey! What is that supposed to mean?!" Seconds turn into minutes and more as Ghost drives onward without so much as a murmur in my direction. Retreating back into my thoughts, I realize the hour is much earlier than I presumed. Seems like Ghost didn't sleep at all in favor of working out. Without any other vehicles around, we fly into a gas station at a worrying speed, beneath a sky of purple and orange. The single attendant inside is a lanky kid, too invested in his phone to notice Ghost slip through the wall and appear a few minutes later with toiletries for us both. He then drags me around the back and through a locked door, depositing me into a bathroom to freshen up.

After treating myself to the luxury of a flushing toilet, I leave the cubicle to look upon the items Ghost has left on the basin for me; toothbrush and paste, hairbrush, body spray. Maybe I should take that last one as an insult rather than a gift, but I'm too thankful to care. Shaking out the hair tie, which is still matted in my hair, I use the brush to sort out the knots in my black and red waves. I leave it loose around my shoulders the way I like it, and then move on to my teeth.

I catch a glimpse of myself in the filthy mirror, my haunted eyes wincing at the state of my reflection. I've never been beautiful but for one brief moment at Afterlife, I'd felt like it. I miss the way Hoax used to look at me like the world didn't exist and there was nowhere else he'd rather be. Or how he'd close his arms around me, like an invisible shield. I've given up talking to him in the hopes he might pop up or give me a sign he's still around. He's gone and I'm left mourning the brief romance we had.

Knuckles rap on the door just before a hand appears through the wood. I hesitate before cautiously taking it, too aware of how quickly I've softened to the milky white eyes on the other side. My instincts scream to protect myself but then I'm reminded that there's nothing left to protect. I've been stripped bare, beaten down and if Ghost can provide some support in helping Hoax, that's a risk I'll have to take.

Without arguing this time, I follow him to his bike and we are soon back on the road. I don't care where we're going, relinquishing all control for a while. Instead, I ease back into Ghost's chest and watch the clouds roll by. I've decided, for this ride at least, to free my mind since there's nothing I can do while flying at 90mph down a highway. It's a new notion to me, yet I slip into the habit easily for a few hours of blissful nothingness. Only when we slow and the towering outer wall obstructs my view of the sky do I sit up and pay attention. I know this place. I've lived in this place.

"Bellemare?" I question, way too quietly for Ghost to hear. He continues down the road that leads to the main gates and I spin in my seat. "They won't let me in, I've already tried," I blurt. In fact, they wouldn't even open the gates so I could talk to an actual agent. I took that as my first warning. Perhaps my second will see me thrown into a human prison and fuck knows, I'd be useless in there now.

Eyeing me, Ghost abruptly twists the handlebars and uses his foot to stop us from toppling completely. Diverting onto a dirt track and into an expanse of trees, he finds an opening to stop and hoists me off the bike.

"Why are we even here? You hate the Mute City," I accuse, finding my footing after such a long journey. Ghost switches off the MV and stands smoothly, a cocky grin back in place on his face.

"Like I said, you can help me with a job. There's rumors of a Mute in Bellemare that can trace an object's origin. I'll get you in, then you can find him and get whatever answers you can on these." Ghost lifts the leather seat and pulls out the pair of manacles he was forced to wear at Afterlife. The ones that suppressed his ability.

"You mean Tracker? I can't visit him like…this," I gesture to myself. Last time I stopped by Tracker's place, I promised he'd never see me again and now I'm on my last life. I shudder at the thought of what he might do if I waltz back into his stronghold. Especially if the MRA officers working for him have already been passed the information about my predicament. For all I know, every soldier inside Bellemare could be laughing about the woman who doesn't belong anywhere.

"Of course you can. You've made it this far, I'm sure you can figure it out."

"And where will you be?" I glare at him as he backs me up against the wall and pushes the manacles into my hands. Overgrown vines should keep us covered from the surveillance cameras but since Ghost's body is filling my vision, I'm unable to check. Whatever he lifted for himself at the gas station invades my senses, the masculine smell of aftershave and an underlying citrus hint. Momentarily disarmed, I forget I even asked a question as his hands rest on the wall either side of my head and his white eyes bore into mine.

"I've got a date," he smirks and promptly uses the length of his body to shove me through the wall. I fall back on a curse, the manacles slipping from my hands. Ghost's mechanical laughter can be heard over the wall, his projected voice following me as I scramble for a hiding space.

"You wanted us to be assholes together, Spitfire. I'm just living up to my end of the bargain."

"Still nothing?" a female voice asks over me. My head remains lolled to the side, my cheek pressed into the metal table as my closed eyes hunt for a hint of darkness. The full force of an overhead lamp makes it nearly impossible but I've had enough practice by now. I remain still, not even flinching when the scalpel is inserted into my abdomen, just above the last incision. It's a cruel torture, to continue their experiments while the feeding tube pushed into my nose and down my esophagus is the only thing keeping me alive. I'm a puppet and Christopher holds all the strings.

"Nothing," the male on the other side of my body confirms. I vaguely hear a heavy sigh but I retreat back into myself, blocking out the world once more. They stopped giving me anaesthetic a while ago, hoping it would jerk my fires back to the surface. I have no concept of time; the day Mania left me is as clear as yesterday yet feels like a lifetime ago. Left me here to suffer without a trace of the man I once was in sight. I lost everything that day. My brothers, my love, myself.

A hard slap is delivered to the side of my face in an attempt to rouse me. I don't move. My limbs are limp, my soul too heavy to respond. If the medical team assigned to keeping me alive weren't so damn good at their jobs, maybe I'd be in hell with Hoax right now. At least then I'd have someone who would never leave me. The tube is dragged back up, a gag threatening to rise when it passes through my throat as it always does. That's the one part I can never get used to. My arms are pulled upwards then, a shoulder bearing the weight of my body until I'm dropped back into the wheelchair. I register that I'm rolling forward until a sharp halt jolts me forward and hands catch me before I crash to the floor.

"What are you doing?" a man roars. Not just any man - Christopher. A slam signals the door closing behind him and the hands ease me back into the chair, remembering to fasten the strap across my bare chest this time.

"We finished today's round, Sir. There's no change in the results and frankly, I don't see the point in continuing." Inwardly, I quirk an eyebrow at the boldness of the scientist, wishing I could see Christopher's face in response. Then I remember, I don't give a shit.

"You're not digging far enough!" Christopher bellows and a sharp stomp on my shin shoves my chair wheeling backwards. My head rolls onto my right shoulder, a long exhale huffing through my nostrils. I don't know at what point I transitioned from hating the solitude of my cell to craving it, but all I want to do is curl up in my bed and be alone. It just about makes this hell bearable. Christopher's voice continues to roar, echoing around the operating theater.

"I'm done waiting! He's not leaving this room until I personally see some results! Cut him open, dissect him if you must. I've been grooming him his whole life for this, I won't let some brooding ruin it for me now." His words intrigue me and I tuck them away for another time when the fog in my brain clears. It's self-inflicted, but necessary. It occurs to me as he continues, that Christopher must believe me to be asleep or passed out. "The flames must be in there somewhere. If he won't give them to us willingly, extracting them is the only way. My plans can't progress without them."

"As I've previously stated, I don't believe we can extract anything unless Pyro wants us to. His fires are a part of his being, not his DNA."

"Then you're obviously not trying hard enough," Christopher growls. A faint scuffle sounds and I'm rolled aside, probably forgotten about in some corner.

"Or," the female interjects this time. "We're going about this all wrong. If you let him work through his emotions and when he's ready, tell him about your plans for his flames, he might just be on board. You'll get a much purer sample with his consent than we could ever just take." A snort resounds inside my head. Yeah right. There is nothing in this whole facility that would convince me to willingly give them access to my fires. I hardly have access to them myself anymore.

"Fine," Christopher snaps back. "But no one talks to him except me. Our asset is our best bargaining chip and until everything is in place, he remains contained." It's unclear if they are still discussing me as I'm suddenly drawn back into the room and moving again, the doors sweeping open again. Cool air sweeps over my face as I'm abruptly halted for the second time. "Don't take him back to his room. It's too…comfortable. Until Pyro agrees to work with us, he can stay in solitary confinement."

The wheelchair is rolling beneath me, down the lengthy corridor to the distinctive 'ding' of the elevator doors opening up just in time. I'm eased in without hesitation and caught by the porter waiting inside. His large hands stop me by the knees and there's a slight pause waiting for the doors to close before he kneels before me. Again.

"Hey buddy, how you holding up?" Enzo asks as he does every time. Out of all the experiments and being spoken about like an object, it's this time of day that tests me the most. The urge to curl my hand into a fist and throw a flaming punch into this fucker's face rides me hard. I just about keep my breathing relaxed and my jaw from clenching, not wanting to give away my façade. I originally hoped if everyone thought I was braindead, they'd eventually leave me the fuck alone but I'm having no such luck.

"Come on Pyro, wake up. I really need to talk to you and you're going to want to hear what I have to say," Enzo tries again. Hearing his voice is enough to remind me of the last time I saw him walking into this very elevator with his arms closing in around Mania. Was she his girl now? Were they sharing a staff accommodation apartment together and laughing at me each night? Stupid, lovesick Pyro that thought he had something special. Someone special. I should have listened to Ghost instead of wasting my life on a fantasy, but he's not even around to say 'I told you so.'

Giving up, Enzo rounds the wheelchair and unhooks the clipboard of notes that are kept back there. The scientist must have slipped it in place at some point, not that I'd have known. I'm too busy trying to will the darkness in me to take back over, to pull me into their depths until I'm unreachable. I feel the sharp talons of my firey demons digging into my consciousness, preparing to drag me under when Enzo's huff distracts me.

"Ahh shit," he mutters. "Solitary confinement? I won't be able to reach you there. Look Py, there's something you've got to know. H-" Enzo's hand presses down on my shoulder and I immediately call for the full force of my fire. It's not as responsive as I'd hoped, but directing it all towards his palm is enough to make him jerk back on a strangled yell. The faintest twitch to the corner of my mouth is the best effort I can make at a smile right now, but it's enough. The fires within frizzle out too quickly, disappearing back into my soul and I physically feel the cage of my being close around them. Well, it was fun while it lasted.

The doors slide open and I am jostled out of the elevator backward. I can only imagine Enzo is using his good hand and maybe the crook of his elbow to push me along, my head jolting all over the place. The air here is different, stale and damp. It's no longer difficult to find the darkness beyond my eyelids as that seems to be all there is. The chair takes a sharp left, the ground becoming uneven beneath the wheels. I faintly remember a place like this when I first came to the asylum, before I was thrown into the Mute pit with Ghost.

"I've just received orders to take over from you," a new voice speaks, a pair of boots stomping loudly as the newcomer approaches. I don't need to be alert to sense Enzo's hesitation, the atmosphere thickening around me. My stomach churns, bile thickening in my throat and sweat breaking out on my brow. I almost groan, my head falling forward and only the strap on my chest keeping me upright. As quickly as it started, the side effects of Enzo's ability vanish and I gasp in a fresh breath. That's the second time he's altered the enzymes in my body and I vow it'll be the last.

"Okay," is Enzo's only reply. The gravel crunches as he swivels, leaving me alone with my new keeper. One who abruptly breaks into a mechanical laughter and punches me in the face. My head rears back and he takes another shot, easily breaking my nose. Now Enzo's gone, and in the familiar reprieve of anguish, I'm able to call the firey shadows up to consume me. Blackness drags me under, the continued assault on my body becoming detached from what I know to be true. I'm alone, I'm weakened, but I'm not useless. Merely reserving my energy and biding my time.

At some point, I become vaguely aware I've been unstrapped and my body is falling to the ground. Pain splinters from my shoulder to my wrist, my arm taking the brunt of my weight on the rock-hard floor. A boot is thrown in my gut and shoves me into the cell before the metal grate is slammed shut. I crack an eye now, secretly assessing the face that bends down to sneer at me. Thick stubble, shortly shaven hair, tattoos on his knuckles as he curls a hand around the bar.

"My orders are very clear. Either you give us your fire, or I get to beat it out of you," he smirks, still believing I'm unconscious. I catch the glint of his guard's badge through my eyelashes and it's confirmed. His death is marked. The fingers on my hand twitch until only the middle one is sticking up and a small flame spark out of the top, illuminating the gesture. It's the closest I've come in terms of responding to the constant goading, but the guard's bitter expression is worth it.

"You think you're so tough," he spits down at me, resuming his full height. "After I'm done with you, that heartbreak stunt your little whore pulled off will pale in comparison to the real pain you'll know." Without responding, I slowly roll onto my other side to take the weight off my injured shoulder and insult him further by turning my back on him. The wheelchair is carted away, leaving me to my thoughts.

The fog tries to descend, blocking out all traces of Mania but the guard's words float around my subconscious. Why would he use that phrase - the stunt she pulled off? Usually, the images of her standing behind the glass appear when I least want them to, but this time I will them forward. I repay our encounter, over and over in my mind's eye.

She looked me dead in the eye and told me I was 'a bit of fun.' Something to pass the time between her bland lives. She broke me into a thousand pieces that day, shattering all the years of longing for her in a single moment. Now I'm stuck in here and she's god knows where, but what if she had no other choice?

"Oh Mania. What did you do?" I whisper, barely even audible to my own ears. Heat flares against my cheeks, the blissful tingle of it drawing me back to the cell. The jagged rock beneath me is slightly wet, a sound of dripping signaling just how far I've fallen. I can't hear evidence of anyone else down here, but I swear the warmth seeping into me feels distinctly like a pair of hands cupping my face. The fingertips brush my ears, thumbs holding my jaw and the strength of them willing me to not give up.

"Hoax?" I ask into the darkness. My body shivers then but not in coldness. In desperation. If he were here, I'd finally have a reason to drag myself up and start to fight back. I remain still, reveling in the prickly feel against my skin as it seeps down my back. I can practically imagine him spooning me, just as I did to him all those nights in the orphanage.

A smile pulls at my mouth while a sizzling tear scores a line from my eye to my hairline. What I'd give just to see him. To share a nod or clasp his hand. But the longer I lie there, the more I'm convinced I'm only fooling myself. My own flame rose to the surface to play tricks on me, to mock me with my own loneliness. It's been somewhat erratic lately so it's no surprise my turbulent emotions have brought this on. I'm not at one with my fire anymore. We're fractured right down the middle, and if anything can destroy me in this place, it'll inevitably be myself.

Keeping my back plastered to the side of a wooden hut, I slide Ghost's manacles into the baggy sweatpants pocket. I'm not surprised he left me the first chance he could, but that doesn't mean I'm not seething inside. At least he'll need to return for whatever information I may or may not find out. I quickly decided, as infuriating as he is, I feel a little easier knowing Ghost is coming back for me and that I'm not going at this completely alone anymore.

Dark clouds have rolled in, the air churning with a sense of foreboding. The first few drops of rain begin to fall as I dart to the rear of the next hut. There's no sound coming from inside. In fact, as I peer out into the main dirt road, there's no sound...anywhere. My instincts scream to stay hidden but I peer out further, hunting for any sign of life. Soon, I'm standing in the middle of the road, out in the open and exposed.

Dirt roads not made for vehicles extend towards the taller buildings in the center of Bellemare. They lord over the shacks quivering below, mocking us with the use of tile and brick. Bold, red roofs and orange stained walls. Real glass windows with double glazing to keep the heat in. The only time we were graced with such luxury was standing in line at the food bank or during the weekly check-in sessions. Most Mutes avoided the hospital at all costs since the lack of treatment we'd receive only put us at more risk of catching someone else's infections. Those who went in rarely left, aside from me.

Putting one foot in front of the other, I continue on with memories darting by on all sides. Across the other side of Bellemare, nature claimed our merged patch of land. A river flows beneath an abandoned railway bridge where Imp, Ammo and I used to play and spend our days in the woodlands. Three little terrors with nothing better to do.

My eyes struggle to adjust as the rain begins to fall a little harder, but I barely feel it. My breathing grows heavy, and it's not with exertion. Where the fuck is everyone? I keep expecting an army of officers to storm from the buildings, tackling me to the muddy ground. The track beneath me begins to incline and I realize I've subconsciously taken the path via my old shack.

Halfway up the hill, a pile of ash-ridden logs gives me pause. I kick the wood aside with my tight converse, frowning at the shack that used to hold so much life. I often envied Serpentina, the little girl with yellow eyes and a forked tongue who never let me pass without a hug. So innocent, she embraced her life without fault. Then again, she had an entire human family who moved here just to be with her. I take a moment to step through the broken-down door, noting the mess inside. My eyes snag on a chessboard thrown onto the floor, the pieces scattered all around.

I don't walk as I continue my exploration of Bellemare. I run. I have to find someone. Just one person who can tell me what's happened to the only home I ever knew. My lungs burn with dread, my chest heaving. I know the early signs of a panic attack - I'm just surprised out of everything I've been through, this is the catalyst. Stumbling up the hill, a cloud of puff appears before my face and I pull to a stop. A shuddering breath rolls through me and I almost collapse from the sheer agony that accompanies it. Hang on, this isn't just a panic attack. It seems my reprieve from chattering teeth and a bone-deep chill is over, leaving me to practically army crawl the rest of the way to my destination.

I make it to my shack without encountering anyone else, heading inside to yank up the false floorboard beneath my upended bed. The stash of money and random items I've collected over the years lay there, but it's not them I reach for. Pulling out a brand new pair of biker boots, I quickly switch them out and sigh. Sweet mother of soles, they feel like pure heaven in the form of black leather and laces. With that handled, I grab for a backpack across the room and turn my attention to the money, stocking up as I don't plan to ever return. Despite the sides of my wardrobe being smashed in, I find a pile of my old clothes within the wreckage and layer up. Then I head for Tracker's stronghold without looking back.

I stand before his towering, concrete building, the rain pattering across my nose. It's exactly how I remember it. Derelict and depressing. A thick chain binds the door handles together and thick planks of wood cover the windows. In between the cracks, there's nothing but darkness and whatever last thread of hope I was hanging onto dies a swift death. Tracker's connections with the MRA run deep so I'd figured whatever happened around here, he'd have found a way to protect himself.

Regardless, I close the distance between me and the metal door, which is conveniently ajar. Steeling myself, I push inside and immediately look around for the doorman, Specky. I'm not stupid enough to call out when no life presents itself but I'm also not clever enough to make a run for it. Instead, I creep forward to the main staircase and I climb all the way to the top on silent feet. My movements are slightly restricted now I have a long-sleeved top and leggings beneath Ghost's tracksuit, with a denim jacket on top. Should be enough to ward out the chill but for some reason, I'm as cold as ever.

The top floor is as derelict as the others, only the scamper of rats within the walls to be heard. Tracker's office is at the far end, lacking bodyguards but the flash of red in the corner of the hallway tells me the surveillance camera is still working. Even if there is no one behind it. I figure all the ones around Bellemare have seen me by now so I walk beneath the camera and stare up, flipping off whatever bastard might have access to it. The door beside me abruptly flies open and I scream, jumping out of my skin.

"Why am I not surprised after all this time, it's you who couldn't keep your word?" a familiar voice grumbles, referring to how my only bargaining chip last time I came here was that I'd never show my face again. Without stepping out from the shadows, I can see Tracker is skinnier than before, but even stranger is that there's no cheap suit covering his body. Instead, he's only wearing a pair of shorts. His tattoos are on full show as he turns his back to retreat inside, leaving the door open.

"Circumstances have changed," I state as I enter. I can't deny the glimmer of excitement that courses through me at the site of the male I used to hate, or who hated me. He was a creep who always stared too long at my chest and ass and if his brother hadn't gotten there first, I bet he'd have tried it on with me. I shudder at the thought of his twin, Hunter, wondering what I ever saw in him either. I'll put that nightmarish decision down to desperation and lack of options.

"It sure as shit has." Tracker drops into a leather chair that reclines back further than it looks like it should. Without taking his watchful eyes from me, he grabs for a cigar in an ashtray with the cherry still burning and takes a long drag.

The first thing that hits me as I fully enter Tracker's office is the smell. Like a stale slap in the face with a side order of crusty ash. Judging by his makeshift bed in the corner, he's been hauled up in here for a long time with only a small attached bathroom sink for washing in. There are no lights on inside, except for the lamp on his desk and glare from the wall of TV screens. This isn't new to me, as he's always been paranoid about the Mutes growing jealous of his ties to the MRA and coming in search for favors. A bookcase stands slightly crooked, revealing the safe room I knew was there. It's probably where he's getting all his food from and mainly what's kept him alive this far.

"Dare I ask what has happened to Bellemare? It looks like the apocalypse out there," I jerk my chin to the window, realizing they've been covered in foil to block out the sunlight. When Tracker continues to focus on giving himself lung cancer rather than answering me, I look across the wall of surveillance screens instead, not detecting any movement. My eyes pause on the hospital, noting how every window is shattered and doors have been ripped from the hinges. A fleeting memory tugs at my subconscious from the day I left that very building with an indigo-haired spirit on my tail. I shut it down before my heart begins to splinter all over again at the loss of a love I'd only just begun to know.

I hear a dull thud as Tracker tosses his cigar to the ground and stands to make his way over to me. For a man who once praised himself on his appearance, there's a defeated slump to his shoulders and his cropped hair has grown into a matted mess. Instead of stopping at my side, he continues past to reach for a thick, black binder and scrolls through the plastic sleeves inside.

"Thought you were a goner," Tracker mutters to himself, pausing on a page and taking a red marker out of his pocket. I inch closer to look at the long list of Mute names under the heading of 'M,' each with a small image of the person beside it. Tracker pulls the page free from its sleeve and uses his finger to locate me. I've been crossed out.

"What do you mean?" I ask as he draws a bold red line around my photo, effectively bringing me back to life in his binder of forgotten souls. The rest of the page though is covered in red X's and my chest constricts tightly. What the fuck? "Tracker, you're seriously freaking me out. Where is everybody?"

"More importantly," he turns on me with his dark eyes scowling, "Where the fuck have you been? The MRA turned on us, stormed the city and took whoever they wanted. So much for our peaceful nation. They set the rules and we blindly followed, yet it seems we were being herded from some bigger purpose instead." My eyes widen and Tracker grunts, walking off into his safe room. It's too coincidental that I would stumble upon a madman seeking Mutes to experiment on while my home was being attacked, but there were thousands of people here. Surely they couldn't have taken them all? My stomach rolls and a slice of cold cuts through me again. I button my denim jacket tightly over the baggy sweatshirt and wrap my arms around myself before following Tracker's steps.

"So…everyone's gone?" I have to ask, still unable to process what's right in front of me. I saw the abandoned streets and buildings, yet my soul yearns for this to be one big joke. That Mutes will pop up out of nowhere and shout 'fooled you!'

"All of those that didn't have the good sense to hide," Tracker grunts from his new position on the floor. The lights are brighter in here, making me wince as I drop down beside him. "I was already in my office when I heard the announcement over my personal MRA radio, and by then, it was too late to go anywhere else. I hauled up in this safe room as they took over the building and watched through a screen as they bound Spectrum with some kind of cuffs."

"You mean, cuffs like these?" I suddenly remember the heavyweight in my pocket and pull them out to show Tracker. The Mute I would have pegged as unshakable flinches and that says more than any words could. He's terrified. Lying them on the ground, our eyes remain glued to the chrome shackles, a heavy silence falling over us. Tracker has never been my favorite person, but when I think about him being locked in this 6×6 room with no one but himself, an ache in me resonates all too well. Suddenly, the past between us doesn't matter and we're two people lost in a sea of misery, barely staying afloat.

"It must have been miserable for you stuck in here. I know a thing or two about being alone and-"

"You've never been alone," Tracker growls, fury dripping from his tone. "No matter how much we distanced ourselves, all of the Mutes here were a civilization. We should have rallied together to overpower the humans before their technology could overpower us." He's right, of course. With the majority of Mutes having weakened genes and receiving harmless abilities, we tried to comply in hopes of being accepted. But being different and being accepted are two things that will never go together. Well, I for one, have had enough of being used and pushed around.

"We're not beaten yet," I say with conviction, pushing myself up straight. I may not be a Mute anymore, or ever was, but Tracker is right. These were my people. I'll stand and fight in their name until my last breath. We will prove that the Mutes were worth something.

That we mattered. "I was being held at a Mute facility. The humans are experimenting on the less harmful ones, but there's a pit of powerful Mutes hidden somewhere underneath. If anyone ordered a mass abduction, I bet I know exactly who it was."

Turning to Tracker, I take in his appearance properly and he does the same to me. His cheeks are gaunt, his eyes hollow. Since his ability doesn't depict his coloring, he's left with a hair and eye color that are in stark contrast to his pale skin. The tangled hair around his ears has grown so much, it's beginning to curl at the ends. It's his tattoos that intrigue me though, the winged skull on his shoulder baring a lot of resemblance to the one on my forearm.

"There's still time to fix this, but I'm going to need your help." I bend forward and grab the manacles, placing them in his hands. There may only be two of us, but every wave starts with a ripple. And Christopher - he has a whole tsunami of wrath coming his way. Nodding slowly, Tracker seems to absorb some of the newfound confidence he's unknowingly gifted me. So much so, that a small smile pulls at his mouth and his dark eyes focus on mine, glistening with determination.

"Tell me what you need."

GHOST

"**A**fter you," I hold the door open and gesture for Isabelle to enter before me. Smiling sweetly, she brushes her lips over my jawline as she passes, thanks to her six-inch heels. In any other circumstances, Isabelle's skimpy royal blue dress and smooth, long legs would have held my interest for at least a week or two. Unfortunately for her, no woman has been doing it for me since I laid eyes on Mania.

I blame Afterlife for fucking with my head, and Pyro for dangling her in front of me. But if I'm being honest, at least with myself, my attraction with Mania's blood-red eyes was instantaneous. She was so different yet feisty, and didn't give two shits about putting me in my place. Now though, she's weak and frail, yet I haven't grown disgusted by it like the old me would have. Instead, I just want to protect her.

Following Isabelle inside the room, I rest my hand on the small of her back and lead her over to the bar. There's already a tipsy glaze to her light brown eyes and she latches onto my arm for stability. I almost feel bad as I order her another large red wine from the bartender, but needs must. I need to know where Pyro is being held and I must get him back. Nothing else matters.

"Are you sure a delicate flower such as yourself wants to be in a room like this?" I ask, blocking out the background noise which is all man-made. Guttural groans, slapping skin and the low hum of multiple toys, all accompanied by the salty, sweaty smell of a good time. For them, at least. Black wipe-down material covers every wall and blocks out any chance of natural lighting. Chains hang from thick, metal hoops or full-body, cross restraints beside the row of sex swings. In theme with the dungeons, robust lockers house every toy, flogger, whip and restraint on the market hanging inside. Isabelle looks over her shoulder at the role-play dungeon, her smile growing.

"I'm not as delicate as you think," she quirks her eyebrow back in my direction. With her wine glass in hand, she twists on the barstool to watch the show before us and I step into her side. My fingers trail over her neck and shoulders, making her moan lightly in pleasure. I don't pay much attention to the others in the room, the novelty having worn off on me. After all, it was my idea.

Once Camo had started raking in the cash from his string of elusive brothels, we'd started playing poker together regularly at Club Supernova. One night of shots and this place was scribbled on the back of a menu. A strip club and brothel exclusively for Mutes. It's both a niche, and it gives some of us the choice to not flock to Bellemare just to be accepted.

This room, however, is for the real outcasts. Those who tested positive with Mute genetic markers, yet have no ability to speak off. It keeps the humans visiting though, thinking their dicks might be the miracle cure and one of the ladies might start breathing fire or climax herself into teleporting. It hasn't worked, except for Sole who discovered she can swap her left and right feet. Pretty shit ability but it got her a Mute name, moved up to the main stage and she can now put her heels on in the dark.

Returning my attention to my date, I pull up a stool and sit, facing her. Twisting Isabelle's body so her knees are between my thighs, I tip the wine glass, urging her to drink up. My fingers draw circles over her knees, working their way up to the hem of her tiny dress.

"You have a point," I smirk. "Delicate women don't seek out Mute lovers while their husbands are at work." That's a lie because I targeted her, slipping the Bee's brothel business card into her purse in a busy market, but she decided to come here. I just took it from there. Isabelle's face flashes with guilt until I lick my lips, bringing her attention to them. "There's a bad girl in there, waiting to break free." I lean forward, drawing a line from her collar bone to her cleavage, as if her skin would unzip and a horny minx would step out.

"Mmmm," Isabelle moans, biting down on her lip. "Except we aren't lovers."

"Yet," I grin, cringing on the inside. I've never had to flirt and play coy with a woman before. Usually, they jerk their eyebrows suggestively and I'd say 'come on then.' Done deal. Not this time though.

"But first, enlighten me. What could keep a man so busy that he wouldn't be at home, buried in the beautiful woman he's been blessed with?" I return my hands to her knees, pushing them beneath her dress and swiftly parting her thighs for me. Isabelle gasps and then giggles, downing her wine to set the glass onto the bar. Swiftly ordering another, I play into Isabelle's fluttering eyelashes and start to massage her open thighs. She rolls her head to the side, causing some of her carefully styled curls to fall free of her updo. My thumb catches the lace front of her panties, causing her to suck in a breath.

"My husband's work is very important," she mumbles. "He always has such eccentric stories about the..." her unfocused eyes look around and she leans forward to whisper, "the Mutes he looks after. So interesting, so forbidden," she trails her thumb across my bottom lip, her gaze heating. "I just had to see for myself."

"I hope I'm living up to expectations," I grin. Taking her thumb in between my teeth, I bite down hard enough to mark as my knuckles scrape over her soaking wet sex. Isabelle's groan is louder than some of the hookers in the room, the lack of tension in her shoulders showing the alcohol is having the intended effect. "Sounds like your husband is a busy man," I muse out loud.

"Yeah," she sighs. "He does a lot of night shifts, and when he is home, he's always too tired for me."

"Luckily for me," I wink. Isabelle blushes and rises to her feet to step into my body. My hands remain on her upper thighs, my fingers stroking the stretch of material covering her pussy. I have no doubt she has a freaky side and would probably ride me all night if I allowed her to. But this is all part of the plan. I might not be the genius mastermind Hoax was, but seducing the lonely wife is my way back. She holds the answers I need, I can feel it as surely as I can feel how wet she is for me. However, I vowed to myself I wouldn't waste a single day of my freedom out here, while Py is inevitably suffering in there. And as such, I've been doing my homework.

There's not a single building on the grid that has the necessary blueprints for an asylum, rehab, laboratory, infirmary and dungeon pit all in one. Of course, I wouldn't imagine Christopher does anything 'on the grid,' but after nights of researching in closed libraries across the state, I've decided it's just not feasible. There's too many differences in temperature, building materials, structure, equipment, professions. None of it makes sense. But that's where I draw a dead-end and that's why I need Isabelle.

"Well," I continue, lifting her by the ass and planting her down to straddle me, "if your place is free most nights, maybe I'll have to pay you a visit sometime." I grind into her for effect, the drag of my jean zipper making her whimper.

"Only when the portal shaft is closed. Otherwise he could pop home without warning and we've just paid off our holiday home in St Lucia." I grunt, not having pegged Isabelle as a gold digger but it's clearly not a healthy sex life that's keeping her marriage together. Her words have intrigued me though and I raise a hand to her breast, cupping it and rubbing her pert nipple through the satin.

"Portal shaft?"

"Mmhmm. Standard issue, silly." Her head dips as she hunts for my mouth, and I tweak her nipple hard to make her hiss instead. This conversation won't be silenced with my sinful mouth. I cock my head to the side, imploring her to continue with my white eyes. "But only the important officers have access to it at will. The rest have to meet at a central location to hitch a ride," she laughs at some unknown joke. I, however, find myself on the edge of my stool with my grip on her tensing.

"A ride? You mean there's some kind of transport that picks them all up?" I actually let it slip that I know about 'them,' but Isabelle doesn't seem to pick up on it. Instead, she takes a long swig of her wine before smiling widely at me.

"Well, if you classify an elevator as a source of transport," she hiccups and giggles again. Faintly, I hear her gasp and whine that she wasn't supposed to tell anyone but I'm no longer listening. Instead, I race through my memories, picking up on the times I've seen guards come and go inside Afterlife, or how Pyro told me he arrived in one rather than the caged delivery I turned up in. The fucking elevator! It doesn't move up and down an elevator shaft, it just…moves. Between locations.

Snapping back, I plaster an easy smile on and tilt Isabelle's wine glass to her lips once more. As soon as she's greedily gulped down every drop, I take it away and replace it with my mouth. A hot, searing kiss passes between us and it does nothing for me. Not. A. Fucking. Thing.

I only just realized how desperate I was to lose myself for a moment, to hang up the weight of my burdens and let this beautiful woman carry me away. Yet, her curves pressing into me and the caress of her tongue leave a bitter taste in my mouth and scorn on my mind. I don't want Isabelle. I want Mania. Writhing and screaming. Squirming and cursing. Her nails can tear my flesh to shreds to match what she's done to me on the inside, but it's nothing compared to what she's done to Pyro.

Pulling away from the way Isabelle is sucking my face, I take in the glaze to her blue eyes between long flutters of her lashes. She raises a hand to touch her puffy lips, giggling to herself.

"A transporting elevator, huh?" I join in her laughter, tightly squeezing her ass in my hands. She falls into hysterics, swaying forward to lie her head on my shoulder. "Where would someone even board something like that?" I grunt, seemingly to myself but right next to her ear.

"Thorncroft Central Station," she snickers as if it's one big joke. I smirk too, but for an entirely different reason. I doubt she even knows she said it as her legs give out and she clings to my shoulders. "I'm done talking," Isabelle murmurs in a husky voice. I sweep the guard's wife up in my arms, carrying her over to a corner of the spongey floor where the light doesn't touch. Propping her against the wall, I fix a metal chain to her ankle and skate my nails up her inner thigh.

"Get yourself started. I'll be right back," I breathe into her ear. Pressing a brief kiss to her lips, I walk away with Isabelle's fingers trailing down my arm and hand. Pulling a stack of notes out of my pocket, I dump it on the bar with a sharp order to the bartender to keep Isabelle happy, at all costs, and walk the fuck out without looking back.

The star-studded blanket of nightfall has settled over another turbulent day as Tracker and I pull up outside the church in a stolen MRA vehicle. Well, if it's classified as stealing if the vehicle has already been abandoned. Either way, there were tons of them all sitting forgotten with the keys in the ignition, imploring us to help ourselves. Tracker used his ability to trace an object's history on the sweatpants I'm wearing to find our way back to the church, which meant his hand has been on my thigh all afternoon while he sat behind the wheel. Something neither of us have enjoyed.

I step out and stretch my body, immediately regretting it as something twinges in my neck. My back aches and I feel weary yet again, not to even mention the chill seizing my bones. Seriously, fuck mortality. Same as the night before, there's no lights on in or around the church and the graveyard has enough shadows to trick the mind into seeing figures that aren't really there. There's no evidence Ghost is back yet, unless he's headed back to Bellemare in search of me, but I'll let him do the chasing for once. Tracker has parked directly in front of the arched doorway and I join his side to hear him grunt at our accommodation for at least tonight.

Regardless of whatever he thinks, the church is a quaint structure

I'd happily stay in. Not too big or in your face, but a modest building I need to explore properly in daylight. Carved statues stand on either side of the wooden door with a hint of more carvings embedded into the arch overhead. Aged stone scrapes across my fingertips as I stroke the inside wall before moving on to light some of the hanging candles. I've never felt a connection to a building before, but knowing there's a mass of spirits wandering the grounds makes me want to learn its history. To know who's passed through here. To study each name of every gravestone in the hopes that any trapped souls will feel remembered.

I don't head down to the crypt, mostly because being in Tracker's company is awkward enough without stuffing us into a small, darkened room. What's worse is he hasn't spoken since uncovering the manacle's history, the weight of what we've gotten caught up in hanging between us. Any glimmer of belief I held that we might stand a chance against Christopher vanished with the knowledge of what Tracker saw, so I know we're just going through the motions. Continuing on because it's the right thing to do for our kind, but we've already resigned to our defeat.

I finish lighting the candles with a matchbox I found on a windowsill while Tracker heads back out to the car. Pulling a kneeling cushion out from beneath a pew, I settle down on the floor, still in eyeline to keep a watch on Tracker. It's not that I don't trust him now we've found ourselves on the same side of a war we can't beat, but I wouldn't put it past him to make a run for it. I wouldn't even blame him. Regardless, he pops the trunk and retrieves the supplies he brought from the panic room and returns to join me.

Sitting on the stone steps before the altar, Tracker opens a cardboard box and sets about making a meal right in front of me. First he pulls out a plastic briefcase which, when he opens the lid, displays the mini camping stove concealed inside. In a large metal bowl, I watch Tracker measure out oats by the cup, add long-life milk and a healthy dose of honey. I can't look away, memorized with the ease that he's adapted in order to survive. This is the Mute who ordered a hit on his own chef for overcooking his steak. Having a decent ability in Bellemare didn't just make you popular, it made you powerful, and

Tracker abused his power on a daily basis. Yet here I sit as he hands me a bowl of mouth-wateringly sweet porridge and sets about making us some tea.

"Well," I say, trying to fill the silence as it begins to weigh on me. "This is…" Then again, maybe the silence is best because I don't know what the fuck to say. Tracker pays me no mind, only leaning over to place a plastic cup by my foot and snatch the metal bowl back.

"Save enough for me," he grumbles. I'd been so hungry, I didn't realizehow quickly I was wolfing down the meal we were supposed to be sharing. Come to think of it, I'm skinny because I'm lacking muscle mass from, you know…dying, whereas Tracker is skinny because he's been living on rations. I lift my tea to my cracked lips, sipping the steaming liquid as I let my eyes roam over him.

His bare legs poking out of his baggy shorts make me shiver and the huff that passes through his nose says he noticed. At least he's pulled on a hoodie and combed his hair through with his fingers, the curled ends reaching his shoulders. In another world, with some manners and a personality transplant, I easily could have gone for Tracker instead of his brother. But that was back when I knew I wasn't going to find any better. Now though, I know the truth of what real love feels like and the thought of settling for less disgusts me.

I look away, spotting the stars through a gothic-style window. It's pointless wishing Hoax would be up there, smiling down on me because I know for a fact, if he's not still on earth then he'll be in hell. Not suffering, but since the Big Man upstairs sees Mutes as an abomination, they have to go somewhere. It's possible Azella is with him, teaching him how to channel his anger into torturing souls like she did for me. Fuck, I miss Azella too. And Pyro, and Imp and Ammo and everyone else I've lost over the years. I'm starting to think Pyro's gift of life has been a curse since I'm still sitting here, miserable and heartbroken.

"For fuck's sake," Tracker moans and I return my attention to him. His gaze is fixed on my shoulders and I now realize I'm shivering. Not just a little bit, but with huge judders raking through my body and my teeth clashing together for the sound to bounce around the church. "Come here." When I don't immediately move, Tracker rolls his dark eyes and moves over to me instead. He removes the now spilled teacup from my hands and pulls me onto his lap. I don't relax but I don't move away either, causing him to sigh deeply.

"I didn't realize until today how much it's fucking sucked being alone. And if you die of cold, I'm going to have to fight this thing for no other reason than pure stubbornness."

"What reason does me being alive give you to fight?" I ask, my voice a shaky whimper at this point.

"I owe you," Tracker states. He looks away for a long while and I think he's not going to elaborate until his arms tighten slightly around me. "I knew I was antagonizing Hunter when I used to flirt with you, or stare at your ass on purpose when he was looking. We were twins, we had a common rivalry with everything and he suddenly had a hot girlfriend. I had no idea he would turn his anger onto you the way he did, and you had every right to make him pay for putting his hands on you."

My eyes widen, fixed on a crack in the floor as I process his words. Has Tracker been feeling guilty all of this time about antagonizing his brother? Is this why he continued agreeing to help me, despite his dickish attitude? A shiver works its way from the top of my neck and finishes in my toes. I don't pay it much mind, trying to think of a reply to give Tracker for his confession but not knowing what to say. Hunter was a woman-beating cock, no amount of teasing can turn someone into that if it's not already embedded in there somewhere. Instead, I wriggle down and lie my head in the crook of Tracker's neck.

"For survival's sake, I'm going to pretend you're someone else." The rumble of a bitter laugh vibrates from Tracker's chest, his own body easing beneath me.

"I'm gonna pretend you're anyone else," he retorts and I'm happy with that. Closing my eyes, I call on my imagination and am surprised when Hoax isn't the first image that greets me there. No, it's the flames dancing in Pyro's eyes at first, then his self-assured smile and soon, the entirety of him. His open, accepting arms. His cool smile and raging affection. The ideal contrast, packaged up specifically for me.

I've pointedly not thought about Pyro until this point for one simple reason. It hurts too fucking much. As much as I miss Hoax, the fact he's already dead makes it easier to mourn for him. Yet Pyro...I broke him. I left him grieving for the love he continued to give me until I saw it flee from his eyes. A lump of sorrow rises in my throat and threatens to suffocate me like it does every time I catch myself wondering if he's okay. Usually, I'd distract myself to think about anything else, but not this time. I embrace the pain and welcome it. I deserve to suffer for the way I turned a blind eye to what was happening, choosing to live in the present like I always have. The future was a fickle concept to me before his flaming eyes gave me a reason to think otherwise, but old habits die hard. That's my curse.

After the ache eventually gives way, I focus on Pyro's fires. The robust strength I'll need to lean on and the warmth I'll pull into myself to keep going. Instead of being consumed by guilt, I'll choose to honor the love we had. It's still here, thriving on my end. I love Pyro more than I thought I was capable of, if for nothing other than his constant sacrifices for the girl he'd never met.

"What the fuck is going on in here?" Ghost's booming voice cuts through the church, echoing high up in the support beams. I jolt upright and Tracker groans lightly. He's slouched against the altar, seeming to have drifted off to sleep but the hulking, moody Mute in the doorway has him shoving me aside to stand.

"You'll move away from her if you know what's good for you," Ghost snarls with more venom than I've ever heard him hurl at me. My eyes widen and the deadly undertone of promise hangs in the air. "Move. Away." Another growl comes but as I stand to walk towards him, Tracker holds an arm out to stop me.

"Don't," Tracker warns me. Some silent conversation is being passed between the two over-possessive males, the air around us thickening with testosterone. I roll my eyes, attempting to barge past him but his hand curls around my forearm and tightens sharply.

"Tracker, I'm presuming," Ghost states, taking a single step into the church. "You don't know me yet, but if Mania isn't by my side in the next ten seconds, you'll become overly familiar with my right fist." To his credit, Tracker doesn't bulk in the slightest. Even though the tense muscles of Ghost's frame are starting to heave. Tracker lowers his arm but I'm having too much fun seeing Ghost this wound up, so I remain still anyway.

"I know who you are, for the most part. I've seen everything you did while wearing the cuffs," Tracker gives me some serious side-eye and I frown. Suddenly, I remember how Ghost finger-blasted me behind the bleachers at Afterlife and I gasp. Heat of a whole new kind claims my cheeks, embarrassment clawing at me. My eyes fly to Ghost's but if he's reliving the same memory I am, his shadowed eyes don't show it. I open my mouth to say something, any damn thing to fill this awkward stand-off when Tracker edges in front of me once more and my eyeline is blocked by his back. "You killed her once, I won't let you do it again."

The air rushes out of me, almost in a laugh if Tracker's tone wasn't dripping with seriousness. He's defending me. Once upon a time, the Mute in front of me would have offered me up to his twin and taken pleasure in watching me being beaten down. Nevertheless, Tracker seems intent on rectifying that. Little does he know, where Ghost is concerned, I can fight my own battles and pissing him off is my specialty. Stepping out into the clearing, I feel Ghost's gaze spear me rather than see it.

"You sent me to find Tracker and here he is," I state accusingly. "He's traced the history of the manacles and we've got a lot to discuss. So leave your ego at the door and get the fuck in here already. I'm freezing," I lie, not half as cold as I was a small while ago. When no one moves, I step forward and click my fingers at Ghost, pointing to a pew on the left. I then do the same to Tracker, directing him to the right. With whatever is happening between the MRA and Mutes as we speak, there's no time for this macho bullshit. After a beat, the boys reluctantly comply and I take my spot by the altar, deciding to remain standing.

"Talk then. I've got news of my own," Ghost growls. The carefree fucktard that dumped me at the Bellemare boundary seems to be a distant memory and I'm surprised to find I miss him. Anything is better than the side-eye daggers he's giving the only Mute who can help us right now. Tracker isn't fazed though, having a lifetime of experience in dealing with bad attitudes, so he straightens and relays the information back to me as if we're the only two in the room.

"The manacles have only had one previous owner," he states and the fight suddenly goes out of Ghost's shoulders. "A male with eyes like burning steel. Lava coursing through his veins and a fiery temper to match. It took them years to break him, but he did. Eventually. Not having access to the very abilities we are carved from is enough to destroy even the toughest of us all, without the torturous experiments he had to endure." Tracker looks away, wetting his dry lips. "I really hope you know what you're getting into Mania. Our city wasn't purged for nothing, and now this. We're in deep shit here."

"How many are we talking?" Ghost interjects, hanging on Tracker's every word.

"Thousands," he responds, not looking anywhere other than at me. He clicks his fingers, the sound echoes like a whip's crack. "Gone."

"Well at least my news is more hopeful than what he came up with," Ghost scoffs and stands to walk away. What a douche. I fist my hands and storm after him into the graveyard, my steps hindered by the multiple layers of clothes constricting my body.

"It's not Tracker's fault what he saw!" I half-shout and thump Ghost on the back. Probably not the best idea but I can't believe after everything I've been through today, he's shrugging off Tracker's words as if they are useless. Quicker than my eyes can track in the dark, Ghost spins and pins me against a stone cross signaling we're standing over someone's grave. Sorry about that, whoever's down there.

"If that is what he saw. What if this is a trap?" A dry, humorless laugh leaves me as Ghost's white eyes hunt for mine in the dark. Shadows dance across the sharpness of his jaw and the tightness of his shoulders. We're sharing the same air, but it's thick with tension and laced with a dangerous undertone. Luckily, the multiple layers shielding me from the cold are also stopping Ghost's grip from digging into my skin.

"I'm not even going to justify that with an answer," I begin to wriggle in his hold to leave but then change my mind and remain right in his face. How dare he send me for answers and then question the ones I get. Nothing was going to be good enough, but I thought he'd at least grunt in approval or something.

"What possible reason would Tracker have to sit in his office for months on the off chance I might go looking for him? And what would anyone gain from trapping me? Christopher doesn't want me back at Afterlife and even if he did, at least that would be a solid lead." I don't let the rejection of not being wanted reflect in my voice, even if it is by someone like Christopher. Ghost has already seen too much weakness through my frail and defeated state, and I hate proving him right. That I'm nothing but a pathetic waste of air. Our noses brush as he growls down at me once more.

"I have a solid lead." I don't bother asking what it is since he won't tell me anyway. Instead, I remain in his hold, waiting to find out what else he wants from me. I don't know if Ghost realized how far his head has dipped, bringing his lips a breath away from mine. His thigh between my legs presses in closer, his body crowding me until nothing else exists. A low snarl of hatred rattles in his chest but I don't think it's aimed at me, but more at himself. He wants me, but he hates himself for it too. That's fine by me, let the bastard torture himself for being a pretentious prick. I won't fall for his bullshit anymore.

"You two finished?" Tracker asks casually from the doorway of the church. He's flicking something out of his nail and leaning against the jam, but the way his eyes are glued on us shows it's an act. Instead of moving away, Ghost pushes into me even closer until my chest can't rise to draw in a breath and his lips graze my ear.

"I send you for info and you bring another male back to bid for your attention. Were the three of us not enough for you?" Then he's gone and I stagger forward to stop myself from falling. I huff loudly, the evidence of my irritation becoming a cloud in front of my face. I thought I was the only one just getting a grip on my newfound hormones. Evidently not.

PYRO

I've become so dulled to the pain, I only hear the crack of the whip across my back instead of feeling it. My new jailer has been taunting me through the bars, too much of a pussy to open the door and fight me one on one. What I'd give to barbecue his ass. But my fires have abandoned me, ignoring my pleas until I gave up calling for them. Another crack echoes around the cell, quickly followed by a huff.

"It's no fun when it just lies there," he grumbles, referring to me as the 'it.' I hadn't noticed he wasn't alone until a female voice rings out, making my stomach churn.

"Your methods clearly aren't working either. Maybe it's time we start doing things my way like I've said since the beginning." Her words aren't a question, but sharply delivered with an edge of sarcasm. Her high heels make two clicks against the stone floor and I listen to the scrape of a key being pushed into the lock. I call for my fires with urgency now, refusing to let this Mute or human or whatever she is close enough to disable me for good. I can make a fiery whip of my own and hang Tate with it, burning her throat into dust, if they'd just come to me.

Delving deep inside, I hunt and scream internally for the smallest flame to come to my aid. Nothing. The lock's bolt shifts with a twang and within a few more clicks on her ridiculous shoes, her tiny hand lands on my shoulder. The shift in my core temperature is the only hint that my fires were still there at all, but Tate has seen to them being well and truly squashed until she deems fit.

"Get up Big Guy," she tries to soothe me with too much familiarity. "There's something you need to see." My teeth grit, the only warmth I have left currently running down my back in bloody rivets. I may not have my fire, but I still have my fists. Twisting on a groan, I allow Tate to ease me upright before cranking back my arm and throwing a punch towards her face. Stupidly, I didn't account for her hand still being on my shoulder and as she jerks, a bolt of ice shoots through my arm. I cry out this time, ruining all pretenses that I've become numb to pain entirely. The limb drops heavily into my lap, pinpricks running along my skin while my veins seize up with frost spawning inside.

I vaguely realize I'm being lifted into the wheelchair as I nurse my arm against my chest and the straps are tightened into place. As quickly as it started, the pain is distinguished by the release of Tate's hand and I slump forward on a gasp. Fucking half-Mute and the involuntary effect she has on me. A burning itch still tingles over the base of my skin and I start to scratch violently, grimacing that she got to me.

I'm wheeled into the elevator where two other guards are ready and waiting, electric batons in their hands. The asshole with the whip stands on the other side of the threshold, giving me a full-bodied grin and wave as I glance up at him through my hair. He can smile now, but I've seen his face and made a silent vow that I won't leave this place dead or alive without his blood coating my skin. My vision dances with possibilities as the doors close and after a brief trip, reopen in an intensely bright hallway.

I squint, halting the scratching on my arm in favor of shielding my eyes. Smooth, laminate flooring glides beneath the wheelchair as I'm pushed forward, blinking heavily to clear my vision. The checked pattern under the wheels gleams back up at me until I'm able to look side to side. Closed glass doors, old metal filing cabinets, forgotten cardboard boxes filled with brown files. Given the fact it seems utterly abandoned as well, I'd swear this was one of the police station levels in the shootout video games I used to play.

My suspicions are confirmed when I'm wheeled into an interrogation room, parked at a metal table and one of the guards grabs my wrists to cuff them to a loop in the center. My back screams in protest to my new position, the slashes cut into me flaring up with a new flood of sticky heat. I hold back my groan, desperately trying to retreat into the hardened shell I'd created around myself. One where no pain, words or heartbreak can touch me. The echo of Tate's heels clicking their way closer makes me wince, the darkness closing around me faltering and dissipating with each step.

"Look," she sighs, sitting down opposite. "You're making this much harder than it needs to be. Just give Christopher what he wants and save yourself...this." Tate waves a hand all over me, hinting to the wounds I now bear on the inside and outside. My eyes slowly rise to her face and I take in Tate properly for the first time. Her hair is a mess, shoved into a bun at the back with tendrils escaping all around her face. She's wearing an oversized jumper, as opposed to her usual fitted suits. Large glasses hang over her unfocused eyes and she rubs a circle over her temple to signal a headache.

"What the fuck happened to you?" I grumble, my throat scraping like sandpaper. I try to reposition myself but there's no chance of me getting comfortable while pinned across the table. I try to stand on shaky legs, only with the intent to ease my back but a sharp zap from a baton thrust into my side makes me collapse into the chair again. I throw a look over my shoulder at the smug-looking guard. He's one of the ugliest fuckers I've ever seen, his nose is at an awkward angle and the acne scars riddling his skin leaving large craters of welts. Tate brings my attention back to her with a drum of her fingernails on the metal table, her voice full of annoyance.

"You and your friend did," she huffs. "But mostly, I've quickly come to realize that there's no end goal here. Either we do as he says, or we're screwed. You're feeling the latter." There's no point asking who she was referring to. Christopher is so powerful around here, he doesn't need more than a pronoun to instill fear in those desperate for his approval. Tate, though, is apparently no longer one of his lackeys jumping through hoops. My head sways and I put it down to either blood loss or Tate's lingering touch.

"If you no longer care about Christopher's cause, why are you here trying to convince me to join it?"

"Because it's easier to give in. There was never a place for us in this world. Do yourself a favor, he's going to win either way." The defeated expression on Tate's face angers me further. Despite being a traitor, she was a Mute once and if she had a backbone, I might not have been in this mess. Hell, maybe no one at Afterlife would if she hadn't proven to Christopher we were weak and gullible. Oblivious to my spiraling thoughts surrounding her, Tate reaches around to a satchel I hadn't noticed she carried in. Producing an iPad, her lilac eyes level me with a nauseating amount of pity before she sighs. "And if you had given him what he wanted, I wouldn't have been forced to do this."

Spinning the tablet on me, I'm presented with an image from a highway camera. There's a time and date stamp, not that it means much to me since I don't have a clue how long I've been locked up now, but that's not what concerns me. In the snapshot, a male with dark coloring is seated beside Mania in the front of a navy car with the MRA logo printed across the hood. I ignore the minor details because my gaze is fixated on the male's hand firmly clasping Mania's thigh.

It's impossible to understand the hurricane of emotions that rile up inside me. There's rage, obviously. A blistering, hot rage flooded my system with an acidic bitterness. The need to kill something or someone blinds me, but at least the image isn't as clear now. Underneath it all, something I'm unfamiliar with shimmers just out of reach. Resentment, maybe, or acceptance. A slither of my psyche had been holding onto the hope that Mania wasn't completely lost to me. That she might be waiting somewhere in the asylum for me to be released.

I've spent more than a few nights wondering what went wrong. If I could have done more or whether I should have never bothered. Most times my mind would drift into fantasies of what it'd be like to see her again, imagining the words we'd share. In fact, I must have played out every scenario possible, but the image before proves I missed one. The relaxed expression on her pale face speaks volumes. She's over me, she's moved on and she truly is the heartless bitch I've been trying to convince myself she's not.

Tearing my gaze away, I choose to focus on a smear on the two-way mirror beyond Tate's head. Is Christopher behind there waiting for me to simply relent? Fuck that and fuck him. My fires are my essence and no matter how shattered my soul is, I will never hand them over. At this point, they're my only 'bargaining chip' as Christopher said himself in the lab. This is all a big game to him. He's the King, Tate's the sullen Queen and every Mute in existence are his pawns.

"Pyro," Tate leans forward to place a hand on my bound wrist. I growl like a caged animal but she doesn't remove the hand I'm going to disintegrate as soon as I'm able. "I'm trying to do you a favor here. It's better for everyone if you let go of her and your stubbornness now."

"You wanna do me a favor? Withdraw your ability and we'll see how stubborn I can really be." Tate's brow furrows and she stands slowly to move around the table.

"Uncuff him," she orders the guard behind me. There's a brief argument passed between the pair until the other goon is called inside and told to close the door. I don't turn around to watch but my ears are pricking as the guards try to intimidate Tate with their size. It's clear to even me she outranks them but everyone around here seems terrified to get on Christopher's bad side.

"Are you fucking crazy?!" One of the guards whisper-shouts and I'm inclined to agree. I don't need my fire to render her unconscious with a flick of my wrist. Snatching the keys for herself, Tate releases me regardless of the protests over my shoulder and spins the wheelchair around to face her.

"Pyro," she says softer this time. "I haven't used my ability on you since you were a resident of Afterlife." My eyes widen then, too many questions racing around my weary brain.

"What do you mean - *were* a resident?" I ask gingerly, deciding to pick my battles. Instead of answering my question, Tate lowers herself down to hold my gaze and asks her own.

"You don't have control over your fire anymore, do you?" A moment passes where we just stare at each other, Tate's face flickering with understanding while I promise her a torturous death with my eyes. Thinking of heartless bitches, Tate could lead the whole lot of them. She'll already be planning how to use this information to her advantage, earning herself a promotion. Out of the two of us, she'll be set for life and I'll be out on my ass.

Standing stiffly, I track Tate's every movement as she turns to the guards and lashes her hands out to touch them. Instantly, two sacks of shit crumple into heavy heaps on the floor at my feet. On the way down, I heard a crack resounding out from the mess of limbs and I grimace involuntarily. Tate bends down to retrieve one of the walkie-talkies hooked to their belts and holds it to her mouth.

"Claire, please report to Pinehurst station immediately. Your services are needed." My head snaps up, realization setting in.

"Of course you'd call your friend to revel in my lack of ability," I grit through my teeth. "What you going to do? Have her trap me inside my mind while you do whatever you like to my body?" I'd meant in a violent sense but Tate's eyes drop to my crotch and I stutter. Great going Py, give them more ideas. It's not like I could do anything if the ex-Mutes decide to gang up on me, although I wish them luck in getting any response from my dick. I wouldn't be surprised if he shrivels up and drops off at this point.

Without responding, Tate returns to her chair across the room and we sit in an awkward silence. I roll my ankles beneath the table, testing their mobility. Dropping my ice-burnt arm to my side, I flex my fingers and wait for the exact moment Tate is distracted by the door opening to move. Bolting out of the wheelchair, I grab the electric baton I was eyeing and hold it up in her direction with the spark zapping. Claire halts in the doorway, wide-eyed and Enzo crashes into her back. Motherfucker. I've changed my mind. He's going down first.

"Woah, woah!" Enzo holds his hands up and I take a step forward to stab the air in warning. "I'll call for backup."

"No," Tate shouts, standing in between me and her colleagues. She's close enough now that I could attack for her real but the way she stops Enzo from radioing out for help makes me pause. Clearly, she doesn't want witnesses to whatever they're about to do to me. I eye the mirror, now seeing it as my only way out but it'll take some force to shatter. "Pyro didn't knock out the guards, I did. Come inside and shut the door, he needs our help."

I scoff at Tate's words, keeping my stance solid but the others do as she says. The door is closed and they edge around the other side of the table gaping at me.

"Oh, Tate. What have you done?" Claire breathes, quivering like a leaf. She's dressed the way Tate should be, prim and proper with a thick plait of brown locks drawn over her shoulder. It's a stark comparison to Enzo's blue scrubs, his ever-watchful dark eyes glued to me. His cornrows are tied back and I have to wonder if he and Claire just came straight from a hair-braiding session. The four of us stand, assessing the situation from our personal standpoints. It's Claire who breaks the silence when I think she's about to crumble. "Tate. Seriously, what have you done?"

"They'll be fine," Tate spears a look towards the guard's resting forms. "I've hindered the left sides of their brains until we're ready for them to wake up again. I need you to make sure they have no recollection of being unconscious or what they heard just before. Pyro can't access his ability, which is game over for all of us." A sharp intake of breath from both Claire and Enzo makes me equally curious and determined to not let them get to my fires. 'Game over for all of us' sounds like a win to me.

"He'll know you've tampered," Claire states and I roll my eyes at the irrefutable 'he' again. It's like they're all scared to even mutter Christopher's name in fear he'll pop up at the mere mention. Tate scoffs and I leave them to their conversation.

"What's he going to do? Abandon me in the asylum while starting a lockdown protocol. I was set up in order to get rid of the annoying one. He was never part of the plan." Freezing, I contemplate what Tate just said with the chilling realization she's referring to Ghost. The lockdown, Ghost leaving while I remained behind. We played right into Christopher's hands. The ache of loss inside has my heart on the verge of cracking all over again, my eyes trailing back to the forgotten iPad that's finally gone into saver mode.

Lowering the baton, although I'm still on full alert, I take everyone's hesitation to frisk the guards for more keys than I would know what to do with, but I feel better hanging them on my person. I fill my grimy sweatpants pocket, all the while with no one stopping me. Tate comes near me and I jerk upwards, zapping the baton in her direction. She slowly lowers, lifting a torch from the belt of the guard closest to her and hands it over to me.

"Here. For your cell," she breathes in defeat. I scowl and this only makes Tate frown further. "I can't release you, but if you let Claire have a look inside your mind, we might be able to find out why your ability isn't working."

"So you can hand me over to be tested on some more. No thanks," I spit. Surprisingly, Claire steadily approaches me, concern filling her pale blue eyes.

"We're not the bad guys here Pyro," she tries to reassure me. "We merely did what we had to in order to survive. Took part in some clinical trials, donated samples in order to have a place to stay. Mutes are the result of a science experiment, but the research didn't stop with our existence. It only increased. It's not just us three who need your ability, it's everyone. Mute and otherwise."

"Why me? Throwing flames is hardly worth all the hassle Christopher is going to." Claire and Tate sigh in unison at this, sharing a sorrow-filled gaze that has my hackles rising.

"You have no idea of your potential. Our survival rests on you." It's clear that's all I'm going to get and despite myself, now I'm more curious than ever. Out of everyone in the room, it's Enzo's gaze I hunt for. Never one to be misogynistic, but if anyone here was to assault me while I'm under Claire's hold, it'd be him. He gives me a firm nod like we've passed some kind of bro-code. One I reciprocate with a clear threat from my red eyes.

Keeping my new loot grasped inside my pockets, I lower myself into the wheelchair on a relented sigh. It's not like Claire hasn't seen everything my brain has to hold anyway, but I must admit if I can find out how to get a hold on my fires again, it's a risk I need to take. It seems they are my downfall as much as my lifeline but ultimately, I'm nothing without them. Taking a steadying breath, I close my eyes as Claire's hands gently clasp the sides of my head and within an instant, everything goes black.

Staying low, we creep beneath the long line of windows around the back of the motel. The concrete is rough on my fingertips but if I weren't feeling my way along, I'd have to rely on Ghost in front to guide the way. No doubt he'd walk me into a nettle bush for shits and giggles. Not even the birds are awake yet, the only audible sounds coming from pesky crickets and the odd truck on the highway we veered off to get here. Tracker takes up the rear of our line, his boots biting at my heels when I pause for too long.

"This is ridiculous," I murmur to myself, not for the first time. Ghost hears me anyway and I slam into his ass when he halts. The dirt skids and my mind paints the image of him swiveling around to narrow his eyes at me. Just in case I'm right, I hold up my middle finger and squeak when he suddenly grabs it. Tracker grabs a hold of my side protectively but with a twist of his wrist, Ghost tumbles the three of us into the chosen room. I find myself as the filling in a Mania-sandwich between a tangle of limbs and instantly wriggle to army crawl free. My clothes become twisted and a leg of my sweatpants rides up but I don't pay it any mind.

"You were saying?" Ghost questions, finding a lamp to flick on and brush himself down as if I'm infectious. His cocky smile drops when I fold my arms, not impressed in the slightest. Just because he was able to sneak into the reception and steal the occupant's number, drawing them out with the ruse of a free dinner, doesn't mean I'm any happier with our current surroundings. Hideous bedspread. Check. Paper-thin walls. Check. The stench of underlying mold somewhere. Super check.

"I was *saying*, if we are going to break in somewhere, I don't see why it can't be a superstore so we can actually choose our own shit." Stomping over to the wardrobe and swinging the door open, I grimace at the clothes I find inside to prove my point. I know I'm being a brat but Ghost's hot and cold attitude makes me feel all kinds of unreasonable. And maybe I deserve to be a bit shitty when my humdrum life has become a whirlwind of theft and depravity. Shifting through the human's charity bank donations in Bellemare is one thing, but being limited to what's available to take is denting my personal style. I mean, we're stealing anyway. It might as well be worth it.

"And risk getting caught on CCTV?" Ghost snorts from across the room. He ensures the ugly, floral curtains are drawn together tightly and checks the bedside tables for anything of use. It won't be money he's looking for, since he has plenty which he can't spend due to our appearances. That's exactly why we're here at all. We can hardly go searching for this magical elevator of his with a huge Mute banner flashing over our heads. Joining my side at the wardrobe, Ghost uses his bicep to barge me out of the way. "You're lucky my ability is actually useful in high-pressure situations." He cocks his brow over his shoulder at Tracker, implying he is a lesser Mute and my hackles rise.

"Real useful," I roll my eyes. "Especially when Tate is around." This riles him the way I'd hoped, his teeth gritting hard enough to crack. Turning on me in the expanse of the wardrobe doorway, his ragged breath seeps into my skin. Anger crackles through my ears, yet the shudder that claims me isn't through fear. I want Ghost to take out his anger on me. I want him to bring my internal punishment to the surface, to mark me. Bruise me. Give me more reasons to hate him because fuck knows, the previous ones don't seem as strong anymore.

My throat tightens at the mere thought of his hand wrapping around my neck and excitement laces through me. Biting the insides of my cheeks, I notice the moment Ghost feels the shift in the air between us too, and it only makes his white gaze grow darker. Remaining centimeters away, Ghost's eyes continue to search mine for an eternity, hunting for something. I wish I knew what it was so I could give him the exact opposite, hoping it pushes us over the precipice we're toying with.

"Move," his deep voice rumbles through my core, encased in threat. I should do as he says, I know this. I'm only human now after all and Ghost is...not. Definitely not, with his milky white eyes and chaotic longer hair hanging over the cropped sides. With his bulging muscles and the corded veins disappearing beneath his rolled up sleeves. This isn't a male I should mess with on the best day, but I can't resist.

"Or what?"

"Or you'll be proving my suspicions that Pyro and Hoax meant nothing to you." Just like that, a bucket of ice-cold water floods my veins and my playful smirk turns into a scowl. He has no idea how deep my feelings for Hoax and Pyro run, or how agonizing it is to be away from them. Picturing Hoax's face, remembering Pyro's warmth. The anguish rises up within me so fast, it kicks the breath out of my lungs and fractures me in half. Again and again.

"Fuck. You," I spit back when all other words fail me. Regardless of the point he just made, Ghost takes a step closer and I edge backwards, becoming tangled in the clothes. Narrowing his eyes and cocking his head to the side, Ghost raises his hand as if to grasp my chin before changing his mind. When his eyes dip to my lips, it's me that turns my head away to break the tension between us. His words stung but I reckon they weren't entirely for me. They were aimed at himself, serving as a reminder of why he should hate me - although his hatred is clearly slipping.

"Shall I step outside so you two can screw and get it over with?" a voice breaks through the silence and I balk at Tracker's suggestion. I spot him leaning against a small dining table with two foldable chairs, pretending to pick at his nails. He's sure changed his tune from the

Mute who refused to sleep last night in case Ghost choked me out in my sleep. I suppose a day of listening to our bickering from the back seat of the MRA car has eased his mind that we're both as bad as each other.

Dismissing Ghost, I turn to grab every hanger with female clothing attached and lift them off the rail before padding over to the bathroom. There's no way I'm changing in here with the both of them watching, especially not after Tracker's comment has made me acutely aware of how vulnerable Ghost makes me without warning. Finding the bathroom light is a challenge on its own, a stupid plastic pendant on a piece of string, and any composure I had left vanishes.

"Don't forget this," Ghost's foot stops me from closing the door. His smirk is back as he hands me a plastic case with a woman's razor displayed inside. His white eyes dip to my exposed leg and on following his gaze, I'm horrified to see the thick coating of hair clinging to my leg. Holy. Crap. On second thoughts, *now* any composure I had left has vanished. This delayed puberty thing is no joke. I've been so wrapped up in layers and rushing freezing cold showers these past few weeks, I can't say I've felt my own legs and now I'm wondering what the rest of me might look like. I dread to think what's nestled between my thighs and Ghost's low chuckle says he's read my mind. A flush claws its way up my neck and settles in my cheeks, a shudder of embarrassment consuming me. Is this what women have to put up with?

"Winter warmth, asshole." I clutch the razor and turn back into the bathroom, but not before Ghost can have the last word.

"It's not even halfway through autumn yet, bitch tits." Slamming the door too harshly, considering the occupants of this room are supposed to be out at dinner, I dump the clothes over the closed toilet seat and switch on the shower. Cranking the dial as hot as it will go, I take to pacing while waiting for the steam to billow thickly around me. In the end, my fingers itch to do something so I take a toothbrush off a shelf beneath an oval mirror and aggressively brush my teeth. Stripping off once done, I'm beneath the spray and moaning softly as a male's voice makes me spin away on a squeal.

"Use these," Ghost demands from beside the bathtub. He dumps handfuls of makeup and bottles into the basin and then whips the white curtain closed between us as if I disgust him. I frown, still covering myself from my initial scare while my heart races from what I hope is fright and not anticipation. My eyes dart around, trying to spot his shadow through the material but when I finally peek, he's nowhere to be seen. Sneaky bastard.

I quickly lather shampoo into my hair until the realization sets in that Ghost could walk in on me at any point, and he had. Yet he hadn't spared my naked body a second glance, so what's the use in rushing? Who knows where my next shower might come from. With relaxed movements this time, I decide to pamper myself a little. A full-body shave, fruity lather coating my skin. Right up until rising off some mudpack I'd found in a tub in the corner, when suddenly my mind conjures an image of Pyro standing in his Afterlife shower with his hands pressed into the tiles and his head hung low.

My hands pause over my face and a sob builds from nowhere, becoming lodged in my throat. I shut off the water, my shoulders hanging heavily as I get out and wrap a towel around my middle. Despite gearing up for some daring rescue that will no doubt fail, I'd let Pyro's sacrifice slip my mind and I hate myself for it. As dominating as Ghost's personality is, it was me who briefly lost focus of what matters. Of who matters. I try to imagine what Hoax would tell me if he were here and come up empty. I'd like to ask Ghost since he knew his best friend better than I got the chance to, but my stubbornness won't let me.

I pick up a tube of spray-on hair coloring laying on top of the pile, glancing over the other bottles of makeup and who-knows-what underneath. Taking full advantage of the hairdryer in a holder on the wall, I dry my waves before attacking them with the purple spray. I look upon the pile of clothes with disinterest, no longer caring about the menial items. Still, the woman staying at this shitty motel has better fashion than I gave her credit for and I'm soon swishing the skirt of a black dress side to side. The front is buttoned from hem to bust and tiny, yellow flowers decorate the material.

Something about the dress awakens an entity in me. Like slipping into a different skin, my mindset has followed suit and is finally seeing clearly now. Pyro may still be trapped because of me, but he also has no idea about Hoax's body - I'm presuming. I already know in my heart he will never want me back, but I need to help him bring Hoax back, even if it kills me. Pulling on a thick pair of tights, I turn to the cleared mirror with a new sense of determination. For all the good it will do, this is my shot to deem myself worthy of the love I was once freely given, so I need to give it my all. And to do that, it's time to get into character. Fake it 'til you make it, right?

I'm soon staring at my appearance, unsure if I like the reflection or not. My skin now has a golden glow thanks to the hash job I made of smearing foundation all over my face, neck and chest. The purple hair jars against my red eyes until I find a pack of brown contact lenses among the pile of beauty products.

A beast of a man appears in the mirror behind me, but I'm more prepared this time as Ghost takes a menacing step towards me. The frustration in his gaze wavers as he assesses my reflection and spares a quick glance down to my ass.

"Are you fucking ready yet? You've been in here for ages," Ghost growls, lacking the usual conviction. I don't respond as I am also busy gaping. His white hair has been sprayed black, making the cropped sides blend flawless into the five-o'clock shadow he's sporting across his jaw. He seems to have used the same contacts, making it too easy to forget he's not the standard Ghost I can't be near for too long, for multiple reasons.

"You found some hair dye too?" I ask, only to fill the silence when he doesn't comment on my appearance. Not that I question why that irritates me so much. His response is a grunt about shoe polish and his hand closes tightly around my arm to drag me back through the door. His party trick is getting old when I could easily open the door via the handle like a regular being, but I sense this is more of a power play for my benefit. Either that or he wants any excuse to touch me. I can't deny the way my skin tingles beneath his palm, or how the rough contact makes my pulse spike. Upon seeing Tracker, all effects of Ghost's close proximity are forgotten and a choked laugh bursts from me.

"Save it," Tracker scowls. His almost black eyes trail the length of my body in the lamplight, one eyebrow hitching. He's unnecessarily altered his look too, most likely to avoid being recognized than anything else. A beanie hat covers his curly hair and he's wearing a basketball jersey complete with baggy shorts, high white socks and high-top sneakers. Sure is unrecognizable alright, considering Tracker must be somewhere in his 40's. "The couple must have a teenage son, and he wasn't going to fit into anything else."

I follow Tracker's hand flick to Ghost. Other than his hair and eyes, he doesn't appear too different from usual. The dark t-shirt hugging his body is a few sizes too small and a pair of stretchy skinny jeans that leave nothing to the imagination glide into a pair of Chelsea boots. I smirk, hoping the circulation is being cut off from his dick so he can tuck away his big dick energy for a while. Then the heaviness in the room settles on me again and I'm equally ready as I am dreading moving.

"Time to head out," I take charge and hold my hand palm up for Ghost to get us out of here. He raises a brow at my hand and turns away with a light scoff. I spot Tracker looking up, vying for patience while Ghost pulls out his phone and lifts it to his ear.

"Camo, it's me. We're going on a road trip, be ready in an hour."

GHOST

Thorncroft Central Station.
A central pillar of transport in the town of Thornberry and built by Edward
Thorncroft himself, the first mayor of this rural suburb. As a major stop in
the NorthWest Railway service, commuters have graced our humble
town-

I crumple the leaflet in my hands, throwing it overarm into the trash can on the other side of the platform. A few humans stop to watch its straight dunk and appraise me with surprised smiles. I duck my head away, still uncomfortable being this close to them out in the open. Not because I'm scared or some shit like that, but because I'm on the verge of putting my hands to better use than flicking through every leaflet this station has about itself. Behind the contact lens and can of spray paint, I'm still the Ghost everyone should fear. Degraded, outcast, slightly unhinged and eager to make the world pay for what they've done to my kin.

Camo and I have scoured the layout of each platform both on paper and for ourselves, yet this bench is as far as we've gotten in finding some hidden portal. I figured it wouldn't be easy to locate but still, if it was being used as the central location for every guard's shift change, I thought I'd at least have spotted some of the bastards from Afterlife by now. My mind churns with 'what ifs' and 'maybes,' all of which Mania is currently voicing from right beside me.

"Are you sure you checked all the fire escapes on this level? What kind of door do you think we're even looking for? In theory, it should be a sliding door to imitate the elevator. When I've been inside, the door always slides open." My eyes slide to her with a bored expression.

"No shit," I drawl. We've gone from a morning of not speaking, to Mania trailing around after me and saying every damn thing that comes to mind. If I'd known what kind of door we needed, I'd have been there by now. "How long is he going to be?" I scrub a hand over my face, referring to the Mute who is disposing of our MRA vehicle and taking his sweet time about it. If I didn't think his ability would come in useful, I'd have been combing the underground tunnels and incomplete tracks by now.

"Just like the last time you asked. I. Don't. Know," Mania rolls her concealed eyes at me. A couple approaches us to ask Mania if she can take their photograph kissing in front of the train and willingly hand over their phone, which she accepts. Snapping a few shots in both landscape and portrait, they wish Mania a lovely afternoon and she returns to me almost skipping. My scowl, however, may be permanently etched in.

"What the fuck are you doing, playing human like that?"

"Err, blending in. I thought that was the point of this," she flicks her purple hair. I try to resist looking at her for too long but like they have the rest of the day, my eyes drag over her face and body. Something about being anonymous and hiding in plain sight has me feeling all kinds of strange and not in a healthy way. I could bend Mania over this bench, lift her dress, slam home inside her and the most I'd get done for is common indecency. It's a naughty, forbidden fantasy that brings a smile to my face. Not to mention, hot as fuck.

Deciding to follow her example, I rest back on the wooden bench and sling my arm over Mania's shoulder. Easing her into me, I ignore the rigidness of her body and spot Camo on the opposite platform as the train acting as our barricade rolls out of the way. I give him a small wave and remain seated until he's made his way over a walkway to join us. He sits a little further down the bench, leaving his elbows on dark jeans. Camo doesn't usually ditch his suit but I'd given specific instructions to blend in, hence the reason he's camouflaging his olive-green hair and eyes in favor of brown. Tracker also arrives, giving my arm around Mania a look of disgust.

"How cozy," Tracker comments and kicks my foot with his muddy sneaker. Playing into his oversized teenage look, his whole jersey is filthy and there's a grease mark on his cheek.

"You were meant to ditch the car, not fuck it," I grin, withdrawing from Mania as I stand. She fits into the side of my body a little too easily, a feeling I can't get used to if we stand any chance at finding Pyro. A little distraction I can handle but the way my moods are swinging from broody to horny will threaten our whole operation. "Let's go." I lead the three of them along the platform and across a bridged walkway while trains pass underneath. Smooth tarmac ramps and the factory iron-cast railings prove this is one of the more recent additions that would probably have had a cynic like Mr. Thorncroft turning in his grave. I'm sure back in his day, you jumped from platform to platform and if you got electrocuted, that was one less mouth for the town to feed.

The opposite platform must be the busiest, as this is also where the long line of alternating coffee shops and waiting rooms are. Large, glass windows show the hordes of humans huddled inside, hiding from the incoming chill of the season. After my comment to Mania on it being merely autumn, she's stubbornly gone without more than a light jacket over her summer-style dress and tights, contradicting her need to dive into one of the passing coffee shops for a large travel mug of steaming liquid.

I approach the only door I've seen staff members in high-vis jackets using while scoping the area, a thick metal fire door with a keypad lock. The camera above moves electronically as I imagine a hefty man sitting behind the controls with a joystick in one hand and a doughnut in the other. Resting against the wall, I urge the others to do the same with a glance and check my watch casually. If there's a discreet way into the rumored tunnels underneath, this has to be it, and if I were to create a portal into an asylum, that's exactly where I'd put it.

"Now what?" Mania asks through chattering teeth. She looks anxious enough to get us caught and I don't know whether to slap the jitteriness out of her or to pull her into my arms and banish that cold once and for all. Instead, I fist my hands by my sides and growl back at her.

"Now we wait." I expect her to question me further but she must realize that's all I'm going to give. My eyes scale the interior of the building, up to the mix-match of original wooden beams and sheets of glass leading to an open skylight at the top. The platforms either side of the station are shielded but you're shit out of luck if you're waiting in the middle for the central lines to Bakersville and Chester's Ridge. I risk a sly glance up at the camera again, seeing it's still trained on me.

Crossing my arms, we remain there as announcements are made for upcoming services and the trains come and go, yet the camera remains fixated on us. Shit, maybe we're not as disguised as I thought. Until I'm sure we aren't being the highlight of someone's afternoon snooping, Camo can't blend us into the wall while I drag everyone through it. My foot taps impatiently, the need to get moving driving me insane with suspension. It's occurred to me that given the employee accommodation at Afterlife, the guard changeover might happen every few days or even weekly, and if we miss it, we can't keep coming back around without raising suspicion. Opening my mouth to moan about something and anything, the tell-tale *ding-dong* of the tannoy rings out around us.

'Attention all passengers, the next scheduled train on platform two is not scheduled to stop at this station. Please stand back and remain behind the yellow lines until the train has passed. Thank you.'

Given we're on platform one, I watch the complicit humans take an exaggerated step back and women clutch their children tightly in fear the approaching train might rear off the tracks and attack them. All except one. My gaze snags on the female who is now standing apart from the crowd, her bare feet planted on the yellow line. Her face is tilted downward out of view beneath a mass of disheveled black hair, her clothes smart if they were pulled straight. I spot her heels discarded by a briefcase on the ground, the scene playing out before me as if in slow-motion. She looks up instinctively, her eyes snaring mine in a dare I can't comprehend as the rhythmic drumming on the tracks grows closer and she takes a confident step in front of the train.

My gut drops and my sharp intake of breath is echoed by Mania's sharp scream. She tries to move forward but I grab her wrist, pinning her back against the wall. A faint electronic buzz of the camera moving catches my ear and before I contemplate on it too hard, I pull her through the door. Mania gasps, fighting against my hold but I throw her backwards, ignoring the pounding on my back as I reach through to grab the other two and yank them by the collars to join us.

"What are you doing?! We could have-" I clamp my hand over Mania's mouth, assessing our surroundings. We're in a damp hallway full of pipes, the end disappearing into a darkened staircase. There's no one around and more importantly, no cameras. I hadn't thought about Camo blending us into the surroundings when I made the snap decision to move, one Mania is giving me a death stare for. I release her mouth, ignoring the other pairs of curious eyes as I tower over her, my words practically hissing with frustration.

"Since when did we care about saving humans? It's their fault Pyro is stuck in an asylum and Hoax is dead. Focus on saving the ones you claim to love, than wasting your bleeding heart on those who wouldn't waste a second trying to save you." Stalking away, my ears prick at the trio of shoes following and I breathe a sigh of relief. Thank fuck she isn't going to throw a bitch fit and dig in her heels when we've finally got work to do. Pausing at the staircase, I turn to jerk my chin at Tracker and then point to the railing. "Look to see if men in blue shirts and black ties have come this way."

He doesn't refuse my order, placing a hand on the metal and briefly closing his eyes. Almost instantly, they snap back open and he gives me a grave nod. Concern floods his expression and I'm sure I don't want to know why, but he jogs down the steps before I get the chance to ask either way. Mania barges past and Camo shoots me a wink, remaining casual as fuck like this is a day trip out for him. I find myself at the back, the heavy fall of my boots ringing out against the metal steps louder than anyone else's. As much as I want to be leading this show, it's probably best Tracker uses his touch and insider knowledge to guide the way.

We level out in an underground tunnel, the air stale and the scratchy claws of rats within the walls. The tunnel spans as far as the eye can see on both sides with a third exit directly in front. The tracks look beaten to shit, the wooden slats in between decayed and broken. Graffiti tags line the curved brick walls and the clusters of cigarette butts and empty glass bottles suggest this is a regular yob hangout. These surroundings aren't much different than my room at the bunker, and selfishly, I suddenly crave my solitude. What I wouldn't give to lose myself with a few cans of spray paint and to know I've left my mark in some hidden corner of the world. My hobby seemed like a convenience to pass the time while my brothers were too occupied to spend time with me, but now I see it for what it was. A way to leave my mark and prove I was here.

"Anything worth mentioning?" I ask Tracker after he's bent down to touch the rails on the ground. He stands with a head shake and I grit my teeth. "Fine. Let's split up. If you find anything, send a message." I tap the burner phone in Mania's jacket pocket, reminding her of the device we picked up on the way over here. "Anything at all." I hold her eye, waiting for her patronizing nod before stalking away. I take the right side and a quick look over my shoulder shows Camo heading opposite while Mania and Tracker go left.

Keeping to one side of the tunnel, I'm careful not to disturb the stones with my boots, remaining on high alert. Small spotlights along the ceiling cast my own shadow in a dizzying pattern, like a vulture circling around me. The trek feels endless when in actual fact, I can't have been walking for longer than twenty minutes. Still, the repetitive wooden planks on the floor are starting to draw me into a trance. Running a hand through my hair, I falter and wonder if splitting up was for the best, but since it was my idea I can hardly run back now.

Chatter sounds from further down the tunnel and I roll my eyes, figuring we've all gone in one big circle. Moving closer, I hiss as someone grabs my arm from nowhere, burning a handprint into my skin. I spin, finding no one there as a uniformed guard rounds the corner and I dive sideways through the wall. Dirt weighs down on me like a sack of bricks, filling my mouth and nose as I look for an air pocket between the earth and the concrete. Distorting the particles of the wall, I manage to wiggle my face through to the other side and draw in a panicked breath. If anyone were to look my way now, they'd see my hovering face within the concrete. Luckily, however, the first guard and his two friends are enthralled in their conversation.

The guard at the back is heaving all of his weight against a cart on wheels, pushing it along the tracks by sheer force. The others have a hand on either side, putting in minimal effort of helping out. One of the wheels is dented, causing an ear-piercing squeak to screech every time it flips over on the rail and the contents inside judders. Wiggling my ears free, I try to focus on their words when a single arm flops out of the cart and I freeze. The guard closest leans over to lift the cover and that's when I see it. Bodies. Heaps of bodies. A glimpse of neon blue hair catches my attention before the limb is tossed back inside and the cover closed once more. They can't be...Please tell me that cart isn't full of...Mutes.

The load on my back is threatening to crush me completely so I pull myself back into the tunnel, ducking low in case a guard should check over his shoulder. Hopefully, he'll mistake me for a gigantic rat and I'll move before he can get a closer look. The guards, the cart and the squeak continue on, rounding the tunnel in the direction I came from. Grabbing for my phone, I hunch over in an effort to hide the light in case any more guards are on their way and tap for Mania. The dial tone rings out. My shouty-caps messages go unanswered. My heart kicks up a notch.

Without any other choice, I take after the guards, keeping just enough distance to not alert them of my presence. I move when the squeak ricochets off the curved ceiling, I breathe into the sleeve at my wrist. Every moment I don't feel the phone in my hand vibrate is a moment I'm closer to causing a distraction to lead the guards back my way. But if Mania is in trouble, that wouldn't help either of us. I shake my head, mentally cursing her name. I swear, she'd better be safe so I can kill her, otherwise I'll never forgive myself.

"Well, it's a door. Now what?" I ask Tracker while smoothing my hand over the solid metal. I'd bet my last breath it slides as well. I could try for a high-five if a) I didn't think Tracker would reject me and b) trepidation wasn't clawing its way up my throat, trying to strangle me from the inside. It's unlikely but possible Afterlife Asylum is on the other side of this door. And then what...I have to convince my ex-soul mate that his best friend isn't fully dead and he's the only way we can get him back, so I can see if there's really something between Hoax and I. Not exactly the love story I fantasized about when I was still naive enough to dream. Tracker joins my side, assessing the tracks that disappear beneath the huge double doors before raising his fist as if to knock. I slap his hand away in panic, using my body as a barricade.

"Problem?" Tracker asks, cocking an eyebrow.

"No, I...We need to wait for the others. Just in case." I can tell he doesn't believe me but after a lopsided shrug, he turns and heads back the way we came. Calming my pounding heart, I shove aside my anxiety before racing to catch up to Tracker's side. Spotlights line our way, highlighting small alcoves along one side where vertical ladders prove possible escape routes if necessary. My nose still hadn't adjusted to the stench of mildew and no matter how many times I tug the jacket sleeves down over my hands, I can't banish the chill consuming me. I can't deny the comfort Tracker's stoic company is bringing me though, something I never imagined I'd think.

"The old Tracker didn't take orders, he barked them. You sure have changed." I comment out loud with a weak smile.

"No shit," Tracker scoffs but then his façade shatters on a long sigh. "The first few days after everyone was taken and the clever few that hid were hunted down, I just watched from the safety of my office, like it was like a sitcom or something. I was so…detached from it all. And it was at that point, I realized how worthless I really am. My ability drew people in, and I abused it to get what I wanted from women and the MRA. But when the time came…"

"None of them stayed with you," I finished when I was sure he wouldn't.

"I waited like a fucking idiot for a guard to come and escort me away. They'd protected me before, I thought they would again. Stupid fucking idiot," he mutters the last part. "Anyways, what I'm trying to say is…thanks, I guess. For coming to find me. For needing me." I stop still, unsure if I heard him correctly. Did Tracker just thank me? If I was in a teasing mood, I'd play dumb to make him say it again but the tension within the tunnel doesn't call for it.

"Tracker, I-" a squeak punctures the air and we spin in unison. Tracker moves to stand in front of me but I don't wait for him to take the force of whatever is coming our way. Grabbing his arm, I drag the pair of us around the next bend and shove him into the first alcove I spot. Voices grow louder and I press myself in closer, the matching thrum of our racing hearts beating against each other. Tracker wraps his arms around me but not in anything other than a protective way, I think.

Time freezes as the voices and sound of wheels creep closer. My breathing heaves in shallow pants until Tracker's hand snakes up between us and gently closes over my lips. His palm is clammy yet I press into the warmth, allowing my eyes to shut before I have a heart attack. At least that's what I imagine the palpitations in my chest are the stirrings of. The repetitive squeak, squeak, squeak stops and my shoulders sag in relief. Whoever it was has passed. Pushing away from Tracker, his hold on me tightens and I frown in confusion.

Jerking my head aside and out of his hold, I shudder to a stop as a pair of yellow-tinted eyes pin me with a glare. They're dull at first, barely visible, but the longer I stare the brighter they become. Soon, luminescent, golden orbs have me trapped in their sights and I'm unable to pull myself away.

"Something wrong, Detective?" a voice rings out but those eyes have me trapped, unable to move under their scrutiny. Tracker must have spotted them too, his arms around me stiffening.

"Mutes," a thick voice laced with hatred echoes around us. It came from him, the one with the eyes boring a hole through my skull. Footsteps descend upon us before a full scream has left my mouth and Tracker is ripped from my grip. I reach for his basketball jersey, my fingers biting at the fabric but I don't get a tight enough hold to drag him backwards or myself closer. Tossing him aside, the guard steps towards me and I bolt, leaving Tracker in favor of finding help. My chest constricts to protect Tracker the way he has been doing for me, but what use am I in this hollow human shell? I'd be dead before I could land a single, awkward punch and he would soon follow. Ghost and Camo are my only options, yet my feet barely make it more than five steps.

The band of a strong forearm winds around my waist, lifting me off my feet and I scream bloody murder. Kicking wildly, wriggling fruitlessly, I'm carried back and dropped into the cart before a fist slams into my skull. My body flops back on the plastic cover beneath my fingertips, my head ringing and spots blurring my vision. Hands close around my throat, cutting off my air supply and one lone tear escapes my eye. I clasp onto the arm pinning me in place, not bothering trying to pull it away. There's no use when I'm this weak. This feeble. And I can't deny it's the least I deserve after hurting Pyro the way I did, forced or not. I can only lie here as the darkness ascends, praying to a god who hates me that Hoax is waiting on the other side.

His indigo eyes burst to life in my mind, the warmth of his breath brushing my lips. The Mute I was unable to touch, yet he touched my soul with his love and I gave him nothing in return. A few fucks and a shit load of resistance, yet I know he loved me simply for me. Heat sweeps my veins, the lightness of my head drifting me from my body. I lazily roll my eyes to the side, glimpses of the scene around me filtering through. Tracker on his back, unmoving. Ghost has appeared, his face barely recognizable behind a mask of blood and rage. My heart expands further, somehow knowing his rage is burning for me.

My hands, still holding the hairy arm digging into my chest, tingle before a blinding flash of light explodes behind my closing eyelids. I jerk with the force of it, faintly realizing I'm not being held down any longer. The sweet precipice of my death claiming me clears as a full breath racks my body, slicing through my lungs as if the air around me is shrouded in broken glass. I splutter, twisting onto my side and clutching my mid-section. The material under me crumbles and the lumpy contents hidden beneath drag me down as I squirm. Suddenly, hands are on me again, heaving my limp body out of the pit I'd created and tossing me like a rag doll into the abyss. Air rushes past my ears, my responses still trailing behind as I'm caught and huddled close to a steel-iron chest.

"I need you to run," Ghost's voice comes from nearby, and before I get the chance to answer, I'm planted on my feet and shoved forward. I stumble and obey, peeling my eyes open as I flee from whatever carnage is happening behind me. Blood-curdled cries fill the air, accompanied by the grunting of fully grown men attacking each other like savages. I can only guess that it was Tracker who pulled me from the crate and if Ghost is still standing, that means we're winning. Scrambling around the next sharp bend, I slam into a body and scream. Camo's once-again green eyes widen, his hands raising innocently.

"Shit, Mania! What the fuck's going on?!" He looks over my head, peering into the darkness.

"Ghost, Tracker!" I pant, pointing backwards. "Guards and a Mute, attacking. Help them!" I urge him, trying to get around him but he moves to stand in my way.

"You can't go running off," Camo states, the hint of a scowl just visible in his features. "What if there's more guards back there and then you're alone. Stay behind me, out of sight but close enough so I know where you are." I nod weakly at his logic, hiding behind his back. A ripple washes over me and I can tell we've been concealed by his ability because as we walk back towards the bloodbath, no one stops to notice us. I peek around his jacketed shoulder despite myself, needing to see what's happening.

Ghost is crouched over a guard, giving him a tour of his knuckles while Tracker evades two more. Tracker isn't a natural fighter, having been protected well by his contacts for years, but he's quick on his feet and playing a good offense. Ducking and weaving, throwing in jabs where he can. The Mute, the one I presume is called 'Detective,' leans against the cart, intent on watching. One of the guards breaks away from Tracker, turning his attention on Ghost's hunched back and I scream his name in warning. Ghost freezes, looking around for me in the dark and the moment's hesitation is all the guard needs to gain the upper hand.

His boot roundhouses into the side of Ghost's face, knocking him flying. I wince as Ghost's shoulder takes the brunt of the fall, the scrape of skin on gravel undeniable. I try to run to him but Camo catches my wrist, pulling me back into the cloak of his ability. No one seemed to notice, too intent on pulling out their batons and attempting to taser the Mutes I'm rooting for unconscious. Ghost is fast though, fast enough to roll out of the electrical current and kick the guard's feet out from beneath him. Snatching the baton, he digs it into the guard's side and keeps it there until he's pushed himself upright. A relieved breath escapes me, but it's short-lived as the guard tasering Tracker slams his boot heavily into Tracker's gut.

"No!" I cry out, confusing Ghost again. He shakes his head, raising the baton high into the air and charges at the remaining guard. This one, however, came prepared. The metallic glint of a gun catches the light a moment before the deafening crack of a shot rings out inside the tunnel. The curved ceiling amplifies the sound with the fierceness of thunder, booming all around and making me dizzy. The skid of boots refocuses my eyes and I blow out a breath to see Ghost is still upright and grappling with the guard until the gun is tossed aside. Then, the two lay into each other the old-fashioned way. Fists flying and blood spraying between grunts of exertion. I strain in Camo's grip, my muscles heavier than lead but I know I need to move. I need to do…something. Bucking and jerking, I yell at Camo to release me.

"I can't do that," he grunts, his punishing hold around my front threatening to crush me inwards. Fuck whatever bro-ship he has with Ghost to keep me safe, I refuse to stand by and watch another Mute I lo…athe get hurt because of me. I'm the one who needs to find Pyro and I'm the reason we're all here. Sinking my teeth into Camo's arm, the copper of his blood fills my mouth and he releases me on a curse. I can't pretend to feel guilty, not when Tracker is slowly rolling onto his side and I skid to a halt beside him.

"Come on, Track. We need to get you out of here," I groan as I try to lift his dead weight. His injuries in the dim lighting don't look too bad but the taser seems to have really taken it out of him. On the third attempt, Tracker uses all his strength to help me sit him upright. "That's it, we can do this. I'm not done needing you yet." I grip Tracker's forearms and heave but it's Camo who drags him to his feet after joining my mission to get Tracker out of here. The dull thud of a body falling behind me must be the guard, so as Camo bends to dust off Tracker's legs, a smile graces my lips.

Bang. Warm liquid sprays all over my face. A faint breeze gliding over the tip of my hairline barely registers. My eyes widen, my heart stops. At such close range, this time the gunshot has deafened me. My ears ring, my mind whirling to catch up with what I'm witnessing. The split second where Tracker's eyes lose all traces of life and his body drops to the floor feels like an eternity. And there he lays, crumpled at my feet with a clean bullet hole piercing his forehead. Behind the place he stood mere moments ago is the Mute with luminous green eyes and the handgun he's lowering to his side. Camo stands slowly, also weary of the enemy opposite. The scream I know I should be releasing doesn't come as shock takes over. No…it can't… we had the upper hand, we…

I slowly look around to Ghost as he steps in behind me, needing to rely on him for strength but it's not his concealed eyes I see staring back. The guard standing there instead raises an eyebrow, daring me to try something stupid. I can't comprehend what's happening as my brain struggles to function. I hunt for the real Ghost, spotting another heap on the floor but I can see the rise and fall of his chest, reassuring me he's still alive. For now. The shudder that rolls through me claims every inch of my body, filling me with icy dread.

"Hey, Detective Dipshit," Camo calls out. My brow furrows at this, my head twisting back around as Camo grabs and swings me in front of him to close a hand around my neck. "You missed one."

Claire's palms gently ease away from my temple, her fingertips catching my head as it lolls to the side. My memories whip around as if trapped in a blender, flickering on fast-forward behind my eyelids to catch up to this moment. By the time I've blinked my eyes open, Claire has crossed the interrogation room and is muttering to Enzo and Tate. Using the arms of the wheelchair, I push myself to wobbly feet and clear my throat for their attention. I get it immediately, but pity mares their expressions. I saw everything Claire did. Relived the single worst moment of my life, experienced the fresh heartbreak as if it was the first time. But I couldn't focus on the final details surrounding Mania's face or the agony that claimed me, so I'm really hoping Claire got the answers we were searching for.

"Did...did you see anything about...my fires?" I croak out. With the help of the table, I shuffle a few steps forward. There's no use being combative now she's taken everything she wanted and if the others were going to harm me, they would have done it while I was unconscious. After witnessing my own downfall, I'm ready for some answers.

"Yes, I did Pyro," Claire replies with far too much sorrow. Any energy I have is currently being used to shove down the tsunami of emotions that will consume me later. Now though, I need to focus.

"And?" I growl, impatience clawing at me. I take a step forward and the fact no one flinches tells me all I need to know. My fires have gone.

"I can only tell you what I saw," the brunette states, avoiding my gaze. "Mania was standing on the other side of the door, telling you that she didn't-" I swipe my hand through the air, not needing to both hear and see that scene twice in one day. Ordering Claire to get to the point, she rests a hand on top of mine and I grit my teeth. Shit, it's bad. "From what I saw, the moment your heart broke, a fiery strand ignited between the two of you and then it snapped. I don't believe you noticed but my guess is, you shared a bond with Mania. A physical bond that was connected to your fires."

"So both my heart and my ability are broken. Fucking perfect," I grunt. Withdrawing my hand, I move to shove my way out of the room. I didn't think I could crave a damp, dark hole in the ground but here I am, ready to return to my cell. Enzo steps in front of the door and Claire reaches out to touch my arm again, intent on trying to tame me like a feral bear.

"Not exactly." I roll my eyes, twisting to glare down into her blue eyes. I hate riddles on the best of days and had I been able to, I'd have incinerated her hand by now. Jerking her touch away from me as if I did anyway, Claire steps in beside Tate for moral support. "The strand snapped, but only on your end."

"What the fuck is that supposed to mean?!" I roar, my head pounding. Claire looks to her friends for support, stuttering beneath my narrowed gaze. It's Enzo who answers for her, talking slowly as if he was explaining physics to a child.

"Imagine a piece of string," he mock demonstrates with his hands. "If you cut it in half, it doesn't simply disappear but instead, there are now two halves. In your case, however, you broke the bond from your end so your half is minuscule and hers...well she has the majority."

"What? No, she broke the bond. She broke me!" I shout louder than I anticipated. The truth is out now though and I can't deny it. Mania took the love I so easily gave her and stomped all over it. I have to believe that's what happened, because any alternatives will shatter the self-pity pretense I've drowned myself in while god knows what has been happening beyond my cell.

Enzo slowly shakes his head, clearly knowing more but the door bursts open then, slamming into his back. Guards storm the room, grabbing all of us roughly. I don't hear any protests from the semi-Mutes, in fact a trio of resigned sighs are the only other sounds against stomping boots. My arms are wrenched behind my back and my wrists are cuffed before I'm shoved out of the room. I struggle for show but with the knowledge that my fires are gone for good, there's no point starting a fight now. Brute strength is Ghost's department, and I can't be sure if the personal show I received was real or a ruse. I wouldn't put it past Christopher to change tactics and use his minions to mess with my mind.

Checking over my shoulder, I spot the three in question being dragged in the opposite direction. The direction I'd arrived in. The guard on my left rams his shoulder into me and I scowl at him.

"Where am I going?" I ask, not expecting an answer but he grumbles back anyway.

"New orders." is all I get. Being tugged along the hallway, I comply after bringing the heel of my barefoot down on his steel-toed boot, petty as fuck but the sharp jolt shooting up my calf was worth it. Even if it didn't affect him, the pain it caused gives me a focus other than pathetic, unaltered misery. Fuck, I've fallen so far. At the far end, the sliding door of another elevator opens automatically and I cast a quick glance around for security cameras. It doesn't matter if I'm being watched either way but I've decided burying myself away isn't going to do any good, not now I've had a snippet of answers. I should keep my wits sharp since I don't have the power of my fires to fall back on.

To my surprise, I'm pushed inside the elevator and left alone as the doors slide closed behind me. The moment they do, I jerk against the cuffs, struggling to get them the fuck off me. When that proves fruitless, I stumble back against the wall and start randomly stabbing buttons with my thumbs. Nothing happens, the smooth ascent of the elevator taking me higher as if these damn buttons aren't even connected. Throwing myself backwards in an effort to smash the cuffs off instead only serves to slide the metal further into my wrists and jar my shoulders painfully. The doors reopen then and I wince, bracing myself for the entourage inevitably waiting to taser me to the ground. That's how these bastards work. Yet nothing comes. At all.

Creeping into the silent room before I'm trapped in the elevator again, I brace myself for an attack that never comes. A glass coffee table in the center of the lavish suite captures my attention first, mainly because of the silver key sitting upon it. Apprehension forgotten, I skid over and grab the key awkwardly, taking far too long to release myself from the cuffs. By the time my arms snap forward like the release of a band, the raw ache in my neck and shoulder is deeply embedded. Stretching my arms in wide circles, I slowly turn to take in my surroundings properly.

Matching cream sofas sit either side of the rug my toes are sinking into, the satin cushions a pebble gray like the suede drapes hanging beside a wall of windows. A flat-screen has been mounted above a false fireplace on a stone feature wall. Back towards the front door, there's a small kitchenette with black cupboards and chrome handles to match the utensils spread across the countertops. I spot a bedroom through an open doorway and reflected in a vertical mirror is the heavenly sight of an en suite.

Gunning for the gleaming tiles and white porcelain enticing me, I strip out of the disgusting, soiled sweatpants I've been stuck in and dive into a wide shower cubicle. Cranking the dial to scolding, I can't help the guttural moan that leaks from my throat. It stretches on and on of its own accord while water pours down on me from a square shower head. My deprived skin roils with blistering redness and I couldn't be happier. Throwing my head back and opening my mouth, my tongue lolls out like a stray seeking to drink from the rain. The heat has nothing on the ferocity of my fires at full capacity, but it's a fucking start.

A small voice in the back of my mind warns me about this being a trap but I drown that thought with another pleasurable groan as I spot the array of shower gels all neatly lined up on a glass shelf. Washing myself thoroughly five times over, I turn my attention to the red hair tickling my shoulder. I'd given up on living, never mind moving since Mania crushed my soul to dust so the thick layer of hair covering my jaw also comes as a shock. When I finally manage to part with the water, and only because it started to run cold, a rummage around the bathroom cupboards reveals a pair of clippers and a pack of razors.

I emerge into the master bedroom a new man, tying a plush towel around my waist. The lengthy mirror shows the extent of my weight loss since I've been imprisoned, my abs sticking out painfully. My tattoos are lacking vibrancy with the ashy skin underneath and my eyes snag on the winged skull in the center of my chest that I share with Mania. The cracked, decaying skull being held afloat by the wispy wings of our broken love. So fitting. Other than being gaunt, my face looks mostly the same yet there's something missing. Vitality, I suppose. I can't look at the pitiful display I've become for a second longer so I turn my back on myself and pad across the bedroom.

I've never seen a room like this with my own eyes before. In fact, I'd doubted they'd existed at all and were only fashioned for entertainment purposes. How anyone can live in such excessive luxury while there are those starving and being exploited is beyond me. That's not even taking into account how the Mutes are being forced to live. Heading over to the king-size bed, I drop down and look around. I'm half expecting a guard to jump out of the wardrobe and force me back to the dungeon I've been calling home, so I just sit there. Waiting. Wondering.

Soon, my body has completely air-dried so I approach said wardrobe, finding no guard inside. Instead, there's rows of suits, shirts and jeans. All laundered and pressed to perfection. Grabbing a few hangers out, I spot the clothes tags and realize, no not pressed, but new. The next dresser holds sealed packs of boxer shorts, pajamas and socks, and without anyone around to stop me, I continue to help myself. I suppose I should be focusing my time on coming up with an escape plan, but what I'm escaping for and where to, I have no fucking idea. So I don't bother.

Returning to the living area, I jolt at the person moving across the window panes until I realize it's my own reflection. Outside, pitch blackness hides all clues of my location. Grabbing the TV remote control from a sofa pocket, I remain standing while flicking on the device. A welcome screen starts up, listing a range of options for me to choose from. Information, room service, lobby, chat function, candidate list, map, catch-up TV and live drone footage. I quirk an eyebrow, my hollow stomach turning at the sound of room service but I scoff. It's not like I'm going to go from Christopher's prison to being delivered a steak and chips on the same day. I'm under no illusions that I'm still nothing more than a prisoner, regardless of the mind games being played here.

Instead, I click on the lobby tab. The screen morphs into a mind field on an olive green background, long lists separated into groups rotating and changing before I can understand what I'm seeing. Algorithms and numbers confuse me, yet I stride closer to get a better look. In the top right-hand corner, framed in a white box, is a dollar bill logo with a bold 4,000 beside it.

"Thing of beauty, isn't it?" a familiar voice states and I spin around. I'd been so entranced by the screen, I hadn't heard the elevator doors slide open but Christopher doesn't balk at my instant scowl. Wearing a three-piece suit on surprisingly broad shoulders that are at odds with his sagging face, he's made a feeble attempt at slicking back his thinning hair. Icy, blue eyes pin me in place and his easy smile is far too relaxed for him to be in any danger from me. And he knows it. Gliding inside, Christopher flicks his cane along more for show than the need of it. I fist my hands, automatically calling for my fires to engulf them in flame but of course, they don't respond. Dammit.

"What am I doing here?" I ask, since that's the only question that matters. He boldly walks up to my side and eases the control from my clenched grip. My chest heaves in the t-shirt I plucked from the wardrobe and despite myself, I take a step away. I can't kill him when I'm certain I'll never find my way out of here without his permission, which I also won't get, so I'll remove myself from temptation's way. The asshole in charge doesn't pay me any mind, his attention squarely on the screen.

"You, my boy, are going to bear witness to a brand new beginning. One that gives everyone a taste of what they've been begging for. Years of trials and preparations have been leading up to this point." I can practically feel the excitement leaking from the old man beside me, his blue eyes sparkling.

"I still don't see what the fuck any of this has to do with me not being in my cell anymore. I've known you long enough to know you always have an ulterior motive. So you can either start talking, or I'll be shoving your free clothing up your ass one at a time." My threat is empty and Christopher knows it since he doesn't pay me any mind. He navigates through the lists popping up and disappearing across the screen, seeming to understand the statistics if his chuckle is anything to go by.

"You were supposed to be my champion," he mutters absentmindedly, "but I'm nothing if not adaptable. You can be my mascot instead." I don't like the full, teeth-baring smile he turns to give me but almost instantly, Christopher's attention is back on the screen as he loads up the map. I gape at the image in confusion. It's a labyrinth of sorts, and it's fucking huge.

"Tomorrow marks the first official day of the Mute games. I've taken the liberty of loading some funds onto your account. Backers choose which candidate to sponsor based on who they'd like to win. The more funds a candidate receives, the more aids we send their way. It's as simple as that really. There will be a chance for you to meet the other backers soon but for now, make full use of the chat function to discuss your favorites."

"Other backers?" I ask tentatively, not following.

"There's close to a hundred thousand humans staying in hotel rooms just like this one around the labyrinth's exterior. Speaking of which, I have many important greetings to make tonight so I should be on my way. You've found yourself on the winning side Pyro, take full advantage of it." Christopher places the control back in my hand and heads for the elevator while my mind is still playing catch up.

"Wait," I call out as he steps into the same elevator he arrived in. "You said this gives everyone what they've been begging for - what is that exactly?" A cruel smile turns up the edges of his lips and Christopher leans onto his cane.

"Candidates get to fully be themselves, with the chance to live as the proclaimed winner at the end. Backers, well they get their fix of blood and gore no other reality show could ever provide. You should take the time to check out our final contestants. They might just sway your mind to play along." The doors close then, as if they were waiting for him to finish speaking and I click onto the candidate list. I already know in my gut I'll wish I hadn't looked but Christopher picks his words carefully and for a reason.

The list is split into five columns across the screen and scrolls down well into the hundreds. Each name is numbered but I don't pay attention, apprehension clawing at me as I press the controller's button repeatedly until the screen stops moving. There, in the very last two slots, are the names I already knew in my gut I would find, but my blood turns to ice regardless.

#6832 - Ghost
#6833 – Mania

I lay limp, fractured. Some of my bones possibly are. I'd fought tooth and nail, literally, after Camo handed me over to the Detective. The guard took my sudden outburst as an invitation to beat me senseless before loading me into the cart with the others. I willed for my mind to drag me under, to render me unconscious, but that would have been too easy. Instead, I'd shifted onto my side and curled my fingers into Tracker's hand, silently crying for him. For the sacrifice that wouldn't have been needed if I'd left him in his safe room. And to think he thanked me for rescuing him barely ten minutes before he was killed.

From then on, I allowed myself to be passed around without any more resistance and all the while, keeping Ghost in my sights. Tossed from the cart, I'm injected, swabbed, stripped, hosed down and re-clothed. If a cropped corset with lace fringe and matching booty shorts constitute as clothes. I appreciate the central silver zips against the black leather and the killer, thigh-high boots tying the outfit together, but my anxiety only heightens with what this could mean. I've had my brief taste of pole dancing and it's definitely not my vocation in life. Pokey fingers remove my contacts before a photographer snaps images of me from all angles. And only then am I transported via elevator from the warm building and tossed out onto the cold, hard ground, just before a heavy mass of limbs is chucked on top of me.

A pained moan sounds and I bring my attention to the state I'm in. My neck is at a crooked angle against a stone wall, the ground damp and my body held immobile beneath Ghost's. I don't bother trying to move. Instead, I slide my fingers into his hair, softly combing the leftover flakes of shoe polish from his white locks. I need Ghost back. I'm relying on his rhythmic breathing and body warmth. For what, I couldn't say. Possibly just to rely on him saying something inappropriate in all situations. Or to keep him close to my side, whether he enjoys being there or not.

Ghost groans again and movement stirs in the shadows. I curl my free hand around his shoulder, for all the good it would do, and cringe at the feel of blood and shredded skin embedded too far beneath my fingernails to be cleaned out so easily. The semi-oblivious trance I had drifted into clears instantly and I glower at the approaching figures, bracing myself for another fight I won't win. Pressing in on us from all sides, heads cock and I shrink under the weight of their scrutiny.

"Turn it on, idiot! You're scaring her," a voice whispers and there's the undeniable slap of skin on skin. Suddenly, the figure in the middle illuminates from head to toe like a human torch. No, not human...*Mute*. I gasp, my eyes flicking around the faces at last. The range of hair and eye colors are undeniable and stupidly, a sob locks in my throat. Relief courses through me at their softened gazes and the understanding that we're all the same here. Well, for the most part but I'm not able to announce my mortality now. Ghost's head lifts lazily, murmurs incoherently to himself.

"Here, let me help," the male offers, stepping forward. He crouches and takes Ghost's hand before closing his stark blue eyes. The veins in Ghost's hand begin to glow, the soft light traveling up his arm and across the expanse of his bare chest. I track the glow, creating a spiderweb effect across his entire body and I'm unable to resist stroking a throbbing vein trailing up his neck. Vitality thrums between my fingertips and I suck in a breath. Reaching his temple, Ghost slowly blinks open those milky white eyes and the glow begins to retract all the way back to the Mute who caused them. Using their clasped hands, the male then heaves Ghost to his feet while I push him up from underneath and then join his side. Ghost leans into me and I stagger sideways before he reaches out and pulls me into the curve of his body.

"Might take a few minutes to get your balance properly but you should be all good now," the male grins kindly.

"Appreciate it…" Ghost trails off expectantly.

"Doc," the male nods. "This here is Firefly, my son." My eyebrows shoot up as Doc steps back into line with the others but I quickly hide my surprise. With every generation diluting further, it's not often for the Mute genes to run in the family. Besides, Mutes don't tend to procreate if they can help it. Being hunted and shepherded like livestock isn't the best of lifestyles to give our children. Firefly nods at me knowingly, like he could read my every thought and I duck my attention to the others. Everyone is scantily dressed, the males in nothing but dark jeans and the females a mix of tiny shorts, stockings and bralettes.

"Thanks, to you both," Ghost grumbles. His tone is groggy still and he eyes those around us with suspicion. I follow his lead, now seeing there's not as many figures here as I originally suspected. Five, maybe? With no further engagement, Ghost decides to fill the silence again. "Someone wanna tell us where the fuck we are?" I nudge him but don't move away as his arm tightens around me protectively. These Mutes didn't have to come to our aid and I won't have him sounding ungrateful, but it's also ingrained in me not to trust so easily anymore.

"What are your abilities?" a young lad elbows his way to the front to ask when it's clear no one wants to answer Ghost. I catch sight of his juvenile face beneath a mess of black hair, his features smeared with dirt but it's the difference in his once-white clothes that interest me. Whether they are hand-me-downs or he's lost a lot of weight since originally obtaining them, the baggy rags hang off his slender frame now. The kid is shushed but he looks back in annoyance, ready to defend himself. "What? We gotta know otherwise it's a waste of time and food," he moans to whoever is arguing with him in hushed tones.

I cock an appreciative eyebrow at the kid's balls but Ghost doesn't seem as impressed. Regaining the full extent of his strength, I feel the tension radiating from him before his hand slides over my hip and tucks me impossibly closer. Heat sparks against my frozen skin where his fingers brush the hem of my shorts. Now isn't the time to take my attention away from the Mutes crowding us but that doesn't stop me from placing a hand over Ghost's and locking my fingers in between his. He's all I have left, all I have in these uncertain surroundings and honestly, I just don't want to let him go.

"Mania?" I frown at the voice cutting through the Mutes, hunting for its origin. She calls for me again and a memory flickers to the forefront of my mind. Legs swinging over a bridge, laughter ringing out around the metal structure of an abandoned railway bridge. The others part for her to approach me and my mouth drops open.

"A…Ammo?" I ask hesitantly. Ghost keeps his bruising grip on my waist as I try to meet her halfway but I shake him off, needing a closer look to confirm my suspicions. In Firefly's glow, a well-built female with tattooed arms bursting from her tank top steps into view. She's acquired fitted cargo trousers and a pair of bulky biker boots which sets her apart from the scantily-clad females hovering behind her. Shaven scalp and hollow green eyes, Ammo hasn't changed at all in appearance but there's a hardened air about her.

"Holy shit," she breathes. Reaching up, Ammo curls a strand of my hair around her finger, her eyes drinking me in. "I thought I'd never see you again. You look so…so…"

"Deceased?" I drawl, realizing she won't have seen me with tattoos, blackened lips and the dark craters beneath my eyes. It's a wonder she recognizes me at all. Ammo chuckles, reaching up to smooth the pad of her thumb over the crack in my forehead. I don't worry about her fingers against my skin, knowing she needs to cock her thumb to take off the safety before any invisible bullets can spray from her finger guns. It's a thing of beauty how Ammo can say 'bang' and an instant later, there's a hole exactly where her fingers were aimed. Imp and I had a theory about her ability having more to do with controlling the force of air pressure but really, it's anyone's guess. Mutes don't come with handbooks unfortunately, or my life would have been a thousand times easier.

"No girl, you look hot as fuck," Ammo eyes me appreciatively. I get the impression her cheeky wink isn't completely platonic as her bronze gaze heats beneath bobbing eyebrows. Ghost notices too, tugging me back to him from the small space I'd created between us while talking to Ammo. I don't argue, relying on his body warmth to keep me from freezing my ass off.

"Again, where the fuck are we?" he asks no one in particular. Ammo snorts, holding her arms out wide.

"Welcome to the Labyrinth newbies. You're lucky we decided to take this route to our hideout. You'd never have survived the night without some assistance." I shoot a glance around us for the first time, no longer concerned with those gathered around us but instead with the surroundings themselves. We're crammed between two walls I'd originally thought were wider, the scent of rotting flesh burning a trail to the back of my throat. My eyes must deceive me in the amber glow of Firefly's light, but I swear the vines cascading down the stone walls are...moving. Clawing their way over the heightened ridge, blocking out the damp stone underneath. That in itself is enough to tear my eyes back to Ammo, a thread of panic leaking from my lips.

"Why, what happens at night?" I ask, glancing up to the sky. The royal blue hue shining among the stars hints that dusk has recently fallen. Ammo clicks her fingers for Firefly to shut off his glow, since she seems to call the shots around here (no pun intended). Linking her arm through my free one, Ghost is forced to follow as I'm dragged along. The teen who questioned our abilities protests but a narrowed glare from Ammo has him falling back in silence.

"They're with us," she states with unwavering finality. Throwing a sideways smirk my way, Ammo softens her tone for my ears only. "I'll tell you everything once we're back in the hideout, but we don't have long. The game starts in the morning." Questions burn through my mind and I fight to keep my lips sealed. The way the whole group moves together as a unit, combined with their lowered voices tells me there's something to fear nearby. And considering their leader can shoot bullets from her fingers, I should be fucking terrified.

A female by the name of Talon, with stunning teal hair flowing down the back of her pinstripe corset, permits us access to a hidden trap door. Lengthening her fingernails on one hand, she shapes them into keys and pushes into what I thought was a crack in the ground. Slowly twisting her hand back and forth, I hear the undeniable sound of locks popping free but the thought of her nails scraping against the rock has my skin prickling with a cringe-filled shudder. Lifting the trap door a moment later, Ghost is ushered inside among the others, where he stops at the base of the ladder to ease me down.

Firefly leads the way, his glow back in full force but something tells me that's only for our benefit. The other Mutes nudge past him, disappearing into the darkened staircase below. Ghost's hand doesn't leave mine for a second as we descend, leveling out into a network of tunnels with Ammo trailing behind. Firefly takes us to a door of woven branches and props it open with his foot, gesturing for us to enter. The open plan room inside takes me by surprise, fully furnished with a lit fireplace that beckons me inside.

Wooden beams support a rounded ceiling above the open planned room. Wooden furniture indicates different areas, from the stools around the fireplace, a kitchenette and a sleeping corner of cots. Cream walls blend into the neutral tones of the dirt floor. Only the vines trickling between the cracks hint at the coldness of stone passageways up above. It's basic, yet warm and inviting as the Mutes get busy with their separate errands.

"Doc, Firefly and Climate are preparing to hunt for supper and extra supplies, Champ." The teen reels off on his way passed, tapping a hand on Ammo's shoulder. I should stop referring to him as a kid, considering he's the same height as me, but the mess of black curls and acne coating his juvenile features don't quite translate into manhood. He carries himself with the confidence I'd expect from someone twice his age and untold wisdom behind his all-seeing, black eyes.

"Champ?" I question. Ammo nods sharply to the male and then throws her arm around my shoulder.

"Reigning Champion," she grins widely. "Any chance your man-slave can help with the hunt? We've got a lot of catching up to do." Instinctively, I tighten my grip on Ghost's hand before sighing. Ammo won't open up to anyone she doesn't trust and for both of our sakes, I need to understand what's going on around here. Namely, how to get the fuck out.

"Would you mind?" I ask Ghost, feeling like a grade-A crap sack. His expression is blank as he regards me but the firm stroke of his thumb on the underside of my wrist says it all. He's as reluctant to release me as I am for him. Ghost has become my lifeline in an instant, although I'm unsure what he's getting out of keeping me close. If anything, I'm just a liability. "Please?" I ask when he doesn't move closer or away. Leaning over me, Ghost's lips brush my ear and send a shiver of longing through me.

"It doesn't take a genius to figure out why Tracker isn't here, so don't think for a second I'm leaving this room without you." His words sounded like a threat but then Ghost places a featherlight kiss on my cheek, confusing me further. "Trust no one," are his parting words as he suddenly moves away and I stumble sideways. Instead of helping with the supper as Ammo asked, he plants himself on a tiny, wooden stool and uses a poker to prod at the fireplace.

Sliding my eyes to Ammo, I shrug apologetically but she looks ready to burst out laughing. Her arm is still on my shoulders so with a gentle tug, I'm drawn towards a series of feathery nests that must constitute as their beds. I'd strip out of my thigh-high boots if they weren't doing a fantastic job at sealing in the little heat I have. Nestling down on the cot, I rest my weary head in my hands and feel Ammo nudge into the same nest. So much for personal space.

"So," she says, leaving that single word hanging between us.

"So, what?"

"So, spill the beans. Who's the guy and how long have you been screwing him?" My head shoots up and my cheeks flame.

"Ghost? Fuck no," I say with a little too much enthusiasm. His milky white eyes slide to me from his spot by the fireplace before he resumes his absent-minded prodding. Clearing my throat, I fight to lower my tone. "It's...complicated."

"Babygirl," Ammo snorts, placing a hand on my bent knee, "I've been stuck here with only myself to create gossip. Give me something." Sighing, I smile weakly and run a hand over my face.

"Well, I'm kinda in love with his two best friends, one of who is dead and we're trying to save the other," I chuckle to myself at the sheer un-funniness of it all. Being beside Ammo reminds me it has only been a year since I was living in Bellemare, carefree with my best friend with the hobby of trying out the various ways I could kill myself for sport. My eyes trail back up to the heavily muscled, tattooed man hunched over in all his shirtless glory. One year, two heartbreaks, three men. I must have sincerely pissed someone off in a past life for that hand. Noticing Ammo hasn't responded to my bombshell, I'm shocked to see the tears welled in her eyes and her tough-girl façade crumbling.

"Shit, Mania I'm so sorry. Losing someone you care about is never easy." A dry laugh escapes me as I rush to reassure her I never had Hoax in the first place.

"It's not like that, really. He was already dead when I met him," my voice trails off at the anguish that has gripped Ammo's features and realization dawns on me. "Oh," I breathe. "Ammo. Who did you lose?" This is a girl who spared no tears when her own mother passed. We were hardened orphans and death was as common to us as breathing. The closest thing we had to a parent was-

"That reminds me. Imp," I seethed through gritted teeth. Ammo's misery disappears as if it hadn't existed in the first place, replaced with a roll of eyes.

"I don't even want to know what she's done now. More fool you for trusting her." I'm not even mad, Ammo is right. The two of them didn't get on at the best of times, so up to the point she went missing, Imp only stuck around for me. And I let her because in a place like Bellemare, where the MRA patrolling officers were always lording over us, we needed all the entertainment we could get.

"Yeah well, lesson truly learned. Anyways, you promised answers. Start with how you are the reigning champ of a game that hasn't even started yet." Ammo barks a laugh, moving to sit opposite me and block Ghost from my view.

"You may just be entering the first publicized event, but nothing of this magnitude happens without thorough trial runs and test rats. I've been in this dump since I was taken from Bellemare, seen it expand and evolve from a merger maze to the labyrinth hell you've found yourself a part of. If anyone can survive this, fuck knows it's gonna be me and my crew."

I look past her to the Mutes busying themselves around the room. Doc, Firefly and the male I haven't properly met called Climate must have gone to hunt for whatever there is to eat around here. Talon is standing at the small kitchenette, stirring a large pot of vegetables with a wooden spoon, thankfully. The female at her side, with flowers cascading through her dreadlocks, retrieves a stack of bowls from a cupboard.

"We don't need numbers," Ammo reassures me after following my gaze. "We just need the Blacksmith."

"Are you going to make me ask each question individually or…?" I quirk a brow at Ammo. Luckily, she doesn't dive beneath my jokey tone to the frustration and tiredness lurking underneath. Clearly Ammo is doing us a favor by taking us into her hideout and offering to feed us, and I'm in no position to entertain the bitterness crawling towards my voice box. But if Ammo could tell me the full story of what the fuck is going on, that'd be swell.

"The labyrinth is split into sections which open one at a time, but it's ever-changing so don't become complacent. The Blacksmith is the only one who can wield weapons, and luckily for us he's sitting pretty in a cage waiting for someone to find the keys and free him. Whoever frees him becomes his master who he must serve until the end, so we have to get there first. However, never lose sight that this is entertainment for those up in the towers. The more entertaining you are, the more commodities you're gifted with." My mind is spinning by this point, information overload dulling all of the questions I know I should ask.

"Holy shit!" A voice sounds from across the room. I lean to peer over Ammo's shoulder to see the teen marveling at Ghost, who is currently passing the scolding hot poker tip through his hand and back. "He can walk through walls too!" Turning back to me, Ammo's smile is menacingly wide, like the freaking Joker on steroids.

"And with my fearless Babygirl here who can't die, we can march ourselves right up to the finish line." Ammo slaps me sharply on the thigh before jumping up to high-five Talon. The group huddle together by the kitchenette, chattering excitedly while utterly unaware of the dread flooding my system. Icy tendrils lick at my skin, threatening to seep inside and freeze my barely-beating heart. My gaze locks with Ghost's for one resounding thought to be silently communicated between us. Shit on a stick.

PYRO

"Psst." My eyelids flutter from the fragile sleep I'd barely begun, an inaudible sound catching my ear. I spare a quick look at the alarm clock to see it's just after four in the morning and will myself to slip back into the semi-conscious dream flittering behind my eyelids. Mania has jumped onto my back, her laughter ringing out as I run through a forest of the brightest greens I've ever known. Hoax and Ghost follow after, chasing us down as part of the game. Although, it's not a game and as they grow closer, their hands lash out in an effort to dislodge her from my back.

"Psssst!" the sound comes again and I jerk upright this time, clearing the foggy haze consuming my mind. I quickly reach over and flick one of the many switches beside the bed. The one I randomly chose sparks a useless LED light above the wardrobe but it's enough to show me there's no one else in the room. I frown, sure I heard something but my sleep-deprived mind must still be playing catch up from the damp dungeon I was imprisoned to. Switching the light off once more, I lie back slowly while listening intently to my surroundings.

"Pyro? Is it you in here?" I freeze, unmoving. The voice is vaguely familiar, coming from the darkest corner in the room. Scanning the area from my reclined position, I'm sure there's no one there but I answer anyway.

"Err…yeah?" The answering huff of breath covers something like 'oh thank fuck' and I slowly edge myself up the headboard. I opened my mouth but realize I don't know what to say so I shut it again. The voice doesn't come across as threatening. If anything, it's similar to the hushed voice from… "Bleacher's guy?" I ask on a whim.

"I prefer Shadow, but sure. Whatever works." His easy-going tone renders me at ease briefly, until I remember he's somehow connected to the Afterlife Asylum and my hackles immediately rise back up.

"Why are you looking for me?" I ask, my eyes trained on the dark corner.

"I've come to warn you," he says and now I'm even more suspicious. Christopher has a fascination for playing games and I have no doubt I'm one of the star attractions in his twisted mind. However, Shadow's following words aren't what I expected at all. "You need to bet on Mania."

"What?" I jerk up right now, my face set in a scowl. "Why the fuck would I do that?" There's no way Shadow knows that very thought is what kept me from falling asleep straight away in the memory foam mattress and plush bedding. I keep the satin cushions around me for comfort, yet all the while I laid there, turmoil banished any reprieve of sleep.

"She won't survive the labyrinth on her own. She'll need all the help she can get." I'm sure he's trying to convey sincerity in his voice but I can't help but think everything is already a trap. "Unless you're ready to see your ex die in full HD, and this time she won't be coming back."

"Why?" I ask despite myself. I shouldn't care, I shouldn't still love her. But it's ingrained in me, even after she broke my heart and caused my fires to flee. I still love her and I fucking hate myself for it.

"Because she's human now." That bombshell knocks the air out of my lungs. I don't want to believe it, but all of the recent revelations keep churning in my mind. Nothing makes sense anymore, so who am I to question the latest droplet of bad news in my ocean of theories? I'm thankful for the silence Shadow gives me but I knew it wouldn't last long. "She didn't just break you, she broke herself. Rumors say she's on her last life, which is exactly why Christopher has put you up here in his penthouse suite to watch it all happen."

"This is all a ruse to get my fires," I nod, the understanding dawning. I knew it. This penthouse is still a prison and my only source of 'entertainment' is a trap to coax my fires out, if they're still responding. Christopher never takes his eye off the prize, just changes his route to get it. Shadow grunts in agreement.

"Trust me Pyro. It's in your best interest to give them to him. If you ever want to see-" Shadow's voice is cut short and I sit straighter, hunting the darkness.

"Shadow?" No response comes. For as long as I sit there, missing the brief encounter of his company, I replay Shadow's words. Over and over. Mania's human, in a Mute maze with no ability and no second chances. It's all so far beyond fucked, I relish the times I only would daydream about Mania with my dick in my hand. Simpler times. I'd give anything to have Hoax with me now. Not only because he'd be able to infiltrate the network and shut it down before any deep-pocketed human could get their fill of violence, but for his company.

Grabbing the controller, I flick on the TV screen across the room and enter the virtual lobby. A surprising amount of people are on for this time of the morning, entering their bets and discussing their favorites. I slip into the chats, lingering in the back like a creep. The same names keep popping up and soon enough, the front runners are made obvious. Defibrillate, Cartograph, Appendage and for some reason, someone called Slow-Mo. I head back to the list of profiles, clicking on each one in turn to learn more about their abilities. By the time I've reached Appendage's and witnessed a 3D demonstration of his detachable limbs, I lie back on a sigh.

I lie there for a long time, battling with myself on what course of action to take. If I bet, I'm playing into Christopher's hand and resigning myself to his game. If I don't, Mania won't make it five minutes into the game. I don't question Ghost's ability to take care of himself, and that fucker left me stranded. He chose his own selfishness over me. His best friend. His brother. I might still hold a barely lit flame for Mania, mostly because I'm so damn confused as to what happened, but not Ghost. That shithead looked me in the eye and walked away, so I'll happily watch him suffer.

Running a hand through my hair, I groan and hop out of bed. There's no chance of me going back to sleep and the shower is the only one calling my name now. I don't think I'll ever tire of the feeling a simple shower can bring, washing my anxieties down the drain. After remaining in there far longer than intended, I pull on pajama pants and head for the kitchen. A coffee machine is waiting with the cup already beneath the dispenser so I flick it on and pace while it warms up.

The heavy drapes are still open from last night and if I keep my head tilted upright, all I can see is the sun rising over a barricade of skyscraper hotels. Purples, pinks and yellow smear together across the sky like an artist has hand-painted each stroke with a wispy brush. Mornings in the underground bunker deprived me of moments as peaceful as this. Just me, the landscape and a coffee brewing. As long as I don't look down.

Yet I do. My head sinks into my chest and I take in the sight beneath me in the small rays of morning light. The labyrinth is massive, far bigger than I'd imagined. Even after examining the digital layout until I was able to fall asleep, I wasn't prepared for the intricate pattern of darkened passages spread out before me. Hotels stand shoulder to shoulder, looming over the pit tall and proud. As I scan over the many lit rooms and the figures standing behind the floor-to-ceiling windows just like me, I can feel their hunger for violence. Excitement emanates through the walls, closing in on me from all sides to prove how truly insignificant I really am. I'm a needle in this haystack of power plays, but I'm primed and ready for whatever damage I may still be able to inflict.

Brewing a coffee on the way back, I return to my bed to assess the screen. I don't get comfortable though, preferring to perch on the edge of the mattress and soak the chill of the air conditioning into my being. I didn't even put sugar in my coffee, as a lame attempt to quell the guilt burrowing deep within my chest. I've heard the voices in the back of my head arguing while I try to block them out. The angel on my shoulder soothing me with words that I've suffered enough to deserve a small slice of luxury. The devil, however, he's a truthful bastard and I don't like what he has to say.

A timer has appeared at the top of the screen, counting down the fifteen minutes until 6 AM. Bets begin pouring in, the repetitive chiming drilling into my skull until I kill the TV's volume. The chat functions are flying with so many messages I don't have time to read a single one before there's ten in its place. My gut twists, indecision clawing at me. My instincts scream at me to put all my money on Mania, to give her any advantage possible. Whereas my heart, that cold bastard says fuck playing into Christopher's hand and Mania made her choice. She refused the unconditional love I was openly willing to give her, and broke me in the process.

Switching to the list of candidates, I scroll through the names slower this time. I can't fathom how so many Mutes have been captured and brought here, until my eyes snag on several names I recognize. Recall, Road-Rage, Flexi, Copycat, Brainwave and Duracell. They're from the asylum, the ones who were sold in the midnight auctions. My world grinds to a halt, yet the timer doesn't. I'd imagined all kinds of scenarios of those auctioned off becoming living pin dolls for Christopher's experiments, but they're here? Have they been here all along? The timer turns red, entering the two final minutes before betting closes.

Sipping my coffee in an attempt to calm the tidal wave plowing through my vital organs, I rub the pad of my thumb over the controller's buttons. Scrolling all the way down, I select the name at the bottom and Mania's profile flashes onto the screen. A 3D image of her in a tiny, leather corset and shorts with boots covering her legs slowly turns before me like an avatar. Our matching tattoos call to me; the winged skull on our chests, the animal head on the back of our hands and the many others that Canvas matched perfectly. It's almost as if he knew to imprint me on her. Now I've started, I can't tear my gaze away from her blood-red eyes that should only look my way. From her cocked eyebrow to her hand-on-hip stance that screams fuck the world; she was, and always will be, my girl.

In all this time, I've been unable to come up with a valid reason why Mania would do this to me. To leave me here, defenseless and alone. Whatever Christopher promised her obviously hasn't worked, given her current predicament. *At least she's not alone*, I remind myself bitterly. She has Ghost. Jealousy rises up in me so fast, I struggle to suck in my breath and my grip tightens around the controller. Who's to say they weren't both in on stabbing me in the back, all part of their plan to be together? Ghost has been envious of my connection to Mania since the day I first saw her, and now he's betrayed me in the worst way.

With merely twenty seconds left on the clock, my thumb flies over the controller at rapid speed as I place all four thousand dollars on Recall. Something the silver-haired woman said to me at Afterlife floats to the forefront of my mind. "You can't save everyone Pyro, particularly not the ones who don't want to be saved." I blow out a shaky breath, dropping the controller to the floor. Betting has ended, and Mania has a grand total of zero dollars besides her name. Yet I squash any hint of self-doubt with the strength of my anger. She doused my fires and now she's going to burn.

Asiren blares through the hideout, jolting me out of my damn skin. Only the weight of a thick arm wound tightly around my body stops me from jumping out of the feathery bed altogether. It's a miracle I slept at all, but I must have needed it if I didn't feel Ghost slide in behind me. The roughness of his jean zipper bites into my lower back as he crushes me into him. Among the racket overhead, I hear the clamor of other Mutes rising from their own beds and I struggle out of Ghost's hold.

"Come on, we need to get up," I elbow him when he reaches for me again. On a deep sigh, Ghost sits up and wipes the sleep from his eyes.

"I know. I just wanted one more minute before it all goes to shit." I frown at this, reaching out to grab his hand.

"Everything's going to be okay," I lie and Ghost's hitched eyebrow shows he doesn't believe me either. Well, it was worth a shot. Standing, Ghost allows me to drag him up and we head for the washroom. Talon exits, giving me a weak smile before extending her nails and scratching the length of Ghost's arm with a wink. Something primal awakens in me at her boldness, despite our fingers being intertwined. Instead of releasing him as I intended, I push open the bathroom door and drag Ghost inside. Catching sight of

Talon's teal eyes, I give her a cocky wink before slamming the door shut.

"Um...what do you-" I spin on Ghost, halting his words with a shove to his chest. It doesn't move him the way I intended, so I push again until he takes the hint and walks backwards. The backs of his thighs hit a pine vanity and I nudge him to sit down, bringing his gaze eye level with mine.

"One more minute, before it all goes to shit," I agree and crash my mouth against his. I'd expected to catch Ghost off guard, but his response is automatic. His hands grip my head, his fingers tangling in my hair as he lays claim to my mouth like it is his last meal. His tongue demands mine to fight back, as if I stood a chance at maintaining control of what I started. I'm utterly at his mercy, a slave to his firm chest heaving beneath my hands. Trailing south, I explore the ridges of his abs the way I've wanted to for far too long. Our lips meld together to share the taste of desperation and despair, which only makes me kiss him harder in search for more. For hope and reassurance he's got me.

Pulling back from our kiss, Ghost's white eyes grip me in a stare that is almost accusing. As if he blames me for opening the can of worms he's carefully kept a lid on, knowing full well the passion between us won't be able to go back in.

"I need you to go," I breathe when I can't handle Ghost's scrutiny any longer. He waits to fix an impassive look across his face before delivering a sharp nod.

"You'll need to release me first," he gestures to my nails which are embedded in his hips. My grip is bruising, yet I don't move. Instead, I pass my tongue between my puffy lips, distracting him for a moment. "I'll wait right outside," Ghost adds absentmindedly. Slowly, I shake my head and Ghost's eyes jerk back to mine.

"I need you to go, as in - leave. You can walk straight through the labyrinth walls and escape. You can find Pyro and tell him how to bring Hoax back. There's no way I'm surviving the games Ammo described. I probably won't make it through today," I shift my head to the side. I'd come to this realization last night and my certainty of the fact has only increased. I'm going to die today and I'm not sure what's waiting for me on the other side. Ghost's hand still tangled in my hair tightens painfully until he's forced me back to face him. His eyes scream pure murder, but not at me. *For* me.

"Listen to me and listen good," he growls, laced with threat. "I am not leaving this hellhole without you. You are m…" Ghost trails off, his eyes wavering. "You're Pyro's girl and we're going to get you back to him in one piece. Understand?" I nod shakily, not delving into the intensity crackling in the air. Ghost can keep up his pretense but the tingle on my lips from his kiss say everything he doesn't want to. I glance at his mouth again, wanting to reclaim the truce we can't seem to voice but the banging on the door drives a physical wedge between us.

"Be right out!" I call. Instead of either of us leaving, Ghost and I avert our eyes while relieving and washing ourselves. I find a stash of bamboo toothbrushes, minty paste in clear tubes and a stack of face cloths in the vanity, allowing me to feel marginally more myself by the time I emerge. Doc cocks an eyebrow but says nothing at Ghost trailing behind, his back bumping me along. We tag on to the line of Mutes exiting the main room, leading us back to the ladder and up to ground level. I don't stop to ask how they know where to go as Ammo is up in first place, her strides that of a confident reigning champion.

My boots scrape on the uneven ground while my eyes dart around for a hint of recognition. There is none. Each path looks exactly the same as the last. Narrowed stone walls covered in vines, randomly spaced alcoves, outstretched vines seemingly looking for a victim. It occurs to me as my legs grow weary from the terrain that we haven't encountered a single dead-end and I have to wonder how Ammo remembers it all. We finally take a hundredth turn and enter a huge circular cavity in the earth. My eyes dart all around, the opening giving me the first real look of where we are.

Hordes of Mutes are approaching from stone archways all around, not bothering with each other in the slightest. A swirling pattern has been carved into the ground, giving me the impression of a black hole ready to suck us all inside. The cracked ridge on top of the rounded walls suggest there was once a dome here which has been removed. I tilt my head upwards at the fading pastels of a sunrise, the feathery clouds seeming further away than usual. A hand brushes my side and I startle at Ghost's touch until he guides me forward.

"There's so many more Mutes here than I thought," I murmur as we reach Ammo. She snorts a laugh at me over her shoulder.

"Give it two days, there'll be barely anyone left." My eyes widen and I take a step towards Ghost on instinct. Not sensing my reluctance, Ammo turns and starts frisking my body. Her hands explore everywhere, including the center of my thighs and up my ass, making me highly uncomfortable so I give her a weak shove away.

"What the fuck are you doing?!" I balk.

"Trying to find your number," Ammo replies without pausing her search. Her thumbs forcefully brush under my breasts and trace my ribs until she finds what she's looking for. "Ahh, here it is." Lifting my arm up, and mentally thanking Ghost once again for the heads up on my body hair situation, I peer at the place Ammo's thumb had stopped to see a small number stitched into my corset. I have to squirm and squint to make out the gold numbers - 6833. Ammo lets out a long whistle and looks around, pointing me towards a curved wall across the other side.

"Head that way. Your digits will be carved into a stone on the wall somewhere. I'll leave you to find your man's number," she quirks a brow at me and diverts her eyes to Ghost's crotch. My cheeks flare as she strides away chuckling. Then I remember the old me wouldn't have given a shit, and she's the badass bitch I need to start channeling if I stand any chance of making it through the day.

Dropping to a crouch, Ghost grips my shoulders as if to push me away. Except he doesn't, which makes our position even more precarious. Searching with my eyes at first, I can't see a number like mine on his so I trail the roughness of his dark jeans with my fingers, from hip to hem and totally avoiding his crotch. Pushing him to turn, Ghost stays exactly where he is and I shoot him an annoyed look.

"If you'd just asked, I'd have told you I found a number sewn inside my fly when I went to the bathroom earlier. I just didn't know what it meant," Ghost shrugs. I jump to my feet, smacking him in the chest.

"Why didn't you say that?!" I gape. Despite the situation around us, Ghost smirks and the bastard I first met with Pyro shines through.

"I started to, but then I was intrigued at how far you'd go." I stomp away in the direction Ammo pointed, knowing without looking he'll be right behind me. The Mutes swarming around don't pay me any mind as I stand before the wall and notice the numbers carved into each stone, just like my old friend said. Luckily, they are in numerical order so I can trace mine all the way to the bottom right-hand corner beside an archway. Turns out Ghost's is right above mine and I watch him push his stone in for it to release from the wall. He eases the stone out to reveal a hollowed out drawer inside. I repeat the process, finding mine also empty and we share a confused look.

"Nice!" a voice beside us calls out as he peers inside his drawer and pulls a map out. I squint in an effort to peer through the paper, although I wouldn't know what I'm looking at anyway, before he folds and pushes it into his back pocket. Whirring sounds as a sea of drones lowers down over us, each one spinning its camera lens in an effort to pick out the Mute it's evidently hunting for. In the center, a ribbon-wrapped box drops from a drone directly into a Mute's hands. He reads the tag with a smirk and a nod, then begins to beatbox. Three guesses what his ability is. The sound grows louder, filling in background music among the mumbles of alliances.

"Nothing?" Ammo asks on our approach, reading my mind. "Ahh, tough luck. I got this lock picking set. Pretty handy, huh? Sometimes they drop or leave messages in your drawer with a task and possible reward." She sticks a thumb in Beatbox's direction. "It'll be hard to get back after this point but if you want aids, you gotta be popular."

"How do I become popular?" I ask, like a child on her first day of school. Ammo's sly smile makes me wish I hadn't asked.

"Like this," she comments, raising her hand. The scene suddenly plays out before me in slow-motion as Ammo's thumb slides back. My mouth drops open on a silent scream but I'm powerless to stop her. "Bam." With time speeding back up to the present, I stand in stunned shock as chaos erupts. Not between the Mutes, but from somewhere in the distance. I spare a glance up, spotting a smattering of towers framing the edge of the pit as far as the eye can see. Roars and cheers, mixed with an equal amount of angry shouts, sound just before a body collides with mine.

My head connects with the floor and the weight that lands on me is bone-crushing. I strangle out a cry, although the Mute is ripped off me before I get a chance to fight back for myself. Ghost is hoisting me to my feet a moment later, cradling my head against his chest. I peer out from the position he has me pinned in, spotting the body slumped on the ground among the Mutes either attacking each other or running for cover. The female's lifeless eyes stare in the abyss, a clean bullet hole pierced through her forehead. Did Ammo know her? Or did she merely want to get the games underway? Either way, I just caught a glimpse of an Ammo I don't know or like.

Ghost isn't waiting around for the apparent bandits that took us in last night. He steps backwards and draws me through the wall, all the while not letting me out of the cage of his arms. His feet are moving, carrying me against him until my shock fades and I yell for him to stop. Skidding into an alcove, Ghost searches me for injury but I grip his chin and bring his focus back to my face.

"We can't be seen ditching Ammo and her crew at the first sign of trouble," I reason. "We have no idea how to handle the labyrinth, or how to get to the finish. We could be chasing our tails endlessly, not to mention we don't have a hideout or know where to get food. We need them, Ghost." A harsh breath passes over my face and his forehead lowers to rest on mine. I must have misread the situation, tilting my mouth up, hunting for some closure that earlier wasn't a fluke as Ghost takes a step away.

"Fine," he growls. Suddenly I'm on the other side of the wall again, being shoved behind his back. Mutes are on him in an instant, taking their pound of flesh without realizing Ghost will hand them their asses for even trying. His tattooed back ripples, his shoulder blades flexing with each punch thrown and each Mute is soon rendered unconscious. I tuck my hands into the back of his jeans in an effort to reassure him I'm still there and realizing a little too late he's totally commando underneath.

Peeking around his frame, I take in the destruction covering the stone ground. True to her word, Ammo has already taken out a pile of Mutes and climbed the pile of their crumpled bodies. She's busy posing for the drone hovering over her, flexing her biceps like a hench, female bodybuilder. Of those stupid enough to hang around, no one dares to approach her, deciding to turn on each other instead. A whistle catches my ear and I follow it back to Ammo's kid accomplice - Remy. He's waving down another drone, this one with a package around the size of a shoebox attached. The strings holding the package automatically release before the device lowers within reaching distance and he catches it with a whoop.

"Smells like we're having curry tonight!" he beams and Ammo hops down from the top of the body pile with a chuckle. Instead of heading over to him, she makes a beeline for me, causing any last strangling Mutes to flinch and scurry away. She ignores Ghost, grabbing my arm around him and hauling me to her.

"See, Babygirl. Stick with me and I'll get you through this, no sweat." Ammo begins to walk away with her hand still clasped around my arm, until Ghost clears his throat expectantly. Tilting her head back to meet his eye, a predatory smile peels Ammo's lips back over her teeth. "Didn't see you around much, Ghost." The stare-off between the pair grows tense while I stand awkwardly in the middle. Trying to twist out of Ammo's grip breaks her trance and she moves to throw her arm over my shoulder.

"That's okay Big Man, I'll take care of more than just dinners," she teases him and I balk at her insinuation. Clearly the year we've been separated has changed Ammo in more ways than I realized and the days of falling asleep together under the stars have just taken on a whole new meaning. Ghost opens his mouth to protest but Ammo holds her free hand up to silence him. "No need to thank me, you're more than fucking welcome." She leads me away now, my panicked eyes looking over my shoulder in a silent plea. *Don't leave me alone with her, ever.*

GHOST

I let Ammo guide Mania away, following close behind. Mania has been right about so many things this morning and the day has barely begun. My automatic reflex to shield her from the bloodshed her friend caused won't do any good until I know what we're up against. I don't know the passages or understand the dynamics taking place around me. If anything, there had been an air of calmness before Ammo initiated that first shot. Then it was a free for all and I was powerless to do anything but run.

We walk back in the direction we came, now on full alert and braced for an attack. Somehow, the journey back to the hideout doesn't take half as long, so Climate, Talon and Flora are already waiting for us there. Remy has jogged up ahead, with Doc and Firefly joining behind as I approach the open trap door. The whole gang together again and just in time for Ammo to enter first, dragging Mania down with her.

The crew's leader is a fruit loop in herself. Claiming ownership of Mania as her new plaything leading her people into a spontaneous attack. Or maybe it wasn't as impulsive as it seemed and I'm not privy to their plans. Either way, the only reassurance I have to fall back on is Ammo's infatuation with Mania, which requires her being safe. So as much as Ammo's possessive bullshit irks me, I'm satisfied with the knowledge she'll protect Mania where I can't.

Regrouping in the same room we ate and slept in last night, the Mutes around me drop to the floor and spill the contents of their pockets. Firefly uses his glow to banish the shadows when no one stops to light any candles, giving me the impression we're not staying for long. The embers in the fireplace have long since perished, snuffing out the trap its warm glow falsely provided. All that's left is the bitter truth of the murderers and thieves at my feet. Their movements are rushed, their voices quiet yet laced with palpable excitement.

"Jackpot!" the younger shit exclaims. His messy black hair blocks me from his eye line and the scowl I'm giving the back of his head. I can't fault his cocky attitude since I've used it as a coping mechanism my whole life as well, but I don't open fire on other Mutes and dance back home with my mind already on dinner. I regard the map clutched in his hand, noticing it as the one pulled out of a drawer beside Mania's. Three guesses of where the poor fucker who received it is right now. Ammo plucks the piece of paper from the kid's grip, flattening it out on the ground. She then grabs for Firefly's hand, using his finger to trail the map's passageways until she finds what she's looking for.

"First check-in is tonight, over in the far east corner." I peer over her broad shoulder, spotting the red square printed over the right side of the map and labeled as 'Day One Safe Zone.'

"Check-in?" Mania asks. She's knelt beside her friend, and as much as I know I shouldn't check her out right now, the curve of her ass in those tiny shorts catches my attention. She's the opposite of the humans I used to go for. Too much damage for a start, yet as my eyes trail the delicate lace trim brushing her pale, tattooed skin, I have the strangest urge to help her. To smooth out the cracks in her skin and start over, free from the shit she's had to deal with. Alone. She must know the way she's crouched with a dip in her back and the tilt of her ass is taunting me because she draws the hair over her shoulder and glances up at me. Holy hotness.

Even the concern penetrating her blood-red eyes can't detract from their lash-framed beauty. Her pursed, blackened lips reminding me of the inferno her unexpected kiss awakened this morning. I could taste her turmoil. I could feel the desperation of her shattered heart. But instead of running in the opposite direction, I embraced her.

"Yeah," Ammo agrees. Also noticing Mania's bare shoulder, the butch female reaches up to tuck a loose strand of hair behind her ear and I glare daggers. "For the first five days, there will be a safe zone we need to be in at sunset. Otherwise," Ammo makes an explosive action with her hands and adds sound effects to be dramatic. "Then we come back here to recharge and start again. The labyrinth changes overnight though, so any progress we've made to find the keys will be lost." I walk over to the fireplace, taking the stool I claimed last night.

"You said you've won all of the practice runs. Can't you find the key you need and get us out of here by morning?" Laughter at Mania's question rings throughout the room and I will myself to find a modicum of patience.

"I also said the labyrinth has grown and constantly changes, Babygirl. Besides, you don't want to be out there after dark. Speaking of which, we need to get out there while it's still daylight. Doc, take Remy and Firefly to raid the pockets of the dead before Incinerate starts dragging them away. Flora and Climate, see what you can find out about the cage's position. I'll look for stragglers with Mania and Talon, you can start key recon with Ghost." The teal-haired female perks upright, fluttering her clawed fingers at me in a girly wave. Fuck no.

"I'm staying with Mania, end of story," I growl without standing. I don't need to when my body radiates 'don't fuck with me on this.' Collecting up the map and stuffing it into her back pocket, Ammo rises to her feet on a sigh. The others jolt up and disperse, busying themselves with shit that doesn't really need to be done and Mania eyes me worriedly. Approaching me slowly, Ammo tries to make herself look muscular in her tank top by crossing her arms and pushing her biceps out. I restrain from rolling my eyes considering she could shoot me where I sit, but I still won't back down.

"Look," she says, feigning boredom. "We're clearly both Alphas here. But you're in my house now so you'd better Beta the fuck up and do as you're told. Otherwise, you'll be out on your ass and anyone who's not with us, is against us." Pushing myself up right now, I tower over the Mute. She stands tall but her height is swallowed by my shadow, my eyes blazing with an unspoken dare.

"She stays with me." I put emphasis on each word, daring Ammo to fight me on this. I could break her fingers before she raises them high enough to do any real damage but just in case, I alter the density of my legs and feet for a sly shot. Her gaze regards me and the others around the room sneak looks in our direction. The silence thickens with held breaths, wondering if she'll concede or if there'll be another body to clean up.

"Have it your way, friend," Ammo smiles tightly but her expression is the opposite of civil. "We'll start hunting for a key with you and shoot any stragglers along the way. Doc," she clicks her fingers, dismissing me. "Talon will etch the map on me so you can take it. We'll all meet in the passageway south of the safe zone just before sundown." There's a strange pause where the others nod some secretive understanding but I don't have time to contemplate it as Mania shoots over the room and into my arms. I crush her into me, glaring at the Mute who tried to separate us only moments ago. Now however, Ammo smirks knowingly and goes about her business.

In less than five minutes, Talon has used a pointed fingernail to scar the map into Ammo's forearm and the stolen trinkets have been passed around. Me, though, I have Mania's hand clutched in mine and for reasons I don't have time to contemplate, I refuse to let go. Even when it proves awkward for her to climb the branch ladder to ground level, I simply scoop her up and carry her the last few rungs. The Mutes with their orders disperse after a united handclasp with Ammo. Holding out her blood-smeared arm, which Doc partially healed, we follow the scarred lines of Ammo's skin from one path to the next.

My bare feet work over the cracked stone, my chest prickling with a chill that my apprehension is keeping mostly at bay. All of my instincts are centered on the female tucked beneath my arm. I have to keep her safe. I must deliver her back to Pyro, earning myself his undeserving forgiveness and the three of us will bring back Hoax. It's the four of us or nothing and in no scenario in my mind can I ditch her now. That must have been one hell of a brainwashing kiss, or maybe she's unleashed the lust I had so carefully buried.

We walk most of the day and my alertness has waned until I hear a scuffle around the next corner. Ammo notices it too, stopping suddenly with her handgun raised. Talon's stance lowers, her nails snaking out into whips and Ammo cocks her thumb back. The pair sneak forward while I hold Mania back, happy to let her friend die before we do. She tries to dodge out of my grip but I raise it to the back of her neck, gripping her tightly in warning.

"I hate being so weak," she whispers while wriggling. I use my steel-like grip to turn her in my direction and crash my chest into hers. The height of her boots help but I still have to lower my head to snag her in a glower.

"Weakness is an affliction of the mind," I snarl. Mania lowers her head, taking my words as an accusation but there's no chance to correct her as the wall behind her shudders. Masses of rock crumble and fall in our direction, causing her to buck but I don't move a muscle. Making us transparent, I use the veil of rock passing through us to crash my lips against hers and swallow her screams. She tenses and quivers as her confusion ebbs out and realization dawns.

Gripping her by the thighs, I hoist Mania onto me and walk her out of the rubble, our lips not leaving each others for a second. I'm surprised I was able to hold off this long after the teasing, intoxicating taste I had this morning. She fits against my body better than any clothing ever could, her long limbs molding around me until I push her against the remains of the wall. "I've got you," I breathe when we finally come up for air. Mania swallows thickly, opening her mouth to reply when Ammo's shout cuts her off.

"Time to go, lovebirds! The labyrinth is moving!" It's only as I place Mania down, her hand in mine, and turn to run that I see the drone hovering in front of my face. The crashing of rock and thumping of my heartbeat in my ears must have disguised its faint buzzing of flight, but the red flicking light beside the camera lens makes me frown. Shooing it aside with my hand, I rush to catch up to Ammo and Talon since they're the ones with the map. The sky has begun to darken and my heart thumps wildly with the worry of what that will bring. Mania's footsteps falter and I pause to toss her onto my back, running as more rocks tumble down from overhead.

Bodies skid into view from adjoining pathways, causing me to lose sight of Ammo but as we're all running in the same direction, I ignore them. Remaining impassive, I jog straight through the Mutes and ignore their cries of anger at the lengths of my powerful strides. By the time the crew are in my sights, all of the others are back in tow and fleeing for their lives. A flame-lit cavern at the end of the passage beckons me onwards, my arms pumping and Mania's grip around my neck chokingly tight. I can't hear anything other than the grinding of stone and the wasted shouts of those behind me who should be reserving their energy for running. Out of the corner of my eye, vines lash out, grabbing Mutes around the throat and restraining them against the crumbling walls.

A female with billowing orange hair appears, darting in and out of the bodies with impressive speed. Her foot crosses the threshold of the carven, a relieved cry leaving her throat as Ammo flicks her wrist, turning the cry into a strangled scream as the female collapses to the floor. My gut flips and Mania's grip on me tightens as she sees it too. Ammo thunders over the threshold, her biker boots splashing in the blood seeping from the girl's head as a drone inside makes an announcement. 'First place - Ammo.'

By the time I've vaulted over the body, all that remains of the orange-haired girl is a mangled mess of limbs. Even her vibrant hair has dimmed with congealed blood and bile rises in my throat. Gently placing Mania down, I hide her eyes in my chest with a deep sigh. What a fucking waste. The sky overhead sinks further into darkness as Mutes all but fall into the cavern, panting and heaving the meager contents of their stomachs onto the floor.

Ammo is beaming, congratulating her team with hard pats on the back until an ear-splitting scream sounds over the crowd. She looks around the same moment I do, spotting Talon tangled in the vines within the passage. She's managed to slice through multiple stems, which lay upon the ground around the cocoon they've now fashioned around her wriggling body. The color drains from Ammo's face and she catches my eye.

"Save her," she pleads, all cockiness vanished. I glance up at the sky outside the cavern's entrance, then at the body splayed over the threshold. I shouldn't do anything to help Ammo, not after the number of lives she's single-handedly taken from our kind today. Yet as I look back into Talon's panicked teal eyes, it's that thought that occurs to me. She's one of us.

"Stay here," I warn Mania with a brief kiss to her hand and then turn transparent as she tries to grab for me. Remy appears from nowhere, flanking me as I take off to save his friend. It's almost pitch black overhead, the moon hidden behind thick layers of cloud. I jump over the orange-haired girl, pushing myself as fast as I can until I'm skidding to a crouch down by her side. Bracing my hands on a free portion of her shoulders, I use my ability to drag her out of the vines that fall through her. They're still wriggling though so I jerk away, pulling Talon to her feet. Mutes are still darting past us, making it to the cavern with cries of celebration.

Bracing myself to run, sharp movements on either side of me fill my chest with pure dread. The dulled glinting metal and the barely audible slices of razor-sharp spears protruding from the walls are nothing, however, compared to the word Remy blurts at me, a cruel smile on his juvenile face.

"Pause." Talon at least has the decency to look apologetic as she stretches a hand out towards the cavern and her fingernails shoot out to latch onto the entrance. I try to move but I'm utterly frozen, my own voice screaming inside my ears. I can't even manage a frown as Talon winds her arm around Remy, who mutters 'fast-forward' and the pair shoot into the cavern at lightning speed. My arms judder in their cocked position from pure will to move but it's useless. I'm rendered immobile. Incapable of growling as Ammo's arms wind around Mania, holding her back from running to me. Let me guess. Remy stands for Remote Control, is my last thought as the metal-spoked walls snap shut on me from both sides.

PYRO

"Nooooooo!" My scream is drowned out by the symphony of cheers that tear through the building below me. I drop to my knees, the towel tied at my waist twisting and getting caught around my thighs. Droplets from my hair drip onto the carpet, my constricted breathing coming out in short pants when I'm close to passing out. I have no idea what the fuck just happened. After a whole day of watching Ghost and Mania walk through the labyrinth hand in hand, I'd resigned to a scorching hot shower to ease the tension building in my chest. I was easily in there for over an hour, seeking comfort from the heat but as I emerged from the bathroom, the screen was filled with Ghost's pained expression just before he was crushed inside the metal-spoked walls.

Cowering over, I let the extent of my pain release in a series of soul-destroying screams and breath-stealing sobs. The first tear that falls causes me to hiss from its molten heat. Like a drip of acid scoring my cheek, I feel the intensity of its burn right through my skull. Then, I force them to fall harder. Let the rivets scar so deeply, everyone who casts a glance on me from here on out will know I've suffered. I've lost, mourned and endured the worst pains imaginable all because I gave my love so freely. What kind of cruel trick of fate is that? Yet I know in my heart, if I had my chance to do it again, I wouldn't change a thing. I'd love them harder, hold them closer, make every fucking second count.

I remain on my knees with my shoulders hunched and hands clenched, the voices leaking from the speakers giving me a focus. Or more specifically, the gut-wrenching cries that can only be from one person. Mania. Tilting my head back, a fresh wash of agony assaults my heart at seeing her face. Contorted with misery and rage, she's fighting with everything she has to be free from the lanky blonde restraining her in place. I saw him emerge from their den, glowing like a damn Christmas tree before branching off to the darkest part of the maze. His arms have hers trapped by her sides and his hands splayed across her bare midsection. Through the overwhelming emotions riding me, jealousy spikes at the edges of my being. It's different from the jealousy I felt with Ghost though. This one is dangerous and the lightbulb fuck-wit has just marked his own death.

The drone inside the candle-lit cave flies closer to the Mute Mania has been hanging around with. Olive green eyes and spikey hair, wearing a fitted tank top and dark jeans with holes ripped all down the legs. She gives her comrade a single nod to release Mania, who barrels forward and slaps her olive-eyed friend around the face. I watch the exchange with interest as the butch female begins to laugh, not even flinching. It's not lost on me how she slides her arm around Mania's shoulders and turns her into the drone's camera, as if she wants her conversation to be seen by all.

"Ahh Babygirl, don't do me like that. This was for the best. You'll see, I promise." Mania stares daggers at her friend and for a brief moment, I was sure I saw the flicker of a flame in her red eyes. However, by the time I've wiped my eyes free from the glaze of tears, it's gone and I decide I imagined it.

"Fuck. You," Mania snarls. The wobble in her voice betrays the anger she's leaning on, and I feel her grief right down to my core. The Mute restraining her doesn't falter though, her smile growing even wider.

"Oh come on, that guy was a douche and you know it. He called me out in my own house, I couldn't let that stand." She reaches up, tucking Mania's hair behind her ear. Her eyes take on a wistful look as she cocks her head to the side, speaking as if telling a well-rehearsed story. "Do you remember those nights when we were kids? We would lay on the rail bridge and you'd tell me of the boy you'd always dream of. Said his fires ignited feelings inside you didn't understand," the manly female snorts a laugh and points in the direction of the sealed walls. "That ain't him."

I blink a couple of times, gripping my towel as I rise to my feet. Numbness claims my body, making my movements jerky as I head over to the dresser. I can't even contemplate what to do with myself but first, I need pants. Wallowing naked just seems so much more depressing, even though there's no one around to see. Or so I thought. Dragging my heavy feet into the living area, merely to put some distance between me and the screen, I'm startled to see the TV on and a suited Christopher reclined on the sofa before it.

"About time, my boy," he says without turning to greet me. Lifting a glass tumbler, he signals for me to join him, casually as fuck. My fingers twitch to close a hand around his elderly neck and squeeze until he stills, but what would be the use now? I have no one to live for, no one to fight for. Unless that's exactly why he's here at this precise moment. Because he has leverage and I have something he wants, albeit buried deep, *deep* inside.

"Bring him back," I state without moving. "You have multiple Mutes at your beck and call. You do your experiments and play God with our genetics. If anyone can bring him back, it's you." Christopher makes a choked noise in his throat, like a strangled laugh and beckons me over to join him again. I make my way over, snatching his decanter of whiskey from the coffee table before dropping into an armchair. If I keep my gaze on him, I can block out the light of the TV screen and ignore the scuffles of a fight I can hear, for the most part.

"If you'd just given me what I wanted, your friends never would have entered the labyrinth in the first place." Christopher's icy blue eyes watch me closely, hunting for a trace of the guilt he's just surged within me. I keep my features impassive, not giving the old man what he wants as usual. But still, the truth in his words cuts deeper than any blade could ever reach and when I'm alone later, I'll let my own selfish actions consume me.

"Tell me what you need me to do. Then you bring him back, in one whole piece and unscathed. Do we have a deal?" I swallow thickly, knowing I've played straight into his hands. He put me up here for a reason, to watch as Ghost and Mania struggled to stay alive until I gave in. I never had a choice. Christopher sits forward to place down his glass and pulls a capsule out from beneath the table. It's around two feet long and a foot wide, clear inside with a magnetic conductor on either end. He lifts it with surprising ease, standing to drop it into my lap. The whiskey from his decanter sloshes as I jerk it out of the way and the weight of the capsule drops into my lap with a thud. Damn, how the fuck did he even lift it at all?

"Fill it with your fire. Then I'll see that Ghost re-joins the labyrinth."

"Not good enough," I bark. "You want my fire, then he'll be revived and free to exit the fucked up maze you've created. Hell, bring him here so we can drink and watch them together."

"And the girl?" Christopher asks, tilting his chin up to the TV screen. I stupidly follow his gaze, instantly regretting it when I see the darkened patch forming around one of Mania's eyes and the trickle of blood leaking from her split lip. Fuck. I search for the other Mute with the spiky hair, and upon spotting her, I frown to see there's not a mark on her. I'd at least hoped Mania had got a punch in, but in her current state, she'd most likely broken her own hand instead of doing any real damage.

"Leave her like she left me," I state, swinging my eyes away. I can't keep chasing my own tail when it comes to Mania. She made her choice, and I wasn't it. My answer seems to appease Christopher more than I'd thought it would, the sly turn of his lips causing me to narrow my eyes.

"I'm afraid withdrawing him completely is out of my hands. Only Mutes can enter the labyrinth, and until he's found the way out, it'll be up to Ghost to save himself. However, I can agree to his safe return to the games and I'll throw in some useful aids as a goodwill gesture." Goodwill fucking gesture, I scoff. However, I'm hardly in a position to bargain any further. I just need the knowledge that my brother is alive, and then it's on him to find his way out. A subconscious part of my psyche also knows that from what I've seen today, he won't leave Mania to fend for herself so in theory, this will be helping them both.

Pulling myself to my feet, I hold the capsule with my hands braced on either end of the metal prongs. Closing my eyes, I will my fires to come to my aid just this once. Nothing. Not even a flicker. Undeterred, I try again. I push so hard, my hands tremble and my eyes are scrunched so tight, I'm seeing spots. Yet I can't muster a single spark on behalf of my best friend's life. I'm vaguely aware Christopher has moved and upon taking my next, huffed break, I find him holding the TV control.

"Maybe you could use a little extra encouragement," he says cryptically. Pushing a button on the controls, he runs back through some of the previous footage from today. I'd chosen to watch only the drone that was following Ghost and Mania, punishing myself instead of checking on Recall - the Mute I actually betted on. Christopher seems to know exactly what he's searching for, stopping on a moment I must have missed while in the shower. Something slams into the other side of the stone wall and a chunk of rock dislodges from the top, hurtling straight for the pair I still care about, despite myself. My heart slams in my chest, even though I've seen past this point and know this isn't the moment that Ghost is killed.

Yet I was wholly unprepared for the reaction Ghost has to the hail of stone falling all around and through him. He grips Mania, yanking her to him and delving his tongue directly into her mouth. Stunned shock ripples through me. I know he had wanted her the whole time we were at Afterlife, but I thought our bro-code was solid. As he draws her further up his body and pushes her against the shaking wall, I squeeze my eyes closed once more. This means nothing. He's still my brother. My betraying, traitorous brother who is right there, kissing my girl for the whole world to see.

Anger, hatred and jealousy course through me with the force of a tornado. My body jolts involuntarily from the inside, my hands cutting into the metal pushing against my palms. My eyes fly open just as they begin to burn like hot coals in my head and the smirking cuntish face Christopher is pulling becomes bathed in a red glow. My hair ignites a moment later and the ferocity of my heat scorches hotter than usual. The last time I even came close was when I went nuclear when Hoax died, and as the need riles up within me to do it again, I channel my fires towards my hands.

The glass of the capsule glows blue and orange as my flames delve inside, swarming together and thoroughly locked in. I'm fascinated, not having seen the true extent of my ability in such fine detail before. Wispy tendrils float around the flames, my eyes easing to see a figure dancing in the center. There's no denying her floating, flame-red hair or the curves of her body as she rolls her hips one side to the other. Mania. She reaches out, her tiny flaming hands pushing against the glass and the metal beneath my palms click into place and I'm cut off from my flames. The wash of cold seeping through my arms and into my chest has an air of finality and this time, I know they're gone for good.

Christopher chuckles like a little lad, marveling over a bowl of berries and cream as he takes the capsule from me and peers inside. The figure is still in there, wrapping her arms around herself as she realizes she's trapped. A frown twitches at my eyebrows, the realization dawning that I've just given away something much more precious than just my fires. Two guards appear out of the elevator at that exact moment, their boots eating up the marble floor to retrieve the capsule. Christopher moves to follow and I grab the crook of his arm.

"What about Ghost?" I ask, dread sweeping through me. Christopher plants the TV control into my hand and twists free of my grip.

"Turns out that kiss earned your so-called friend a fanbase of swooning women. I wouldn't be stupid enough to permit the death of my second favorite to win now, would I?" He laughs at himself, stepping into the elevator and pressing a button inside. "Check camera thirty-three, and Pyro? Thanks for your donation to my cause. I have the ideal candidate to benefit from your generous gift." I stand, stunned and confused long after the doors have slid closed. Then, when I'm sure Christopher isn't going to return again just to laugh in my face some more, I move over to the screen.

Bringing up camera thirty-three, I see my best friend there, slumped against a wall and looking bored out of his fucking mind. The room is mostly dark except for one flaming torch attached to the wall above his head. From the angle of the camera, I imagine this one isn't a drone but is a permanent fixture in the corner of the room. Confusion starts to make my brain spin so I rewind the footage, all the way back to the moment the ceiling opens and Ghost falls inside. There's a heavy crunch of metal on metal, making my stomach roll with just how close he came to being kebabbed before the floor gave out. He lies in a mangled heap for a little while before shaking off whatever trance he was under and dusting himself off.

Shutting off the TV, I slump back into the bedroom and fall face-first into the mattress. Of course I'm relieved Ghost is safe and alive, but the undeniable knowledge that I've been played wells up in me and there's nothing I can do but lie here. Still broken, still alone and so much more pissed off than before. Strangely though, one thing Christopher said repeats in my mind and just before I drown in a puddle of my own self-loathing, I spare a moment to contemplate that. *'Only Mutes can enter the labyrinth.'* So if Mania's on her last life, what other ability does she possess?

"You're making a big mistake," Ammo repeats for the fifth time. I keep my back to her, kneeling on the ground and waiting for the walls to open back up. They can't stay closed forever because they're the only way out of here and if they don't open soon, Ammo will probably start another blood bath. Backers can't support their favorite Mutes if there's none left. I was surprised she defended me from Talon after I openly attacked the bitch for what she did to Ghost but that doesn't mean I'm going anywhere with her. That Mute is not the one I used to know. The labyrinth's trail runs have changed her, just like the guys who have splintered and stolen pieces of my heart have changed me.

There's a deep rumble beneath my fingers as I pathetically try to pry the walls apart, and as if by magic, they begin to open. The metal spikes inside have retracted, allowing me to dart between them as soon as they are wide enough. Ghost wasn't the only one who got caught in the crosshairs of the speared trap. Chunks of flesh, organs and brain matter smearing the walls slowly trickle down and leave a slimy mess across the ground. My chest squeezes and the tears begin to fall again as I hunt for evidence Ghost is really gone. I know I shouldn't, that I'll never be able to scrub the sight from my mind, but I push on regardless.

I scramble right up to the last point I saw him, frozen in place and panicked. His white eyes locked with mine as he took his last breath. But as I scan the area, there's nothing to imply he was here. No white hair, no tattooed patches of skin, no swatches of dark jeans. Even Ammo grunts in confusion as she catches up and tries to pull me beneath her arm again.

"Get the fuck off me!" I yell, shoving her away. She has the audacity to look hurt as Firefly approaches, his glow illuminating our tense stare-off.

"Just come back to the hideout. We need you for what tomorrow brings," she starts but I'm already shaking my head and backing away. I don't want to hear it. Without any reason to stay and nothing of Ghost's to tie me here, I start running as fast as my shaky legs will carry me. Tears sting my eyes and my feet are late to respond to each uneven slab in the ground, but I don't stop.

"You'll never survive the night in one piece!" Ammo calls out, causing my breath to labor harder. I keep going, aware of a drone buzzing behind me until I turn a sharp corner and hunch over to dry retch. Pain slices along my spine with each heave, yet every time I close my eyes and picture the clumps of discarded skin or intestines in the next alleyway, I retch again. Maybe Ghost's traits were too shredded or covered in blood to recognize. Maybe I should stand here all night in hopes the same fate will take me and I'll find peace in hell.

Hearing others approach, I push myself against the wall and will my breathing to ease. Ammo and Doc's voices pass in hushed tones, followed by trampling footsteps. Resting my head back once the crew has gone, I only then realize a vine has snaked out and sneered my wrist. Jerking away, I claw at the vine until my wrist is free and start moving again. I don't know where the fuck I'm going. Just keep twisting between passages that all look like the one before and ducking aside when I hear voices. Eventually, I come across an alcove and take a rest there. The dent in the wall is deep enough that, with my knees drawn up to my chest, no one would be able to notice I was there.

Despite the ache in my heart, my eyelids begin to droop. My legs feel heavier than lead after a full day of traipsing around and my stomach is hankering for my next meal. Yet none of it matters more than the desperate grasp I have on my last shred of hope. It was a blur, but I'm certain there were no parts of Ghost among the other body parts. He has to be okay. He's all I have left.

I wake in the morning with a start, the feeling I'm being watched confirmed by the drone hovering in my face. I scowl, batting it away but it's faster than my sluggish movements. My back and neck are stiff from the crooked position I slept in, my eyes itchy and squinted. I stretch out my legs, rolling my ankles as the drone lowers down to me again. A compartment in the base slides open, revealing a gold gift box complete with a satin, red bow. I don't move to take it, dubious of its contents, but the drone tilts forward and the box drops into my lap. I reason with myself that if it were a teeny tiny bomb, I'd be dead by now so I gently unravel the bow and pop the lid. A message is printed inside, the scrawny text compressing my chest with the force of a battering ram.

'*Compliments of Christopher Gordon.*' Strangely enough, while I'd been fearing and running for my life, I hadn't stopped long enough to wonder about the who and why I was here, but now it all makes perfect sense. Genetic experiments + raving lunatic = a maze of twisted games and deadly intentions.

Lifting the message, as my curiosity gets the better of me, I find a key card. It's black with an intricate, silver pattern and the weight in my hand hints to the electronic circuit inside. I flip it over, finding yet another message engraved in the back and I let out a huff. Cunning bastard and his riddles. And to think I almost joined his team willingly.

'*Find the exit where it all began*'. I drag my eyes back up to the drone's camera lens and fix a bored expression into place.

"Where do you expect me to stash this? Up my cu-" A roar sounds from the other side of the wall I'm leaning on and I jump to my feet. Deciding my corset cup is a better option, I jam the keypad between my under boob and the leather before taking off. Where I'm going, I have no fucking clue but it won't be anywhere near here. The wall I was resting against moments ago disintegrates into dust and I risk a look over my shoulder in time to see an animal step through. No, not an animal.

I skid through an archway, gripping onto the stone for a precious second to get a better view. He's a beast of a man. Easily eight feet of mocha skin and brawn. Bulging muscles ripple across his torso among tribal tattoos. Flicking my gaze down, along the length of his dark jeans which are sitting awkwardly, I find two shining brown hooves. A Minotaur in the labyrinth? You've got to be freaking kidding me. I know I need to move, but I'm transfixed. Frozen stock still and gaping as his black eyes settle on me. A huff of visible breath heaves from his pierced nostrils and he shakes his shoulder-length brown waves around a pair of girthy, protruding horns. With a flex of his clawed hands flex to form fists, a harsh roar leaves his thick throat.

Go. Fucking go! I mentally scream at myself, moving as fast as my legs will carry me. Tearing through the passages, I spot a few others who must have also heard the roar but they're far in front of me and already disappearing from view. A top tip forms in my mind, one I cringe at but it rings true all the same. I don't need to be fast, I just need to be faster than the slowest person.

The walls thunder and the ground shakes as I stagger onwards in my boots, already panting from exertion. Turning the next corner, I find myself in a circular opening but I don't waste time looking around. Darting across the space, my eyes are fixed on the opposite archway when the roar behind me sounds again. I'm caught off guard this time, my chest having eased as if I might be able to outrun this hefty-hooved fucker. He must smash one of those meaty fists into the rounded wall because in the next moment, the archway I had my eyes on collapses beneath a pile of tumbling rumble.

I struggle to stop, my heart jumping into my throat. Frick it. Skidding out on my ass, I twist to see the Minotaur stomping over to me with long, sure strides. Wriggling back with my hands, my back hits a fallen rock and I swallow. Hard. I'm so dead. The ani-man's black eyes glisten and his lips peel back in a snarl over two rows of pointed teeth. His chest is corded so tightly, each breath looks torturous. Taut veins track the expanse of his neck, drawing my attention to a ropey chain swaying among his black hair. The black rope would be impossible to see if he weren't leaning over me and the pendant wasn't hanging right in front of my face. A key. Ugh, it's so cliché, it hurts.

My eyes fly around in all directions, trying to spot a way out but the Minotaur is blocking my vision. For some inexplicable reason, my gaze trails over his body once more and I have to double-take at the bulging outline locked inside his pants. Oh girl, this really isn't the time, I berate myself but still, I can't look away. His cock trails down his bulky, left thigh and his balls…well, let's just say they haven't been emptied in a while.

So I do what any girl in a life or death situation does. I snatch the key dangling in my face at the same time I slam my foot up into his biscuits. Holy, ow. The brick-like balls have most likely sprained my ankle and I cradle my booted foot in my hand. The Minotaur bellows a pained roar in my face and his gaze doesn't waver from mine, filling me with the certainty that I've just signed my own death warrant. Then, he grips his hopefully injured balls and keels over, rolling around on his side. A minuscule part of me sort of feels bad, but then I remember I need to move.

Pushing to my feet, I make a move to leap over his body when a hand lashes out mid-air and grabs my knee. Yanking me down on top of him, I wriggle as much as I can in his iron grip. The key is pressed so far into my palm, I'm sure I feel the trickle of blood but I don't stop fighting with all I have. My elbow catches his throat. His foul breath huffs across my ear, disheveling my hair further into my face. Rolling until his crushing weight is on top, I don't hesitate to force my hand between us to rip his nose ring cleanout. Blood sprays over my face but the beast falls off me, howling in pain and this time I'm able to make my escape. I don't even think about looking back - I just run for my freaking life.

What seems like hours later, I finally let myself relent to the fact I'm not being chased. I must have put miles between me and the Minotaur, but my overriding fear that I've been moving in circles and am actually only a wall away hasn't let me stop for more than a minute. The stitches in my side are now permanent fixtures and as the sun passes overhead, my stomach is ready to turn in on itself. I can't kept going much longer, but unless I want to start licking the stone walls, the vines scaling the stone are my only option and fuck, what I'd give for it to rain. My throat is drier than the Sahara and I feel like my sweat can't penetrate the layer of grime smeared across my forehead. Fucking gross.

Ripping into a vine with my teeth, I chew on the leathery stem just to put some substance inside me. I've never thought of myself as high maintenance but if I ever miraculously get out of here, I'll be one of those girls demanding pointless shit purely because I can. Maybe I'll get a sugar daddy to wait on me hand and foot with the illusion of sex he's never going to get. I snort a laugh to myself, chewing vigorously. Leaning my ass against a random boulder, I wipe my arm around my sweat-beaded brow and wobble slightly. Hysteria, I decide. That's what this loopy, no longer regarding my own life mind babble has come from.

A soft scrape from high above whips my head up to see the curious gaze of a crow perched on the top of the wall. Oh fantastic, a crow has come to witness my death. I stare back, tilting my head every time he tilts his, taking great amusement in mimicking his actions. A smile graces my lips as he coos and I brace myself to copy when the pointed glint of a spearhead pierces the front of his chest. The bird drops forward lifelessly and I catch him on instinct, utterly appalled and shocked. What the-

"Hey! That's my kill!" a voice shouts and I jump to my feet. Stupidly though, I cradle the bird to my chest. Death never used to bother me. In fact, it was a common occurrence I took advantage of to visit Azella in hell. But in a few short days, I could happily never witness a death again. Of a person or an animal. Still, the bird in my arms is dead and I can't deny that the Mutes have to eat something other than vines. That shit isn't edible in the slightest.

"What are you going to give me for it?" I ask, seizing the opportunity that has fallen into my lap.

"What's your name?" he asks instead of answering my question first. My hackles rise. He knows, just like I do, there's so much more to a Mute's name than a simple word. It's our identity, so in asking me that seemingly simple question, he's actually sizing me up. Trying to suss out who holds more power out of the two of us, and I won't be stupid enough to inform this stranger it's definitely him.

"Mania," I state with my head high. "Deranged mistress of Hell." Okay, that was laying it on a little too thickly but the male's spear wavers slightly. His prawn-shaded pink eyes look from me, to the bird clutched in my hands and back again.

"Bait," he replies, giving me the same kindness. "Hand over my kill so I can cook it, and I'll give you a leg." My eyes widen at the thought of harming my little friend but then I mentally shake myself. Pull it together Mania. This bird's dead and you need to eat. Besides, I'm never going to survive if I only rely on my stubbornness.

Nodding slowly, I close the distance between us and reluctantly pass him the crow. Then, as quickly as my nutrition-deprived body can manage, I rip a vine from the closest wall and loop it around his wrist in a shabby loop knot. To be fair, my movements weren't half as precise and coordinated as I'd have liked, but the fact he stands and lets me bind his arm soothes me a fraction. Wrapping my hand around the other end, I jerk my head for him to lead me wherever he is heading. I don't miss the mild amusement of his smirk before he turns away, complying with my silent order.

We don't walk far when the Mute I've tethered stops abruptly in front of a dead-end. I crash into his back, having been too complacent walking along with some company. It's been less than a day since I found myself alone yet it's seemed like weeks. Let's just say, I'm not handling my captor's position very well at the moment. Tugging at the vine restraint, Bait places his hand flat on the wall in front of us and to my surprise, the stone shifts outwards as smoothly as an automatic door. It's dark inside and I hold back, suddenly rethinking my plan to follow a stranger home.

"Erm, you know what...I'm not actually that hungry. I think I'd better be going. Got loads of…er…allies looking for me. And I need to get back before sundown," I ramble on. Releasing the vine still wound around my hand, I make it two whole steps before an arm around my waist whips me off my feet.

"Is that so, Mania?" Bait breathes into my ear, giving me all kinds of creeper vibes. I buck against him, trying to repeat my ball-crushing success from the Minotaur but from this angle, it's useless. "I think you should come inside. I have a friend who would love to meet you." I balk, wondering just who or what he is reeling me in as '*bait*' for.

"No thanks," I grunt through my struggles. "I'm good." Leaning into his grip on me, I draw both knees up high and then slam them down on his shins. His arm weakens as he cries out, but it's the trembling of the ground beneath us that really makes me pause. Fuck, am I that strong? I hear the sound of cracking before I see it, a thick zigzag splintering along the pathway and aiming directly for us. Bait stills, his sharp intake of breath beside my head confirming my suspicions. That wasn't me.

"On second thought, you're on your own." My boots hit the floor as Bait releases me and takes a step back. My head whips around, trying to place where the continual cracking is coming from. "You can keep this too," Bait shoves the dead crow into my chest and bolts inside his door, slamming it closed behind him. I don't have to shove the mass of blood and feathers off me as the floor opens up and I'm freefalling. My knees crash in the base of the pit, only the thickness of the leather boots keeping my skin intact. My bones, however, feel like they've just taken the brunt of a sledgehammer. I scream, writhing in agony and as if it couldn't get any worse, the tell-tale buzz of a drone closes in on me.

"Mania, you need to move," a voice flitters on the edge of my consciousness. I lash an arm out, catching the drone and forcing it to put some distance between me and the lens.

"I…can't…" I sob, clutching my legs into myself. Leaning all the way over, my head rests on the cold, hard ground and I feel it with certainty. I've given up. Well and truly. Today can go fuck itself, along with the past few weeks I've been forced to endure. What's the point of continuing on when I keep getting lured into the same shit-tastic situations? I'm desolate, I'm dejected and I'm done.

"Mania," the voice comes again, more demanding this time. Lolling my head to the side, I flinch to see a pair of boots and crouched cargo pants beside me. In the time it takes to jerk upright, the figure has gone. I shiver deeply, as if the essence of whoever was just here is passing through me. In my heart, I know who it was but my head won't believe it. There's just no way. Not after all this time and all I've been through, he wouldn't have just found a way to pop back into my life now. I'm not that lucky.

My gaze darts up to the top of the hole in the ground I've found myself in, only seeing a cragged rock face stretching high above me on either side. The crack through the earth is long, creating a new passage to contend with but as I squint into the distance, there he is. Indigo hair, purple eyes. His lean physique covered with intricate, technical tattoos. A strong stance and the body I became one with in hell. Hoax.

"Move it!" he yells and I scramble to comply. A whimper escapes my lips as I urge myself back to my feet, using the wall as a crutch. Hobbling towards him, I gain enough distance to see the concern trapped in his gorgeous eyes when the sudden flare of heat burns at my back. I don't hang around to see if my hair is singed in the way I'm imagining it is, running full speed now with the pain in my legs forgotten.

A hissing sound gets the better of my curiosity and I risk a look over my shoulder. Blazes of fire pour from the walls like a flamethrower, directly over the spot I was just sitting in. Another round of fire blares to life, this one closer and I scream involuntarily. I run the length of the passage, my eyes remaining fixed on Hoax's now. He's my anchor.

My boots thunder over the cracked stone, barely treading as I fly forward. The air whips around my face, causing the tears to spill from my eyes in blurred lines. A relieved smile pulls up at my mouth and I call out his name. My beautiful Hoax who came back for me. Coming within two feet of his pinched expression, I throw myself freely into his body and sail straight through into the wall on the other side.

My cracked skull smashes against the rock and for longer than is healthy, everything goes black. Blinking my eyes open, I peer up at the spot he was and of course, he's nowhere to be seen. I expected to crumple back into a ball of self-pity, but instead, a strange sense of numbness washes through me. Typical sleep and food-deprived brain, creating images that aren't really there. I stare at the blazing fires growing closer, not trying to move this time. They're beautiful really, in all their harshness and chaos. The flames waltz, sauntering towards me to lick at my skin. My inhales become heavy and laced with smoke. Between the sporadic combustions and the slow trail of blood oozing down the side of my face, I'm lost in a trance of my own concoction when a small body trips over my boot and collides with mine.

"Hey, what the-" I begin, thinking this is another trick of my mind but the body slithering her tiny arms around me is real. Craning my face to peer over her head, I spot a group of Mutes high above the rock in the direction the girl fled from. From my angle, it's clear someone is trying to jump into the pit after her, but others are holding them back. More fires are on their way from both directions, ensnaring the two of us here like rats in a trap.

I shakily push myself to my feet, keeping one arm caged around her. She's trembling forcibly, her limbs constricting around me. I sink a hand into her hair, comforting her the best I can when her face tilts up to mine. Two perfectly slitted yellow eyes blink up at me and my heart stills in my chest.

"Serpentina?" I whisper. Disbelief courses through me, along with a hefty dose of suspicion. I tense my grip around her, checking she's real and this isn't another figment of my imagination. No, she's really here and a burst of anger awakens inside me. She's a child, barely more than seven years old, and she's stuck in this dreadful maze. The little reptile must have been herded in with the rest of the Mutes from Bellemare, but as the rest of her family are human, she must have been shepherded in alone. I can't begin to imagine how scared she's been, but even contemplating it makes me heave harder. I fight against myself to loosen my punishing grip around her small body. Scaring her further in her last few moments isn't going to help anyone.

Instead, I turn my back to the approaching fires, shielding her view and rock her slowly.

"Shhh, it's okay little one. We're going to a really cool place where the Mutes all live together. We'll play games and laugh all the time. There's an awesome female down there too, called Azella. I met her when I was about your age, she's the best." I smile wistfully, unlatching Serpentina's arms and legs from me. Bundling her up into a cradle, I try to make my body cover every part of hers as if that's going to shield her from any of the pain about to consume us both. The sound of the rushing blaze heightens like a roar so I pitifully hum a tone, keeping her as calm as possible. Inside, though, an inferno of my own is raging. I'm silently vowing to be Christopher Gordon's personal poltergeist until he dies, and then the real fun will begin. I'll torture him for all of eternity for the lives he's so cruelly imprisoned here.

The first flame brushes my back and I hiss on instinct. But then I still and realize, it doesn't hurt. Turning my head ever so slightly to the side, I eye the orange and yellow strands just before another crevice in the wall opens up and we are engulfed in flame. I twist, keeping Serpentina tucked into me as the fires crash together, although I need not have bothered. The tornado rages in a cocoon, sparing us in the eye of the storm. Growing brave, I stretch a handout, brushing the roaring flames and marveling at the lack of pain it causes me.

Just as quickly as it swarmed, the fires are gone. Disintegrated rock and ash tumble around my feet yet I stand there, unscathed with a quivering ball of a Mute in my arms. After sharing a wide-eyed look, I tentatively reach up to place my hands over her ears.

"What the fuck was that?"

Serpentina has drifted off by the time the Mutes above fashion a rope from vines to pull us up. At least, I hope it's exhaustion that's claimed the small girl collapsed in my arms so I give her a regular shake just in case. Her forked tongue slithers out to grace my cheek reassuringly and I let the reprieve of sleep take her again. Wrapping the vine around my waist with one hand, I then curl it tightly around my wrist. Leaning back, I steadily walk my boots up the rock face while relying solely on the Mute above to not let go. Two females huddle together and rush forward as my boot grazes the top of my rocky prison, reaching out to take Serpentina from me. My instincts to tighten the hold around her small frame isn't a selfish one, but seeing their collective concern soothes me. I brace myself, ready for the rope to slacken as soon as she's safe, but the Male tugging me up reaches out a hand, pulling me to safety.

"Thank you for saving her!" the female with long sandy hair and pale eyes holding Serpentina cries. The girl has awoken with all the racket, throwing herself further into the Mute's hold. It's clear from their bond the young reptile trusts her as the pair sob into each other's necks and the other female, this one with ashy white skin and ebony hair, coos around them. A strong hand clasps me on the shoulder and I jump out of my skin.

"That's quite an ability you have there," the male praises. My cheeks heat at his words and I turn to get a proper look at the Mute who pulled me up. Like the others and despite his older age, he stands before me topless with dark jeans snuggly fitted to his thin hips. His skin and bald scalp are tanned and leathery, like he's spent too many days in the sun.

"Oh, erm, it's not mine," I dodge uncomfortably and his brows furrow. Thankfully, a soft chuckle from Serpentina distracts him as the women sing a strange lullaby in her ear.

"Well regardless, thank you. I can't imagine carrying on without Serpentina to fight for." His hooded eyes, framed by a pair of graying brows, hold a surprising amount of love, yet his smile is pensive.

"Where are her real parents?" I ask, instantly cringing at the trio of pained expressions I receive. "I mean, I knew Serpentina from Bellemare. She was born to a human family." The females look away, turning their attention back to the girl and the male nods, unsurprised.

"We're from Bellemare too. My wife, Dialect, promised her parents we would care for her when the MRA seemed hellbent on separating them." I follow his chin-jerk to the sandy-haired female, realizing the love in his gaze wasn't just for Serpentina. "I'm Summon, by the way."

"Mania," I respond, suddenly aware of how much time we're wasting standing out in the open. "We need to move. The sun is starting to dip." It's strange how quickly I've become accustomed to watching the movements of the sun, knowing my life depends on it. The others begin to shuffle onwards at my words, leaving the female with ebony hair staring at me.

"I'm Monochrome. I know we don't look like much but you're welcome to tag along with us. Dialect has the clue to the next checkpoint and it's not far. We were on our way there when the ground opened up." I fall into step with her, sneaking looks at her coloring now I know her name. Her eyes are as black as her long locks, her skin pure white and unblemished. It's like the color was completely drained from her body and the black leather of her pants and tank top don't help. Summon and Dialect turn a corner and I jog to catch up, not wanting to put any space between us. I'm in no place to pledge allegiance to another group but one look at Serpentina's slitted eyes and I know I'm already invested.

From there on, the group move as one, keeping to the thin edge of the passage. Keeping my back to the wall, I can see the spot where Serpentina fell. A dip of crumbled rock and the tell-tale sign of where she must have slid down. I peer over my shoulder, wondering why the Mutes didn't jump in after her but since the spot I had decided to have my pity party is in full view, I can only imagine they'd left it to me. Her yellow eyes find me over the female's shoulder as we walk in silence and I do my best to give her a reassuring smile.

In front, Summon stops every so often to check around corners before we dart across archways. I don't recognize this area of the maze, spotting more vast spaces between the passageways and less others crossing our path. Where is everyone? The group suddenly slams to a halt and I peek around the wall to see what's fascinating them. A huge cage sits in the center of an opening, and I'm glad I'm not the only one who seems surprised by its presence. The iron bars are easily over ten feet tall, clamped shut by a thick lock and completely empty inside.

"Someone must have beaten us here," Dialect sighs.

"Not that we have a key, even if we did find it first," Monochrome replies sharply. I look away to hide my face, not wanting to give away the chunky metal key currently stuck between my thigh and my boot. I'd shoved it in there and mostly forgotten about it, except now it's burning against my skin. These Mutes seem nice enough, especially since they are keeping Serpentina safe when others would have ditched her at the first sign of trouble, but I've thoroughly learned my lesson. Don't be gullible and make smart choices. Besides, disclosing my one bargaining chip wouldn't put the Mute back in the cage.

Continuing on, we walk the length of a few more passages before coming to a stone intersection. Summon stops, looking both ways a few times before Monochrome moves to join his side. They mutter in hushed tones, the female's black eyes sliding back to me and I freeze.

Quirking my brow, she quickly looks away and that's when I stride to the front of the group.

"Problem?" I ask, my skin prickling with apprehension. As clueless as I am about the labyrinth, I'm done being left out of decisions that are going to directly impact me.

"No, no. Not at all," Summon answers quickly. "The check-in point is that way but our refuge is also close by. We probably have time to run back and grab some food before sunset if everyone needs a break." Monochrome eyes me again and I realize that even though Summon said 'everyone', they namely mean me.

"I'm fine. But what about Serpentina? Can't she go back to your place of refuge while we make the check-in?" This time, it's Dialect who makes a strangled sound in the back of her throat.

"The instructions are clear. Every Mute has to make the daily check-in or they'll be eliminated. She is hungry and weak, but we really shouldn't risk it." Looking down at the girl in her arms, there's so much compassion in their shared gazes it makes my heart squeeze. Serpentina does look rather pale but Dialect is right. A few more hours and they'll be back in their hideout, thankful they're still alive. Nodding sharply, Summon continues to walk and I jog to remain with him.

"I seem to have arrived at the labyrinth later than everyone else. What instructions did you receive?" I ask, keeping my eyes glued to the wobbly ground. When Summon doesn't immediately answer, I risk a look up and find his narrowed eyes fixed on me. He must find whatever he's searching for because he blows out a heavy breath.

"I get my name because I can summon any item I can think of, but only once. The night the guards stormed Bellemare, Dialect and I were separated and I was entered into a different part of the labyrinth to her."

"You mentioned you were from Bellemare," I dodge, not in the mind frame to process everything else Summon just said. It'll come back around later when I have a moment to sit and think over everything that's happened today.

"We all were," he looks over the pair of females huddled behind. "Come to think of it, I do remember you. There wasn't the black in your hair, or around your eyes. You didn't have a crack in your skull or-"

"Yeah, yeah. I haven't aged well," I grumble. Summon laughs softly.

"You used to cause quite a bit of trouble with your pickpocket friend and the one who liked to shoot out the generators." I smile, even though I probably should feel bad. Life in Bellemare was shit enough as it was, without a bunch of dumb kids making it worse. But Ammo had a fascination with the stars and would force a city-wide blackout just so she could see them better. Staring into space made us feel like our problems were as insignificant as the human's petty power plays and I suppose she was right. Didn't make getting through each day any easier though.

"Anyway," Summon continues. "First, I summoned a secure place to hide where no one else could bother us, then I called for my wife. It's the first time I've ever needed to do it, but it scares the shit out of me I won't be able to again. Apparently, the small serpent girl bundled in her arms was included in my call because when Serpentina fell in the pit today, I was unable to call her back out. Then the fire started and I just couldn't let Dialect jump in after her..." Desperation floods Summon's eyes and that similar tightening in my chest comes back. I shove away all thoughts of how it felt to lose my guys, not wanting to re-enter the pit of misery I've just climbed out of, but I understand. Summon looks over at me, his lips pressed together in a rigid line.

"I will protect my wife first, no matter what." His words aren't a threat, just the honest truth and I nod in agreement. Looking back, however, I can already tell Dialect has a similar idea in mind about the little girl wrapped around her body like a monkey clinging onto its mother. I can't even imagine how confusing and scary this must all be for Serpentina, and it makes me hate Christopher all the more. Every time I think I've seen the worst of him, he proves me wrong. At least I have a focus now, and a reason to continue when all hopes of saving my guys are lost. I'm going to get out of here and kill that manipulative fucker if it's the last thing I do.

The sun has begun to dip and our steps hurry, wanting to make good time. In the back of my mind, a voice tells me to skid over that threshold first today so I can be proclaimed the winner. Maybe it comes with a prize and I'll be the one sharing a curry with my new comrades tonight. A smile pulls at my lips as we seem to be the only ones around, shuffling towards an opening at the end of the next passage.

Entering the open space, which has multiple entrances, there is a rounded structure like that of a cave, complete with a closed stone door. 'Check-point' is carved into the stone, just to clear up any confusion. I make it there first, hunting for a handle or keyhole or anything, but frown when there isn't any. Then I take to trying to shove the damn thing open, pushing with all my might until my extremely lean muscles quake. Like an omen, drones descend from overhead, twisting and spacing out until every angle is covered.

Summon joins me, hunting for a way in until Monochrome calls out to us. She hasn't left Dialect and Serpentina, but she's helpfully pointing out two large cylinders across the opening. Edging closer, I check all around them before peering inside. Weird. There's no clues or instructions, just two glass containers around five feet tall and attached to the wall.

"Any ideas?" I ask Summon when he doesn't immediately offer up any solutions. Twisting my head, I see why. A hand clutches the male's mouth and others crowd around those holding Serpentina, but none of that chills me as much as the finger gun pointed directly between my eyebrows.

"Hey Babygirl," Ammo grins. "Glad you could make it. I told you I needed you today."

"Let the others go. You don't need them," I respond automatically.

"You're right, I don't. So why would I bother keeping them alive?" Ammo shifts to place both hands heavily on my shoulders and just then, everything slows. My mind still works in real-time, but the display around me moves at a snail's pace and I'm powerless to do anything except watch. From their position guarding the females, Firefly and Talon's eyes widen at a spot beyond my head. I slowly look aside to see Remy materialize out of the wall, a machete braced across his throat and then a seriously stacked, gloriously tattooed and severely pissed off Ghost right behind. *Ghost.*

My heart jack-knifes but he doesn't meet my eye. Instead, with one smooth swipe of the machete, he slits Remy's throat and time suddenly returns to normal speed. Ghost still has the element of surprise though and in a split second, his blade has soared through the air and sliced through both of Ammo's arms at the wrists. The wrists that were attached to the hands gripping me. Blood splatters across my face like a slap. I scream and jerk back, prying her severed hands from their death-like grip on my shoulders but it's nothing compared to the wail Ammo releases.

Without hesitating, Ghost grabs her arms and shoves her stumps into the two glass cylinders. The blood spews in all directions, quickly coating the inside of the glass and churning my stomach as I chuck her hands away from me. A grinding sound catches my attention through Ammo's screams and I twist to see the door of the cave has begun to open. I look around in shock, taking in the scene but it's Ghost's murderous gaze that captivates mine.

"Blood buy-in," he states in answer to my unspoken question. Ammo jerks against his hold, trying to free her arms which he is holding in place.

"What the fuck have you done?!" Ammo screeches. "She can't die!" I maintain Ghost's stare, half not believing he's here and half in realization what Ammo's plan was. To kill me with the reasoning I would have come back to life with merely a scar, whereas she is now bleeding out and not being quiet about it. Doc rushes to her side, cursing out Ghost but my attention is drawn elsewhere. Mutes suddenly begin appearing in all of the archways, no doubt drawn in by the commotion. Without losing another second, I make a run for the cave and throw myself inside just before a body collides with mine.

'First place - Mania,' a voice booms from the drone. My heart beats erratically, a range of emotions flittering on the edge of my consciousness but I can't delve into them right now. Bodies swarm the cave, pushing and shoving like animals being herded into a pen. Peering as high as my tiptoes will allow, I see the door to the cave slide shut just after Doc has ushered Ammo inside. Pitch black falls upon the Mutes and I know too long in a cramped space like this will start a riot. Especially if Ammo is healed and looking for vengeance. A blinding light switches on via the drone, which scans back and forth over us while I desperately look for Ghost. I remain close to Serpentina and those protecting her, making sure no one bumps into her in the moments of darkness.

Seconds later, hands grip my sides and my surprised shriek is swallowed by the mouth clamping down over mine. I shove at the hard chest pushing against me, needing the confirmation it's Ghost who has found me and not some stranger. His white eyes flash in the drone's spotlight, his face and bare chest covered in a sticky layer of blood. It's not all Ammo's, as I trace the line of his chest with my finger down his sternum and across his ribs, where he releases a sharp hiss. I frown, beginning to ask what happened when the door rolls open and a collective sigh of relief sounds throughout the crowd. As quickly as they rushed in, the Mutes pour out and make a run for their shelters, leaving me standing there in Ghost's arms.

Summon lightly touches my shoulder, his furrowed brow asking if I'm okay and I nod. "I'm all good now. You head on back, I'll see you at tomorrow's check-in," I say with conviction. Ghost's arms tighten around me and his head drops heavily into my neck. Luckily there's no sign of Ammo or any of her posse because Ghost's defeated stance makes him an open target right now.

"Hey, shouldn't we go too? What if we get locked in here?" I ask, momentarily forgetting the Mute crushed around me can walk through walls. His eyes raise to mine, shrouded in shadow now the drone has flown out too, but I can feel the heave of his chest. The tightness of his hold. The close proximity of his lips. His hand slides to my chest and his finger prods my sternum.

"There's no fucking where else I need to be tonight than right here."

GHOST

I brush a blood-stained thumb over Mania's bottom lip, not making a single move when the cave door slides shut and takes every source of light with it. My intentions are clear and she melts against me, the way I've been imagining she would all damn day. And what a hellish fucking day it's been. I didn't try finding her, knowing she has an impressive knack for surviving. Instead, I focused my energy on learning more about the maze, obtaining my machete and locating a spot we can call our own. Then I'd overheard Ammo sniggering to her crew about using Mania as the blood sacrifice, and followed them all the way here.

"I thought I'd lost you," Mania breathes and for the first time all day, I let my bravado slip. There's nothing like a near-death experience to awaken the deepest, darkest parts of your psyche. I want Mania. I need her, and once I've got her out of this maze, I'll just have to tell Pyro how it is now. The three of us are going to get Hoax back and then he'd better get used to sharing.

Trailing my hands all over her, the slickness of Ammo's blood smears across Mania's delicate skin. It's dark and twisted, but so alluring to the right person. Mania has traveled to the underworld and back, literally. She's an angel of darkness, born of ash and bathed

160

in the embers of hellfire. A true queen of survival, and for tonight, she's all mine. Not wasting any more time, I hike Mania up and walk her backwards. Her breath hitches and her thighs tighten around my waist. Pressing her back against the stone wall, I press my forehead against hers.

"How many times did you almost die today?" My fingers carve a path over the tiny corset and down her goose-bump-lined stomach. Coming to rest on the waistband of her leather trousers, Mania shudders beneath me.

"Twice. Possibly three times," she mutters, turning her face away. I take full advantage of the soft patch of exposed neck, biting down hard enough to leave a mark. Her hands are braced on my chest, both for stability but also to hold me at bay. I can feel she wants me from the heat radiating from her pussy, her legs clenched around me tight enough to bruise. Yet she keeps her chest distanced and avoids my mouth when I turn her head back to meet mine.

"They'll understand," I say, barely able to hold off much longer. The need to take her and have her every way I can think of is sending me into a frenzy. Since she was last on my arm, I've been tricked and attacked repeatedly. I've killed more Mutes today than I'm comfortable with but it was all for this moment. To have her back in my arms and this time, I won't let go. Not for Pyro or Hoax or even long enough to see I'll hurt her more than help. I'm a selfish fucker like that.

Without taking no for an answer, I grab her face between my hands and plunge my tongue into her mouth. The sound of my own groaning fills the cave as I finally take her in the way I've been resisting. Brutally. Savagely. She opens up to me, granting me full access to her mouth and her muscles slacken in my hold. Screw the blood, the muck and the lack of a shower, Mania's skin is feather-soft beneath my calloused fingers. I roll my hips, grinding my already pulsing cock at her core, eager to be inside her. This round will be rushed and hasty, but then I'm going to take her again and again. Engraving my touch on her soul and my imprint in her mind.

Mania's mouth doesn't leave mine. Our tongues battle for control, her teeth sinking into my bottom lip. Finding the hooks trailing the front of her corset, I free her from the tight leather and moan to find her completely bare underneath. Her tits are perfect handfuls, or at least perfect for my hands. I massage them firmly, flicking my thumbs over her taut nipples and drawing a hiss from her parted lips. I kiss the length of her jaw, biting and sucking at her neck and collar bone.

"Fuck foreplay," Mania growls, knocking my hands aside. She grabs my jeans, popping the button and fisting my cock in her hand.

"That's more like it," I praise. She needs this as much as I do right now, even if it's just for the distraction. I'm happy to be of service. Gripping Mania's waist, I hold her in place against the wall while she pumps her hand up and down my shaft, drawing a stifled groan from my throat. The blanket of darkness awakes all my other senses, heightening the way she pushes her hand down further and rakes her nails over my balls. Holy hell.

"What happened to fuck foreplay?" I groan, drawing her hand free so I can shove my jeans down to my thighs. Her tiny shorts are next as I hastily push them down, leaving her thigh-high boots on. On my way back up, I trail my fingers through her cunt and smirk at the wetness I find there. She's drenched and ready, and it's all for me. Lifting one leg and curling it around my waist, I hold Mania's ass in a punishing grip and slam home inside her in one, hard thrust. Her shocked gasp is music to my ears, her nails digging into my biceps. I remain there, allowing her to adjust to my size before grinding into her several times.

"You have no idea how hard it's been to resist you." I moan into her ear and kiss her lobe. "I've been lying to myself for so long, pretending your sweet cunt isn't exactly what I wanted. Now I'm not sure I'll ever get enough."

"What's changed?" Mania asks without any conviction. I draw out and slam back into her, making her cry out in pleasure and pain. She knows exactly what's changed, considering we've both tiptoed with death multiple times in the past few days, but she wants to hear me say it.

"It's so much easier to have you than to hate you." I claim her mouth again, halting any reply she might give and take her without restraint. My cock slides in and out of her channel, hitting her G-spot every time if her muffled cries are anything to go by. My hands are being scraped free of my skin by the stone wall as I protect her from its roughness but it doesn't matter. Her tongue fights mine, her chest strained against me as we struggle to get closer.

Wrapping my arm around her lower back, I drop a hand in search of her clit. The downward angle allows me to penetrate her deeper and coax out her orgasm faster. Pushing my thumb over her clit and rubbing rough circles, she tightens around my cock almost instantly. Her mouth moves to sink her teeth into my shoulder and the sharpness of her bite almost has me following in her climax. She marks me with the roughness of a feral animal and I want more. Gripping the back of her neck, I rip her from me before I blow my load and spin her around.

Bending her over, I slam back home into the slickness of her cunt. The globes of her ass beneath my hands feel heavenly and the tightness of her channel from this position has my head lolling back. I could fuck her like this forever if it wasn't for the tightness of my balls threatening to detonate. Taking her slower this time, my fingers dig into her hips and her nails find the back of my legs.

"Fucking....Christ," I hiss through gritted teeth. Leaning forward, I grab Mania by the throat and draw her up with me, her back to my chest. "I wish I'd known you'd feel this right. I'd have made you mine long ago." Her hands reach back, scraping those nails up my thighs and I growl threateningly. Tightening my grip on her neck and holding her lower abdomen in place, I fuck her as roughly as my constricting jeans will allow. In unison, we buck and grind, filling the cave with her cries of pleasure. Taking me all the way in, Mania stiffens just before another orgasm tears her in half. Her sweet pussy pumps my shaft in a vice-like grip until I'm groaning myself. Pulling out of her, I pump my cock hard and cum against the cave wall on a curse. It occurred to me a little too late what Mania being human again could mean but at least I caught myself just in time.

Doing the best I can to clean up, aside from scraping my sensitive tip against the rock, I fully remove my jeans now. Then I turn my attention to stripping Mania of her boots and pull her down onto the ground with me. Lying flat on my back, I take the brunt of the uneven ground with my hands beneath her knees as she climbs on to straddle me. My dick jumps, already hardening when Mania leans over and kisses me with all the words she can't say. I know, because I'm doing the same.

I let my tongue sweep over hers, sealing a promise that I won't leave her again. With a simple taste, I'm hooked on the same enigma that had my brothers reeling. Or maybe it's because of them Mania suddenly means so much to me. She's my last connection to those I love and as she lowers herself back onto my rigid cock, she cements herself firmly onto that list.

Switching off the TV screen, I flop back against the mattress. It doesn't take a genius to figure out what Ghost and Mania were doing inside the cave, but the drone waited to see out today's check-in winner and apparently so did I. For fucking hours. Their satisfied smiles and linked fingers make me instantly regret it though and now I can't scrub that image from my mind. I've loved that female for most of my life. Fuck it, I still love her and now she's with my so-called best friend.

The ostentatious clock on the far wall shows one minute past midnight, meaning another day has broken. Another day of showering, drinking coffee and lying around. Sounds like a hermit's dream but when my only source of entertainment is watching those two either fight for their lives or shack up, it's more like a recurring nightmare. Not to mention how empty I feel inside without my fires. I can't even muster a spark from my finger now. All in all, the Pyro pity party is in full swing and no one else is invited. Padding through the suite, I rest against a desk chair that looks over the labyrinth. Flashing drones fly over the walls, hunting for their targets or ideal vantage points of whatever joys tomorrow will bring for the contestants.

I'd been studying the map on the screen in my downtime, and

now I understand the layout, there is some method to the madness. In the center sits a huge opening like that of a gladiator ring complete with a stage. Each of the four sections surrounding it are divided by their position on the screen's digital compass. While the finish line is at the highest point north, the fire twister Mania found herself in the heart of seemed to remain contained to the southern border. To the west, liquid can be seen through the cracks in the ground and a waterfall that originates from nowhere plunges over a stone mountain.

And somewhere down there, right now, they are together. Watching through a screen puts some distance between the viewer and the truth, as if it were any other reality show. Christopher has been clever in that sense, allowing his bidders to feel at ease while anonymously cheering for death inside their hotel suites. But looking over the labyrinth reminds me it's all real and happening right this second. His hands are on her body. His lips brushing her ear. Her soft giggles as the cocky bastard swoops in as her hero.

Grabbing the chair I'm leaning on, I throw it into the glass with a scream of rage. The wheels fly in all directions and the armrests bend but the glass doesn't even wobble. Fuck. Not that I was planning on jumping to my death but the intention is clear. I want in. I can't sit here while he takes her from me. If we die, we're doing it together but she's always been mine. Any other pretense that I'm over her floods from my system and an ugly, possessive thought riles within me. I'm going to take her from Ghost, dead or alive.

Turning my anger on the room, I inflict as much damage as Mutely possible without the assistance of my fire. The TV screen goes first, smashed into pieces via the coffee table I launch at it. The desk is next, then the kitchen. All the while I bellow like a caged animal, destroying my pretty prison and coating the destruction in a layer of torn-cushion feathers. My chest is heaving, my breaths coming out in short pants. The veins in my neck and shoulders are corded tight enough to snap. Storming into the bedroom with every intent to do the same in there, the TV screen I'd turned off flickers back to life. In the center of the screen, a text box appears informing me I have a message.

'Pick your battles wisely. There's more at play here than you realize. Dress smart, I'll pick you up in an hour. T.'

With narrowed eyes, I take a long moment to release the pent-up breath I'd been holding. My anger is still in full control, blanketing the room in a red hue until I throw my fist into the side of the wardrobe. The pain splintering up my arm gives me another focus. Droplets of my blood rain across the cream carpet as I enter the bathroom and turn on the shower. There's more at play here than I realize. That's what the message said and even though I know it to be true, I'm not changing my mind. I'm alone, broken, empty and powerless. The least I can do is be beside the girl I devoted my heart to.

Yet I find myself beneath the burning shower spray, curious as to who will be arriving to my prison shortly. Staring at the same cream walls was sending me just as insane as the dungeon cell, and I can't deny the smallest flutter of excitement at getting out. This is exactly what I need to escape. Still, I have no intention of dancing to anyone else's tune.

Dressing in jeans, a long-sleeved tee and black high-tops, I slide a cheese knife into my sock and a butcher's knife down the back of my pants. The elevator doors slide open as I'm pulling my t-shirt into place and I'm greeted with lilac eyes through a black lace mask. Her purple hair is pulled into a slick, high ponytail that swishes when she shakes her head at my appearance. A red, satin dress clings to her body, the thin halter neck strap hinting at her exposed back. On the end of her slender arm, she's holding a dry cleaning bag by the hanger.

"Tate," I growl. She rolls her eyes, stepping inside.

"Never one to do as you're told," she clucks with her tongue. "I need you to put this on so you'll blend in." She shoves the bag in my direction and I make no move to take it.

"No chance of that," I drawl, pointing at my flame-red hair. Tate's heels click on the marble floor but she's careful not to move too far into the room. Instead, she sidesteps and hovers close to the wall.

"That won't be a problem. It's a Mute masquerade ball. Everyone will be impersonating their favorite players so it's the perfect opportunity for you to go unnoticed." When I still don't take the offered hanger from her, Tate releases a noise of frustration and stomps her heel. "We've been waiting for this event since you entered the hotel and are putting our necks on the line for you. So put the damn suit on and for once, put your trust in someone who's trying to help."

"Without your help, I wouldn't be in this mess. You're the one who disabled our abilities and trapped us in Afterlife in the first place. Why the fuck would I trust you?" The elevator doors begin to slide shut and I dash forward. Tate steps into my way, raising her hands in warning. I shove her aside, reaching a hand out to catch the door but she knocks my arm aside.

"Pyro, stop!" she cries in a plea. Snatching my wrist, she pushes her ability into me, sending a bolt of ice directly through my chest. I don't back down, despite the blinding agony that's threatening to make me blackout. Grabbing her slender neck, I slam Tate's body against the now-closed doors and squeeze. The firmer my grip, the more the ice in my chest dissipates. "H-h-h," she heaves, flailing uselessly.

"No one is coming to help you. I'm done playing your games." I inhale her desperation and revel in the panic flooding her eyes. I'm not a murderer, or at least I wasn't. Who knows what I am anymore but Tate's messed with me for the last time. If it wasn't for this Mute, we'd have been able to break out of Afterlife long before it all went to shit. I'd be free and happy and loved. Tate's eyelids flutter, her head shaking as much as she can in my punishing grip.

"H-Hoax," she breathes and I freeze. "Al...alive."

"What did you just say?" When I'm sure Tate is about to pass out, I release her and she drops to the floor in a heap. I grab the crumpled clothing bag from the floor and slowly lower to her eye line. "You have until I've finished changing to recompose yourself. Then you're going to tell me everything." Without waiting for her reply, I stride away with a frightening amount of composure. I was going to kill her and I wouldn't have lost a moment of sleep about it.

We step into the ballroom, arm in arm like old friends or lovers. Little do the other guests in attendance know, Tate has changed into a high-necked gown to hide the bruising I left on her frail neck. She wasn't lying about blending in. The Venetian mask Tate brought for me matches hers, except where hers is delicate and highlights her eyes, the black lace of mine has harsh edges and covers half of my face. Ball goers smile and nod as we pass while my eyes scan the sea of rainbow-colored hair and eye contacts. I'm trying to be aware of my surroundings and keep my focus, but everything Tate told me upstairs has my head spinning.

According to Tate, if she can be believed, Christopher has frozen her, Enzo and Claire out of his affairs after he discovered them alone with me in the interrogation room. But she told me about the body with indigo hair that was wheeled in just after I was captured and the rumors she'd heard along the way. It's hard to believe Christopher's right-hand Mute wasn't fully aware of his every move but Tate says her role was to control those in the asylum. It was the last part she said before we left the penthouse suite that really caught my attention. About a whispered voice who came to her in the dark and had told her my fires are being used to spark life back into my best friend. I want to believe it more than anything, but how can I when this Mute has never given me a reason to trust her before.

Tugging me along, Tate cautions me with a hard glare and leads us into the center of the dancefloor. Chandeliers dripping with crystals hang overhead among white netting that covers the rest of the ceiling. Gold lights twinkle around the edges of the dancefloor as if they're floating and upon the stage is a live band and male singer, all dressed in matching white tuxes. Despite being one in the morning, the ball is still in full swing with soppy, love ballads crooning through the couples locked in tight embraces. I scan every face nearby, feeling the tap of the razor blade in my pocket against my thigh as a reminder. Anyone who gets in my way tonight will act as a message to Christopher himself. I won't be caged any longer.

"Stop that," Tate hisses, winding her arms about my neck. I remain stiff, not moving, holding her until she yanks us chest to chest and puts my hand on the small of her back. "You're going to get us caught before we've done any recon at all," she huffs. The Mute's whole demeanor is agitated, her eyes not meeting mine.

"What even is the master plan here, Tate? You say you've told me everything you know and I've told you, I'm going into the labyrinth." Humans are dancing all around us and Tate is quick to shush me, faking a laugh for the benefit of anyone who might have been eavesdropping. Holding me closer still, for her floral shampoo to fill my senses and her lips to brush my ear, Tate spins us in slow circles.

"The plan is to get you to Hoax before he's transported elsewhere and we lose him again. The elevator shaft for the labs isn't in this building, but permission to leave is limited. Events like these have been organized so humans can socialize with those they've been talking to using the chat rooms. A shuttle leaves every half an hour and will take us to the hotel we need. So until then, just blend into the crowd and no one should look our way twice when we make a move to leave." Tate pulls her face back to give me another stern glare. Her specialty, it would seem. Her chest is pressed against mine, the dip in her waist beneath my hand and her heels means our mouths are far too close for my liking.

"Don't get any ideas. I'm taken," I growl. Something fiercely protective has reared inside me since I made the decision to take Mania back for myself and suddenly all of the hatred I'd reserved for her is being shared out between those who put me here. Tate's lips curl up into a smile and her eye rolls behind her mask.

"Oh please. You're the opposite of my type," she scoffs. The song ends and everyone stops to clap before falling back into step for the next sickly love ballad. Tate's shoulders ease the longer we're out in the open with no incident and I find myself curious about the Mute who is acting as my accomplice.

"And what type would that be?" I tilt my head. I have no idea why I asked. I don't even recognize myself anymore. Fancy suits, heists, killing sprees and lying were all traits of Ghost before our apparent role reversal. Tate looks me up and down like the answer to my question is obvious.

"A little less penis and a whole load more balls," Tate quirks a brow and then shifts her gaze across the dance floor. A petite brunette is standing on the edge of the dancefloor, her long braid pulled over a one-shouldered dress. Her eyes widen as she's caught staring at us and I bark a laugh.

"Claire?! Claire has bigger balls than me? She's one of the meekest Mutes I've ever met." I spin Tate away, breaking her stare with the small woman so she isn't the one who becomes distracted.

"Mmhmm. And other than the boys at Hermitage and those at the asylum, how many Mutes have you met?" I regard her small smile and knowing eyes with a frown. Tate sure seems to know a lot about me, especially for someone who told me less than an hour ago she wasn't involved in Christopher's business. Trailing her hand over my shoulder, Tate grabs my black tie and tugs it tightly around my throat.

"Claire may be quiet, but she's survived decades more of experimentations than you have and she's not having an identity crisis. She also doesn't turn in on herself and wait for others to solve her problems." I scowl at her sly smile and twist my face away, hating that Tate is right. My track record proves I prefer hiding away and ignoring the world. I did it for years in the bunker, thinking I had nothing to live for when my brothers were right there. If Hoax really is alive, I've wasted valuable time and potentially put him at more risk. As far as best friends go, I fucking suck.

"Well, I'm ready now. And I'm bored of standing here with you. Are we doing this or not?" Pushing Tate away from my body, I stalk across the dance floor and make sure to shoulder barge Claire on the way past. Uniformed guards are posted every few yards, between separate rooms and bathrooms. I catch glimpses of a restaurant, several bars and a meeting room before spotting a lobby leading to a main entrance. Ducking through the door before Tate manages to catch me in her heels, I'm halfway across the lobby before a group of humans in my way allows her to catch up.

"You need me to access the elevators, dickwad." She shakes her wrist at me, implying the key is a part of her. I grimace, but I knew I wouldn't be losing her that easily. Mainly because I don't know where the fuck I'm going or what I'm looking for. Making it outside, the cold crisp air of the approaching winter instantly seeps through my suit. The speckled paving slabs are playing host to a smoking area in front of a single-lane road. Beyond that is the sheer dip of the labyrinth and a low fence for anyone stupid enough to look over too far.

A shuttle bus pulls to a halt in front of us and the humans all around stub out their cigarettes beneath their smart shoes and queue to board. I nudge my way into the line, about halfway back with my hand clutched around Tate's wrist. She steps into my side, thinking I want her close when in actual fact, I'm feeling around for a chip or anything electronic I can slash out with my razor blade and leave her behind the first chance I get.

Guards step in either side of the shuttle doors, carefully watching each human who steps forward to board. With each one who takes a seat and the line edges forward, the tighter my grip gets on Tate. This was her plan so for her sake, it had better work. The male in front is granted permission to enter the vehicle and I step forward, earning a baton to the center of my chest.

"Hold up," the guard grumbles, catching my red eyes. I recognize this one from my time at Afterlife; bald and stout with a pet peeve for being poked if I remember correctly. His gaze roams over my face and down to my hand that shifts to link with Tate's fingers. A tense moment passes while he assesses my so-called date before removing the baton and knocking the guard beside him with a sneer. "Hey, Pete. Look who it is. Miss Uptight herself, decided to join the Mute Masquerade Ball I see. Must be nice to pretend you didn't betray your own kind for an evening."

Humans behind gasp and whisper in shock, now drawing every set of eyes to us. I raise an eyebrow at Tate, wondering if she expects me to run to her aid but the determined tilt of her chin says she's got it covered.

"Hey Brian, nice to see you again. I just thought I'd show my new friend around and give him the whole Mute experience," she winks at me. Taking a step forward, Tate pauses and raises a finger to her chin. "Oh, speaking of betrayals - how's your wife? Isabelle, is it? I heard she was juggling a few Mute masquerade balls herself. I bet she'd have loved tonight's entertainment." The bald guard's smirk is wiped clean and a look of fury takes its place.

"You little bitch," he spits and I see my opportunity to interject.

Stepping in just before he advances on Tate, the guard's chest bumps my sternum and I glare down at him. Not because I'm that bothered about Tate's wellbeing, but because I want to hear the rest of that story. The guard regards me for a long moment before deciding it's not worth the fight. Stepping aside, I pat him on the shoulder and tell him he made a good choice before entering the bus, all the while his voice carries to me.

"That Mute got what he deserved anyway. The club owner was more than happy to trade Ghost's safety for his." I still at my friend's name, looking back at the guard speaking to Tate. "And then when we finished, we threw them both in the maze anyway." Both guards begin to chortle but Tate climbs the shuttle's steps and urges me to take a seat. My eyes, however, remain pinned on the bald bastard responsible for Ghost being down in the crater just beyond the bus.

"Ignore them," Tate orders from the seat next to mine. She twists her body inwards to face me, our thighs pressed together. "We have business to do first, then you can come back and do whatever you like." The overhead lights switch off as the doors slide closed and the vehicle begins its journey onto the next hotel.

"What do you care if Hoax is saved?" I have to ask, keeping my voice low beneath the bus's rumbling engine. It's occurred to me Tate seems desperate to save my friend, yet I can't see what's in it for her. A clear conscience, maybe? She sighs heavily and relaxes into the seat.

"I know this is hard to believe, but Christopher was a different man altogether when he first picked me up. He had dreams of helping people, making the Mutes equals and creating something we could all be proud to share. But with the money, came power and somewhere along the road, he's lost sight of what he started. He won't be content with bringing Hoax back, he'll use your friend as his new pin cushion so the sooner we get there, the more experimentation we can spare him."

Tate's words chill me in a whole new sense and suddenly, the bus can't move fast enough. How could I have had this power in me all along and not realize? Even worse, how come my love for Mania was enough when we were kids, yet as I sat beside Hoax's body crying, nothing happened? My mind tumbles down the dark avenue 'could haves' when we jerk to a stop. Tate hooks her finger beneath my cuff and gently tugs to signal I should follow. Stepping off the bus, the next hotel looks identical to the last, but I know it's different. My soul can feel Hoax's presence here and for the first time, I allow myself to believe it's true. He's alive.

Ghost doesn't release my hand the entire way back to the safe house he spoke of. With the machete resting over his shoulder, he walks us through wall after wall in companionable silence. The labyrinth is pitch black and through the darkness, the sounds of screams and destruction can be heard. Yet with Ghost keeping us completely transparent the entire way, I'm able to relax. Even if the Minotaur or any other unearthly monsters happen to find us, they can't do any damage as long as Ghost doesn't let me go. And our time in the cave has reassured me he won't be doing that any time soon.

Every passageway looks the same to me, especially in the cover of night but Ghost seems to know where he's headed. Entering an opening, I make out the rounded curve of stone on the outside and the glint of metal from the empty cage in the center. I realize I've been here before, both the black card and the key I obtained yesterday are now laying in the base of my left boot beneath the sole My prize for arriving at the check-in first is clutched in my hand, mini first aid kit in a tin. Either that's genuinely going to come in useful or I'm being mocked.

Ghost leads me through the bars so we're standing inside the cage and turns to face me. Wrapping his arm around my waist, he presses a fierce kiss to my lips that has my toes curling. I knew he'd be a good lover but damn, Ghost has awakened a demon inside me that needs sating over and over.

"Don't panic, I've got you," is all the warning I get as he alters the density of the floor and we free-fall downwards. A scream is ripped from my throat, earning a chuckle from Ghost when he lands artfully in the underground tunnel, his hold not loosening for a millisecond. I slap his chest, taking in the long line of mounted brass holders and lit candles on either side of us. Pulling me along, Ghost knocks twice on an iron door before entering anyway.

"You took your time," a graveled voice states as soon as we enter and I flinch. A male is hunched over a workbench, smoothing his hands over liquid metal. His bronzed skin, and my god there's so much of it, is scuffed with dirt, hiding the faint network of radiant veins throbbing underneath. Orbs of smoldering steel gray swing away, rendering me frozen in place. With a brief glance, he returns to his work on a patterned sword of some sort.

"I had a wrong to right," Ghost smirks and shoots me a wink. "Figured you'd appreciate your freedom for a while. Mania, meet the Blacksmith." The male doesn't look my way a second time and as Ghost places down the machete, it all clicks into place.

"You freed the Blacksmith," I mutter, more to myself. Scanning the room, I notice everything that can be made with metal, is. The doors, drawers, cupboards, basin, table, chairs. An elaborate, yet unnecessary fireguard sits before an empty fireplace. Our source of light and heat radiates from the extensive amount of candelabras molded into the brass beams crossing over the walls and let's not even mention the chandelier. Branching off from the main area, iron doors with intricate swirling patterns imply there's more rooms to this junkyard-challenge home.

"Come on, let's eat." Those four words have my stomach responding in a desperate gurgle. Ghost walks me over to a steel pot hanging above a makeshift fire pit. Lifting the lid off the pot, the delectable smell of a bubbling stew slams into me and I groan. Ghost retrieves some bowls and a ladle from the kitchen counter, dishing us up two healthy servings.

"There's some stale bread in the bread tin. Not the best but better than nothing," The Blacksmith grumbles. He doesn't look our way, swinging the sword off his bench and shoving it into the fire until it glows molten red, then returns to his work. Ghost fetches the bread and some spoons, and we sink down together in the corner.

"Where did all of this come from?" I ask, blowing on the chunk of beef I've pulled from the stew. My mind is struggling to catch up with what's happening around me as the food consumes my thoughts, but Ghost's answer breaks through.

"Perks to being a star attraction," he points his fork in the Blacksmith's direction. "This was where he lived prior to the games starting." My eyes widen and I take in the furnishings again. The Blacksmith must have been here for quite a while before he was somehow forced into the cage above ground, and I bet that was a feat in itself.

"Better?" Ghost asks, taking my bowl in a blood-stained hand. I nod with a weak smile. Now my insatiable hunger has subsided, the thick layer of crusted muck coating my skin.

"I'm disgusting," I grimace down at myself. "Any chance of a built-in shower around here?" I was joking but Ghost's wink makes my eyebrows shoot up. "Wait, seriously? There's a shower?"

"No shower," the Blacksmith grumbles and my heart sinks. "Just a tub."

"Just a tub? *Just* a tub?!" Ghost pulls me to my feet with a chuckle, his whole demeanor the polar opposite of what I'm used to. I half expect him to throw me against the wall at any second and clamp his hand around my throat while delivering a threat. The fact my thighs clench at that thought says everything about my current post-climax mind. After placing the bowls in the basin and promising to come back to them in a while, Ghost leads me through the nearest iron door and into a quaint bedroom. It's what I'd imagine a hobbit house looked like, if the hobbit was a love child with the iron giant.

The same beams translate in here, crisscrossing over the walls and ceiling to surround us in a sea of diamonds. Images carved into the steel tell a story I don't have time to explore, but on the surface that of a male with too much time on his hands. One who's broken, bored and so utterly alone, my own heart aches. Ghost disappears into the adjacent room and the sound of running water turns my attention his way. A vast bed covered in furs separates me from the Mute undressing me with his eyes from the door jam.

"Huh," I comment, tracing one of the bed knobs with my fingers. All four match, a tiny bird is trapped inside a solid cage but in each one, the bird's position changes. In this one, his beak is open in a silent scream and his wings braced for flight. "It just occurred to me that if the Blacksmith can manipulate metal at will, why was he sitting in that cage waiting to be freed?" Ghost closes the gap between us, toying with a strand of my hair against my neck.

"Not everyone is like us, Spitfire. They don't have anything worth fighting for and the simplest pleasures can have them jumping through hoops. Or in this case, staying where he was told." I frown, pressing my cheek into Ghost's chest.

"I don't feel like I've fought much," I sigh. "More like glorified surviving."

"Hey, look at me," Ghost tilts my head up to meet his milky white eyes. "You are a survivor *and* a fighter. You wouldn't have made it this far if you didn't want to. Things may seem bleak today, but tomorrow we'll be one step closer to understanding how to beat Christopher at his own game."

"So wise," I tease, scraping my nails across his skin. "This is a new look for you."

"And I hate it. The sooner we get to Pyro, the sooner I can go back to being the jokey asshole you really want. Come on, join me in the bath, and then I'll be ready for dessert." His eyes skate down to the apex of my thighs and my cheeks heat at the clear meaning behind his words. Oh hell yeah.

The bath was heavenly. So much so, I had butterflies of excitement before I'd even dipped my toes into the clear water in the iron tub. But then a thickly corded arm wound around my waist and a naked Ghost sunk into the water with me. I braced myself for him to tease me into a state of frustrated bliss, tethering on the edge of an orgasm, but he did me one better. Ghost's firm fingers deftly smoothed the kinks out of my back and shoulders before washing my body and hair. I was liquid in his arms by the time he'd finished massaging my scalp. Exiting the tub before me, Ghost holds the only towel out to wrap around my body and pulls me into his arms.

And that's how I found myself being laid carefully onto the mattress in the Blacksmith's bed. My limbs feel like Jello and my head rolls into the pillow as sleep calls my name but Ghost has other ideas. Namely, keeping good on his promise. Opening the towel, his lips trail kisses from my ankle, all the way to my upper thighs and then back down the other leg. I groan softly and pout through the haziness of my drooping eyelids. Ghost chuckles, spreading my thighs and brushing his thumb over my clit so I suck in a breath.

"Make me come so I can go to sleep," I murmur, feeling my growing wetness that has nothing to do with the water droplets from the bath still coating my body. Ghost drags his tongue over my seam in one, long movement and I gasp.

"So romantic," he taunts. I fist his hair and push his head into my pussy, needing to feel that tongue against me again. Putting his jokey nature aside, Ghost grips my waist and delves his tongue into me. Repeatedly. I mewl and grind shamelessly as he fucks me with that expert tongue. Moving his hands downwards, he spreads my lips, splaying me to his invasion. The next thing I know, Ghost swaps his tongue out for two fingers and his lips have closed around my clit. The sounds that leave me are just short of possessed. I cry out, my back arched and my hands fisting the covers.

Ghost finds his rhythm, pumping his fingers into me with a curling motion to stroke my G-spot every time. I buck against the tightness of his mouth over my sensitive bud, not relenting for a second. The familiar flutters in my abdomen and legs begin to build and when what I imagine to be Ghost's thumb starts to circle my puckered ass hole, I know I'm a goner. His thumb pushes inside me just as my walls clamp around his fingers, spearing my orgasm into something much more dark and turbulent. I scream his name, shattering for the Mute who came back for me. Who saved me.

My climax drags on, pulling more strangled cries from my throat as Ghost drinks in my pleasure. Literally. His hand is whipped away to tilt my ass up into his hungry mouth and he sucks the cum from my pussy like a starving man. He eats me until I have no more to give, although he manages to coax more wetness from me and laps it up. I'm powerless to do anything but enjoy the ride, rocking my hips in time with the wave of ecstasy owning my body.

"Holy shit," I gasp heavily. Ghost rolls me onto my side and climbs up the back of me. His arms wind around my body in a tight grip, making it hard to catch my breath but I cling onto him all the same. With my cunt dripping and pulsing from his assault, I bury my face into Ghost's bicep and somehow through the exhilaration, the sleep comes back to claim me almost instantly.

"Sleep while you can, Babygirl." Ghost kisses my hair and I don't need to be told twice.

PYRO

nsuring the mask covering half of my face is still securely attached, I wander over to the bar and order another whiskey, neat. Noticing Claire was following us, Tate has slipped off to *'discuss the plan'* or some shit, leaving me in my own company for a little while. For all I know, they could be sexing it up in a cleaning cupboard but I'm quite happy here. With the humans playing dress up as the lesser species, I've been able to let loose and dare I say, started to enjoy myself. Gut-punching the male who was talking about Mania's ass in the bathroom stall helped, and the open bar may have somewhat contributed too.

Humans are fickle creatures. So distracted by their fancy suits and unwarranted riches, they don't even realize their enemy is right beneath their nose. And the labyrinth - that's the biggest con of all. Paying to watch people suffer when they are the ones who are suffering with their own lavish boredom. They both fascinate me and make me want to mount their heads on my wall. What a wall that would be. A hand slaps heavily on my back a moment before a gangly, mocha-skinned man in a suit takes the seat beside me. I roll my eyes, turning away from him.

"Tate sent me to get you. She's found the way in," Enzo's deep voice travels to me. I shove off his hand when he fails to remove it quick enough and down my whiskey.

"I'm not going anywhere with you. You stole my girl." It's petty, sure, but I have every right to be. The moment Mania left me, Enzo was there, pulling her into his arms as the elevator doors shut behind them.

"Actually," Enzo chuckles to himself, "I saved your girl when your stubborn ass nearly killed her." I spin on my stool, snarling at the bastard before me. His hazel eyes dare me to start a fight, knowing full well he can alter the enzymes in my stomach and put me on my ass.

"What did he give you?" I ask, the sludge in my mind quickly forgetting my hatred and moving towards curiosity. Enzo looks at me like a raging lunatic and I swipe a hand through the air. "Christopher. What did he give you to trade in your Mute looks? Tate clearly didn't take him up on the offer so why did you?" Questions like these have been burning in my mind ever since I first laid eyes on the three traitors at Afterlife.

As much as it would make my life easier to walk among the humans undetected like I have tonight, being a Mute is who I am. I want them to fear me. I want them to see my flame-red hair and eyes and run a fucking mile, not the other way around. Ghost used to rave on about a Mute uprising to show the humans who they are messing with, and I could never muster the energy to care. Now though, now I'm pissed as hell and I want to see the world burn for what's been done to me, my brothers and my soulmate.

"Acceptance," Enzo tries to palm me off with a generic answer but the rigidness in his features cements his lie. I shake my head, sneering at him like the scum on the bottom of my dress shoe.

"Not good enough. You can't handle being ostracized, that's your own weakness. It's no excuse to turn on the rest of us."

"Turn on you?" Enzo stands quicker than my hazy eyes can track, throwing me off balance. I grip the bar to remain upright and shove at his gut. Enzo grabs my shirt collar and hoists me up above his head.

"Someone's been eating their spinach," I chuckle drunkenly. Enzo's eyes have turned dark and are laser-focused on mine, not caring about the attention he's attracting.

"I did this for the Mutes. Humans are always going to play God with shit they don't understand. I decided to be a part of it to protect my fellow Mutes, help them through their transitions. The alternative is leaving men like Christopher to it, unchecked." I wriggle, kicking Enzo in the shins until he puts me down.

"Bang-up fucking job," I nudge his bicep with my fist mockingly. We're eye level standing anyway so I push at his chest and start to walk away. I knew he'd ram his shoulder into me and take the lead, needing to report back to his master like a good dog. In that instance, I'm the bone being retrieved but I'll take it.

Leaving the bar, we cross the lobby and head for a central staircase. This hotel seems busier than the last, humans bumping into me and wandering in my way with every step I take. The same glimmering chandeliers hang high above, as well as the white marble floor with tendrils of gold to match. A loud cheer rings out and I look over those around towards a room that resembles a casino. It's not machines or chips that have the men inside excited though, it's the screens showing a raging Minotaur ripping a body clean in half with its horns. Grimacing, I sprint onwards to catch up to Enzo as he climbs the stairs.

"In the maze, is that a real Minotaur?" I ask, not thinking that was a question I'd ever need to say. Enzo side-eyes me like an idiot, drawling his reply.

"It's a Mute and probably one of Christopher's most successful experiments to date." I fall a few steps back, my brows knitted together tightly. If that creature out there is an experiment, fuck knows what he has in store for my brother. Like a fire is under my ass, I run up the rest of the stairs, finding Tate and Claire standing at the top. As soon as she spots me, we all move as one to the left, circling the gold railing around to an elevator door out of sight from the lobby. My heart is hammering again, sobering me right up as Tate raises her wrist and presses it against the keypad. The elevator dings on contact and the doors slide open with ease.

"Hurry," Claire ushers us in. We rush to move, the thickness in the atmosphere doubles as the doors shut us inside. Claire's large blue eyes find mine as she chews on her lip nervously. "I was able to get a read on one of the guards on his break. I'm not sure what I saw, but it was like an explosion of fire and light contained in an upright cylinder. The glass blew out and the guard must have shut his eyes because I couldn't see anymore, then we were interrupted." I nod in thanks, trying to ease the panic I can see painted all over her face even though I feel the same way myself.

No one speaks the rest of the way down, letting the elevator music fill in our silence. I remain stationary, fists ready for the moment they're needed, but a glance aside shows the others taking small steps into each other. Tate pulls Claire in for a quick hug and Enzo's arms encircle the pair of them. Must be nice having those you love around, and suddenly I wonder how much of Enzo's complicity has to do with protecting the Mutes, or protecting the two he's shifting in front of to join my side.

We jolt to a stop and I inhale deeply, steadying myself. I'm going to get Hoax back, then I'm going after Ghost and Mania. The four of us together is all I've ever wanted. The doors open to pitch blackness. Not a sound can be heard and that freaks me the fuck out more than if we'd stumbled upon a room of fireworks detonating around the walls. Enzo and I push the females back on instinct, before sharing a stern look and stepping out together. Just as my foot crosses the threshold, a familiar voice shouts through the darkness.

"Don't!" It's too late. Two lightning bolts spark from nowhere, slamming Enzo and I in the chests. We fly backwards, crashing onto the floor as the girl's screams pierce my ears. They join us a moment later, writhing and crying on the floor. I raise a shaky hand to my chest, surprised to find there's no hole or wound because the agony sliced me from front to back.

Small spasms rack my body as the lightning works its way out and a pair of heavy boots step into the light of the elevator, the black leather right in front of my face. I have no control over my limbs but I attempt a pathetically weak punch at his shin, causing a throaty laugh to ring out in mockery. Gritting my teeth against the onslaught of pain claiming every inch of my body, I try to push myself upright. The heel of the boot lifts, crunching down on my fingers and I cry out, collapsing back in a heap on the floor. Bending, the male clasps a hand over my mouth, his boot still crushing the bones of my fingers and somehow, among my own screams of agony, I hear Tate's shocked whisper.

"Chloroform."

Waking with a start, I gasp in a shuddering breath and raise my hand to cover my eyes. The brightness of the sun spearing through the netted curtains makes me wince and as I sit upright, a headache slams into me like my head is in a vice. What happened, where am I and why the fuck am I naked? Squinting through slits in my eyelids, I try to gauge my surroundings, finding myself completely alone.

The room is modest, with the double-sized bed I'm lying in pushed against the back wall. There's a desk and chair, coffee sachets beside a travel kettle and a mini-fridge. The wardrobe and dresser share the same oak finish and of course, mounted on the cream wall is a flat-screen TV. My head rolls to the side, the memories of trashing the penthouse, the ball and the elevator coming back to me. Was it all a setup to ambush me? Somehow, I doubt it since Enzo took the same lightning bolt I did but I can't be certain. Groaning, I reach for the TV remote on instinct, needing to know what has happened while I was out cold.

Rewinding, I find no further progress than Ghost leading Mania by the hand to a new hideout beneath the empty cage. A place the drones can't go and the sheer unknowing fills me with aggravated determination. I need in there before Ghost gets his claws any further into her. All of the years of moaning about my love for her, he sure is doing a good job at pretending he feels for anyone other than himself. If that were true, he wouldn't have abandoned me.

With balled fists, I jump up and stomp across the bedroom to tug the dresser drawers cleanout. Once out of this room, I'll be damned if I'm coming back but I need to be smart about it. Yanking multiple layers of clothes onto my body, because I'll be damned if Mania's ass is splayed across hundreds of TV screens any longer, I find a backpack in the top of the wardrobe. It's like they wanted me to plan an escape.

Once stocked with every toiletry and item that has the potential to be a weapon I can find, I bang my fists on the front door. There's no elevator here, like a standard hotel room and I can only hope I'm not too far away from the elevator I need. When my thumping goes unanswered, I take to calling Christopher every curse word imaginable at the top of my lungs, trying to coax him out from wherever he's hiding. I know he'll have some sort of surveillance on me, but still – nothing. I ram my shoulder against the door, realizing too late it's reinforced. Pain splinters through my shoulder blade, causing my arm to tingle and me to give up. Fine, I decide. I'll find another way.

Grabbing the desk, I shake the coffee station off the top and flip it over. Slamming my boot into the leg at the same time as tugging, the spear of wood snaps free in my hand. There's a vicious point to the end and without hesitating, I drive it through the window. Glass shatters around my forearm, slicing my skull tattoos with several lacerations that instantly begin to bleed. Keeping my weapon clenched in my fist, I hop up on the windowsill, kicking out the remaining glass and peering outside. I must be twenty-something floors up and directly below is the deadly drop into the labyrinth. Looking all around and then up, I spot a balcony directly above me and blow out a harsh breath.

Without thinking about it too much, I push the spear between my teeth and grab onto the top of the window. From there, I use the fancy brickwork to shakily pull myself up. I've really let myself slide in the fitness department and I'm praying one of the drones doesn't spot me because no one needs to see this. The way my biceps are trembling is embarrassing. Latching onto the bottom of the balcony, I claw up the outside without once looking down.

My boots land heavily on the safe side of the railing and a scream instantly penetrates the air. My eyes lock on with a woman's through the glass doors, her limbs frozen but the male thrusting into her hasn't got the memo. Grimacing at the tiny dick he's aggressively trying to penetrate her with, although kudos for effort, I use my foot to smash the glass this time. Her scream sounds again and the ghost of a satisfied smile on his lips vanishes as he spots me forcing my way inside. I grab the robe hanging over the desk chair and throw it at him while the female scrambles to pull the bed covers over herself.

"Oh god," she whimpers, visibly horrified. "You're one of them." Ignoring her, I stalk across the room and try their door. Then I give it a shoulder barge, just in case mine was sealed shut because I was in there. With no luck, I turn back to the couple who are rushing to pull robes and their discarded clothes back on. The open suitcase on the floor is full of crumpled shirts and ties, and given the stale, BO smell clogging my throat, I address my question to the male standing across from me.

"How do I get out of here?" I growl, low and threatening. His messed-up, dark hair is shedding flakes of blue and a pair of discarded tattoo sleeves suggests he was at the Mute ball last night. At least, I hope it was last night. Either way, I bet his blonde date was hoping for more when she agreed to have a nightcap with him.

"You have to call and make a request to leave," he offers with a loud swallow. The woman nods quickly, backing up his words in fear I won't believe him. The way they're staring at me is comical and it occurs to me they really have never met a Mute in person before. They just get their kicks from watching one be tortured instead.

"Call then, if you don't want me to incinerate your face off." I drink in his look of horror with a satisfied grin. This marshmallow-dick of a man doesn't need to know otherwise and for once, I can see the appeal Ghost found in taunting the humans. In fact, he was right all along. The humans should fear us because showing weakness is exactly what has led our species to this - being played against each other in a maze of death and chaos. The man rushes to a phone attached to the wall, that I definitely didn't have in my room, and I stalk closer to listen in. His blue eyes lock with mine and I don't release him from my stare, daring him to give me away.

"Oh, hi there. Um, can I get an escort to collect my guest?" he fumbles and I draw a line over my neck with my finger. "A woman! I mean, my guest is a woman who I brought back...for sex....and now we're done, so um...yeah please can someone come to fetch her?" I roll my eyes and catch the blonde watching us with interest. Pointing to the fumbling jackass, I give her a credulous look and she shrugs, clearly embarrassed with her choice of one-night-stand. He hangs up the phone and I drop into the desk chair, pointing my wooden stick in her direction.

"You'd better get dressed. Looks like you're coming with me," I sigh. Five minutes later, there's a knock at the door and the blonde has squeezed back into a black, form-fitted dress. She foregoes her heels, slinging them over her shoulder, much more at ease in my presence. Maybe it's due to the fact her date used her as my escape ploy, or that I haven't moved from the chair.

We stand before the door, my spear now tucked into my backpack and my hood pulled over my hair. However, as the door beeps and opens outwards, it's not a guard on the other side but a simple bellhop. The cliché kind in a red jacket with rows of gold buttons and a stupid rounded cap. He doesn't seem to care about the extra body filing out but I tip my hood over my eyes anyway, following the woman down the hallway to the elevator. These elevators are giving me a headache so as I step inside, I take full advantage of inspecting the inside of one.

The buttons create the shape of the hotel, four across and fifty stories high with a few single buttons creating the tip. It certainly looks standard, complete with a surveillance camera in the corner. Either that's a recent addition or this isn't the elevator that took me to the penthouse suite. We reach the fourth to bottom level for the blonde to exit, her eyes lingering on me curiously. I raise my finger to my lips in a 'stay quiet' motion as the doors shut and then it occurs to me, I have no idea what I'm going to do next. In no time though, I'm entering the lobby and I make a beeline for the front entrance. I'm surprised how many humans are still around and wearing their smart attire; suits, ballgowns and diamonds everywhere I look.

The ballroom door is closed, leaving everyone torn between the restaurant, bar and casino lounge. Spotting a stocked open buffet, my mouth waters and my feet almost turn that direction but I force myself on. I can't storm in to steal food and remain undetected. Even worse, I can't allow myself to indulge in the human's riches for a moment longer while Mania is starving and suffering in the maze. Passing the lounge, I notice groups of suits still huddled around the huge projector screen like before and my eyes trail to a cushioned booth. I barely looked for more than a second but that was enough for the old man puffing on his cigar to spot me and stand with his arms wide. Shit.

"Pyro, my boy!" that old bastard's voice rings out and I shudder. "Come join us!" I grip my backpack straps tightly, eyeing the front entrance as a team of security step in front of it, their hands on their electric batons. They knew I was here all along. Deciding not to go up against the batons and risk being knocked unconscious and moved, yet again, I stride towards Christopher with purposeful steps. He's the only way in and out of this place. Patting me on the shoulder with a smug grin, Christopher urges me to sit on a stool by their table. The males previously enjoying their brunch flinch as I pull down my hood, revealing my hair and the color drains from their faces.

"You have to see this," Christopher chuckles, placing one meaty paw on my arm and using the other to point behind me. I grimace over my shoulder at the screen, spotting a female Mute trapped in a cave with only the drone's light to go by. She's rambling to herself, scribbling words onto the walls with a pointed rock in her hand. "Bibliophile," Christopher fills in for me. "Can recall every quote she's ever read."

"I'm surprised she made it this far," one of the other men pipes up with a grin. I narrow my eyes on her writing, picking out a few of the quotes she felt she couldn't leave locked in her mind before she died.

It's always the quiet ones you have to watch. They'll dance in your blood, leaving crimson footsteps in the snow, just because it looks pretty. – Rosa Lee. I'd turn this world upside down and meet her in the fields of Mother Moon's sanctuary. – Avery Stone

"Only 200 Mutes left," one of the men around the table frets. "I suppose there's not long left." The group of them huff in agreement, their disappointment palpable and I send a scowl to each and every one.

"You'd be surprised," Christopher bobs his eyebrows at me. "Now the weaker ones have been weeded out, this is when the real game begins. I may also have a few cards up my sleeve, just to keep it entertaining." His cold laugh slips beneath the sound of chatter and a crowded gambling station nearby. Money is being thrown at the cashier as two Mutes fight savagely on the screen before them. The lengths rich, defenseless humans are willing to go to get their kicks makes my stomach roll and bile rise in my throat. It's all so senseless.

"I'm going in." I state and a sharp intake of breath surrounds me. Christopher's icy blue eyes hold their humor, yet an edge of danger creeps in. I don't know what I expected from him, but he simply takes a drag of his cigar and blows the smoke out into my face.

"You're throwing away a perfectly good opportunity here, Pyro. I've given you what all Mutes have always wanted. A place among the humans, a lavish penthouse of your own. Once you leave, you'll be chased and tortured, just like them." He jerks his head to the screen behind me and a growl rumbles from my chest. Rising from the table slowly, I snatch the cigar from his hand and stub it out in his eggs benedict.

"I am one of them," I scowl. Jolting my body to the left, the man beside me jumps with a high-pitched squeal and then looks down at the growing wet patch in his gray slacks. I smile cruelly, reveling in his reaction as the others shrink into the booth. It feels good to be the bad guy for a change and as Ghost has so clearly demonstrated, good guys never win.

"There's no coming back," Christopher warns me again, hoping I'll change my mind for some reason. I have nothing else for him but I can see now how Tate, Claire and Enzo fell for his charm. It genuinely seems like he cares, but I know better. Bending over him, I plant my fists on the table.

"Yeah there is, and you'd better watch out for when I do. I'm coming for you old man." Shrugging with one shoulder, Christopher whistles loudly and in a second, hands wrap around my arms. I don't resist but they wrench me backwards and a needle digs into the side of my neck. As I'm dragged away, I hear Christopher making the announcement, some more Mutes are joining the labyrinth and betting has officially opened, but I drown out the commotion. Hoax may be completely lost to me now, but I'm finally on my way back to Mania and if Ghost wants to fight me for her, he won't know what's hit him.

An ear-splitting noise shrills through the underground hideout, causing me to drop my tin mug and bend over, clasping my ears. The ground around us shakes like a tornado is passing overhead and Ghost's arms wrap around me a moment before a large chunk of the ceiling crashes through our joined bodies. The claxon continues to blare, frying my thoughts and piercing my skull. Prying my eyes open, I make out the Blacksmith's form emerging from his room, tugging his jeans on with his ear pressed into his shoulder.

"We gotta move!" he bellows, fastening his button and then placing a hand on Ghost to soak in his ability as well. Grabbing my boots on the way passed, the three of us scramble through the network of tunnels to a metal ladder and door hatch, just like the one Ammo's crew had. The Blacksmith goes first with Ghost's hand firmly wrapped around his ankle. The ladder is shaking viciously but he manages to raise his hand and melt the lock on the hatch. Molten metal sizzles against the stones as it drips to the ground around me and I allow Ghost to pull me under his arm.

Shoving the hatch open, a blinding ray of sunlight spears the tunnel and through dazed, watery eyes, we make our way up to the surface. The day has barely begun and yet the chaos erupting around me is worlds away from the simple morning coffee I was just treating myself to. The walls either side of us shake ferociously but the snaking vines expand and shift to hold the rock in place. Mutes are running with no sense of direction, screaming and terrified while we stand there gathering our bearings. It becomes apparent the siren is coming from the drones at a high-pitched decibel that makes me want to take a screwdriver to my own eardrums.

Unsheathing Ghost's machete from the back of his jeans, I wait for the flying contraption to come close enough and then slice it in half. The two pieces drop to the ground, sparking and flashing. Still making that blasted noise though. Shoving my foot into my boot and feeling the comfort of the key and electronic card still hidden in the sole, I smash my heel into the drone until it goes dark and the sound splutters out.

"Nicely done," Ghost remarks, carefully plucking his machete from my fingers. I smirk in response but Summon, Dialect and Serpentina dart across our path. Without thinking, I run after them, leaving the protection of Ghost's arms. The small serpent girl is crying into Summon's neck as he holds her to his body, ducking out the way of a loose rock tumbling in their direction.

"Watch out!" I call, even though the male has already dodged it. The trio halt, turning back to me in panic. Closing the gap with the presence of Ghost and the Blacksmith right behind, I cup Serpentina's tear-stained cheek and wipe her eyes. "What's going on?" I ask Summon.

"We have no idea. Dialect received a message from the vines. We need to get to the center of the maze for an announcement. Anyone who doesn't make it before the labyrinth closes in on itself..." he trails off, sparing Ghost a sympathetic look. Summon must have seen what happened the night of the first check-in and I nod in understanding.

"Where's Monotone?" I suddenly ask, looking around for the ashy female. The silence that penetrates the ringing in my ears is just as deafening. Fuck. Another casualty to Christopher's twisted mind. Ghost reaches for me and I twist away, giving him a stern look.

"Protect the girl," I order him. His white eyes flash with surprise and then darken with a protective streak of anger but I shake my head. "You said it yourself, I'm a fighter and a survivor. You only have so many hands. Take her and the rest of us will hold onto you, but no matter what - she is your priority. Got it?" Ghost takes in the girl's pale face, her yellow-slitted eyes blinking horizontally as she gazes up at him. Blowing out a harsh breath, Ghost holds out his hands and after a tense moment, Summon eases her small body into them.

"You let go of my arm, I'm stopping," he growls at me but I just shake my head. We don't have time for this when the labyrinth is about to slam closed on all of us and if it comes to it, we have to protect the child. She hasn't even had the chance to live yet. To make mistakes and learn, to love and lose like I have. It sucked donkey dick, but at least I had my shot. Gripping Ghost's bicep, I tell the others to hold on as well. The Blacksmith clamps his hand down on Ghost's shoulder while Summon and Dialect huddle together, tentatively holding on to his sides. It's clunky and awkward, but as one we begin to move.

"That way," the Blacksmith announces, pointing left. Ghost doesn't hesitate, his quickening pace leaving us all to jog forward before he slips through wall after wall. Summon and Dialect trip over his heels multiple times and I can feel Ghost's irritation pulsing through the veins in his ink-covered arm. True that with the six of us remaining transparent like this, the walls clamping shut wouldn't pose an issue, but if there's an announcement we need to hear it.

With my heart hammering in my chest, we soon find ourselves catching up to a flock of other Mutes racing in the same direction. The walls tremble and slide an inch inwards, causing a collective shriek to pierce the air. Instead of using the walls as our quickest mode of transport, Ghost turns sharply and I momentarily lose my grip on his arm. He spares me a warning glare, pushing on through the crowd of Mutes clambering to burst past the final archway. It isn't lost on me that his choice of direction was a tactical one. He wants the others to see how easy it is for us to pass through their bodies and take the victory of entering the huge opening ahead of them, even though we're far from first.

Entering the safety of the opening with only a few stragglers right behind, the walls suddenly shift, slamming closed over the archway. I spin on a gasp as screams sound from behind the stone and before I get the chance to yank Ghost back through to their aid, another slam sounds. This one even louder and so abrupt, the silence following makes my stomach roll. Choking on a sob for Mutes I didn't even know, I spin to find us in a huge chasm in the ground. The walls seem to loom higher, making the sky feel that much more out of reach. Mutes barge in on us from all sides, sandwiched in like sardines flailing inside their tin can. Ghost pulls me onto his back so I can look over the heads for a reason we're all gathered here and my eyes fall on it instantaneously.

In the center of it all, ten or so feet above the elbowing crowd, a stone stage has grown out of the earth. The familiar sheen of sunlight streaking across the front hints at a glass container, displaying our 'announcement' like a gallery exhibition. Dread and excitement clashes together in my chest, my eyes prickling with tears. My breath locks in my lungs and the whole world seems to stop around me. In that glass box, on that stage, is Hoax.

He's stunning. A man-made of electrifying ink and brawn. The hard planes of his chest heave over a deeply engrained six-pack. Dark jeans are slung low on his hips, displaying a drool-worthy V and unlike the others, he's been gifted with a pair of black converse on his feet. The circuits covering his chest and the wires tattooed along his arms spark as if they're active. An indigo-tinted glow pulses through his ink, trailing up to his jawline where my eyes suddenly connect with his. His stare spears me, sparkling like orbs of amethyst but there's no familiarity in his expression. His hard-cut jaw is clenched firmly, a scowl imprinted between his eyebrows. But nothing else matters. He's alive.

"No fucking way," Ghost breathes and I loosen my grip on his arm to take a step forward. I can't help it, seeing Hoax in the flesh is too alluring. But the second my hand disconnects from Ghost, a body slams into my back. I scream, bucking like a wild animal. My boot connects with hard skin and as I flail to catch Ghost's eyes, I see he's not making any move to save me. This gives me pause but I don't relent my fighting, not even when I'm spun around like a rag doll. Slamming my fists into a solid chest, my eyes barely register the flying skull tattoo there that matches my own. A punishing grip on my chin jerks my head up and a pair of flame-red eyes assault me with their fierceness. My brain can't catch up as my heart jackhammers and suddenly, tears are pouring down my cheeks.

"Please tell me you're really here," I sob, not believing my luck. It doesn't matter what pandemonium version of hell we're trapped in, if all of my guys are really here, together and in the flesh, I might just have a heart attack. The fingers on my jaw soften and any anger Pyro was trying to direct at me vanishes.

"I'm never leaving your fucking side again," he growls. "Whether you want me there or not." I realize my hands are still pushing his chest away and I jump forward, crashing my mouth on his. Everything that's happened, every freezing cold night, every dark corner of my soul, is chased away by a blinding light that bursts behind my closed eyelids. My heart physically clicks back into place, swirling a spiral of warmth through my entire body and chasing away any lingering shadows. Words echo around my mind, chanting a mantra I will never let go of. My soulmate. My lifeline. My home.

Banding me tightly in his arms, Pyro kisses me without abandon. Our lips tremble, the saltiness of my tears leaking through. My whole body is alive and thrumming with his presence, unable to get close enough. His thumbs brush the wetness from my cheeks, not breaking contact while his tongue sweeps over my lips, soaking up my tears. His action is so simple, yet in withdrawing my pain, he corrects so many wrongs I hadn't realized still hurt until now. The layer of numbness I'd learned to hide behind without him comes crashing down and all that's left is my bare soul for the taking. A thousand questions burn at the end of my tongue, but a familiar voice booming through the air tears us apart. I remain against Pyro, merely turning my head to see a drone lower, its speaker loud enough to crackle slightly.

"My surviving Mutes," Christopher's voice bleeds over the crowd and I glower at the offensive drone. Typical of the raving madman to refer to us all as 'his' when it's his mess we're trying to escape. Ghost steps closer, shoulder to shoulder with Pyro, and links my fingers with his against Pyro's chest. Serpentina is safely back with Summon, for now. "Congratulations on getting this far! You have a lot of supporters rooting for you as you enter the next phase of the Labyrinth." I swallow hard, not liking the sound of that. "You'll be pleased to know there will be no more nightly check-ins." The crowd sighs and smiles are passed between strangers but I'm not so easily fooled.

"However," he continues and I grunt. There it is. "Recent developments have caused me to rethink the rules. The finish line, which would have transported you to the oasis where you could have lived freely and happily, is gone. You can blame your newest competitors for this change, as it's their betrayal that means I can no longer facilitate Mutes at my compound. Instead, I've decided the labyrinth will continue to run until there is only one Mute left standing. Then, for better or worse, he or she will be freed back into the world to live out your miserable days in hiding." Christopher's voice hardens, reveling in the effect said-betrayals are causing him.

Mutes gasp and cry out in shock, their eyes searching for those responsible. Yet all I have to do is look up at the hard-set jaw above me. Over Pyro's shoulder, I spot Tate, Claire and Enzo shrinking back against a wall sheepishly. My mouth shapes into an 'O' but no sound comes out. Without Tate, Christopher can't control the Mute's abilities. No wonder he sounds pissed, I bet uprisings have already started in the Afterlife asylum.

"Oh, before I forget," Christopher blares in a chirpy tone again. Twisting, my eyes lock back with Hoax's glimmering indigo ones, his stance and stare not having moved this whole time. The container illuminates in a purple hue, the invisible spotlights honing in on the Mute trapped inside. "While you are locked in here, the labyrinth is receiving an upgrade. Something my boy here and I agreed was long overdue. Hoax will be my eyes and ears on the ground, ensuring you are all having a memorable experience. As soon as we are done, you'll be free to return to your hideouts. Enjoy." A mocking laugh rings out as the drone flies upwards and disappears from view. It doesn't last though as several others zoom overhead to take its place, the red flashing lights on the camera lens drinking in our every movement.

"One left standing?!" a female shrieks.

"What are we gonna do?" shouts another, starting a concerto of cries and hollers. Most are aimed towards the drones but some of the Mutes turn on each other, shoving and arguing. The noise level rises to a high pitch of frightened screams as a male not so far from us starts snapping necks of those around him. The Blacksmith pushes his way forward, materializing a steel blade from his palm to take out the Mute without a moment's hesitation. Females flinch away as he returns back to shadow Ghost but the Blacksmith pays them no mind, his face set in stone.

"We have to get to Hoax," I tell Pyro and he nods once. Grabbing Ghost's hand out of mine, Pyro grips his wrist tightly and tugs him forward. Ghost's ability washes over me while I'm sparing the two a curious glance but Pyro's feet are already moving. His arm banded around my waist drags me along, passing through Mutes who barely notice we're there. My boots manage to catch up with his speed and I look over my shoulder to see Ghost has hands all over his neck and shoulders from the trail of Mutes following behind. The Blacksmith, Tate, Claire and Enzo. I frown at the mocha-skinned Mute, catching his hazel eyes until a conversation nearby catches my attention.

"It's him who's changed everything!"

"He's the one we need to kill!" A trio of burly males are pointing at Hoax, visibly seething. Their chests are covered in ink and it quickly becomes apparent from their identical features they must be related. Triplets, I'd guess. My gut clenches at the deadly intent in their gray eyes and I yell at Pyro to hurry up. It doesn't matter though, because the brother in the center creates a boulder in between his hands and then others help him to launch it directly at Hoax.

A scream lodges in my throat as the huge rock flies through the air and smashes into the glass container. But it's not the glass that shatters. It doesn't even wobble. Electrical sparks fly out and the boulder explodes into hundreds of tiny rocks. All the while, Hoax remains inside, unmoving. Except for his eyes, which despite my movements, are still trained on me. Reaching the base of the stage, I stare up with a trickle of fear rolling through my spine. Those purple orbs aren't just glowing, they're swirling like a poisoned sea of volatile, crashing waves. Something tells me getting to Hoax isn't going to be as simple as smashing the barrier surrounding him. No, saving him is going to be a whole other issue.

GHOST

I materialize just in time for Pyro to land a punch to my jaw. I stagger backwards, dazed and confused.

"What the fuck was that for?!" I splutter, shoving weakly at his shoulder. I can't bring myself to hit him back, not when I'm still reeling that he's actually here.

"That," my brother seethes with a flame dancing in his eyes, "Was for fucking my girl." My eyes widen and I glance at Mania who is peering at me from over his shoulder.

"Look Py, I know how it looks, but you have no idea what it's been like," I start but he punches me in the throat this time. I double over, grabbing my neck while a choked sound involuntarily leaves me. I can't draw a breath, spluttering and pushing a cough through the agony in my throat. A hand grips the lengthy part of my hair and yanks my head upwards.

"Oh I know," Pyro grows at me. He raises his knee towards my gut but Mania smacks him on the back. He doesn't respond to her, keeping his furious gaze on me. "I was forced to watch the whole fucking thing in full HD. I thought you were dead," his voice cracks. "I gave up my fires to save you." The moment his hand loosens on my hair, I shove my way forward and wrap my arms around him. He struggles but my hold is unwavering. Even if he wasn't thinner than the last time I saw him, Pyro was never a match for my strength. Too many nights playing video games while I was in the basement of our bunker, bench-pressing pretty blondes for entertainment.

"I missed you brother," I croak. He stills in my arms, not returning my hug but at least he's stopped resisting it. After a full minute, he shoves at me and I release him with a half-smirk. His expression, though, is bitter.

"You left me," is all he says, then turns his back on me. I divert my eyes away from Mania's red blood pupils, not wanting to see whatever pity she has held there for me. I made my choice. I knew it was a shit one. Regardless of my intentions to gather intel or supplies or whatever I was stupidly thinking the moment I left Pyro behind at Afterlife, we've been bonded since we could walk. No matter what stunts I pulled over the years, we had one rule – we don't leave each other. Nodding, I use my ability to stride through Pyro and start climbing the rocky face of the stage.

"What are you doing?!" Mania calls after me.

"Saving my brother," I call back without faltering. I latch onto cracks in the stone, my feet slipping out from under me every few moments but soon enough, I'm throwing my forearms over the top of the stage. Heaving myself up, I roll just short of the glass wall and push to my feet. "Don't worry Hoax, I'm here. I'm not going to fail either of you again."

He doesn't move. If it wasn't for the occasional slow blink, I'd presume he was frozen still. I hadn't fully believed Mania when she told me about Hoax, not until I saw him standing up here. I mourned for this Mute. I closed his lifeless eyes and carried his limp body from our home. Another boulder smashes into the glass, too close to me for my liking but it snaps me out of my daze. A rogue electrical current lands on my forearm, causing the hairs to raise as well as singe my flesh. I pat it down, cursing under my breath.

"Alright buddy, I'm coming in," I warn as if that'll grab his attention. Reaching out a hand to shift the density of the glass, a flash of blue lightning shoots into my palm. The volts race through my arm and explode in my chest, at which point I drop to my knees on a roar. My cheek grazes the glass as I tumble, the unstable texture telling me it's not glass at all. Another current zaps into my skull. Black spots speckle my vision and I'm not sure if I'll vomit before I pass out or after. Crashing into a writhing heap on the stage, cheers cut through my screams instead of boos, those watching fully enjoying the torture show. Squinting up at the shimmering, electrical bubble, I can't be sure if the container is slightly swaying or if my head is spinning. Moving to roll onto my back, I misjudge my position and plummet off the edge. Fuck my life.

"**G**host!" A hand slaps across the face, jerking me awake but my eyelids are too heavy to lift. I bite down on my lip, groaning and rolling my hips.

"Ooph Mamacita, do it again," I moan and a knee slams into my balls.

"Stop grinding on my fucking leg, you moron. The doors are open again. Time to re-join the land of the living," Pyro snarls down at me. I roll onto my side, cupping my dick and giving him a weak thumbs up.

Hands grab at my arms, tugging me upright. My head rolls on my neck and if it wasn't for the hands flat against my back, I'd have toppled over. I mumble a thanks over my shoulder, spotting Enzo there and jolting forward.

"Hey, take it easy," the Blacksmith catches my shoulders. "We need your ability in check before we leave in case of an ambush on the way out." My brain catches up with the situation around me and I look to see the stone doors are indeed open. Certain Mutes are hanging in clusters by the nearest archway, including the triplets from before. One is brandishing a club, smacking the rock against his palm and daring others to try to pass. Slender fingers slip into my hand and I instinctively pull Mania into my side. Tate and Claire are also still too close for my liking, sticking to Pyro like a fly on shit. I narrow my eyes at them as they begin following Pyro towards the triplets while I hold back.

"I'm not going anywhere," I say. Pulling Mania in front of me, I cross my arms around her and bury my face into her neck. Pyro stops abruptly, sighing before turning back to me.

"We can't stay here out in the open. Who knows what kind of upgrades Christopher is installing and nightfall will be even worse, you know it." Pyro pinches the bridge of his nose, a clear sign that I'm infuriating him.

"As you pointed out, ditching my brothers is a nasty habit I've developed." I quirk a brow, returning my focus to Mania. Running a hand up her back, I shift her hair aside to cup her nape and gently massage the pressure points there. No doubt she'll be feeling conflicted about Pyro and Hoax turning up the day after I fucked her raw, but nothing has changed on my end. The plan was always to get them back and with that came the inevitable strain of conflict. Something I laid awake thinking about all night. If it truly came to it, I've loved my brothers for my entire life and I won't risk our bond. But I reckon with the right amount of stubbornness, I might be able to have my pussy, cake and eat it.

"Don't be dense," Pyro glowers at my hand on Mania's neck. "You've proved your point. Now let's go." I don't make any move to follow his command, causing the Mutes at his back to shift uncomfortably. Good. They should be uncomfortable, because I'm going to gloss my machete in their blood the first chance I get. What are they even doing here, and why doesn't Pyro give a shit at their close proximity to them? He can forgive the Mutes that trapped and tortured him but not his own best friend. That's bullshit. Pyro lazily points towards the clear cage holding an unmoving Hoax with his freaky swirling irises.

"If you can't get in, I doubt he can get out. We know where he is, we'll come back when we have a game plan to get him out." Uncertainty twists in my gut and the prickle along my spine screams of the past repeating itself. Mania looks around me to Hoax, her grip on my waist tightens as she buries her head back in my chest.

"Exactly what I thought last time and look how that turned out," I flick my eyes up and down Pyro's body in mockery. The flame-red eyes I've longed to see hold so much contempt for me, it's almost as heartbreaking as the notion I'd never see him again. Like me, he's wearing only a pair of dark jeans. His inked torso and bare feet appear much cleaner and smoother than mine though. It'll take me more than just one bath to get my skin as supple as his again. Pyro strides over to me and I carefully peel Mania away from my body in time for his chest to bump into mine.

"I'm the one who's always got us out of shit before, now is no different. All you seem to do is fuck up and fuck my girl. I'm back in charge so it's time to get the hell out of my way." I laugh in his face, loud and wholeheartedly.

"Oh yeah? Funny that because *your* girl is over there with Boulder Bro one, two and three." I jerk my chin in the direction of the archway. Pyro twists his neck sharp enough to make it click, a wave of heat roiling from his chest into mine. I wasn't pleased myself when I saw her approaching the triplets in my peripheral vision but I couldn't lose face when Pyro was acting like the big dog. He can be pissed at me all he wants for the bad choices I've made, but we both know I've done the best I can to keep her safe. He's gone in the next instant, a brief wash of cold brushing my chest but my feet are right on his heels with the rest at our backs. Storming over to the triplets with our fists clenched, Mania spares a mischievous look over her shoulder.

"Finished your pissing contest so soon?" she flutters her eyelashes. "I was just making a deal with my new friends here. A blade each from the Blacksmith and they'll lead the way back to the hideout for us. We can never have too much muscle on our side." She reaches out to squeeze the bicep of the shithead holding the club and I mentally lose my fucking shit. On the outside though, I remain the image of calm because I understand what she's doing. We have no idea what's waiting for us outside that archway. Safety in numbers and all that, but none of the Mutes looking at Mania like a piece of meat are stepping foot in our hideout. I'll kill them myself for even thinking about it.

Nodding to the Blacksmith since he is staring solely at me, he shrugs and generates liquid metal between his palms. One by one, he rolls his hands to manipulate the metal into a dagger and gives it over to a triplet. I grab for Mania's hand and Pyro's arm on instinct, preparing to alter our densities in the face of an attack. Three more hands clamp down on me from behind before I do and the Blacksmith shifts to push his foot against mine. To anyone outside of our circle, I look like one big orgy train at this rate. Satisfied with their new weapons, the trio say their thanks to Mania and head out with us right behind.

The first thing that strikes me about the labyrinth's new appearance is the lack of stone. The walls have been coated in a shiny layer of metal and the vines replaced with electrical circuits that hiss like snakes. They jump out at us as we pass, sparking at the ends threateningly. Through the cracks in the stone flooring, energy flows like purple lava and the friction crackling in the air has our hair standing on end. We shuffle as a unit, following the trio in front, keeping to the passageways this time. With my ability shielding us all from harm, I want to understand the changes Christopher has made if I have any hope of surviving them all. No doubt he's been plotting in his office for ways to strike us all down, regardless of ability. The whole 'one only can survive' thing I'm benching for now. One bombshell at a time, thank you very much.

Most of the Mutes used the other archways to disperse around but the few that happen to cross our paths are soon chased away by the sight of the boulder bros. The Blacksmith shouts directions out for them to follow, leading us directly for his hideout. Turning into the next path, I begin to whisper to him about ditching the fuckers when we spot a dead-end up ahead.

"Wait," the Blacksmith frowns. "That's not right. It's definitely this way." We stride closer, hunting for a hidden exit but there is none.

"Are you trying to play us for fools?" one of the triplets turns, holding up the dagger clenched in his fist. Without a protective handle, the sharpness of the metal slices into his palm and blood runs down his forearm. A sharp slice through the air makes me flinch, but it's not one of their blades. This noise is closer, louder and coming from back up the passage. We all turn, hands dropping from my body, to see a metal grate has closed over the archway we passed under. The ground shakes and suddenly, it's moving beneath our feet, rolling backwards towards the dead-end like an accelerated treadmill. I lose my balance and my grip on Mania and Pyro as I jolt forward onto my hands and knees.

I rush to catch up with myself, gaining traction beneath my feet and hoisting myself upright. I have to break into a jog in an attempt to close the distance between us, my arm outstretched to graze Mania's elbow. Then, a blood-curdling scream behind me is quickly followed by a nauseating round of crunching. Looking back, despite the precious moments it costs me, my gut flips and then drops like a lead brick. The dead-end has opened up to reveal a chunky set of saw blades, rotating in such a way for the deadly spikes to have maximum impact but never touch. All of which is covered in the shiny, red blood of Boulder Bro two, his wide eyes and gaping mouth all I see before the blades crush his skull into nothing. The explosion of blood makes me flinch, chunks of brain matter speared on the sharp spokes.

"Ghost!" Pyro bellows and I jerk back into action. My stunned shock has lost me precious moments, the floor beneath my feet wheeling me straight to my death. I momentarily consider telling Mania and Pyro to stop running because I can allow them to pass through, but what if there's nothing underneath and I'm stuck there, holding them among the blades until I run out of energy? Instead, I run at full speed, pumping my arms to catch up to Claire. The brunette has fallen behind, her brown plait swishes as she struggles against the speed of the conveyor belt. The others have made it back to the grate and are holding on with all their might. The horror in their eyes doubles as I storm past Claire, fully intent on letting her meet her end at the hands of the man she so recently worshipped.

"Save her!" Tate screams and I flip her the middle finger until Mania joins in.

"Save her or I'll let go and do it myself!" I groan, falling back a few paces to grab Claire's arm and drag her forward. The ground picks up its pace, throwing me off balance. I stumble to stay on my feet, my grip on Tate bruising.

"I fucking hate you," I seethe.

"Likewise asshole," she spits back. With our mutual disdain agreed,

I pull Claire the rest of the way back to the others with her steps only faltering half a dozen times. Rolling my eyes, I shove her into Tate's open arms and latch onto the bars, ordering everyone to hold on. I don't wait to check how many hands are on me before dropping us all through the bars into a heap of heaving chests onto the ground. As if it never happened, the grate raises and the floor on the other side halts. I distinctly hear a drone buzzing away while I search for Mania and drag her into me.

"Let's not do that again," I pant. Another arm winds around Mania's waist, tugging her away from me and for now, I let him. Pyro's petty glare doesn't pack the same punch when I almost became ground beef so he can have his turn with her for now. When I've regained my fucks though, I fully intend on fighting him for it.

Pyro does not release my hand once as we scour the maze for a way back to the Blacksmith's home. Every turn we take, grates close behind us and dead ends seem to move position. Ghost stopped dropping through the ground in search of the tunnels when Enzo's grip on his outstretched hand slipped and Ghost was almost buried alive. Just another reason for him to hate 'Christopher's cronie', as he keeps calling him through his tuts and muttering. Besides, if Ghost kept going off alone and anything were to happen, we'd be screwed. I already feel terrible about the triplets I asked to help us ending up shredded, and I didn't even know them. Walking among the tortured souls of hell was one thing but actively seeing Mutes die multiple times a day isn't something I will ever get used to.

Tugging me around the next bend, I finally snap and twist my hand free from Pyro's grip. He wheels around with knitted eyebrows, his anger simmering just beneath the surface.

"What's wrong now?!" He widens his eyes at me like I'm being awkward purely for kicks and I fold my arms.

"Did you come here for me or to get me away from Ghost?" I ask, ignoring the broad chest that steps in behind me. I was hoping we could have this conversation later and in private, but I'm sick of being dragged along just so Ghost can't catch up to take my other hand. Pyro looks between us, his face contorted with rage and something else I can't pinpoint. Jealousy or misery, along those lines. Tate, Claire and Enzo duck their heads, walking on but the Blacksmith stays by Ghost's side as is standard it seems. Opening and closing his mouth a few times while trying to formulate an answer, a flash of movement further down the passage catches my attention and saves him the bother.

"Hey! Summon, wait up!" I call out after the Mute, breaking into a run without caring if the others are right behind. With Ghost passing out and rolling off the stage, I didn't get a chance to see them leave earlier. Following Summon around a tight corner, I slam into a chrome-coated wall and fall back on my ass. Touching a hand to my nose, the slow drip of my congealed blood trickles from my nose and I check the crack in my forehead hasn't grown anymore.

"Shit, Mania," Ghost drops to his knees, taking my face in his hands. It wasn't so long ago he'd have been the one, arms crossed and brooding against the opposite wall and Pyro would have been comforting me with a soft caress.

"I'm fine," I lie, letting him pull me upright. "I saw Summon without his wife or Serpentina." Ghost's eyes flash with alarm, the same way mine had when I first saw it too. That, and the flicker of relief that he might know the way back to his hideout and we could have joined them there. The darkness of night has crept in like an omen for what's to come and we all crowd around to share worried glances.

"What are we going to do?" Claire asks. Both Tate and Enzo wrap an alarm around her, the three of them huddled close in comfort. I rest my head back against the metal and sigh.

"I'm going to have to look for somewhere safe we can hide until morning," Ghost starts but I wave his words away.

"We discussed this. You can't go walking into another trap, one that may be even you can't escape."

"Beats standing out here as idle targets. If this is the upgrade the labyrinth got, I don't even want to cross paths with that damn

Minotaur." I shudder at the thought, picturing steel horns and metal hooves.

"Wait a second," I straighten and point at the Blacksmith. "This place is now made of metal, which you can manipulate. Can't you maneuver the walls or make us a bunker or something?" His steel-coated eyes look around in thought and the excitement that stirs within me is bordering giddy. The answer has been trailing us this whole time if only we'd stopped long enough to catch our breaths and realize it.

"Metal yes, electricals no," the Blacksmith sticks his thumb out to point at the purple sparks emanating from the electric vines further down the passage. He pushes his way through us to where I stand and places his hands flat on the metal wall. I shift out of the way, choosing to stand by Pyro and watch. There's no right way to handle all the shit we've been through, but while he's being a jackass, I'll stand right here in solidarity.

Tense moments blur into minutes and the giddy knots in my stomach have died a painful death. A loud screech pierces the night air, high-pitched and crackly. The sound makes us all flinch, looking for its origin until Enzo points it out. A mechanical bird lands on top of the chrome wall, its joints buzzing as its head shifts from side to side. Flashing red lights blink from its eyes, like those of a camera. As it spreads its wings, a pair of small fans appear to lift it higher into the sky and sweep it out of view. Looks like the drones have received an upgrade as well.

The wall shudders briefly before dripping downwards, pooling and seeping into the craggy ground. I edge back on my tiptoes to avoid the metal touching my boots. Not caring in the slightest, Pyro sweeps me up into his arms and holds me there until the liquid has drained into the rock. I wind my arms around his neck, savoring his touch while he's not content on treating me like a possession instead of his so-called soul mate. Stubble lines his jaw, gently tickling my cheek. His deep breaths roll over my forehead and his arms relax. Instead of holding me, he's hugging me and it's better than I remembered. So much so, when we begin to move, I refuse to let go and he carries me for a while. I want to embrace this moment; feel his warmth, inhale his scent, run my fingers over his neck, in fear that once he puts me down the connection will break again.

With the rhythmic heartbeat pounding against my palm and the calmness all around, I can close my eyes and pretend we're somewhere else. Anywhere else. But then Pyro drops me to my feet and I'm jolted back to reality. It could be a worse sight before me though. In another rounded opening, the Blacksmith is drawing all of the metal from the nearby walls and working it into a shelter for us. The veins lying just beneath the surface of his bronzed skin strain beneath the pull of his ability and begin to glow like magma. Some of the material melts down into dull gray rivers, trickling towards the center, while other pieces come off in whole chunks and fly towards the structure like the pull of a magnet. It's not pretty, it's not even a real shape but soon the structure is complete. Ghost holds out a hand for me and an arm for everyone else to touch so he can walk us inside without the need for a door.

Of course, it's pitch black inside and lowering onto the smooth, metal floor isn't the comfiest of places to be, but at least we're alive. And exhausted. And annoyed as hell and starving. Other than that, this is perfect.

"Make a fire for us Py, it's going to be a long night freezing our asses off." Ghost grunts, shuffling in beside me without releasing my hand. My legs outstretched, bumping feet with someone who I hope is Pyro, since his response comes from directly opposite.

"Haven't you been listening dickhead? I gave up my fires to save you. And now we're all going to freeze together."

"Sorry my near-death experience was such an inconvenience for you," Ghost retorts straight away. His tone is laced with sarcasm and I can tell he's in one of those irritating moods. "But now you've mentioned it, let's air our baggage. What you really want me to be sorry for is not actually dying so Mania wouldn't have rode my cock like a bucking bronco." Gasping, I slap Ghost's arm and he laughs. I'm thankful there's no light for him to see me blushing and I can't imagine what Pyro's expression is like. On the topic of light though, the flames in Pyro's eyes have brightened enough for me to see them in the dark and I quirk an eyebrow. Ghost grunts as if he's just won a bet with himself and continues goading Pyro.

"You have no idea how good coming-back-from-the-dead sex is. I know you're basically a virgin again since it's been so long, but I'll tell you. Mania's pussy clenching around my shaft like-". A spark of light shoots across the shelter, spiraling through the air and landing on the bridge of Ghost's nose. His face lights up in panic, but the flame continues to wiggle upwards until it crosses the length of Ghost's eyebrows and then fizzles out.

"Let's see how attracted she is to you without eyebrows, fuck face," Pyro bites back.

"Why yes, I'm sure she'd love to fuck my face. I don't need eyebrows to use my tongue," Ghost chortles at himself. I bend my knees and drop my head into them with a groan. Similar sighs can be heard from the others who are also stuck in here, sharing the same consensus. This is going to be one long night.

Morning can't come soon enough and the news that dawn has broken is music to my ears. I dozed off somewhere between Ghost singing a tune about gnomes and him playing chopsticks with himself against my thigh. As Ghost pops back into the shelter, telling us it's safe to leave, I scramble for his arm. The bliss of inhaling a lungful of fresh air is doused by the pounding of rain beating upon my head. My half-corset soaks through instantly but anything has to be better than the tiny, metal shack. Not to mention stuffy and I need to find the first available private corner to pee in.

"I need food before I take a chunk out of one of you," I groan, clenching my stomach. Ghost winks, wrapping his arms around me from behind. His slickened skin slides over mine, spreading his warmth across my back.

"You know you can always feast on my dick," he mutters in my ear, followed by a fake yet convincing moan. Grinding his morning wood into my ass, I elbow him off me but can't deny, as always, he's immediately lifted my mood.

"No but seriously," Ghost addresses us all in a circle, "cannibalism isn't far off and you know who's going to be first." Each of us look around at the other before back to him with matching frowns. "What?

No one is going to say it? Fine, I'll be the bad guy." Ghost sighs dramatically and rolls his eyes. "Claire has put on a few pounds around the middle lately. Between Pyro and the Blacksmith, we could have a spitfire going within the hour."

"Ghost!" I gasp at the same time as Claire, who promptly covers her stomach. His resounding chuckle tells me there was a joke about to follow, most likely to do with spit-firing Claire and then spit-roasting me but I turn my head away before he can make it.

"When are you going to get it into your thick skull?" Pyro growls. "I don't have my fires anymore." I gape at him as well, as if that's the big issue here.

"Keep telling yourself that," Ghost shrugs. The Blacksmith steps up, grabbing him by the forearm.

"Count me out, I've had enough of your quarreling for one night. I'm going to stay behind, catch up on some rest." Now that I look closely, he does still look drained from last night. Dark circles hang beneath his burning-steel eyes and a yawn pulls at his mouth as Ghost deposits him back inside the metal hut. Then, Ghost turns and leaves, whistling a tune through the patter of rain.

Giving Claire a sympathetic look, I follow because we need to stay together and she reluctantly trails at the very back. I don't blame her half as much as I blame Tate for our time at Afterlife, and Enzo's helped me enough to scratch himself off the list entirely. Their presence doesn't bother me but some time alone with Pyro and Ghost to sort our shit out is needed sooner rather than later.

Taking to the labyrinth on tired feet once more, we trudge around beneath the curtain of rain as if it's hovering over only us. I wrap my arms around myself, rubbing my arms. Surprisingly, Pyro gently tugs my hand down and holds it inside his. Warmth seeps through our palms, moving up my arm and expanding throughout my body. I peer at him, his eyes concealed by the damp red fringe hanging low over his face. Maybe Ghost is on to something about Pyro's fires. Too bad Mutes don't come with a manual. I stop in my tracks, tugging Pyro back and Enzo bumps into my back.

"Twenty percent!" I shout to be heard over the rain. Ghost turns around, wiping the wet droplets from his face to quirk a brow at me.

"Christopher once told me Mutes only access twenty percent of their ability. That they become complacent and don't continue exploring it after discovering what they can do." Tate rounds my side with Claire tucked into her body.

"Well yeah, that's what all of his experiments were originally based on. It's why Claire can not only gain information from people or certain objects, but she can delve into memories. Even the ones you've forgotten." The brunette pokes her head up to nod along with Tate's words, finding her voice from somewhere.

"One of the scientists has the ability to alter appearances. As payment for volunteering, Christopher asked her to change our looks so we could fit in with the human world. Enzo and I were the original test subjects. Tate joined later on but she refused to be altered. From there, we decided to stay to help the others through their experimentation stage. He never said anything about an asylum or keeping Mutes against their will. It all just…escalated," she shrugs.

I sigh heavily, deciding in that moment I'm letting go of any anger I'm harboring towards the three refusing to meet our gazes. I did the same in their position; I jumped at the chance of somewhere welcoming to stay. The simple truth is there's no place for Mutes in this world, except maybe a labyrinth that'll remove us from existence. Regardless, we're all in the same boat now and if anyone knows Christopher's mind, it's them.

"Well, no better time for redemption than the present," I tell them with a half-smile.

"What's going through that pretty head of yours, Spitfire?" Ghost walks towards us, falling into my other side.

"Enzo can alter our chemical reactions," I step aside to face him. "Can't you make it so we don't feel hungry anymore?" Enzo's mouth opens and he frowns deeply, mulling my words over in his mind.

"I mean…I could give it a shot I guess." I smile fully now and nod. I'm sure a sated Ghost is much less Hannabal Lecter than a hangry Ghost and we might just all make it through the day without losing a limb to his appetite. Pyro grumbles under his breath about not being a test subject and I roll my eyes. Pulling my hand free from his hold, I offer it out to Enzo.

"Here, do me first." Ghost groans and I elbow him in the gut. His arms wind around me anyway, probably in support in case Enzo's ability precedes him and I end up writhing on the floor. The mocha-skinned Mute's eyes lock onto mine, a question held in their hazel depths and I nod firmly. If this works, we can scratch another problem off our long list of shit to contend with. Taking my hand, Enzo closes his eyes in concentration and a wave of nausea rolls through me. I gag, but as quick as it rises up, it disappears and my stomach stops growling. The intense cramping in my abdomen subsides and as I withdraw my hand, I roll my shoulders and twist my torso.

"Holy shit," I mutter. A fresh rush of energy floods my system, revitalizing the aches and pains I'd grown accustomed to. "I feel amazing," I beam. "How did you do that?" Enzo turns his face away from my praise, his cheeks pinkening.

"Enzymes are generally used for breaking down so I tried to adapt them; I envisioned a type of enzyme that builds up instead. From there, I think I dabbled in some cell regeneration but it's hard to be sure." My eyebrows raise and I bounce on my heels a few times, feeling the press on the key and black card I'm still carrying around in my sole. The labyrinth has changed so much, I probably don't need them but they seem too valuable to toss. Enzo pushes his newfound ability into Claire and Tate next, before Pyro steps forward to have his turn. By the time Ghost has reluctantly offered up his elbow for Enzo to touch, adrenaline is buzzing around my system. I feel high on it, needing to break out into a run and feel the race of my heartbeat. The rain hasn't stopped but I couldn't care less now. I'm ready to go.

Yanking his elbow back once the job is done, Ghost grimaces and dusts off the patch of skin Enzo has touched. I punch him in the arm, glowering at him.

"Thank him then. Enzo's done you a favor." Ghost crosses his arms, twisting his face towards the sky so I can't stare him down. How am I attracted to such an overgrown child? I reach up, trying to pry his face back down but Enzo cuts in to save me the bother.

"It's fine, honestly. It's the least I can do. I'm just glad we've got an alternative to starving. I doubt it'll hold off the need for real food for long. But it'll do for now." Giving him a quirked smile, I return my focus to the open passageways on either side of us. Resolution spurs me to stand tall and address the group.

"Let's make the most of extending our abilities today, finding out what other tricks we can rely on if need be. Then we'll regroup, focusing on weak spots in the maze and ways to free Hoax."

"What's got you all taking charge all of a sudden?" Pyro asks with a narrowed gaze. I give him a coy shrug with one shoulder and start to walk, letting the rest follow me for once. Hopefully not into a death trap but I'm only human, or an ex-communicated Mute or whatever. Regardless, I feel fan-fucking-tastic, Pyro is here, Hoax is alive and with Ghost on my team, I feel ready to take back control. I'm going to lead my group of rejects to victory and save Hoax from himself. Destroying Christopher in the process will be a bonus.

"Do you hear that?" Ghost asks for the millionth time, yet I can't find it in me to ignore him.

"You're not having gastro cramps," I groan back. As the largest and most likely to fend off an attack, Ghost is taking the lead upfront. The passageways we've found ourselves in after walking for most of the morning, to no avail, are narrow and damp. Moving as a single file line, Mania is in front of me, Tate and Claire behind with Enzo taking up the rear. We attempted to go back for the Blacksmith but soon lost the metal shelter. I just hope he can muster enough energy to melt his way out or that Mute is long dead. Ghost stops abruptly and like dominos, we all slam into each other one by one. "What the hell?!" I shout, just stopping myself from crushing Mania into his broad back.

"Listen," Ghost hisses and we all freeze. At first there's nothing but the buzz of a nearby drone flying over the maze, but then my ears prick and I hear it. Ever so faintly, like a mirage to my senses, I hear the sound of running water. No, not running. Crashing. I share a look with Ghost, noting the panic in his eyes as he clearly envisions a tsunami headed our way, but I've seen the map. I know what that sound is.

"Take us toward it," I order him, placing a hand on Mania's shoulder and encouraging the others to do the same. He thinks about refusing but after a moment, the veil of his ability washes over us and he leads us through the walls. I wasn't prepared for the number of bodies littering the next passage over. Crimson red stains the shiny walls and blood seeps through the rivets in the ground. Further down, a Mute with glowing orange eyes stops at the sight of us, his hands clasped around the ankles of a dead Mute he was dragging away. We continue to move as my mind plays catch up. How could we not have come across any other bodies before now, yet here they are? It's as if the maze has been using the dead ends and grates to steer us away from them, or to let the Mute we just saw clean up before allowing access to that passage again. Whatever happened down there was a massacre and I shudder to think what that means for us.

The sound grows louder and I edge closer, trepidation washing away in favor of a stronger emotion. Excitement. The thundering water pounds through my ears and as we appear through the next wall, my heart flips at the sight. I'd presumed in the update, the waterfall would have been removed like all other natural elements, but it's even more beautiful than the camera portrayed. Even in the rain, I itch to dive into the cascading rumble of water spearing from the rock mountain towering above. A glistening pool at the base beckons me closer, although Enzo, Tate and Claire hang back.

"It's okay," I tell them. "I saw this on the live feed. There were Mutes swimming in it who were still here when we arrived."

"So you say. I can't imagine why Christopher would leave this place un-adapted by Mute-eating piranhas," Tate says without taking her eyes off the water.

"Well the piranhas can have my juicy ass, there's nothing that could keep me from enjoying this," Ghost shouts, already butt naked and running into the water. We all watch closely and a part of me secretly wants to see something actually chomp into the cocky bastard. He's always been able to keep up his arrogance in the face of any situation and I've not-so-secretly hated him for it. Although I know him well enough to know it's not because he doesn't care, but because he can't handle the anguish the truth may cause him. Bringing a smug nature is his role in our group, so for the sake of balance, I suppose I'm not entirely annoyed he hasn't lost it.

After a few minutes of watching Ghost splash around and doing naked handstands in the shallow area, which is an image I never wanted imprinted in my mind, I unbuckle my jeans and run in after him. Diving forward, I catch his neck just as he bobs back up and take him under, throwing a knee into his ribs. His fist connects with my gut and as I breach the surface for air, he tugs my ankle in the direction of the waterfall. I kick against his hold, trying to swim away but he's relentless. The instant the brunt of the waterfall hammers into my back, I yell out and manage to land my foot into his face beneath the water. Releasing me, I swim away, only to hear his booming laugh resound from behind the waterfall.

"Just like old times, Py," he shouts and I roll my eyes, fighting a smirk. Damn him for being a loveable shithead when I'm still pissed about him and Mania. He hasn't even apologized, I remind myself but a voice in the back of my mind says he never will. Ghost doesn't apologize for his actions so I'll just have to make him pay in other ways.

"Hey Mania," I call with a devious plan in mind. "Come on in." She hesitates for a moment, looking back at the others who make their way to the shallow pool. Removing their boots, Tate and Claire dip their feet in and Enzo tugs up his jean legs. With their attention averted, Mania strips and I try to be a gentleman, but damn. There's no way I can resist staring at her gorgeous body. Her breasts are the perfect size for her body, small and pert between the expanse of ink. Every time I see the winged skull in the center of her chest, a slither of warmth finds me at the marking we share. My eyes travel the length of her pale skin to the apex of her thighs, smooth and flawless.

She tips a toe into the water, finding it lukewarm against the chilly winter air rolling in and smiles. That smile melts any last reservations I had about being mad at her. She is, and always was, my girl. It's time I proved that to her. Swimming over, I hold out my hand and she strides forward to take it. The instant her fingers slip into my palm, I tug her down onto me. Her surprised squeal is silenced by my kiss; a quick, demanding steal from her lips with the promise of what's to come. No more delaying or taunting. I pull her into the cradle of my arms, telling her to hold her breath and then sink us beneath the water. Kicking powerfully, the hurricane of water pounding over us is deafening until we breach the other side.

Ghost is resting against an outcrop in the rock, his eyebrows shooting up at the sight of us two together. I laugh internally, turning Mania away and swimming us over to the opposite side. A circular skylight at the top of the cave allows us to see fairly well thanks to the midday sun. Droplets of water shine from the jagged, rocky spikes before dripping into the otherwise calm water.

Ghost says nothing, not even when I push Mania up against the cave wall and thrust my tongue into her mouth. She, however, groans and the sound is amplified around the cavern. Her body slides into mine like it was made to be there. I run my hands down her sides, my thumbs grazing her breasts. Lower down, I curve her hip bone, smoothing my palms around her thighs to hoist them around me. All the while, she doesn't stop caressing my tongue with hers, filling my ears with her breathy moans at my simple touches. It's been far too long since we've been together. In fact, we didn't get the chance to explore our connection before and by the throbbing of my dick against her core, I can't hold off waiting to have her anymore.

Thrusting forward, with the help of the water, I slide all the way home in one move. She tenses around my intrusion, her teeth sinking into my bottom lip. It's me that groans this time as I adjust to the tightness of her sheathing me so smugly. I rock gently, allowing the flow of the water to control my movements, until she's relaxed her hips from their position crushing my waist. I don't let her go far though, gripping her ass and tilting her into my next thrust. It's slow and luxurious, every nerve ending in my dick coming alive inside her. Kissing her until she breaks away for air, I turn my attention to her jaw and neck. She's so soft beneath me, yet firm and unmoving in her posture. She doesn't wriggle or shy away, instead Mania meets me thrust for thrust.

Dipping my head lower, I take her nipple into my mouth and her hand pushes into my hair. Her back arches into me and she hisses when I bite down, before licking the tender bud better again. I roll my tongue back and forth, bringing my hand around to tease her other breast. Mania moves with me, shifting her hips into me and digging her nails into my ass to urge me on. Strangled moans fill the cave, bouncing off the walls multiple times so I can't tell where one ends and the next begins. I grin to myself, switching my hand and mouth to give her other tit my attention when a ripple of water alerts me to someone else's presence.

"I'd have made her come twice by now," Ghost mocks in my ear. I release Mania's nipple with a pop to glower at him, his face the image of smugness.

"Maybe she's being put off by your ugly face," I snap back.

"Maybe the pair of you should shut the fuck up while I picture Hoax, because he never let his macho bullshit come between me and my orgasms," Mania groans. I frown at her closed eyes and the look of bliss on her face and wrench her chin down to me. Her blood-red eyes open lazily, a playful smirk playing across her blackened lips. Running my fingers between her cleavage, over her sternum and down her inked abdomen, I flick over her clit. Mania gasps but any sense of victory I felt is stolen when Ghost claims her mouth, despite my cock being buried inside her. I grind my thumb over her clit roughly and fuck her harder, burying myself deeper. Anything to get her attention back on me.

Although she doesn't stop kissing my so-called best friend like she's fucking starving for him, her hands roam my chest. Her nails drag over my nipples and abs, no doubt scoring marks all the way to my cock. Lifting her leg, which Ghost grabs and raises to rest on my shoulder, Mania reaches underneath to roll my balls in her hands. With her open to me, every slam has my rounded head pounding her G-spot and she finally breaks the kiss to scream out.

Ghost only moves to slip in behind her, his hands coming around to massage her breasts and his mouth on her neck. I ignore him, focusing on Mania's face instead. She's begging me to make her come with her pained whimpers and pleading eyes. I falter in my rhythm because as much as I want to, I don't know what else to do. And the cocky bastard hitching his eyebrow beyond her head knows it. I refused to fuck anyone who wasn't her for so long, I don't have the experience to pleasure my soul mate the way he does. In that moment, I feel like I've failed her more than I thought possible. She was carved from my very essence, perfect for me in every way, yet I can't please her.

"Little help here?" I growl, turning my head away from them both. My thrusts have all but stopped and the heat flaming my cheeks has nothing to do with my ability, or lack of.

"On it," Ghost replies. I vaguely notice his hand shifting from her breast and disappearing beneath the water. Mania grips my face, and with a hard tug, manages to make me look at her.

"No," she says and Ghost's smile slips. "Ghost can stay, but only to watch. You can do this Pyro. You're enough," she whispers before placing her lips on mine. My resolve cracks, her words slicing me open and instantly healing me so thoroughly, I can pretend I was never broken. *You're enough.* I've needed to hear those words from so many people in my lifetime, but coming from her, they're everything. This time, I don't hold back. I shove her into Ghost and I fuck my girl because that's what I've spent years dreaming about. I take her mouth in a savage dance of bonding and lust, pinning her hips in place against my best friend. Cried moans fill the entire cave and I'm sure they'll hear it beyond the waterfall. The water splashes vigorously and Mania's leg drops to the crook of my arm.

Continuing my assault on her clit, she's tightening around my shaft and screaming my name in no time. My elation is short-lived when my own need to explode rises within. I want to prolong our time here, not knowing when our next moment of isolation might arise. Reaching over, I grab Ghost by the shoulder and use him to keep us afloat. If he insists on being here, I'll use him as a support post. Slamming into Mania over and over, her caress on my face shifts to claws digging into my back. I'm on the verge of finishing so I try to pull out but a slender leg around my waist won't let me. I try to protest, my words halted by Mania's mouth crashing on mine and as I press the length of her body into Ghost, she comes again and I know I'm also a goner.

The soul-shattering tremors of my climax subside, yet the rumbles through the rock continue to reverberate. A drone watching overhead, flies out of harm's way through the skylight but doesn't disappear as the first speared rock separates from the ceiling and hurtles toward us. Pyro throws me aside and kicks off the wall, but not before the rock crashes into the water and he releases a pained scream. He paddles towards me, winding an arm around my waist although clearly injured. The rocks continue to fall, splashing the water in all directions so I can't see where it is safe.

Removing Pyro's arm, I link our fingers and tuck him beneath the water as another hand grabs my nape. Ghost uses his weight to shove both Pyro and I downward, while stones fly through us like torpedoes hunting for a target. My lungs scream for air and black spots dance across my vision but I continue to kick, not releasing Pyro once. With Ghost keeping a tight grip on our necks until we've cleared the waterfall, the three of us breach the other side, gasping and spluttering.

"What's happening?" I croak to Enzo, who's rushing into the water to help us. Pyro and Ghost shoot hands out to cover me, but my nakedness isn't the priority right now. I take Enzo's hand, stumbling out of the water and Tate is waiting for me with my clothes.

Wriggling into the shorts and shoving my feet into my boots, I tackle the half-corset with wet, wrinkled fingers. The metal hooks click into place from sternum to abdomen and by the time I get to the last few, a hastily dressed Pyro and Ghost are kneeling to tackle each of my boot zips. A spray of water crashes over us from a fallen boulder, the entire waterfall seeming to be coming down and as I glance up, I see why. An army of parrot drones are hovering overhead, shooting lasers from their beaks towards the cliff face.

"Oh come on," Ghost groans, following my eye line. "We didn't even get to play well-hung drunken pirates and the seductive siren." His pout is adorable but I'm more concerned with living through today. Grabbing for his and Pyro's hands, I break out into a run for the exit. A grate closes as soon as we pass through, Enzo's dreadlocks grazed by the metal. He huddles Claire and Tate into him, the six of us running in two smaller groups. Walls slam closed in front of us, forcing our way through the maze as the tell-tale buzz of a drone bird follows. Wet, red hair plasters itself over my eyes and my feet stumble over the rumbling rock below. The maze moves us whichever way it deems fit, until we spill into a huge, stone field. I realize too late the faint tingle of a forcefield rushing over my skin and as I meet Tate's eyes, she's felt it too.

Unlike any space we've been in before, this one is rectangular with clearly outlined square bricks on the ground. We're not the only ones; it would seem most of the remaining Mutes have already been pushed in this direction. Their rainbow spectrum of eyes look around in fear and confusion while I hunt for any sign that Serpentina is here. More than that, safe. The various doorways shift, closing over so we're all trapped inside. Ghost's grip on my hand tightens as he tries and fails to use his ability. Just like in Afterlife, we're all powerless here. Drones band together and a projected image splutters to life between them.

"My marvelous Mutes," Christopher's wrinkled face beams. His gray hair is slicked back and the hint of a suit tie can be seen, but it's his smug smile I can't tear my gaze away from. A mixture of boos and hisses sound from the Mutes, although I doubt the projection is a two-way stream. "Congratulations on still being alive," the old man cackles. Interference surrounds him, as if a room full of humans are laughing and cheering him on. No surprise there, Christopher loves a good show. "However, it's come to our attention there are more defensive abilities remaining than mundane ones. It's time we evened the playing field. Or should I say, the minefield." With that, the image disappears and a collective gasp travels through the chasm.

The squares on the ground illuminate in shades of purple, blue and green. Before anyone has time to understand what to do, the army green blocks lower an inch into the ground and chaos erupts. My ears burst, filling my head with a high-pitched ring I can't shake. The brick explodes, limbs and blood spray into the abyss. The noise in my ears is nothing compared to the icy chill of fear clutching at my chest, blocking all air from entering my lungs. From our vantage point at the back, we have a clear view of the carnage, but we also have less choice of squares to choose from.

A ten-second timer begins to sound from the drone birds and Mutes flee in panic. Many flock in our direction, leaping onto the walls in an effort to escape. A sharp electrical shock shoots them back into the minefield, writhing on the ground with jerky movements. Ghost grips my hand to the point of breaking my fingers, desperately trying to get us out of here to no avail. It's Pyro who takes the initiative, but not in the way I'd have hoped.

"Stand on a different color to me," he orders Ghost, dragging the two of us forward. Planting himself on a vibrant purple square, he then swoops me into the cradle of his bunched arms. Tension rides the length of the corded veins in his neck and the flame dancing in his eyes glows brighter. "If my square even judders, I'm throwing her to you. Be ready."

"What?!" I balk. "No way, let me down!" I shout. Twisting my neck to Ghost on a lime green square, he's nodding with his arms outstretched and ready. I don't have time to marvel in the fact the pair have actually agreed on something as the timer reaches one. Explosions ring out again, screams being cut short. Being further in the field means chunks of rubble rain over me, scratching my back and arms. I don't know what color went, but I twist to see Ghost is still standing and I release a breath.

"Ten, nine," the timer starts again. Body parts haven't finished flying through the air before we're moving again. Protests lodge in my throat because being stubborn isn't going to help anyone right now. The odds of the three of us surviving this look none existent. I search over Pyro's shoulder, spotting Enzo with Tate and Claire hoisted over his shoulders in a similar fashion. Although, if one of them goes, they all do and my gut twists at that thought. Not for any selfish reason like Ghost might conjure up; their stoic presence has become reassuring. The notion that we're all the same and none of us are safe from Christopher's twisted wrath.

I can't count how many mines detonate, each one blending into the next while Pyro jumps from square to square. All the while, I struggle to be released, refusing to let their damsel in distress bullshit carry me through this. The ground has fallen away where the bombs have taken out chunks of earth and now it's not just the colors Pyro is competing with, but the sheer jumps between pillars. He halts, his breath sawing out in ragged puffs and his arms halter.

"I..." he heaves. I take my eyes off the ground, clinging onto Pyro's neck. His eyes are focused on me and the mix of pity and love I find there breaks my heart in two. "I can't make it."

"It's okay," I try to smile. "We're together. That's all that matters." He doesn't reply to me and a flicker of regret passes over his features. Turning his head away, he addresses the Mute a square behind him.

"Take her." Without a moment's hesitation, I'm passed into Ghost's arms as he barges passed and leaps through the air. I scream, for many reasons, with my body momentarily lost to the air until I land heavily back in Ghost's arms. Scrambling over his shoulder, I desperately look for Pyro. Another mine is triggered, too close for comfort. Clouds of ash hinder my vision and I call out, a gut-curdling cry until the smoke subsides and I see Pyro still standing across the gap separating us.

"Leave me here, go back for him!" I yell at Ghost, bucking for him to put me down. The timer is counting again and tears spill in hot rivets from my eyes. "Ghost! Save him!" I beg, hellbent on dying here and now if it's with the knowledge Pyro sacrificed himself for me.

"Spitfire," Ghost breathes in a far too soothing voice. "I'm surprised I made that jump once, and it was only by force of will. I won't make it twice and Pyro is heavier than you. It's not my fault he didn't join me for cardio practice," he says but there's a falter to his voice. Despite how he's clearly trying to hide his own emotions, I rear back and crunch my forehead into his nose.

"You selfish motherfucker!" I scream, grabbing my head. Fuck, is his nose made out of steel or some shit?! Finally releasing me, the timer counts '*three, two*' and I leap. I sail through the air, the ruminants of an explosion nearby knocking me off course. Flailing, my nails scrape the rock until my fingers graze an outcrop in the rock. Grasping with all my might, with the pain of my splintering nails shooting through my fingers, I manage to yank myself to a stop. My shoulder tears yet I hold on, slowly pulling myself back up. I hadn't realized the drop was so steep until I had to drag my stupid ass back up it. An eternity later, a hand clasps my wrist and thankfully hauls me the rest of the way.

Wobbling on weak legs, I fall into Pyro's arms for a short respite before pushing away. His mouth moves towards mine until I crack a sharp slap across his face.

"Don't you ever, ever do that again," I scold. Pyro's embrace around me doesn't waver, not even as his face reels to the side. "I'm not some precious princess that needs saving. I'm all too familiar with dying, and as much as it fucking sucks," my voice breaks, "we're a team. We live together or we die together, but there's no world for me if you're not in it. I've just got the three of you back, I can't survive losing any of you again." This time when Pyro's lips press against mine, I don't resist him. His gentle touch breaks through my anger, stripping me bare. A rush of emotions are creating a tornado inside me, and his soothing kiss becomes my anchor. I grasp his face, savoring the delicate wobble of his bottom lips that betrays how scared he was for me.

Breaking away with tears pricking at my eyes, my heart hammers in my chest as I risk a look down. Smokey blackness meets my gaze and I swallow hard. I used to pray for death. I reveled in it during the days where hell was my only home. But now I have something to live for, something real and irreplaceable. Through the pulse hammering in my ears, I vaguely notice the drone has stopped counting and in its place, Christopher is making another cheery announcement.

"Wow! Wasn't that a thrill!" I scowl at the parrot drone with his mouth wide open to relay Christopher's message. It's perched on a wall across the other side of the field, zeroing its camera lens eyes on each of us in turn. Counting those still standing, I imagine. Gently, the stone gaps rumble as rock grows up from the earth until the floor is complete again. Sticky coatings of blood smear the stone, the freshly rancid copper smell making me gag.

"Since we've reached the lucky number 50, the game has now come to an end. We sincerely hope you all enjoyed that as much as we enjoyed watching it, and I'm happy to say the top three Mutes on the leaderboard will now be announced. These three will, from now on, be known as our Elites, and will receive special gifts for their ranking. The tasks they face from now on though, will be even more treacherous than before!" I share a look with Pyro and Ghost before searching for the others and not spotting them. "These lucky Mutes are Smokescreen, Brainwave, and with all the women up here rooting for her happily ever after, Mania." My gut twists and I let out an expectant sigh. Resting my head against Pyro, I feel Ghost's arms wind around me from behind now he can join us.

Following the sound of grinding rock, a doorway opens to our left and the Mute I spotted before with glowing orange eyes and a navy boiler suit strides in. He begins to drag the pieces of discarded bodies to a central point, creating a pile while paying us no mind. Breaking free of the hug I plan on returning to at the next possible moment, I look around the vast space. The remaining Mutes are fleeing and through the rush of bodies, I spot two quivering females crumpled together against the wall. Claire's braid has unraveled and Tate's tear-stained eyes spot me rushing over.

"Where's Enzo?" I ask in panic, scared of the answer. Claire's sobs double and I have my answer. "No. It can't...he can't..." I trail over, searching the limbs and maimed faces left around. As much as I need to see it to believe it, I also know seeing Enzo mutilated will scar my brain for good.

"He tossed us aside just before-" Tate's voice cracks. Claire is inconsolable, no matter how hard her friend cradles and soothes her. Enzo helped me when no one else would. He was nothing but compassionate when I gave him no reason to be. Trying to find the words to console her, despite the ache in my chest expanding and swallowing me whole, a parrot zooms towards me and stops short of landing on my head. Clutched in its claws is a large black box tied with a red bow. Dropping the package into my hands, I turn away from the sobbing females to place it in Ghost's hands and make short work of tearing the ribbon open.

Beneath an unnecessary layer of red tissue paper, a map lies face up. The paper is thick like card and the image laser-inked on, showing one clear path with a vivid blue line. At the top, my destination is printed in bold lettering. *'Minotaur's lair – key required.'* Flexing my toes on instinct, I feel the weight of the key in my boot. I haven't heard of or seen the Minotaur since our last encounter but I can only imagine taking over his lair will include the task of killing its current occupant.

"We have to go," I tell the guys before turning to the two females on the floor. "Come on, before night comes and fuck knows what else."

"I can't," Claire cries in a new round of wailing. My heart cracks for her with each strangled sound, but with everyone's abilities subdued for now, we can't afford to get locked in here.

"If you don't, Enzo will have sacrificed himself for nothing." My tone is cold, even though I was nearly in the same position myself. I know if someone was trying to move me away from the scene one of my men had died in, for me no less, I'd have to be physically restrained. Thankfully, my cold tone does the job and Claire allows Tate to pull her upright. "We have a place to go now. I'll keep you safe," I promise with no way to back up that claim. The guys step in behind me in solidarity and their presence bolsters me more than words could right now. With the map in hand, I take the lead, all the while praying we don't have to fight a minotaur at the end of this trail. Monster or not, I can't bear any more bloodshed today.

GHOST

"You've had a key stashed in your boot this entire time?" I ask, still confused as to where we are. The hulking, slab of rock before us hasn't received the same makeover as the rest of the labyrinth. A perfect outline of a keyhole sits central and Mania pushes the iron key into it, ignoring my question. Locks and bolts judder inside the wall, sliding from one side to the other before the wall releases. Prying it open with her skeletal fingers, I place a hand on Mania's shoulder. "I have a bad feeling about this."

"It's sunset and we don't have any other options. Christopher said my trials will be twice as treacherous now." Her red eyes flick back to me and we share a shudder. "We need to take any hope of refuge we can get." Releasing a sigh, I ease her aside and take the lead. My ability still isn't as reliable as I would like, flickering in and out randomly. With the fear I'll get stuck halfway through a wall, I prefer to put it on the back burner for now.

Inching inside the darkness, I pause to listen for movement. When nothing happens, I reach back to pull the torch from Mania's hip and edge forward. In the glow of artificial light, smooth tarmac shines down a sloping decline. The tunnel has been purposely hollowed out, creating a concrete burrow in the base of the mountain. Clasping

Mania's hand in mine, I guide her onwards while Pyro takes up the rear with the sniveling females. Another door halts our movements; this one large enough for an elephant to comfortably pass through. Without a keyhole insight, I shove my weight against the rustic panel and am instantly rewarded with a blast of heat. A light switch on the inside wall illuminates the space and I stand dumbfounded.

For a monster, he sure lives in luxury. A sofa on a sheepskin rug faces inwards towards the door. On a carved rock to resemble a fist, a finely-sculpted chess board is propped and halfway through a game. Red velvet curtains hang over a canvas print of a seaside sunset. Fake plants reach from their patterned pots to the ceiling where naked bulbs hang. Everything about the room screams a measured personality, but that's not the type of hoof-handed manic I was envisioning.

"Where's the Minotaur?" Mania breathes and I shrug. Wherever he is, he's not here now and the mold growing on the dishes in the sink show he's either a messy shit or he hasn't been back in a while. My stomach growls, diverting my attention from the image of a Minotaur trying to wash up with hooves for hands and I stride across the room.

"Food, shower, bed. In that order," I state, and I didn't mean alone. I rifle through a wicker basket brimming with root vegetables, grabbing out an array to start peeling and chopping. Pyro automatically joins my side, boiling some water over the stove.

"I didn't know you guys could cook," Mania quirks a brow at us. Instead of grinning smugly, I frown. It just occurred to me we haven't had a single 'normal' day with Mania since we met. As she returns to the others, who have settled in a mopey corner on the sofa, I share an idea with Pyro in a hushed voice. He pauses mid-washing up in thought, before nodding. It's the most of an agreement I'm going to get from him in his current mood so I'll take it. A cupboard under the basin provides a stale hunk of bread, which I hollow out to use as a bowl for the vegetables. Pyro pours in the broth he's made from the leftover peels and I shove it into the oven while working on rectifying the bread. Somehow, with some oil and salt, I manage to fry some life back into it by the time our makeshift stew is ready.

"Dinner's up ladies," I call. Settling on the ground, we pick at the food with the few forks Pyro cleaned. Dunking a stick of bread, Claire forces it past her lips through pure force of will. "It's not that bad," I scoff and Tate shoots me a warning glare.

"I think we're just going to turn in," she grumbles. Picking Claire up from the floor like a ragdoll, the pair slink off and disappear behind one of the doors. Mania heaves out a heavy sigh, her eyes downcast.

"The likelihood of us all surviving this," she mutters and I cut her off by placing my hand over her mouth.

"Nope, not tonight. We've survived another day, we're safe in this gigantic bunker and we're together. That's enough cause to celebrate." Peeling my hand away, I try to soothe out the hitch between her eyebrows but it's engraved in too deeply.

"Together," she huffs bitterly. "Together without Hoax." I grimace, suddenly hating myself for forgetting about Hoax. Pulling her into my side, I kiss the top of her forehead.

"He's alive. That's more than we had yesterday. And by tomorrow, he'll be fighting for your attention as much as Pyro has been." I feel the instant she softens at my words, stealing the small bit of hope I was faking. Mania's face tilts up, her lips curving and her tense posture easing.

"Let me guess, you don't need to fight because you're just so damn irresistible?"

"You said it Spitfire, not me," I wink. Pyro rolls his eyes, taking our finished meal back to the sink. On his way passed, he hoists Mania away from my body and eases her upright.

"Come on baby, let's find that shower. Don't think I haven't noticed how you keep wincing when your shoulder is pulled." His fingers slink over the back of her neck, over her shoulder and he gently kneads her skin. She hisses but leans into him as they walk and I hop up to follow. Trying a few of the huge doors, Pyro finds the bathroom but I stumble into the bedroom. Holy bedhead. Now this is what I imagined a monster's lair to look like. The Minotaur's bed takes up most of the room, his mattress a mess of fur throws and pillows like a nest. A hefty wood wardrobe and dresser stand tall against the concrete wall and the ceiling is easily double the height of me. I raid the contents of the dresser first, even though the few clothes I find are torn and stink of wet beast. Moving onto the wardrobe, I open the door and stumble back.

A heap of mutilated bodies tumbles out at my bare feet. Shock hits me first, and the stench second. Looks like I've found the Minotaur's stash of meat. Holding the crook of my arm over my mouth and nose, I start to kick the body parts back into the wardrobe until my gaze catches on a pair of legs. Teeth marks mar the flesh across the waist but it's the pair of blood-smeared black Converse on his feet. Kneeling down, I pry them free before spotting more legs within the pile. The Minotaur must have had a thing for torsos. Finding a pair for Pyro and Hoax too, because fuck not having shoes when there's some going to waste right here, I then stuff the legs back into the wardrobe and shut the door.

"What you got there?" Mania asks, walking in with a towel wrapped around her middle. Her hair is dripping water droplets over her shoulders and into the hint of her cleavage.

"Footwear," I grin, holding them up by the laces. Mania scrunches her nose up and Pyro steps in after her. His towel is tied around his waist, his skin lined with water as well. There's no way they both could have showered in that short time but I shove down the jealousy threatening to rear its head. I've had Mania to myself for a while now; it's only going to get harder when Hoax re-joins us. Hoarding the clothes into my arms, I leave the pair in favor of rinsing everything out in the shower before washing myself. Hanging them all out to dry, I'm drying my hair with the only towel left as I re-enter the bedroom.

I still at the sound of groaning, noting how Mania is sitting in her towel between Pyro's legs and his hands are working out the kinks in her neck, shoulders and back. She rolls her head with closed eyes and a blissful smile on her blackened lips. Not wanting to miss out on the fun, I casually throw my towel around my middle and drop onto the bed. Taking one of her feet in my hands, I roll my thumb over the pad and massage her thoroughly. A groan-off begins, alternating between the kneading pleasure we both provide in turn. Pyro narrows his eyes at me while I blow him a kiss, chuckling to myself.

"So what do you guys wanna do tonight?! I bob my eyebrows at

Pyro. Mania rolls her eyes but doesn't outright refuse the dark corner of her mind her thoughts clearly made a beeline for. When Pyro continues to stare blankly at me and Mania's head lolls to the side for better massage access, I mouth 'the plan' at him.

"Oh err," Pyro clears his throat. "How about we call out for some pizzas?" I nod approvingly with a groan.

"Extra meatilicious with a garlic-stuffed crust," I agree. Mania eyes me curiously as I move onto her other foot. "There's a new action movie starring The Rock's lesser-known cousin, The Pebble. He's not as ripped but he does a decent impression to show the family resemblance. We can crash on the beanbags in Py's room, watch it on his big screen."

"As long as you keep your grubby hands to yourself," Pyro adds and I bark out a laugh. I didn't miss the double meaning in his words, but the fact he's still protective over a damn PlayStation he blew up months ago is typical.

"I'll pass the memo on to Hoax when he brings the Ben and Jerry's." That one felt raw in my throat but Mania bites onto what we're trying to do here.

"What, sharing myself between the three of you isn't enough? You want to compete with Ben and Jerry as well. Spoiler alert, you'll lose." Pyro finally breaks a smirk and we all visibly relax.

"Harsh, Spitfire. I at least hope they make you cream twice before the real fun begins." I trail my fingers up her inner leg, dipping beneath her towel. Her breath hitches as I stroke the length of her pussy, which is gloriously wet already. One look at Pyro, though, has me retreating but not before I stick my fingers into my mouth and marvel at her taste. I've already given my cock a pep talk in the shower about behaving. After the vulnerability Py showed in the waterfall, I've decided to take a step back from showing him up in the dick department. That doesn't mean I won't take Mania aside to fuck her senseless when he's not looking, but he'll never get on board with sharing her if I am always her go-to cum drum.

Returning to massage her feet, Mania kicks my hands away and reaches out to pull me closer. My head rests on her thigh and her fingers tickle over my chest in rhythmic circles. "Stop fawning all over me, you guys have injuries too." She points to the various bruises littering my torso and I shrug off her concern. I look up into her beautiful face, marveling at how someone so delicate can have the three of us chasing our tails for her. She brushes Pyro's hands away too, easing back into him.

"I've had worse, but if you're offering some special attention, I've got a real ache in my co-"

"We're fine," Pyro growls to cut me off. I smirk at him, enjoying winding him up the wrong way as a part of our foreplay.

"Speak for yourself," I grumble back, sliding my hand beneath Mania's precariously open towel. Grazing my fingers over her clit, she sucks in a breath, bringing the smile back to my face. Catching the interested glint in Pyro's red eyes, I tilt my head to the side. "What do you say Py? Shall we give our little Spitfire here a reason to sleep soundlessly before we tuck her in?"

Now that I've caught his attention, a small flame ignites in his eyes and he gives me a sharp nod of approval. Pulling her towel open, the full glorious display of tattoos covering her pale skin is revealed. The collection of demented skulls on her left thigh and the floral flourishes I know span her lower back both mimic the ink on my right arm, wrist to shoulder. Warmth spreads through my chest that we share such markings, claiming her as mine long before I did. Circuit wires track the lengths of her legs down to her ankles, and not to mention the winged skull in the center of her chest in the same place Pyro's is. If I ever see him again, I owe Canvas one hell of a handshake for the skilled work he did on Mania's body and the way he unknowingly tied her to us all.

I lazily trail patterns across Mania's abdomen, working my way south. Her head rolls back on Pyro's shoulder as I strum my fingers back and forth over her glistening opening. Spreading her thighs wider with my shoulders for a better look, moisture pools into my mouth, salivating for a taste. With a small shimmy forward, my mouth closes around her small bud, pulling a soft moan from her lips. I take my time, lazily drawing my tongue back and forth. Each time, her breath hitches I can't contain a grin of satisfaction. Mania's body is an instrument of pleasure and I'm all too happy to be her conductor. Giving in to her pleas, I spear two fingers into her cunt, the flowing juices slickening my invasion .

Catching Pyro's curious gaze seems to snap him out of the trance Mania's rotating hips had put him under. His hands slip around her front to take her breasts in his palms, rolling her pert nipples in his fingers. It should have irritated me, or sent a surge of jealousy through me like it would if he were anyone else, but it doesn't. Instead, I nod my head in approval and snap my eyes closed to focus on the flutters rolling through Mania's pussy. As much as I approve of what's going on here, it doesn't mean I need to see it.

The feminine moans filling the room become muffled from what I imagine is Pyro's kiss, giving me the challenge of breaking them apart. Pumping my fingers at rapid speed, I suck and flick my tongue over her bud until I know she'll feel me tomorrow with every step. Fingers claw into my hair, pushing me impossibly closer as Mania takes over and sneaks her own pleasure. Grinding her pussy into my face, I feel the tightening of her pussy and abruptly withdraw my fingers, replacing them with my mouth. The full glory of her orgasm fills my mouth, my tongue lapping her up like my new favorite ice cream. Guttural screams echo around the huge room, bouncing off the walls and blending into the next. I eat her relentlessly, only easing once her explosive climax begins to fade.

Panting breathlessly, Mania's grip on me relaxes and she melts into Pyro's body. I risk a glance upwards at their matching red eyes, although Mania's are already fluttering shut. Her chest and neck are flushed red and the satisfied smile on her face warms me. It's good to see her smiling at last.

Rolling aside, I grab Mania's hips and whip her down the bed with a shocked gasp. Pyro grumbles but shuffles down as well, pulling a thick fur blanket over the three of us. With her back to me, I push my nose into Mania's hair and inhale the pomegranate shampoo she used. It must be the maze that's turned me into a soppy shit, filling my mind with the notion that I don't need any other female than the one crushed in my arms. My brothers are everything to me, but I can't deny the endless amount of sex and revolving door of women-only deepened the empty hole inside. Yet now, in the face of death and losing those around me every day, I've found a woman worth living for. One worth saving, even above myself.

Hot breath fans my neck and I wriggle between the two bodies crammed on either side of me, despite the size of the Minotaur's bed. I stretch out, muscling some room for me to shuffle my way out. Creeping to the foot of the bed and then towards the door, I look back to see Ghost loop an arm around Pyro, who mutters my name. The smirk on my face doesn't falter the entire time I slip out and head into the bathroom.

The clothes Ghost had washed are hanging from the shower rail, still a little damp but so much more comfortable than the tight corset and tiny shorts Christopher has had me in all this time. The sky blue t-shirt hangs off one shoulder and low past my thighs. Along with the belt from Ghost's jeans, I manage to fashion the oversized item into a dress. My thigh-high boots complete the look and with such a simple change, I feel ready to take on the day.

After a thorough clean, I convince myself the Minotaur's toothbrush is in decent enough shape to brush my teeth and I take the time to smooth my fingers through my hair in the gigantic mirror. By the time I've stepped back into the bedroom, the boys are awake. Ghost is nursing a swelling eye and Pyro paces over to me with a look of panic splashed across his face.

"You can't wear that." I scrunch my nose up, following his eye line from my chest to my waist. Shrugging my bare shoulder, I rest my hand on my popped hip and push my tongue into my cheek. Overall, the pose screams 'bite me' and I really hope he does.

"Corse she can." Ghost joins us, his gaze much more appreciative. "Sexy yet understated." Shooting me a wink, he brushes a kiss over the crack in my forehead and moves towards the door. Returning to address Pyro, an abrupt hissing sound cuts off my words. Frowning, I hunt for the source of the noise, spotting vents I hadn't noticed in each corner of the room. I smell the gas instead of see it, quickly rushing to tuck the lower half of my face into the shirt. Pyro is on me in seconds, holding the material against my face rather than reaching for a shirt for himself. Ghost disappears through the wall without a moment's hesitation, leaving us to fumble with the door handle. At least he was considerate enough to fetch Tate and Claire without being asked.

Breaking free, similar hisses echo around the bunker, clouding our vision. Pyro's step falters, his body leaning on mine heavily. Wrapping my arm around his waist, I limp the pair of us towards the exit, hoping the others will meet us there. My head feels all kinds of woozy as time seems to slow down around us. Staggering under the increasing weight of Pyro's body, a flash of white makes me smile weakly in relief, until I see the two pairs of Converse in each of Ghost's hands.

"Where...are...the girls?" I breathe out, coughing on my own words. Dryness clogs my throat, a wheeze rattling inside my chest. Ghost's eyes are dazed and unfocused, his body swaying side to side. Unless that's me. His eyebrows furrow though, as he places a hand on my shoulder and steps us through the main door.

"Who?" he asks, passing a pair of shoes and a t-shirt to Pyro. I heave in the fresher, albeit damp, air of the tunnel, smacking him across the arm.

"Tate and Claire," I splutter. "Go get them!" The roll of his eyes tells me Ghost knew exactly who I meant but had no intention of saving them. Sighing, he disappears once more and I lower myself down before I pass out. The stone is cold against my back while I take deep breaths to clear my screaming lungs. My thoughts race, escaping before I can fully stop it from blending into the next. It comes to me too late that I just ordered Ghost back into the gas and that he may not make it back out, but as soon as my heart skips a beat, he appears again. Luckily, with a spluttering brunette clinging onto his arm and an unconscious Tate slung over his shoulder.

Light seeps from beneath the door, illuminating the Converse clutching Ghost's feet and I curse him for taking the time to put them on. I push up onto my knees as he lays Tate down, checking the lilac Mute's pulse and breathing. She's alive, but without the knowledge of what gas is now pumping around her system, I can't be sure for how long. Just then, an all too familiar hissing fills the space all around us, both seeping beneath the door and from overhead.

"We need to move," Pyro says, scooping up Tate. The five of us navigate the darkness of the tunnel, all holding onto each other. Breaching the main door thanks to Ghost, I instantly know something is wrong. For a start, there's no sun. The sky is shrouded in a blanket of darkness, but I know from the rest in my bones that I slept for a long time. Perhaps it's possible I slept all day but judging by the way a tall Mute with billowing raven hair runs by with her wide eyes glued to the sky, I don't think so.

An explosion erupts from deeper inside the maze, the ground below us rumbling as rock and metal fly overhead. Unable to turn back into the shelter of the tunnel, we crouch and run with no end goal in sight. Metal grates slide closed behind us, effectively herding us in the direction the maze wants. Every turning presents a new round of screams which we veer away from. Ghost's hand doesn't leave mine for a moment, with Claire only keeping up by her grip on his other arm and Pyro storming ahead without Ghost's protection, all the while carrying Tate. Her purple eyes glance over his shoulder as she comes to, the frown maring her brow evidence that she still hasn't caught up with the present.

Pyro skids to a stop and with Ghost's ability in full swing, we skid straight through him to where the ground gives way. I scream, rearing back at the same time Ghost does as he drops his shield. Pyro's hand clamps down on the collar of his shirt and for the first time, I'm so glad he decided to wear one. Tiny rocks skid into the crater below, the one the maze was seemingly trying to shove us into. Purple liquid crashes below, splashing against the sides and doubling back as if it has a life of its own, trying to escape the crater it's stuck in. Just beneath the surface, electric eels writhe. Their bodies pulse with shock waves that spark each time another one gets too close. I swallow thickly, thankful as Ghost drags me a few steps back and shakes Claire off to surround me with his meaty arms.

"Starting to get the feeling this shit is personal," Ghost muses, almost to himself but I heard it. My gaze flicks up to the parrot drone sitting on an opposite wall, the camera lens in his eyes trained directly on us. I can only imagine Christopher is sitting in his large, leather desk chair with a whiskey in hand and killing himself laughing at the display we are putting on for solely his benefit. Flipping off the bird, I twist and lead us back to the metal grate a few feet behind. Ghost helps us to pass through and I risk a look upwards once more.

A surreal glow surrounds the sun, like an eclipse that won't be ending anytime soon. The parrot keeps close, dotting along the walls on clawed feet. We have only walked the length of one passageway when Ghost pulls me to a stop, his head tilting curiously.

"What is it?" I ask. Tate squirms to be released now she has roused fully, practically jumping from Pyro's arms to crush Claire into a punishing hug. Satisfied she can stand on her own, Pyro joins us as Ghost hums in the back of his throat. Suddenly, his arm flashes out and his fist crashes into the wall. Although, it's not the wall, because the resulting shriek of pain gives way to a figure stepping out from the shiny chrome. The color seeps away, revealing a Mute with cropped hair the shade of olive green, no shirt, low-hung jeans and bare feet. He clutches his nose but nothing can stop the pouring flow of blood Ghost's fist has erupted.

"You slimy little shit," Ghost starts but I put a hand on his chest. Those green eyes regard me with such disdain, I can only now believe the Mute before really did betray us. I'd hoped I misread the situation but apparently not.

"Good to see you again, Camo." I smile sweetly, stepping forward with fluttering eyelashes. However, the moment his hand lowers from his nose, I level a blow to his throat, causing him to splatter blood all over my t-shirtdress. Doesn't bother me though, because the look of panic that he might be asphyxiated choking on his own blood and the fact Camo is also stuck in here is all I need. Ghost whoops, using his hand on the back of my neck to spin me into his kiss. It's hard and fast, coated in the coppery taste of Camo's blood.

"Let me guess, you're the one who made your not-so-clever deal with the MRA and got these two tossed in here like yesterday's trash?" Pyro steps up next. Looking over my shoulder, I take in the clench to his sharp jaw and the not-so-subtle fire dancing in his eyes. The brighter it grows, the warmer my chest becomes until I'm rubbing it uncomfortably. Ghost frowns, lifting my hand away and I gasp at the spiral flames spinning around my forearm. They swirl upwards, circling my wrist and lacing through my fingers but not once does it burn me.

As I flex my fingers back and forth, another sensation builds in my chest. This one is much more potent - rage. It consumes me with the ferocity of a forest fire, burning deeply into my core until all I can think about is expelling the heat from my body. I vaguely register being shaken and a distant voice screaming my name but I can't focus, can't see beyond the flames dancing across my vision and in the center, there's Camo.

"Pyro!" the voice comes again and something tugs at my subconscious. That's not my name. Squinting through the haze of red, I see my brother's white, panicked eyes and collapse in his arms, *Mania*. Gasping, I buck out of Ghost's arms, patting myself down. The rage is gone, as have the flames and any evidence of what just happened.

"What the fuck was that?!" I ask, but deep down, I already know. That wasn't my rage, my revulsion or my ability.

"I have no idea," Ghost answers as Pyro simply stares in confusion. "One minute your arm was on fire and the next, you passed out and Py was in some kind of trance."

"It's like I told you," Claire interjects, her attention squarely on Pyro. "The breaking of your bond was only one-sided, so the flame connecting the pair of you didn't just vanish. It snapped on your end and ricocheted into her." Five pairs of eyes slowly turn to stare at me, Camo's included as he's remained standing there for no reason at all. Anyone else would have split by now but he seems as curious about Claire's revelation as the rest of us.

Our awkward silence is sliced apart by the incoming stampede of feet and screams, and another explosion not long after. Ammo crashes through us without a backward glance, her stubbed wrists pumping as fast as they can in an effort to escape the mechanical bull chasing the back of the crowd.

"Oh shit!" Ghost shouts, spotting it at the same time. Without any regard for Doc or Firefly who are also barging past, Ghost whips me onto his back and uses his ability to run through them.

"Hey! Wait for me, fuckface!" Pyro bellows, rushing among a few others to catch up. I jerk around in panic, tracing his flame-red hair until he latches onto my ankle. Only then does a breath of relief sag through me, but not for long. The bull roars in a classically animated way, tinged with a slight crackle. While those around swerve sharply around the next bend, Ghost races straight through the wall and the bull connects with the other side. Metal grinding on metal makes me cringe as the robot skids aside, chasing down those still running.

"Wait, Tate and Claire!" I shout, digging my ankles into Ghost's hips like a horse. His intrigued glance back and cocky smirk are at odds with the crescendo of screams that fill the air. I huff in frustration, not surprised by Ghost's lack of consideration for others but still. Does nothing dampen his playfulness? The answer to that filters into my mind, the moment the walls crushed inwards and he truly thought death had come for him. Squirming to get down, I stand in front of Pyro with folded arms, hoping he'll back me up. "We need to go back for them."

"Oh come on," Ghost protests, whining like a child. I shouldn't find his pout and puppy dog eyes sexy but goddamn my libido for popping up at the most inappropriate times. Biting down on my lip to prevent smiling, I step back into Pyro for the strength of his hard chest to bolster me. "They're going to have to die at some point anyway. Christopher said only one will get out, and besides. You're one of the elite three, they're in more danger with you than anyone else." My mouth drops open at that. I reckon he'd meant for his reasons to ease my guilt, but the opposite has happened.

"What does that mean for the two of you then?" I ask in a small voice. Pyro immediately hugs me from behind, as if that will banish the tendrils of fear coursing through my limbs and settling in my chest. Suddenly, the sounds of screams are drowned out by the rushing in my ears and it's hard to breathe. The only way I've been able to keep going lately is by compartmentalizing what I need to know and benching the rest. But Ghost is right. We're all doomed regardless. And I'm putting them in harm's way just by being nearby.

"Don't you dare," Pyro growls into my ear, making me flinch. "Don't even think about running away from us. I can feel it in your stance, you're getting ready to bolt." I realize then my knees are slightly bent and my fists are clenched. His arms band around me like restraints, holding me in place. Taking a long stride forward, Ghost sandwiches me between the two of them and cocks his head. All jokes aside, there's a dare in his white eyes.

"There's nowhere you could go that I won't find you," he threatens. Raising a hand, he catches the tear that escapes my eye and I drop my forehead against his chest.

"So we're all fucked, then" I sigh in defeat. There's no use arguing. They've made up their mind and now any point in fleeing seems pointless. Both of them would only get themselves killed coming after me.

"Completely and utterly fucked," Ghost agrees, resting his chin on my head.

"And together," Pyro adds. I smirk despite myself as he leans into my back.

"Not yet," I mutter. Linking my fingers on one hand with Pyro's at my side and the other curling around Ghost's waist, we stand there for a moment, drawing comfort from each other. "Once we have Hoax, the rest won't matter." A screech shatters through us, breaking our bond as we hunt for the source. Sitting on an archway a few feet away, the parrot drone squawks again. I narrow my eyes at it, sure it's the same one from before. The zoom of its camera lens eye focuses on me, its beak opening to release yet another god-awful scream. This time though, its call is answered by the reverberating whack of the bull crashing into view.

"I think we made it mad," Ghost whispers. His ability washes over us but something about the glowing purple eyes of the bull fills me with unease. I'm missing the obvious here, but I believe I'm about to find out what exactly that is.

The bull charges forward, blowing smoke from its nostrils and grunting like a boar. The squeak in its joints are at odds with the animalistic way its huge head sways back and forth as it runs. We remain stationary, waiting for the bull to pass through us, hopefully it gets bored and trot off. Mania tenses but over her head, Ghost has already begun laughing at the robot's attempt to scare us.

Just as it reaches our feet, the bull abruptly stops and smashes its hooves into the ground. Over and over again. Weary of its strange behavior, I begin to pull Mania and Ghost away when the stone at our feet cracks. Or rather, the stone beneath Ghost. The same purple lava we nearly fell into before surges upward in a wave with one lone electric eel soaring through the middle. Bolts of lightning burst from its snake-like body, the current powerful enough to knock Ghost's ability off course for a split second. But that's all it needed. Circuit wires shoot out from the walls, wrapping around my arms and whipping me off my feet. My back slams into the wall, causing agony to temporarily blind me.

Ghost goes next, his yell forcing my eyelids open. Pinned to the opposite wall, his body jerks against a constant flow of electricity pulsing through him. His body flickers as he struggles against the punishing hold, a frustrated growl ripping from his throat. And in the center of it all, Mania stands alone and terrified, facing off with a mechanical bull twice her size. A cloud of smoke huffs from its nostrils, enveloping her in a warning.

"Run!" I scream at the same time as Ghost shouts "Don't move!" The smoke clears for her indecision to become clear, her fingers trembling but she dares not take her eyes off the purple ones glowing down at her.

"Stay calm and close your eyes," Ghost says calmer this time. "Bulls are triggered by the color red, that's all this is." I'm not sure who he's trying to convince but it sure as shit isn't any of us.

"It's electronic, you fucking idiot! Consider it triggered because that's what's it's damn programming tells it to be," I grit out, struggling against the wires. The hefty, metal head tilts and turns towards me, the pointed ear beneath a chrome horn shifting. Is it... listening to me? Sensing her widened red eyes flicking in my direction, I jerk my head in a 'get the fuck out of here' gesture while addressing the bull directly.

"Yeah, that's right. You're nothing but a piece of machinery, a colossal chunk of computer crap." I try to kick my leg out, intent on planting my foot in its face if it weren't for the wire snaking around my knee. Ghost groans, his drawl meeting my ears.

"Smack talk really isn't your forte Py," he rolls his eyes through the zaps of electricity thrumming through him. The bull's head rears his way and Mania risks a few slow steps backwards.

"You think you can do a better job, be my fucking guest," I seethe. Even when we're both in deep shit, Ghost can't help but prove how much better than me he is at bloody everything. Most of all, keeping his cool when I'm ready to detonate.

"Hey, you motorized rodeo," Ghost chuckles and Mania shifts back further. "There's dildos out there with more hardwiring than you." He smirks despite the clench to his jaw.

"Oh yes," I agree with heavy sarcasm. "That was so much better." A wire wriggles up my body, closing around my throat as the bull whips his purple eyes back on me. The way it regards me is too lifelike and unnerving as shit, but I'll take the brunt of his attention as long as Mania keeps moving. The cord tightens, cutting off my airway and I swear the bull shifts its head enough to reveal the hint of a smirk.

Darting my eyes away, I just see Mania disappear around a bend and chuckle to myself. Raising my middle finger, the bull roars through its speaker and charges at me. The full weight of his head rams into my middle, his horns penetrating the wall either side of my trapped arms and in the next moment, it's gone. The vines release and I fall to the ground, choking on the pain carving me in two. My temple connects with the stone, instantly heating with the slice of oozing blood. Thundering hooves hammer through my skull as the bull chases after my girl, yet I can't move.

Without giving me time to recover, a hand grips my wrist with an instant electric shock before dragging me forward. Ghost pulls me into him, cradling me in his lap like a child. If I were semi-in my right mind, I'd shove away his hands from lifting my t-shirt to check me over. I'd refuse his help and fight against his overbearing affection, but that's Ghost all over. Full of shit and never serious, but his heart is pure. I was wrong to doubt his loyalty, knowing deep down once Ghost accepts you as his kin, his claws are in for good. Peeling my eyes open, I dismiss the pain in favor of muttering one word.

"Mania." He nods once in understanding, pulling us up to our feet. We're beyond the point of cliché. She's all that matters. From broken boys to damaged men, the three of us have been close but fractured all these years until she brought us together. Completed our bond in ways I still don't understand, but I need to. Putting one limp foot in front of the other, with Ghost holding me up despite his limp, we push onwards. Each step is sluggish and full of protest, but it's a step closer to her. Wherever she is.

"Woah there," Ghost heeds for the tenth time as I stumble into him yet again. Somehow, even with the live static radiating from his skin, keeping the hairs all over my body standing on end, Ghost has recovered much quicker than I have. It's not just the raw ache in my abdomen of where the bull rammed into me. The bones in my legs feel like they're going to snap with each step, breaking free of my shins. In fact, the growing tension riding through my knee caps causes me to whimper and I begin to beg for the release.

"I...fuck, Ghost, I can't," I choke past the sob trapped in my throat. My ankle rolls and I collapse, hitting the ground hard. Ghost fumbles to catch me but there's no use. Crouching down, he holds my face in his hands, filling my vision with his furrowed brows. "Something's not right. You need to go." I shove at his chest, ignoring the way he's already shaking his head. "Ghost! Go get our girl and come back for me. I need to wait out whatever's wrong with my legs." Instead of moving, his white eyes flash and a satisfied grin takes residence on his face.

"Say it again." I frown, confused until it clicks into place. That was the first time I've openly agreed to share Mania as ours. Growling, I push at his shoulders, refusing to get into this now when she's out there somewhere in danger.

"I swear if you don't go right now, I'll find a way to burn your dick off and then she'll never want you again either way." Ghost chuckles, standing slowly.

"For once Py-face, I don't think my dick is the only thing keeping her interested." He winks and salutes me, as if I'm not writhing on the floor in pain and he's got all the time in the world. Strolling away, faint purple tendrils still snake around his limbs like glow worms disappearing into his shirt sleeves. "Even though it is a huge advantage. Fucking massive, actually." His voice fades out as he moves further into the maze, leaving me with the echo of his laughter. I shake my head at myself, cursing him out under my breath.

Slowly, I stretch my legs outward and hiss at the pain that flares up at the smallest of movements. The more I try to shift the circulation to my feet, the less they move altogether. Throwing my head back against the wall with a snarl, whirring sounds and a glint of silver drops down beside me. I shoo the mechanical parrot away to no avail, its camera lens eyes shifting to focus on my face.

"I've had my fill of fucking robots for today." I growl. Jerking its head, the parrot's metallic beak opens to reveal the speaker hidden inside.

"And here I was thinking you'd appreciate the company, my boy,"

Christopher's voice leaks from the offensive creature. I squeeze my eyes shut, pinching the bridge of my nose. My day just got a thousand times worse. "It's comical watching you try to continue when it's so obvious what's happening. Actually, scratch that. It's rather pitiful."

"What the fuck are you taking about?" I growl, sick of this conversation, this game, this constant bullshit of always being kept in the dark. Yet I can't bring myself to ignore his goading. Maybe one of the bullshit snippets of knowledge Christopher imparts on me could present a clue I need.

"She stole your fires, Pyro. Before you gave me whatever was left, which was only enough for one use by the way." I scoff at his tone, noting the hint of hurt he fakes. "The more powerful she becomes, the weaker you will be. Seems like all I need to do is keep giving Mania reasons to tap into your fires and you'll regret ever turning your back on me. We could have been quite the team-"

"Fuck your team," I cut him off. Willing my legs to move results in jackshit, so I take to punching the parrot instead. My hand came off worse for sure, but the propellers beneath its wings whirl and it takes off, a haunting laugh trailing behind. I swallow thickly, realizing the upper half of my body has grown stiff. Trying to lift my arms, they remain flopped by my sides. But I don't fret. In my self-induced coma, I see everything so clearly now. My fires aren't gone; they've simply transferred into Mania in her times of need. Christopher may have taken what was left but there's still a chance they can save her. They have to, otherwise my very existence has been for nothing.

Lungs burning, legs pumping, I keep running even when I'm sure there's nothing behind me. Grates slam down in front of me, steering me whichever way the maze sees fit and to that end, I can never be safe. Rising heat, that has nothing to do with exertion, wells within me until I'm puffing on smoke. My vision slips in and out from Pyro's, spotting the parrot drone beside his legs. His rage clogs my throat as he punches the damn robot, causing a shock of agony to shoot through my own knuckles. Gasping, I jolt back into myself just before I slam into a wall. Pressing my palms on the cool surface, I take a moment to collect my thoughts. I can't keep going blindly, not knowing what I'm looking for. Just a way to continue surviving I suppose, which isn't much different from the way I grew up.

Spinning around, I find myself trapped in another passageway with a grate at the far end. One, lone archway sits halfway down, allowing the hum of other people to drift outwards. Relief and worry hinder my cautious steps as I near. Peering around the opening, an electrical vine lashes me in the ass and I jolt inside. The wall instantly slams down to lock me inside, not that I bother trying to escape. My eyes are locked on a pair of glowing, indigo ones across the huge chasm. Hoax hasn't moved a muscle since I last saw him here, standing tall and protected on the stone stage.

The handful of Mutes before me run from side to side, most of them I recognize. Claire's brunette braid swishing as she struggles to keep up with Tate, a pair of yellow-slitted eyes peering out from the cradle of Summon's arms and even glowing magma veins from the Blacksmith's bronzed arms. Camo jumps out of the metal thanks to a jolt of electricity from the sparking cables trying to entrap him. Ammo is among the survivors as well, slamming her stubs against the wall and screaming to get out. I can't make sense of what's happening until a grate across the far side rises and the mechanical bull steps inside. Shit.

Its purple, glowing eyes seem to find me among those rushing in between and that's when I see the slight tilt to its head, at the exact moment Hoax does the same action. His gaze is curious and unsure, yet with a flick of his wrist, the bull takes a step forward. I gasp, taking in the purple sparks of cables, the pulsing lilac liquid between the cracks in the ground. It's him. It's all him.

The bull takes another menacing step forward and my breath locks in my lungs. Then he charges. With nowhere to hide and no other bright ideas, I dart through the eruption of chaos, heading for the stage. I have to get to Hoax, convince him to stop this. Thundering hooves collide with the stone, shaking the ground beneath my feet. Smoke plumes from the bull's nostrils, all for show but just as menacing. I don't stop moving, because I'd be as much as a target standing still, but as he nears close enough for his horn to graze my bicep, a scream is torn from my throat.

"I don't think so, Chrome dome," Ghost hollers, slamming into the bull's side. The metallic body splutters in and out of transparency, luckily just long enough for me to pass through the center unscathed. Ghost, however, skids across the ground, writhe with pulsing electrical currents claiming his body. I hesitate to go back for him, but the bull recovers much too quickly. Spinning with renewed fury in its gleaming eyes, I'm running before the first crackled roar slices through the air like a thousand bullets.

Leaping onto the side of the stage, I clamber up the side as quickly as my skeletal limbs will allow. The rock crumbles beneath my finger when the bull collides with a spot my feet just moved from. I falter, slipping enough to slam a boot into the bull's head and boost myself back up.

"Hoax!" I cry out. "Hoax! It's me, Mania. I'm coming to save you!" My fingers graze the top of the stage and I flip myself over the ledge, panting heavily. Screams pull my attention to the Mutes down below. The bull has changed course, heading directly for those stupid enough to have their backs pinned to the walls. Cables snake out, wrapping around their bodies and locking them in place. Standing tall in the center, Ghost holds his hand up to beckon the bull towards him and I curse his name. Charging straight ahead, the bull passes through his body until a surge of electricity seizes him, causing his foot to get stuck halfway through the bull's hind leg. I roll my eyes at his shouts, sparing his flailing arms one last glance before turning to the one controlling the maze.

"Hoax," I call again. He continues to ignore me so I take a small step forward, conscious of the shimmering force field he's contained within. Looking around for a way in, or maybe a loophole when my gaze lands on Tate. Tied to the wall, her hand is clutched to Claire's as the pair face each other, their foreheads pressed together. "Tate!" I scream and her head snaps to me. "It's all Hoax! You need to deplete his ability!" That was probably the wrong thing to shout, as Hoax's eyes lazily turn to meet mine.

"I'm too far away!" Tate's reply comes but I dare not look away from the Mute I've longed to be this close to since the day he first appeared in my life.

"Then lower the force field long enough for me to get in!" I shout back. A moment passes where I know she's looking at me like I'm insane so I spare a brief glare her way. "Do it!" Tate releases Claire, raising her hand. Cables lash out in an effort to restrain her, but not before the bubble around Hoax wobbles. A second more and I see my opening, a tear down the side just big enough for a tiny body to slip through. AKA, me. Diving inside, the force field closes at my back and I crash into Hoax's chest.

Topless, tattooed and oh so tasty. Somehow I'd forgotten the firmness of his chest, the rhythmic beat of his heart and the electrifying energy that radiates from him. I brace my hands on his pecs, marveling at the warmth and firmness that greets me. It's been months since I've seen him this close, never mind being able to touch him. The time I spent with him in hell only served to deepen my desire and make me crave the sweet male who watched over me. But it's the time without him that's proven how I truly felt about Hoax. I fell for him the moment he appeared in my hospital room and now we're back together, I know in my heart it's all going to be okay.

"Please, stop this," I beg him, peering up into his purple eyes. "We're together again now. Me, you, Pyro and Ghost. We can get out of here, start somewhere new." His jaw remains tight, the glow in his eyes dimming back to their usual indigo hue. Slowly raising a hand, Hoax touches at the skull tattoo on my bare shoulder. He traces the outline absentmindedly, no doubt remembering the day Canvas gave me my ink and unknowingly linked me to the three of them. I sigh at the contact of his fingertips trailing from the neckline of the shirtdress to the back of my neck and I smile at long last. Tilting my head and pushing up on my tiptoes, our lips are a breath apart as he continues to stroke my nape.

"Starting new sounds good," he mutters and I nod. Wrapping my arms around his waist, I use Hoax as the anchor to save me from myself. Everything about Hoax, from his scent to his strength makes me swoon. Moistening my lips, I prepare for his mouth to ascend on mine. "But I have no idea who this 'Hoax' is."

My brain doesn't have time to wrap around his words as the hand on my nape tightens and a bolt of electricity erupts from his palm. Agony, fully-fledged and crippling, claims my body. I slam my cheek against his hard chest, using him as the crutch to keep me uptight. When he twists away, I cling on to Hoax as tightly as I can, refusing to be tossed aside. Through slitted eyes, I squint at the inside of the force field. Images from all around the maze stare back at me, giving Hoax a personal insight as to where everyone is. Although, there's barely anyone left outside the chasm other than Pyro. Somehow reading my mind, Hoax reaches out and taps a finger on the image of Pyro lying helplessly on the ground. At his touch, the ground cracks open, consuming my flame-haired soul mate in one, swift movement.

"No!" I scream. "Why are you doing this?!" The first tear rolling down my cheek opening the floodgates for all the others. I keep my grip tight, refusing to let go as I scan the images through watery eyes. This can't be all of it, just the areas we've been shepherded into like cattle. At the top, the outline of a building sends chills through my body before I've fully registered what it is. Pain explodes at my back where Hoax has rammed me into his force field. The tick in his jaw betrays the anger in his eyes. It's not me he's battling with, but himself. Instead of releasing him as he'd hoped, I knot my fingers together at his back and with one sharp tug, knock him off balance. Hoax catches his footing before we both fall but that was exactly my intention.

"I'm not leaving here without you," I say quietly, placing a kiss to his surprised brow. Then, I yank us both over the edge.

GHOST

Sparks burst from the top of the stage as the clear dome Hoax was shielded in shatters. I watch the pair of them sail towards the ground at top speed, unable to do anything as the bull continues to drag me along. It slams into the wall where I reach out, grabbing onto a cable. Before it moves again, I twist the cable around my arm, the sparking end held tightly in my hand. The head of the robot shifts aside, looking for its next victim and I jam the sparking wires into the crevice at its neck. The roar it releases is freakishly lifelike, the watts of electricity raking from its body into mine. I embrace the pain, focusing on my ability until I'm able to shift the density of my foot enough to pry it free from the metal leg. Only then am I able to scramble upright and see what has become of Mania and Hoax.

The Blacksmith is standing a small distance away, a web of metal chainmail extending from his hands. Mania rolls out of the net unscathed, albeit holding her head and swaying slightly. Hoax is right behind, his eyes glowing twice as bright and his hand raised. The bull reacts immediately, making a beeline for Mania who is still blinking away her haze.

"Blacksmith! The bull!" I shout, taking off after the robot.

Retracting his web, the Blacksmith turns his head and shares a nod with me. With an outstretched hand, a metal chain whips towards me and I manage to catch it, despite the lash against my forearm almost making me drop the blunt end. I skid to a stop, holding the chain tight with the Blacksmith on the other side and the bull slams into it. It's no real surprise I'm whipped off my feet and dragged across the ground, although the scene of stopping and lassoing the bull looked cool in my head. Instead of wasting more time on my heroic fantasies, the Blacksmith extends a metallic cord around Mania's waist and whips her out of the way just before the bull chases into her. I, however, release my chain and skid to a stop, directly in front of Hoax's feet.

"Hey buddy! Good to see-" Hoax's feet slam down on my chest, catching me off guard. I heave out a cough, recovering quickly enough to grab his ankle and whip him down to the ground beside me. I draw him into the strongest of bear hugs, just needing a moment to embrace him before I kick his ass.

"Why does-" Hoax struggles against my chest, "-everyone keep hugging me?" His teeth are gritted, his lithe body wriggling free far too soon.

"Because we love you dude. Remember love?" I rap my knuckles on his forehead, hoping someone is home. By the blank stare I receive back, evidently not. The ground beneath us cracks, giving the electric eels swimming through the purple-tinted waters room to leap upwards and bite my ass. "What's up with these rapey eels man?! They're obsessed with me. Unless this is some repressed attraction you've been hiding from me; I can't say I'm surprised."

This time, I'm sure I earnt the punch to my face but can't withhold a chuckle as Hoax straddles me. His fist comes down again and I buck my hips, knocking him too far forward for it to have any impact on the top of my head. Mania skids down by our side, grabbing both mine and Hoax's hands in hers.

"Get us out of here, Ghost. We need to get to Pyro." Her blood-red eyes are filled with concern and my smirk drops. Hoax shoves himself away from the pair of us, holding out his hand as the bull charges past. Gripping onto the end of the loose chain still stuck around its neck, Hoax is yanked upright from the ground. With a few calculated steps and a leap, the purple-spiraling chain draws him gracefully up on the bull's back.

"Motherfucker!" I yell, pulling Mania up with more care than I thought I could muster. "I wanted to look that cool!"

"How about we worry about staying alive first? Then you'll look so freaking awesome when we're torturing Christopher."

"Deal." Tucking her under my arm, we make a run for the nearest wall. I can't depend on my ability working but my girl needs me, so I'll be damned if I'm not going to try. Mania digs in her heels and ducks out of my hold, leveling me with a stern glare.

"We can't leave without Hoax. We might not be able to find him again." Her eyes hold mine and despite the refusal on the tip of my tongue, I know she's right. The heavy footfalls grow closer and instead of relying on my ability, I shove Mania backwards and hope for the best. My body's density falters at the last possible second, allowing me to pass through the bull. I breathe out a sigh of relief, then realize I've just shoved my girlfriend to the ground for no reason. Picking her back up, I press a quick, forgiving kiss to the top of her head.

"Well he's busy trying to kill us at the moment. What would you propose we do to get him out of here?" Mania's eyes dart around, full of renewed determination. It's a hot look on her, one I look forward to seeing while she ties me up and teases me to insanity later. Wishful thinking and all that. She calls out, pointing over at the pathetic pair who have been strapped to the wall and enjoying the show since I arrived. I groan, but keep our fingers linked to follow her anyway, all the way to Tate and Claire's panicked eyes.

"You're up, bitch tits," I state, trying to pry at the cables cutting into their flesh. It doesn't escape me that they have been placed in such a way, not to damage any vital organs or to cut off their breathing. Either Hoax has a soft spot somewhere deep, deep down or he's only hellbent on killing the ones here to save him.

"Here," the Blacksmith drawls, growing an ax from his hand. Cutting the females down, he turns his smoldering eyes on me. "Thanks for leaving me for dead, asshole."

"I wasn't exactly reclining on a beach and sipping margaritas myself, asshole. Once we left that shelter, the maze had no intention of letting us find it again."

"Just get us the fuck out of here and we'll call it even," he states with the hint of a smirk. The Blacksmith is as much a realist as me, but the thought of escaping is a pretty dream. One that we'll strive for until our last breath. The bull comes for us again, its hooves wearing down the stone under the sheer weight of crashing metal. And at the top, like king of the fucking world, is my brother. The bull rears up, slamming down and this time, the ground shatters beneath it. They recover quickly, jumping aside as a thick crack heads straight towards us. We jump for cover in all directions as the crack passes and climbs the wall we just freed the females from. Crumbling rock and metal tumble down like rain from the darkened sky, almost drowning out the small cry of help that reaches my ears.

I hunt for the source, clambering forward to peer into the crack. A hand slips beneath the purple crashing waves roaring below, but not before I spot the skull tattoo inked on the back. Without thinking it through, I throw myself into the liquid, diving into its darkened depths. The eels find me instantly, their bodies lighting the way with each spark of electricity thrown into my sides. I take the brunt of pain as long as they continue to illuminate the body slipping lifelessly away. Bubbles escape my mouth as I keep pushing myself downwards, kicking my legs despite the scream in my lungs to turn back.

My hand grips the back of Pyro's t-shirt and I instantly spin back on myself. Dragging him back to the surface, the purple hue begins to fade to black and my legs lose the power needed to get us the last few inches. My fingers grace the freedom of cool air before the liquid tosses me aside. Crashing into the rock, my grip on Pyro slips and after a quick gasp of air, I'm back down after him. This time I wrap my arms around him, kicking with every last drop of energy I don't have until we breach the surface.

"Little help down here!" I yell. Help of the wrong kind descends in a length of sparking cable, snaking down the rock face. I start to back away from it when a head pops into vision up above, her black and red hair flying around her erratically.

"Grab on!" Mania calls. I open my mouth to protest when the

Blacksmith moves into view and I do as I'm told. He helps Mania heave us out of the gloopy liquid as the eels leap in an effort to get me one last time. Using my feet, I help scramble up the rock with Pyro laying uselessly over my shoulder. I flop him down on a ledge a few feet below ground level, beckoning the others to hop down out of direct sight of the bull I can still hear charging around. Mania, the Blacksmith, Tate, Claire and a few others I don't recognize heed my advice, filling the ledge on crouched feet. Mania takes over with Pyro, giving him mouth-to-mouth while I get to work pumping his chest. After a few tense moments, nothing happens and I thump my fist down on his chest instead.

"Ghost!" Mania barks, clicking her fingers for me to continue giving him CPR.

"I'm so sick of losing one of you. You have his fires, spark that eternal flame shit already so it doesn't matter if he dies or not. He'll just bounce back either way." The death stare I receive should have skinned me alive as Mania also sits back on her heels and sighs.

"Does this look like I just 'bounced back'? I've been dying inside since I was eight years old. My senses dulled so much, I couldn't even connect with my own emotions." Her red eyes flick towards the purple sloshing liquid below but not before I see the tears gathering there. "Even if I could create this everlasting bond like he did, I wouldn't know how."

"Just love him," I shrug and her head snaps back to me. This time I reckon she's going to hit me, although the mixture of hate and sorrow in her stare is enough to shred me open anyway.

"I do fucking love him!" she snaps. A bald male with leathery skin hushes her, his head bobbing up and down like a meerkat to see what's going on above the surface. If it wasn't for the small girl huddled in his arms, I'd be adding him to my shit list for that alone.

"Obviously not enough. Love harder!" I coax the anger out of her since that's what always worked for Py. I never thought I'd be arguing with my girl about loving my brother with more vigor than I know she has for me, but we're beyond possession now. She's ours, for as long as we have left. Mania growls deep in her chest, directly where an orange glow begins to shine beneath her t-shirtdress. The next time she blinks, there's a flame dancing in her eyes and I smirk. This is the answer to everything. If I know Mania and Py are bonded again and their deaths aren't at the forefront of my mind, I can concentrate on getting us out of here. They're the true soul mates, the ones who set us all on this path. At this point, Hoax and I are afterthoughts.

Bracing herself on Pyro's chest, the flames in Mania's eyes are unleashed by her tears. They swirl a dramatic pattern around each other, like the two entities Mania and Pyro are, always tethering on the edge of joining together. My hand twitches to reach out and take it, hoarding Mania's love for myself but my selfish days are behind me. Even if this cements them as soul mates and I'm forever on the outside looking in, I'll take it. Wow. I never thought I'd see the day I put others before myself, and I can't wait for Py to wake up so I can rub it in his face. The flames near his chest so I rip his shirt open, giving them full access to bury into his heart. Skating across the top of his skin, I reach out to grab Mania's hand and give her a nod of my head. No more waiting, do it.

"Wait!" Claire pipes up. The fires die an instant death so close to entering Pyro, the glow remains reflected on his pale skin for a beat before disappearing completely. I snarl at the brunette, who I hadn't noticed had snuck forward to clasp Pyro's temples between her hands. "The more you use his fires, the more you're hurting him." Mania rips her hand from mine, slapping them on her thighs with a groan.

"What the fuck am I supposed to do with that?!" she screams at the sky and I agree with her sentiment. Just in case the big fella upstairs is sneering down at the abominations maring his perfect planet, I toss up my middle finger in solidarity. It's then I realize no sound is coming from the chasm overhead, except for the whirring drone-parrot hovering nearby and watching our every action, so I point a finger up at the noisy, bald Mute to have a look.

After passing the child to Claire, he peers out of our hiding place just as a lilac, holographic scythe slices through his neck with frightening accuracy. There's nothing holographic about the way his head departs from his body though, dropping into the liquid below before his body tips aside and follows. A trio of female screams cuts the air in two before I can stop them.

"Keep working on Pyro, I'll handle this," I tell the Blacksmith through the cries. Raising my hands, fully expecting them to be sliced off at the wrists like Ammo's, nothing comes so I stand to gaze upon a blood-soaked Hoax with the bull patiently waiting at his back.

"Look man, I know we've had our differences and all. I'm, well me, and you've got that whole broody tech nerd thing going on." I pull myself up from the ledge until we are eye level. "But we're trying to save you while you kill us off. What's the end goal here? What are you gonna do when you're the only one left, stuck in this huge maze by yourself?"

Hoax's blank expression doesn't change, his grip on the opaque scythe not faltering. The tatts I once ridiculed him for stand strong now, putting on the front he's more machine than man while his glowing eyes assess me like a stranger. I nod to myself, understanding now. If it looks like a duck and quacks like a drone, he's a goner. Another empty vessel being used for Christopher's gain, and to that end, he is thoroughly lost to us.

Quickly glancing around the chasm, beyond the blood and spare limbs lying around, I spot the archways are now open again. With enough of a distraction, there's a chance the others could escape and find a way to wake up Pyro. Clicking my fingers behind my back at the Blacksmith, I point to the exit and really hope he's got the message as I sink my fist into Hoax's nose. He stutters back in surprise, the scythe blinking in and out of sight. I take my chance, grabbing his wrist and spinning him by the arm now trapped at his back. Smoke pours from the bull's nostrils, giving those scuffling to their feet behind me a curtain of cover.

"I'm really sorry about this bud. I promise, this will hurt me way more than it'll hurt you." I apply a little more pressure to Hoax's wrist until the bone snaps with an echoing crack. Even I wince, thankful the bone didn't break the skin or I might have just gagged. Hoax, though, doesn't even flinch. Wrenching his arm back further, I shove him into his bull and quickly turn to help lift Pyro from the crater. Mania hesitates, her hand on my arm but I push her to follow Claire and Tate.

Bringing my attention back to Hoax, cables shoot from the ground and encase my arms behind my back. I struggle uselessly as he rounds on me, his eyes flashing in and out of focus as if he's a hologram himself.

"Don't you think it's ironic that the shithead who can internally fix any device on the planet is now being used as one and can't even fix his damn self?" I groan, the cords tightening. My fingers tingle as all of the blood drains from my arms.

"You talk too much," he grunts, leveling a kick into my gut. I stumble back, fully preparing myself to fall into the crater when a pair of small hands on my back stop my fall. Steadying me, she works to free my arms and jerks the slithering wires away from us. Hoax doesn't react to her presence other than a slight head tilt that the bull mimics. Me, though, I'm furious.

"I told you to go," I grit out through clenched teeth. Hoax takes a step forward and I push her behind my back, sidestepping the pair of us away from the opening in the ground.

"If he'd have wanted us dead, we would be by now," Mania whispers. Her hands remain on my shoulder blades, using me as a shield. "We can still save him." I shake my head, walking her backwards now. Hoax and his bull follow us step for step, a cruel smile tilting up his lips and confirming my suspicions. He can't be saved because he isn't my brother. Not anymore.

"I promised Py I'd save you, and that's exactly what I'm going to do," I say over my shoulder. Before she can answer, I dive into Hoax, knocking him to the ground. "Now run!" My fists smash into his face, each time coming back with more blood coating my knuckles. A vine snakes around my neck, choking me back but I refuse to be dislodged. I keep pounding any flesh I can reach before the vine yanks me back again. Bringing my foot around, I thank the Minotaur once again for the gift of shoes and kick Hoax's temple. His eyes dim before they flutter closed and the vine drops away. I pat his cheek, wishing him sweet dreams when the rasping of my name meets my ears and it's at that moment, I realize the bull is gone.

A gasped name torn from my throat. Haze claiming my vision. Blazing pain rooted in my sternum. That's all I know until I lift my hands to my abdomen and feel the thick bull's horn skewering me into the wall. My hands come away sticky and covered in red, pulling another shocked whimper from me. After everything we've been through, this is it. My final moments on Earth. Still seeing double, I glance around at the scene, trying to make sense of the sounds hammering through the pounding in my ears. There's screaming I can't place, a mechanical sound from the beast pinning me upright, yet the tiny voice of my subconscious seems louder than it all. I failed.

My head lolls aside, the warm line spilling from my mouth and dropping crimson down my shirtdress not a good sign. The bull judders, drawing another scream from me as it jerks and collapses, taking me down with it. The horn is wrenched free and in its place, a pair of hands try to cover the wound. White eyes flare with worry before Ghost rips his t-shirt off and presses the material onto my abdomen.

"Ghost," I reach for him.

"Stay with me Spitfire, I'll fix this. I'll-" he fumbles, alternating between applying pressure to my abdomen and stroking a blood-covered hand across my cheek.

"It's okay," I fake a small smile. "We did our best."

"No, no, no! Don't talk like that." His head lowers to my chest, mumbling words I can't make out. I drop a hand into his hair, stroking the longer part just like the night we arrived in the labyrinth. We'd laid just like this, with his body over mine waiting for the monsters to creep out of the dark and consume us. I knew then we weren't the masters of our own fate. We never stood a chance when the man orchestrating our pain is holding all of the cards. And in the middle of it all, we tried to find romance and love. Scratch that, we did find love and it was worth every moment of suffering just to know someone will mourn me when I'm gone. That I mattered enough to leave a scar on not just one, but three hearts if Hoax's spirit counts too.

"Ghost," I say again, bringing his white eyes back to me. "It was easy to fall for Pyro and Hoax, but you," I splutter on the coppery taste filling my mouth. "I never saw you coming." My eyelids close and Ghost shakes me vigorously.

"Hey, you can't go. There's something I need to say." I smirk, wanting to tell him I'm not surprised but the words don't seem to come out. Curling me into his arms and pulling me into his firm chest, I tilt my ear to hear his next words. I want them to be embedded in my soul and with me for all eternity wherever I end up. "You're the hottest corpse I've ever had."

The laughter that rocks my core sends a fresh wave of pain hurtling towards my wound, ending my chuckle with a sharp hiss. Through cracked eyelids, I see Ghost's smirk drop to a frown again.

"Smile for me Ghost," I beg. "Let your smile be the last thing I see." Ghost complies, despite the sadness filling his eyes. Gripping onto his biceps, I snuggle further into his chest. "I fucking love you, shithead." His chuckle fills my head, easing me into the afterlife as his words fade out. After all, dying is what I do best.

"I love you Spitfire. More than-"

PYRO

I jolt upright on a strangled shout. A red layer hindering my vision, the taste of ash coating the back of my throat. I pull myself upright, fists clenched and anger burning. No, not just my anger. *I'm* burning. Flames dance around my arms, caressing my muscles and seeping inside. The depths of my core ignite and I take my first, contented breath for too long. I'm back. But something's missing.

I can make out the silhouettes of figures all around, my mind screaming to defend myself from an impending attack. Base instinct veers me onward, fanning the flames coating my skin. I welcome its warmth, embracing the fires that have finally returned to me.

"Hey, hey! Cool it Pyro, it's us," a voice says to my left. I twist to make out the raised palms, my first instinct to set fire to the lengthy digits I spot, but something holds me back. I shake my head, blinking quickly to clear my eyes of the red curtain hovering there. Slowly, the Blacksmith's face comes into focus with Tate and Claire peering out from behind him. Snuggled in Claire's arms, a small girl turns her pair of yellow-slitted eyes on me. Her forked tongue flicks out, beckoning me forward to stroke my thumb over her cheek. A tear falls as I do, moistening my knuckles while I do a quick headcount.

"Where's Mania and Ghost?" I ask, the dulled flames kicking back up a notch so I quickly withdraw my hand.

"Cool it, flame boy. We're here," Ghost walks up behind me and I sigh in relief. Spinning around, the sight before me is anything but relieving. With Hoax thrown over one shoulder, Mania cradled in his arms and a trio of parrot drones hovering behind, I stand open-mouthed while Tate rushes forward. She rounds Ghost, pressing a hand on Hoax's back while I lift Mania into my arms.

"What happened?" I ask, failing to find a heartbeat in her chest.

"Too much," is the only answer I get. Water instantly wells in my eyes, burning an acidic path down my cheek. Ghost lashes a hand out, catching the rogue tears in his palm before they drop onto her, maring her perfectly porcelain skin. Instead, they burn holes into Ghost, who reaches up to wipe the rest away from my face. Mania's red hair has fallen over her face but I dare not shift them in fear I can't control my renewed flames. It's taking all my control to simply hold her close to me.

Hoax stirs, causing Tate to step away as Ghost drops him heavily to the ground. The Blacksmith steps in without being asked, binding Hoax in a thick chain that grows from his hand. Opening his glowing, purple eyes, Hoax attempts to call the cables hanging limply on the walls to his aid but Tate's done a number on him. Claire relaxes, stepping into our circle and whispers reassuring words to the whimpering child in her arms. I suppose we're all that's left of the labyrinth. Ghost heaves Hoax up to his feet, throwing an arm over his shoulder while punching him in the gut.

"I'm never going to stop punishing you for what you've done here today, whether you were acting on someone else's behalf or not." Hoax shoves at him, clearly hating being held so Ghost tightens his grip. The scene is as necessary as it is ridiculous, and I'm done. Growing a fiery whip from my hand, I slash the parrot drones in half in one smooth lashing. Metal drops out of the sky and for good measure, I ignite a path of flame to melt down the remaining pieces.

"Is your ability working?" I ask Ghost without looking at him. I can't take my eyes off the female lying in my arms. The one who should have been mine. My soul mate. My lifeline. My queen. Ghost grunts in confirmation and I now raise my face. Pressing my forehead against his, I mutter at him to get the others out of here without taking no for an answer.

"Py, don't be stupid-" Ghost starts and I cut him off with a glare.

"She's gone. Hoax is demented and I'm as broken as ever. This ends, right now."

"And what am I supposed to do? Sit around licking my own asshole while Hoax sits, chained up and forced to watch?" A shudder rolls down his spine at the visual image he's painted for himself and I roll my eyes. "Mania died for us to be together again. I say we return the favor and find her in hell." Hoax jerks at the idea but I simply shrug. Ghost is big and dumb enough to make his own decisions, and hopefully, we'll find Hoax's spirit down there to reconnect him with his body. Hoisting Mania higher to rest her head on my shoulder, I clasp the Blacksmith's shoulder.

"Take the women and the child, get them out of here. Run as quickly as you can, I can't hold off much longer." Even as I speak, the fury welling inside rises to a dangerous temperature. The muscled wall of my chest begins to peel away from the inside, flaying me internally as the tears come again. The Blacksmith passes over the chain to Hoax's restraints and gives me one, last nod. The group disappears around a corner and I close my eyes on a sigh. It's on him now, because fuck knows the four of us were never going to be allowed to leave together. This is the only way.

A hand curls around the back of my head as Ghost pulls me into his chest. The growing pressure of my flames makes it impossible to talk now, not that there's anything to be said. We're still those three lost boys, hunting for a family, for a place to belong. Yet, in my arms, here it is. Everything we hoped for. A reason to live and die for; the answer to our suffering. Wherever Mania is, I will never stop hunting for her. Never stop loving her. She's our missing piece, and if we can't have her alive, then she'll complete us in death.

MANÍA

I blink through patches of time. One moment I'm on the ground. The next, I'm moving. The sky is dark, then it's ablaze. Words don't register, places aren't recognizable. I'm placed down, picked up, passed from person to person. Warm chests against my cheek are at odds with the coldness of death sweeping through my being. I'm not alive, that much is clear. But something has me clinging on. Figures fade and blend, soon replaced with others.

I turn in on myself, hunting for solitude from the confusion. What I find instead, is a burning sphere. Pushing myself closer, curiosity flaring, I marvel at its beauty. The ball hovers in my subconscious, alight with flaming energy. Purple sparks dart in and out of an almost invisible circumference protecting the fires inside. As it spins on its axis, I note a hole directly in the center in the shape of a skull. Thick, black smoke begins to seep from the hole, spreading outwards in wispy tendrils. Almost instantly, the fire shrinks as the smoke stretches upwards, consuming the very flames of my soul.

My subconscious knows what's going to happen, even though rational thought is far from present. The fires will be distinguished and this time, it'll be for good. Not just for me, but for all of us, and that's something my heart can't let happen. Not when Pyro's flames have given me so much to live for. Love, a reason to live, a family. I scream inside my own head, a high-pitched sound that rocks the *fireball off balance. The purple sparks begin to glow brighter, linking to a circuit around the sphere in an effort of protection but it's useless. Black cracks delve deeper, splintering and suffocating from the inside. All the while, the ball slowly spins, hovering on the edge of my being. There has to be a reason it's appearing to me now; a way to save the sphere and ultimately, our eternal bond. The next time the skull-shaped hole turns around, I decide on what to do. I throw myself inside.*

Heat explodes across my body, my face protected by whoever is holding me. Prying my eyes open a crack, I see it's not just one person shielding me from the inferno raging overhead, but three of them. Rock and metal shatter all around, raining down on us like meteors. I squirm to get free but the grips on me are bruisingly tight, keeping me immobile. Groans of frustration leaks from my cracked lips, causing a pair of eyes above to shoot open. No, not eyes - orbs of smoldering, fiery coal. A fresh wave of fire bursts from Pyro's body and burns even hotter, making me wince even though the flames don't penetrate my skin.

Just like I saw in my half-dead state, a glowing sphere surrounds us. Pyro is the catalyst, radiating flames from vibrant oranges to luminescent blues. Staring at a point by their feet, Ghost's eyes have turned completely white as he shakes with the force of containing the fires, creating the dome overhead. On the outer layer, purple circuits connect like pulsating veins, solidifying us inside. They're combining their abilities to work together, and they're doing it for me.

Unable to speak, even if I knew what to say, I tentatively reach up to cup Pyro's cheek. My movement catches Ghost's attention too, his irises rolling back into position as he crushes the three of us tighter in his huge arms. Hoax stirs then and I realize he wasn't hanging his head in solidarity, but rather he was half-conscious. His dazed state must allow him to act from impulse rather than whatever brainwashed bullshit I see flare to life back in his glowing, indigo eyes. Bucking against the meaty chains holding him in place, Ghost quickly slams an elbow into the side of Hoax's head and he flops against Ghost's shoulder again.

"Can't...stop," Pyro grinds out, tensing as he tries to reel his fires back.

"Don't," Ghost replies for me. "This feels...right." I quirk my lips, nodding slightly through the fog still passing through my mind. A bitter, ashy taste in my mouth tells me this wasn't just a close call, but that I did actually die as I thought. Yet here I am.

Giving in to his fires once more, they expand in a raging tornado. Pyro throws his head back on a scream, his anguish piercing my heart and cracking it in two. A tendril of fire breaks off from the rest, curling in a pattern between the four of us. This flame then splits into four, shooting into each of our chests. I gasp in shock, the fire seeping into my heart and mending the years of fractures lingering there. Renewed power thrums through my body, providing me with a heady strength I've never known. I shove out of Pyro's grip this time, standing tall and slipping my hands into his and Ghost's. Chaos reigns all around, yet I feel more invincible than ever. The eternal flame. It has to be.

In one last effort, screaming upwards until his voice gives out, Pyro shoots his flames into the sky, shattering through Ghost's shield. The light soars into the darkness until only a speck is visible, then they explode. Giant fireworks of red, orange and yellow, one after the other. A smile grows wide across my face at the spectacle. I tilt my head back on a laugh while Ghost whoops and Pyro savages my body for another squeeze. I feel like he's going to take a while to let go and I'm fine with that. Even Hoax has stopped struggling, his dazed, indigo eyes trained on the large embers drifting back down towards us.

As they do, slashes of sunlight penetrate the dark sky, spearing the night like laser beams. My smile falters and I tug on Ghost to stop cheering. Instead of the ash I was expecting to gently trickle back to earth, the fires pick up speed, tumbling down like meteors. The first crashes just a few feet away, tearing a scream from my throat as the walls around us shake and begin to crumble. The ground judders beneath our feet, slicing open through the center of our huddle. I grab for Hoax, pulling him across the opening crack when he tries to duck the opposite way. Although, it's not a gaping hole I find underneath but grass.

"I don't like the look of this," Ghost mutters and I follow his eyeline. The crumbled walls have broken down into a sea of tiny stones that congregate together, flowing in a rocky river and leading away from us. We follow, needing to see where they're traveling to, despite the clawing of my gut telling me nothing good awaits there. With each step we take, the maze continues to disintegrate, but unlike before, not a single rock tries to attack us. It's almost as if the maze itself is…disappearing. We break into a run, desperate to see this is the end of the labyrinth. My heart hammers in my throat and I risk a glance upwards at the sunny blue sky sweeping across the horizon until there's no evidence of night left. The ground continues to soften until I skid to a stop, staring at the grass beneath my boots.

"Hoax," I call out so Ghost will stop dragging him along. "You saw everything from inside that bubble. What's happening?!" The cascading river of rocks is tuned out by the rumble of laughter and I spin around to see the last of the barriers come down around us. Right before my eyes, an oppressive, concrete building comes into view. A canopy hangs over several picnic benches, casting a shadow over the notice board pinned onto the wall. I look side to side, already knowing what I'll find but I need the confirmation. A basketball court to the right, a circular running track to the left. Abandoned gym equipment, empty bleachers and a tall, barbed fence. Minus the hordes of Mutes, it's all here. Afterlife. We've been in Afterlife Asylum this entire time.

The laughter grows from inside the doorway as Camo steps out, his arm around a grinning, bubblegum-haired Imp.

"I've waited so long to see your faces when you realize the truth. At one point, I thought you'd kill yourselves before I got the chance. Lucky me, I guess." Camo shrugs. White strips band across his nose from where Ghost and I went to town on his face, his cropped hair a duller color than its usual olive green. Like Imp, a gray tracksuit swamps his body.

"You won't be feeling lucky when I turn your chest cavity inside out," Ghost takes a step forward and I grab onto his forearm.

"Wait," I tell him. There's no way I'm not getting my answers after everything we've been through. "He obviously has a story to tell. Let us hear it, then he's all yours."

"Ahh, but it's not their story now, is it?" Christopher's voice booms from the speakers attached to the walls. I grit my teeth, glaring at the cameras staring our way. No doubt he's sitting in his guarded tower, feeling as invincible as ever. Camo waves a hand over the outer wall, allowing his ability to drop and reveal Tate and Claire being held by two Mutes. The one gripping Claire's mouth I've seen before, dragging the dead bodies into a heap to burn them to dust. The other is new to me. A huge stack of muscle with tattoos covering his head and stone-cold eyes. The tumbling rocks barrel his way, absorbing into his very skin and somehow making him bulkier. His grip on Tate is unmoving and she whimpers, her purple eyes locked with mine.

Beside them, the Blacksmith stands tall with Serpentina cradled in his arms. The three carry their prisoners inside, not a trace of sorrow in the Blacksmith's festering eyes. If I didn't know him better, I'd say he was a male without a trace of remorse. One who has been…broken. We run for the doors as they begin to close, ignoring the mocking laughter leaking out of the speakers, for them to slam in our faces. Ghost bangs his fist the loudest, trying to make his way inside but even his entry is barred by the undeniable glimmer of a forcefield. I swivel on the camera with fire flooding my veins.

"Come on then. Start talking you fucking asshole!" I spit. Pyro drags me back a step into his body, winding his arms around my front in an act of comfort. I don't want to be comforted through, I want to kill this taunting bastard for thinking he can own the Mute world and abuse it as he sees fit. The veins in Pyro's arms glow like magma has replaced his bloodstream and as I force myself to calm down, they dim back to normal.

"The premise is simple, yet you four made it so much more fun," Christopher starts as if retelling his favorite bedtime story. "We took samples of every Mute who entered my labyrinth, watching closely for the extent of their ability to be revealed. From there, they became obsolete and their deaths served to earn more funding from our generous bidders. Now I have the money and the means to rear a Mute civilization to be respected."

"You mean feared," Pyro states from behind me. Christopher's booming laughter is an answer in itself.

"Two sides of the same coin, my boy. My Mutes will not be left up to chance or pot luck. They'll be engineered and trained for a purpose."

"Like taking over the world, no doubt," Ghost snorts. "Too bad an old fucker like you won't be around to see it."

"I wouldn't be so sure, there's a mutation for everything these days. I've had teams of researchers working solely on Pyro's eternal flames while you lot have been enjoying the wonderful world of Hoax's imagination. Thanks for the demonstration on how it works, by the way." I share a look with my guys, pursing my lips and dragging them a little closer. I need to keep Christopher talking. I need to get as much information as possible and if there's one thing I can be certain of, it's Christopher's need to gloat.

"What's that supposed to mean - the world of Hoax's imagination?"

"Ahh, that's the best part! It was Hoax that gave me the idea all those years ago in the orphanage. We would take him away from the others to practice honing his ability in ways we could use. During these sessions, he would use the computer code to invent scenarios which he then tried to bring to life. Trigger the alarm clock to boil the kettle, simple childish ideas. But that's how I knew he'd comply again. He doesn't need his consciousness, it's a basic instinct to create a world where he isn't the victim anymore." I look over to where we've abandoned Hoax, restrained and confused in the middle of the yard. No longer angry for a cause he doesn't understand, he simply looks...lost.

"Thanks to the Mirage twins, Camo, Skyscraper and Incinerate, it was practically a done deal. We created the beauty of the labyrinth right here in our backyard," Christopher finishes, sounding all kinds of proud with himself. I lock those names away for later, moving them directly onto my kill list right below Christopher.

"And the bidders?" Pyro adds. "I was in those hotels, there was no faking it." There's an echo of a clap through the speaker, followed by a grunt of agreement.

"The hotels are real, as was the footage from the maze they enjoyed. Only the placement of the labyrinth wasn't as close as they were led to believe." The three of us share a sigh of defeat, leaning into each other.

"So now what? You're going to keep us locked out here like dogs?" Ghost asks and I really wish he hadn't. Now they're not being disguised or whatever, cords shoot up from the gaps in the concrete slabs at our feet, ensnaring us in turn. Ripped away from each other, my back slams into the wall, my arms and legs wrapped tightly enough to cut off my circulation. All the while, that condescending laugh reverberates around my skull.

"I wouldn't dream of giving my champions anything less than a royal homecoming. Oh no, I have big plans for all of you yet." I can hear the mockery dripping from his tone and something inside me snaps. The flare of pain consuming me is suddenly drowned out by a flood of fire swamping my system. My vision bleeds red, my breaths growing ragged. A growing voice in the back of my mind is coaxing me to 'do it,' if I knew what *it* was.

"Mania!" Pyro shouts before a vine wraps across his mouth as a gag. My eyes flicker his way, the grip pinning him in place making my blood boil hotter. Smoke heaves through my mouth, churning directly from my chest. I'm going to do it. I'm going to self-combust and take down this entire asylum with me.

Whether from regaining his ability or brute strength, a pair of milky white eyes appear in front of me. Ghost's strong arms wind around my waist, ripping me directly from the cords. His lips press a kiss on my forehead, despite the fever-pitch temperature I know is coating my skin. I recognize the hatred burning through my veins is reflected in the fiery glow of his, Pyro's and even Hoax's across the green. I'm controlling their emotions. We're all one now, and that means no matter what is done to us, we'll never be apart again. Dipping his head to my ear, Ghost's words are a soothing balm to my soul.

"Don't give them the best of you, Spitfire." I tilt my head, contemplating his words. The best of me? This is the worst of me, and Christopher deserves it. They all do. The Mutes who betrayed us, the scientists, the entire human race. I'm going to see that they burn to ashes long before they enter the reprieve of hell. Shooting a red-stained glare at the camera lens, my voice comes out husky, laced with the demon I was always supposed to be.

"You've been marked, Christopher Gordon. We're more powerful than ever, and believe me when I say, we're coming for you."

"Feisty as ever Mania," comes the responding chuckle. "I can't wait to see you try."

ACKNOWLEDGEMENTS

Thank you for reading book two in All My Pretty Psychos Series. I've had so much fun writing it and I really hope you enjoyed it just as much! This is a dark reverse harem romance which will ultimately (eventually) have a HEA at the end of the trilogy so hang in there!

There are so many people that I need to thank for helping me to make this book a reality.

Morrigan McKay, Avery Stone, Maya Morrison, and Unlikely Optimist - My Sprint Room Team - I can honestly say that they are the only reason this book got finished. If you haven't had the chance to read books by these amazing authors, I highly recommend you giving them a chance.

Sam - not only are you an amazing PA, who I would be lost without, you have now helped make my words even better. You are a great editor and I'm so proud of you for completing your course. I don't ever want to share you!

Oriane Seiner, Amy Hayes Hartung, and Jenny Milam Hays AKA My Betas - you girls are amazing. You read my rough words and give me the feedback I need to produce this book. I'm lucky to have each of you.

Emma Luna - as always you have knocked it out of the park and made the Kings just as sexy as the Queen. Thank you for making my book so pretty.

To my beautiful children - thank you for being so patient with me and being so understanding when I don't have as much time for family time. Every word I write is for you. I love you.

To my amazing husband - Not only do you support me and encourage me to follow my dream, you are there by my side while I do it. Thank you for all your help and support. We make a great team, and I love you."

ABOUT MADDISON

Maddison is a married mum of two, and a serial daydreamer. As a huge fan of all romance tropes herself, it was time to pen the stories which consume her mind most hours of the day.

As a child, Maddison was a jet setter and has lived all over the world, only to return to the south east of England, where she is now happily settled. With a double award in applied arts and art history, Maddison is a creative with a dark passion for feisty females and spicy stories.

If you're a new reader to me – welcome to the mad house! Keep reading for my list of writes, and for up-to-date info, make sure you follow my socials! The reader's group is the best place for reveals, announcements, giveaways and more, and please never hesitate to reach out! I love hearing from readers.

Also, make sure to join my Facebook readers group, Cole's Reading Moles here:
www.facebook.com/colesreadingmoles

facebook.com/maddison.cole.314
instagram.com/maddison_cole_author
amazon.com/author/B086ZQ6SW4
bookbub.com/authors/maddison-cole
tiktok.com/@authormaddisoncole

MORE BY MADDISON

ALL MY PRETTY PSYCHOS

Paranormal RH with ghosts and demons

Queen of Crazy

https://amzn.to/3O4biQt

Kings of Madness

https://amzn.to/3HzvBCY

Hoax: The Untold Story (novella)

https://amzn.to/3xAJhcA

Reign of Chaos

https://amzn.to/3b95PcI

I LOVE CANDY

Dark Humor RH - Completed

Findin' Candy (novella)

https://amzn.to/3bcueOp

Crushin' Candy

https://amzn.to/3n0TASf

Smashin' Candy

https://amzn.to/3Oniuai

Friggin' Candy

https://amzn.to/3QwlmUb

Candy - The Complete Collection

https://amzn.to/3LvatBu

.

THE WAR AT WAVERSEA

Basketball College MFM Menage - Completed

Perfectly Powerless

https://amzn.to/3OqHTQp

Handsomely Heartless

https://amzn.to/3tMoRfu

Beautifully Boundless

https://amzn.to/3MYiiNG

.

MOON BOUND

Vampire/Shifters Fated Mates Standalones

Moon Bound

www.books2read.com/moonbound

.

WILLOWMEAD ACADEMY (CO-WRITTEN WITH EMMA LUNA)

Sexy Student - Teacher Taboo Age Gap Standalone

Life Lessons

https://amzn.to/3tL8eAX

.

A VOODOO'S HAREM

A Halloween Horror Harem

https://amzn.to/3f5xw8F

.

VICES AND HEDONISM SHARED WORLD

A Reverse Harem MMA Romance

A Night of Pleasure and Wrath

https://amzn.to/3Rgg0fC

A WONDERLUST ADVENTURE: A DERANGED DUET

Retelling of Alice - twenty years on.

A vampire menage romance.

Descend Into Madness

https://amzn.to/3wRIqVd

Embrace The Mayhem

https://amzn.to/3AwJWgM

MAFIA TIES SERIES

Deranged: A Dark Mafia Menage Romance

https://amzn.to/41JX66b

BILLIONAIRE BADBOYS SERIES

Billionaire RH

Wreckin' Candy

https://amzn.to/3oHGsFF

www.ingramcontent.com/pod-product-compliance
Lightning Source LLC
Chambersburg PA
CBHW070558170726

48291CB00003B/635